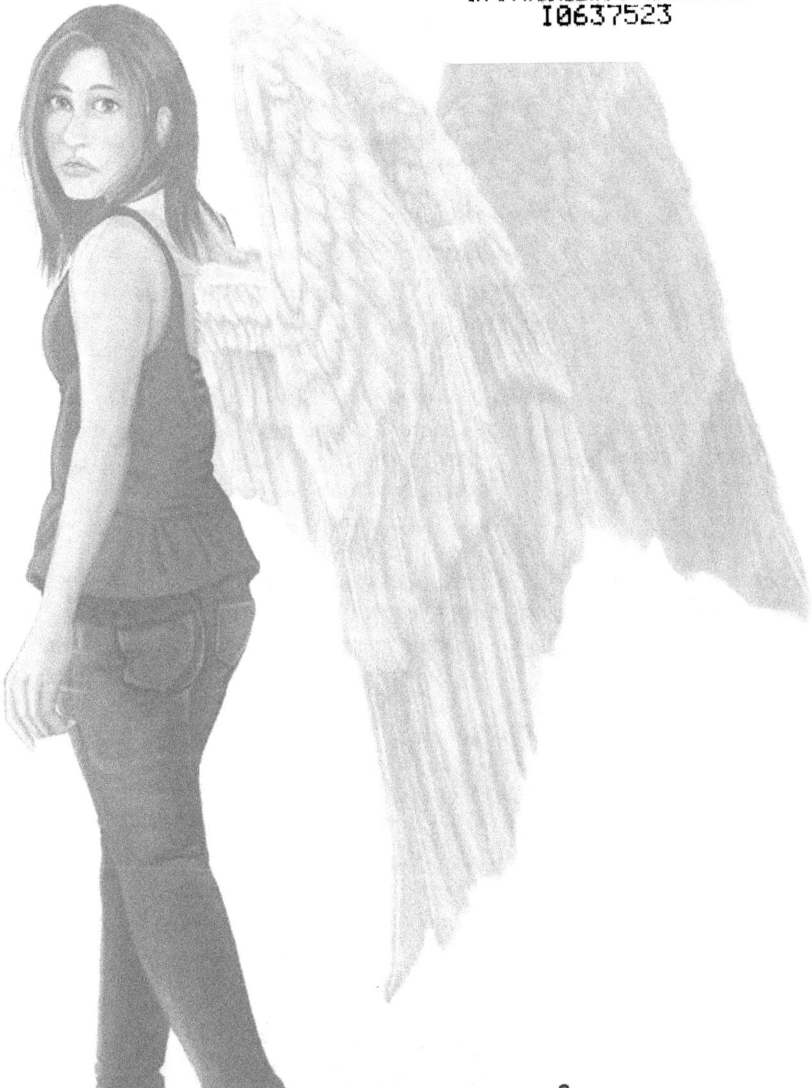

ARCHIPELAGO
MATI RAINE

Published by Fantastic Journeys Publishing,
Boise, Idaho
PUBLISHING HISTORY
E-Book released through Kindle February 2014
Soft Cover trial edition February 2014
Mass market edition XXXXXXX

Cover art created by Lorraine Barraras
Cover Art copyright by Lorraine Barraras
Content copyright ©2013 Lorraine Barreras
Edited by Diamond Preston

Published in the United States of America.

ISBN: 978-0-9855766-7-7

Fantastic Journeys Publishing
Boise, ID

ONE GIRL - LEARNING WHO SHE IS.
ONE BOY - WHO FORGOT WHO HE WAS.

EQUALLY LOST IN A WORLD THAT DOESN'T ACCEPT THEM.
EQUALLY DESTINED TO CHANGE THAT WORLD.

TWO SOULS - STRUGGLING WITH REALITY.
TWO HEARTS - ABOUT TO CHANGE.

IN A SEA OF WHAT IS NORMAL,
WE ARE AN ARCHIPELAGO.

To my mom:
I've always been jumping off branches trying to test my wings.
Thanks for having the patience to catch me when it didn't quite work.

TABLE OF CONTENTS

PART ONE: TO GAIN WINGS

PART TWO: STANDING TALL

PART THREE: HERE LIES THE BATTLE LINE

PART ONE:

TO GAIN WINGS

PROLOGUE

THEY'RE COMING

The ground beneath her feet was solid, but in her mind, everything was crumpling around her. It was so dark, reality couldn't grasp her; the door she knew should be in front of her nose, the jackets she felt her shoulders pressed against, and the wings curled tightly along her back all felt imaginary. But when the distant blow rattled the foundation under her feet, it was the one terrifying certainty she wished she could escape.

"They're coming."

Lilly's heart thundered in her throat, and her shaking caused a wisp of hair to fall into her vision; only her mind's eye could transform the shadowy images into the lilac and brown contrast that she knew was present. Why did she have to be different? Look at what it had caused. She wanted to run to her parents, be embraced by their comforting arms. But her thoughts were rattled by the sound of splintering wood, and her parents' muffled gasps met her ears.

"I've grown tired of your games, Mr. Douglas," sliced a voice, filling the bedroom with a chilling danger as footsteps moved into place. The threat resounded in the silence that followed. "Did you think running away could solve things? Did you think ignoring me would make me go away? You've only made things more difficult by refusing my proposals. I could have helped solve your family's problems."

"Problems? You're the only problem. We don't need anything you can offer," snarled someone; it took a moment for the frightened teen to recognize her father's voice, his protective anger shrouding the person she had known for so long.

"Do you want to haggle with your daughter's life? Or maybe your wife's? I gave you the chance to keep your family, but you've decided to watch it be torn apart. Look around you, Mr. Douglas. This is the cost of refusal. We're going to find your daughter, and you'll never see her again."

"You can't do that!"

The yell was followed by a struggle, a crash, and then finally a thud at floor level. Lilly could hear her mother sob, whispering something, before a disturbing chuckle cut her short. "I assure you, I can do whatever I want. I am going to find the girl, and I have no qualms over disposing of those who stand in my way." There was the sound of metal hitting flesh, and Lilly flinched, trying to drown it out. "Tell me where she is. This is your last chance. Answer and you will be spared." The only response was painful staggered breathing and quiet cries from her parents. To the hiding teen, the draining moment felt infinite, before the voice changed direction and transitioned to decisive calmness. "Kill them."

Those two words ripped Lilly from her frozen terror, and she felt herself screaming at the top of her lungs, throwing the closet door forward.

"STOP!!!"

She collided with something solid, but instead of rushing to her parents like she intended, fear sent her scrambling in the opposite direction with trepidation chasing her out of the room. As she launched herself down the stairs, wings held close to her sides, she anticipated sounds of pursuit. But only her thundering heart reached her ears as she raced across the remains of the broken front door. Even as she ran, shame smothered her soul, burying her in thoughts of what she had just done. Her brave action transitioned into cowardice, and it caused a sob in her lungs as she spread her wings.

Don't look back. Just survive.

Instinct took over where thought collapsed. She was in the air, wings guiding her through the low shadows of the night. Around

2

her, every rustle and hum of the world was muted and dead. The same fear that made her ache for her parents drove her to keep flying into the darkness, where time and distance melted together. Higher and higher she reached into the clouds, cold air biting through her skin as trickles of ice crystals threatened to form on her feathers. Nothing felt as cold as the shame in her heart, however, so frozen it burnt inside. Cities disappeared, mountains pulled into view, and trees reached into her vision with branches like waiting arms. Nothing seemed to slow her. She was mindlessly seeking escape from danger, pain, and reality, and as the night passed into the first songs of morning, she flew away from it all.

Slowly, adrenaline settled, and pain took over. It cut through her with a hot fire beyond anything she'd ever known. Tears made their way in streams down her cheeks, and she dropped out of the sky and into a deserted settlement below, half falling, half flying. Somehow, she found the support of an old brick wall, and there she let the cries fill her heart and mind. The last few days had destroyed everything Lilly knew, and when she thought back on it all, she lost the ability to hold in her dismay...

CHAPTER ONE

THE BEGINNING. THE END.

Staring out at the ocean on a cold summer morning, Lilly Douglas drank in the world around her. Her bare feet were buried in wet sand, her legs braced as a wave of frothy tide washed around her ankles, and a tiny band of seaweed clung to her foot as it fought to stay ashore. The sky was a muted blue with a deep fog obscuring the horizon, and in that moment, everything felt perfect. Even with her wings stuffed uncomfortably inside a heavy jacket, and the water icy with the chills of dawn, Lilly loved being outside, and she treasured the moment given to her. She turned to face her mother, face glowing with childlike wonder, wanting to stay in that moment as long as she could. Today felt like a day she would never forget.

She didn't understand how right she was.

Picking up her shoes, Lilly moved to where a middle-aged woman stood, and hugged her tightly around the torso. "It's so amazing out here, Mum. I wish we could stay longer."

Mrs. Douglas smiled softly and gently led her daughter back up the beach toward the storefronts. "I know, dear, but it'll be too crowded later in the day, so we have to finish our shopping early. We'll come back later in the year when everyone is back in school, okay?"

Lilly nodded, encouraged a little, and moved carefully toward the faucet to wash her feet. The silver nozzle wedged into the bricks looked almost comical at a glance, but it was a necessary placement with the way the sand clung to all surfaces. "Are there lots of people here during the summer?" she asked, flinching as her mother turned on the water.

Mrs. Douglas paused, her face consumed with thought. "Yes, it can get pretty busy here." She seemed to clip her sentence short, and then gave a warm smile. "People like to go to the beach."

Lilly listened to the carefully worded answer, and for the first time, she found herself wondering what was hidden in it. Here, next to the stubby building at the shore, with serenity around her, something felt wrong; as she watched the sand run in rivulets off her toes, that realization nagged at the back of her mind until it sank into her thoughts.

It was August 10, and Lilly had just turned 14. Even at that age, she was an abnormally innocent and sheltered child, free of knowledge that would otherwise taint her. From the day she turned five and her wings started to grow, her life had been enclosed by the walls of their home: a world that her parents carefully constructed. Each day followed a familiar pattern. She spent her mornings with her mother cooking or cleaning, her days doing school work, and her evenings spending quality time with her family, with games or conversation. The only time she ever went outside was at night, when her family would lie on the grass and look at the constellations, finding shapes in the stars. Even then, the sky always called to Lilly with such vehemence it tormented her to stay on the ground, but her young wings were too small to carry even her slim frame.

As a child, Lilly didn't think she was different. In her world, every child was home schooled, every child grew up hiding, every child had no friends, and every child had wings. She couldn't desire anything bigger, but with age, that also changed. Lilly grew curious of what was over the fence, or beyond the window. She would sneak to the sill in the living room and peer through the blinds, watching people walk past. Children laughed and played together, separated from her by a thin pane of glass. Gradually, she started longing to be part of it. But that longing was suppressed by a second, larger need. Each time she looked outside, her gaze moved toward the heavens, where the other winged creatures flew free. She felt caged, and she longed to fly.

By the time she was seven, her desire for flight had grown to the point that Lilly stopped focusing on school. She begged her parents to let her test her wings, unable to be content with her confinement to the earth. She was restless and uneasy, and showed the first signs of rebellion with her desperation to reach the air. At first, her parents refused to give in to their daughter's pleading, and Lilly became withdrawn, heart breaking under the denial. But with time, her depression grew to be too much for them, so they agreed to let their daughter try.

On a cold, cloudy evening, Mrs. Douglas drove her daughter into the mountains, where Lilly made her first clumsy attempts to use her unique limbs. Together, mother and child stumbled through the mechanics of wings, and two years later, she could soar. Lilly felt connected to the sky like a tendon to a bone; it felt like being airborne gave her purpose. Every week she would wait for the nights when her mother would sneak her to the mountains, and her diligence in schoolwork was spurred by the elation that came with escaping the confines of gravity. She became strong in mind, spirit, and heart: a teenager with the glowing soul of a child. Her wings carried her through life in more ways than one: it was her only escape into the outside. When she was in the sky, everything else faded away. Her fears, her worries, and her confusion disappeared, and she found peace among the birds. Beyond the reach of technology that could shake her beliefs, the world was a mystery to Lilly, and in the sky, she saw things that would be unattainable to others. She made up for what was missing by treasuring the experience she alone could have. Everything felt right.

Yet, good things are destined to change. After Lilly started flying, the Douglas' knew they could no longer keep their daughter from the world, and they gradually began expose her to society. When Lilly turned twelve, her parents took her on her first trip to the city; the event carried a chilled sense of danger the young girl didn't entirely grasp. The house was silent as the Douglas' carefully bundled Lilly's wings inside a heavy jacket, and instructed her never to take it off when she was outside. No one must see her wings. No one must know she was different.

Different.

That word entered her vocabulary, and wrapped itself like a snake around her mind. It was a realization that unsettled her with the force of an earthquake. Why was she different? What made her different? As far as she knew, everyone else was like her except—

Her wings.

Different.

She was different.

For the first time, Lilly didn't want to see the outside world. But as she moved forward, it was too late, and there it was. She stepped across the threshold, and with that step, her innocent view of the world began falling apart.

It had continued to crumble ever since.

"Lilly? Are you coming?"

Memories shifted, and Lilly was back to gazing longingly across the ocean, feet dripping with chilled water and sand floating toward the drain behind her like the images emptying from her mind. Gone were the memories of her simple life inside her house. They were replaced by the perilous yet beautiful reality that surrounded her. Lilly slipped her sandals back on, and moved to her mother's side. At least with her parents, nothing could harm her. With them, she was safe. Why would she wish for things to change? This world was not like her, although deep in her heart, she still wanted to understand why.

As Lilly walked along the storefronts, she knew she was missing something. She was beginning to notice things around her that made her question the vastness of existence: maps of California, advertisements for 'amusement parks,' stores selling souvenirs of a place she lived in but hardly saw. Every time she stepped outside, she was terrified, but relieved. Walking along sidewalks, hearing other people speak, seeing all the faces, she felt like maybe, if she understood them, she could belong. One day, she wouldn't have to hide. All the people here were very *different*. Some spoke in other languages, some had skins of different colors, and some had different hairstyles. Surely if they were willing to accept people with pieces of metal shoved through their ears and noses, they could accept someone with wings!

As her understanding of the world grew, so did her confusion, and two years were not enough for her to feel ready to face any of this on her own. She was still a child, looking in on a mysterious place that could destroy everything she believed in.

Curiosity was a dangerous thing.

"So, where do you want to go first?" Mrs. Douglas asked, moving down the first street, and turning to wait for her daughter's direction. Lilly pointed to an art gallery just across from them, and they crossed the street at a brisk pace, slowing down only when they were inside the doors. Once inside, Lilly paused, trying to take it all in. Beautifully rendered artwork stretched to all sides, with details so breathtaking they looked more like scenes frozen in time, ready to come back to life at any moment. Then she turned and pointed to the first art piece to her left, studying it more closely.

"Ma, look at the colors! It's like they painted with sunlight..." she whispered in awe. The painting captured a fall day, with leaves in every hue of orange, red, gold, and yellow. A waterfall roared behind the leaves, reflecting shades of purple and blue. Lilly sighed happily and pointed to a small section of color in the waterfall, gleefully looking up at her mother again. "They used my color, Ma."

Mrs. Douglas leaned closer, and nodded warmly. "Yes, that is your favorite, isn't it? Lilac... Is that what we're going to look for again today?"

Lilly nodded eagerly, staring mesmerized at the picture. "If only hair dye could be this beautiful."

Her mother chuckled. "Maybe someday it will be. But some of the most beautiful things in life cannot be captured even in a painting as lovely as that." Lilly felt her mother's hand fall on her back, gently pressing against one of her wings. Some silent connection passed between them, an unshakable bond between mother and child, and as they moved through the rest of the gallery, Lilly felt warm contentment in her heart. She wanted to treasure every moment of this day, as clearly as that artist held time in his painting. So she let go of her worries, and let herself enjoy the time by her mother's side.

Half an hour later, Lilly stood staring at handfuls of fake hair swatches, her face pulled into a tight frown. This tiny store boasted dyes of nearly every color, but lacked the one shade she was desperately trying to find. Tolerantly, Mrs. Douglas looked through the shelf of semi-permanent colors, but purple was terribly underrepresented.

"Mum, I can't find it anywhere," Lilly finally whispered, exasperated. The longer they stood searching, the sillier her idea seemed. They had come this far, though. It seemed like a shame to turn back now.

Mrs. Douglas frowned, and rubbed her forehead with her hand. "You might just have to just try another color, dear," she responded quietly. Lilly sulked and kept looking. It was a childish goal, she knew that, but she was mesmerized by the images she was already shaping in her head. While the tufts of lilac hair refused to respond to any hair dye, she liked the idea of adding new pigments to her naturally earth-toned locks. The small stripe she had was comforting, and there didn't seem to be any harm in emphasizing it. As the purple faded, there would be traces of pinks, light lavenders, then finally pale white: it would be just like a painting.

So she kept hunting, desperately trying to find the right dye before her mother's patience wore out. Down one aisle, up the next, Lilly's gaze never left the rows of colors. In her focus, Lilly forgot to watch where she was walking, pace quickening with every row. The sprint ended abruptly, when she crashed into another customer and stumbled backward in surprise. Lilly stammered an apology as her hat went tumbling to the floor, while the sound of rapid footsteps echoed from the other aisle.

Before Lilly could collect herself, piercing gray eyes locked onto her and she withered under the gaze. "Oh, I'm sorry, dear. Was I in the way?"

Rational thought fled momentarily as Lilly knelt to retrieve her hat. Her gaze stopped as she noticed the box on the floor next to it. The color was exactly what she was seeking. A glance at the shelf revealed an empty display.

"I..." Lilly felt like she was choking on her words. She looked up at the man's face, then down at the dye he now held. She had the sudden urge to forget the color and flee the store, but she was frozen by his icy gaze.

"Is this the color you wanted?" he inquired slowly, holding out the box.

Lilly felt herself nod, trying to force her hand to take it from him. A rush of courage let her snatch it, grasping it tightly to her chest as she muttered a muffled thank you. The gaze followed her as she turned away, and like needles, it seemed to pierce her wings, which felt all too noticeable inside her hot jacket.

"Lilly, is everything okay? Oh, you found the color you wanted! That's great!" her mother's voice said cheerfully behind her, and a firm hand caught her shoulder. When Lilly looked up, what she saw only spurred on her fear. Her mother's fake smile momentarily wavered when she looked down, and as they paid for the hair dye, Lilly began to shake. Then they were back on the street, moving quickly toward their car.

"Mum...I—"

"Stay close, Lilly. Don't speak."

They moved rapidly down the sidewalk, a quick stride that was almost a run, and Lilly's calves burned by the time she jumped into the back seat of their car. The doors locked with a resounding 'click' before Mrs. Douglas quickly pulled out, leaving the beach behind them in a blur. Without reason, tears began to tumble down Lilly's face, and she began to shake. Mrs. Douglas turned to glance at her with a face that was filled with deep worry.

"Lilly, listen to me. I need you to calm down, okay? We got the hair dye, we'll go home and fix your hair, and that will be the end of this."

"But Mum...I...I don't have a good feeling about this. The way he looked at me... Ma... It was like he knew something."

Silence grew heavy in the car before Mrs. Douglas spoke again, her eyes deeply locked on the road in front of her. "I don't understand how he could, Lilly. It will be okay. It was probably nothing more than a nosy old man. We'll go home and dye your hair, and then we'll leave this business behind us."

Lilly tried to be encouraged by her mother's words, but was too shaken by what had happened. She spent the ride home in silence, and after her hair was dyed, she crept up to her room and curled up on her bed, resting her damp hair against the pillow. From her bed, she could see the stars glimmering in the window, and they offered a tiny promise of safety. Only then did she relax. Here in her room, she was safe. The man was gone. This was their home. No one could reach her here. Slowly, her eyes flicked closed, and she breathed deeply, wings gently curled around her. She let her mind fall into a state of safety, forcing the worries out of her mind. The world out there, it couldn't reach her. When their door shut, nothing could enter. These were the promises she grew up believing, and now, she used them as a blanket of comfort.

No sooner had she relaxed, however, than a knock sent her launching off the bed, echoing in her mind like a roll of thunder.

Someone was there.

No one ever knocked on their door.

Someone was here.

Lilly could distantly hear movement in the living room below; one of her parents moved toward the front door. There was an unfamiliar 'click' of the door unlocking, then a creak as the barrier to the outside world cracked open.

"Good evening, sir."

It was the man from the store. His voice carried through the air, slipping through the crack under her door, and sending a chill down her spine. Lilly could almost see him taking off his hat, a bald patch of nothingness perched inside his wiry hair. She could picture a suit on him, and a business-like manner on his face. It was all clear in his voice. He was here for a purpose, and somehow she knew it had something to do with her.

"Excuse me, but it's late, and we don't make a habit of entertaining guests at this hour," Mr. Douglas' steady voice answered.

"I understand completely. I'll get right to the point. I was down at the beach today and happened to run into your daughter at the store. She was buying hair dye, and the color she was looking for is of particular interest to me. For the past several years I have connected this hair color with teens who—call me crazy—possess certain...gifts."

Lilly's heart pounded deep within her. Her wings seemed like dead weight on her back. It was like their lives were on display, and he was just browsing the gallery. He knew about her wings! But did her hair really have something to do with that? How could he possibly connect hair dye to gifts, in any proportion? It was too odd...too sudden. Thoughts rushed to the surface of her mind, and she almost missed her father's answer.

"I assure you, our daughter's gifted, but in normal ways! Bright student, gets great grades, and she's just going through those phases like everyone else. Lilac suits her perfectly, and she insists on having the hair dye. It's her favorite color, nothing more."

"Yes, sir. I have no doubt she's a good student, but haven't you noticed anything else? The differences I am interested in are much more noticeable than a few straight A's. I believe your daughter may be special...very special indeed."

"I am sorry, but late, and I think you have the wrong house." Like that, the conversation was ended, and there was the sound of the door beginning to close. There was a pause, and Lilly felt as if the man had stopped the door.

"I apologize for coming so late, but I urge you to speak to me again at a later time. Here's my card. I would be grateful if we could arrange another meeting. Have a good evening." The man shuffled, and his departure was sealed with the click of a shutting door. Once he was gone, Lilly rushed downstairs.

"Mum! What's going on? Why was he here? What was he talking about?" Lilly asked, distress slipping into her voice.

Her mother shook her head slowly. "I don't know, Lilly, but I can tell you one thing. We aren't staying to find out. I'm not putting you at risk. We're leaving immediately."

Lilly was even more alarmed. "Leaving? But why?! Mum, Dad. You're scaring me."

Her mother quickly enveloped her in a sheltering hug, and Lilly couldn't help but feel foolish. She was fourteen years old, and shouldn't be panicking and getting scared like this. But seeing the fear on her mother's face only increased her own. "Lilly, it's going to be all right. We just want to make sure you're safe. You're different, and there are people out there who might want to harm you because of that. That man might be one of them. That's why we must be cautious. Do you understand?"

Lilly had nodded, but it felt like her stomach had been punched. The rest of the night was spent loading boxes and packing, and by afternoon the next day, the Douglas' had left town.

Lilly sat cross-legged on the couch, quietly working out the math problems she had in front of her. She was about halfway done with her homework, and now she was growing tired and unmotivated. Yawning, she stretched and watched the numbers melt with her vision's momentary blurring, before returning anew. She couldn't concentrate on math today. She couldn't concentrate on much at all.

Putting her book down, Lilly went to the window and delicately parted the blinds. A sliver of sunlight managed to drift through and rest on her face, carrying the images of the outside world to her eyes. Everything was different here; the Montana air was chillier, and while there were more trees, this neighborhood held none of that comforting foliage. The yards were colorless and bland; the houses close, but the neighbors distant and guarded. Lilly hated this new house. At night she lay awake with the noises of cars and airplanes common and reoccurring. Sometimes, she thought she heard things like sirens or yelling distantly in the night. But they turned into quick silence, like echoes in her mind of imagined terrors.

Lilly let the blinds close and her hand trembled lightly as she returned to the couch. She perched on the edge of the cushions, her back turned to the soft trace of daylight. The house was quiet, with her mother upstairs doing laundry, and her father away at work.

13

That left her alone in the living room, fighting to finish her schoolwork, with panic threatening to rise.

It had been a week since their flight out of Wittier, and so far there had been no sign of the man from the store. Time seemed to bring trepidation more than relief. It felt like they were in the stillness before a storm; a clock was steadily tick-tick-ticking away the moments until it came.

There was a sudden ringing that made Lilly leap from one end of the couch to the other, and on the coffee table, the phone rattled with an incoming call. Lilly's brown eyes scrutinized the screen where the caller ID glowed with the words UNLISTED CALLER.

"Lilly, don't answer it!"

She didn't need to be told twice. Mrs. Douglas came down the stairs and stood staring at the phone with wide eyes, hand hovering over it. She didn't pick it up, stopped from touching it as if it were red hot. Then suddenly it clicked to the answering machine, and the voice they both feared filled the room.

"Hello, I am just hoping I have the number of Mr. and Mrs. Douglas. They left town awhile back, and I was looking forward to speaking with them again. If I have the correct number, I would be extremely—"

Lilly jumped as a snap cut off the phone, and stared in shock as her mother stood clutching the cord she had ripped from the wall. The soft, gentle mother's eyes she once knew were unrecognizable in the ones that now burned their way from brown to a coal-black. There was a flicker of fear as the woman seemed to realize what she had done, but it was already too late to take back the action. In the end, Mrs. Douglas just set the phone cord lightly on the coffee table. "Lilly, stay inside today, please, dear. I'm going to go start dinner."

Lilly knew what that meant, and she crawled upstairs with her books, heart hammering in her throat. It meant, "Lilly, it's not safe anymore. Stay out of sight. We're going to protect you."

She didn't want them to protect her, though. She didn't want them to be in danger. Her child's heart was so scared for her parents, she wanted to just lead the danger away, and not let them be hurt if it came to that. But the other half of her was terrified of the danger, and wanted to run into their arms and the safety they offered. She was so torn, knowing either way nothing good was going to come after this. She whispered a soft prayer and curled up on her bed, staring at the window. Darkness was brimming on the horizon.

Three days came and went, and nothing further happened. Once again, it didn't reassure anyone. On the fourth day, Mr. Douglas came home from work, and Lilly knew something was wrong as he quickly drew his wife into their room. Sitting on her bed, Lilly strained her ears as she listened, and barely made out what was being said.

"He isn't giving up... e-mails today... I didn't respond and he... threatening. The last one... fools in hiding the girl...he'd have to come take her."

"What are we going to do? We can't let that..."

"I don't know. I guess we'll..."

Lilly finally pulled away, and the voices became murmurs. She sighed and went over to the window, looking out into the cloudless night. It was an inky darkness, but even the bright contrast of the stars was obscured by the city's reflective lights. Her eyes looked up to the heavens, tried to imagine the skies from their old home, but that seemed lost to her already. This week had been hard on all of them, both adapting to the new home and trying to shake the growing sense of danger. She wished they had moved further into the countryside, without this city bustle she was unfamiliar with. The changes were draining, and she was too exhausted to cheer herself up.

As she surrendered to her worries, she let her head drop, but surprise shattered her thoughts. People were quickly making their way across the street, right toward their yard.

Lilly scrambled out of her room, and threw open her parents' door. "Mum, Dad, there are people coming toward the house!" she gasped.

Her father flew to the window. "Lilly, close the door and be quiet!"

"Dad, no. What about you? I can't—"

To her surprise, Lilly felt her mother's arms engulf her, and she was scooped off the ground in a hug that was on the borderline of painful. But Lilly was too stunned to fight it. Her hands tried to reach out for her mother, but the voice in her ear scared her to the point of paralysis. "Lilly, please, stay quiet. I love you. I love you so much." She was dropped into the closet, the arms letting go, and then Lilly was staring into her mother's tear-filled eyes. "Whatever happens, do not forget that. Be strong. And *be silent.*"

Then the door shut, and Lilly was staring into the darkness, frozen with fear. Then two final words were whispered:

"They're coming."

The world shifted, turned, and tumbled. Images of her past life collided with the reality of the present, and Lilly awakened to find herself alone. She was in an alley, limbs numb with cold, and her broken heart let forth a burst of agony that rippled through her limbs. She closed her eyes, trying to dissipate her confusion at her unfamiliar surroundings. But as her eyelashes fluttered and she stared at the sky, she knew there was no way to escape the world that surrounded her.

So that was it. In a few short moments, her life was gone, and she was left on the other side of the door she had so longed to go through. Now that she had crossed that threshold, she wanted nothing more than to go back. But the door was gone, along with everything she had held dear. In its place was a world Lilly was a stranger to, and a life filled with fear and danger. There were no adventures, no open skies, nothing she imagined she would find. Cold, terrified, and alone, Lilly lay against the wall and stared at the sky above her. There, the same stars she had stared at with her parents smiled down at her, tenderly trying to comfort her. But Lilly just gazed emptily, and then let her eyes flutter shut.

Back then, she just wanted to fly.

Now, she just wanted to go home.

CHAPTER TWO

FROSTBITE

The darkness was closing around him, and he couldn't escape it. In front of him the forest stretched, beckoning him toward safety, and he forced himself not to glance back. They had to make it! They had to get away! But the hand was falling out of reach.

"Cory!"

The pleading voice cut through him, and he fought for greater speed. But suddenly, the hand was gone, and he turned, trying desperately to find the figure behind him. Instead, terror-filled blue eyes stared back just before a gunshot echoed around him. His mouth was open in wordless horror, but only trees surrounded him. Then everything was falling away, out of his reach, out of his control. He was slipping forward in time, until finally, he sat upright in bed.

Reality fell into place with the delicacy of a train wreck; everything around him announced its presence like bits of metal screaming to a halt. Gone were the darkness, the trees, and the dirt. Nothing surrounded him but white walls, a barred window, and on the dresser to the left, an alarm clock with the time 7:02. Cory stared at those numbers, as if trying to understand them, but in actuality, he was still battling with the remnants in his head. It had been a long time since he had a dream like that, and it shook him up more than he wanted to admit.

It was August 10; somehow, that date didn't feel possible. Nothing felt real in the room he woke up in, but he had grown used to such feelings of disconnection. When he came to this school, even the struggle for survival became a comfort. If he had something to fight for, he wouldn't have to remember; he could forget those sad blue eyes and the desperate desire to run. Sometimes he could get so far from those things, they almost vanished...

But he could never quite escape himself.

His thoughts swirled in his head as he peeled the sheets off his chest and wiped the sweat from his brow. The sound of that gunshot still reverberated in his mind. The images wrapped themselves in a thin veil around his thoughts, threatening to smother him, and subconsciously, his fingers found the edge of his pillowcase and slowly drew it into his grip.

"Cory? Are you okay, Hun?"

A voice drifted warmly through the door, but it stung his heart like fire. His breath was turning into a fog as the temperature dropped, and he continued to fester in his emotions. He had to pull back. He had to control himself.

"Cory?" Trish called out.

"Cory!" echoed a voice in his mind.

His hand jerked and his mouth opened in an angry snarl, his thoughts broken by the sound of ice shattering against the wall. He watched as his pillow fell to the floor, splinters of ice littering the carpet around it, and he stared at the shreds of fabric hanging unnaturally in their icy state. The feelings inside him all turned to hate, interlocking into a solid wall that protected him from the outside. Cory breathed slowly, choking down the memories and emotions until they finally sank, like rocks in a lake. Then, as easily as he froze the pillow, the waters of his soul became ice, sealing all else into the depths. Only then did he get up from the bed to walk toward the door.

"Cory, you're gonna be late for first hour. I'd hurry if I were you."

The voice was gentle, the I's with a soft 'ah' tone to them, but they still had an impact on his bitter mood. He huffed as he yanked the door open, glaring at the face on the other side. "Don't you have better things to do?!" he spat. The girl didn't even flinch.

"I swear, one of these days I'll leave you to fend for yourself." With a scolding huff, she shoved her way into the room and moved to the dresser on the right. "You know what'll happen if you're not there—"

"*Ah*'m aware of the consequences, Trish," he mimicked, earning a slight glare.

"Then get dressed!"

His muscles tensed with the instinct to duck as she threw clothing in his direction, and his scowl gradually deepened. As a sock flopped across his ear, he rigidly exhaled. "Why do you feel the need to do that?"

Her yellow-green eyes gazed back at him, reading his face as if words were printed on it, but she said nothing. He watched her eyes dart to the pillow in the corner of the room, and she gave a tiny puff of air, watching the light fog rise in front of her. "I can tell when something is otherwise distractin' you." She opened her mouth, then bit her lip and moved toward the door, face wiped clean of all emotion. "There's a breakfast bar on the dresser. At least take a bite today." With that she left, shutting the door with a firm click behind her. Listening to the silence left in her wake, Cory stiffly moved to pick up his clothes and get dressed.

On the football field, morning frost stiffening the grass underfoot, Cory stood unmoving with one arm draped against the fence and fingers loosely gripping the chilled metal. His eyes stared ahead at the horizon, where the sun was lazily making its way into the sky. Even with his arms bare, he felt no cold. He never did. It was another advantage of being one of *them*. He sapped the last drops of energy from the grass underneath, leaving the tiny green blades so cold, he was sure one touch would shatter them. He was the liquid nitrogen of the world: his presence drained the warmth around him. Yet unlike that cold liquid, the warmth he stole became his own energy. Perhaps he was selfish, but feelings of guilt had long since ceased entering his mind. Living at this place, this school, only survival mattered, and whatever means necessary to attain it were tolerated and encouraged.

Above his head, strands of barbed wire glittered with cold. Their purpose was only to intimidate, as they were rather useless otherwise. This school, perched on the peak of a barren mountain, surrounded by skeletal trees, didn't need the fence or the wire to intimidate. All it had to do was exist. Cory didn't mind. He fed off the strength of the school, the power of it. He was standing on top of the world, looking down. Around him, he could see a strange beauty in the emptiness, the loneliness. It was the sense of independence, the ability to stand untouched and unchallenged. He was part of this: he was this fence, this metal, wound into the fabric of this school.

Today, he felt something stirring in the bones of the institution. It was a spark, threatening to explode into a raging fire. Something was happening today, but he didn't know what. This sense, as powerful as the rage evoked by his dream, allowed his emotions to float from the depths, bringing curiosity and intrigue. He would learn the source soon enough, when the call to action sounded, and if there was a hunt, the students would begin to stir, bristling for a chase like hounds eager to run; if it was a battle, simple tensions would briefly vanish, with a common goal to fight a new enemy. For once, he regretted being part of the group that was leaving today. A good chase was always refreshing, and it helped him better focus on his goals. But today he had other things to attend to, and whatever it was would have to wait.

Pulling out his phone, he punched the number five, then 'Send,' and he listened to the ring buzzing in his ear. After a few moments, a voice finally answered, giving a growl-like noise.

"What?"

"Send back Oz. We're ready," Cory spoke, clipping his words off with sharp enunciation as he began walking toward the building.

"He is on his way—I sent him to you a few moments ago. Finish training, then go."

"Plan still on?"

"Yes, although I hope you keep yourself in check. Remember, I don't want you caught! I expect you to be back here to check in, but you need to do it discretely. I'm heading out to Laguna Beach today and I can't afford your exposure," the voice growled.

Cory felt a dark chuckle slip from his lips. "Caught? The other three were dragged in with welcome arms. Those Charity brats are too naïve to suspect anything."

The voice on the other end sighed, and seemed to battle with a withheld comment. After a pause, it returned. "If anything goes foul here, your group will be our best chance of success. I hope you realize the importance of this mission now. Your presence at that school could be tested soon. Don't disappoint me."

"Understood."

With a grunt of "I'll be in touch," the phone clicked. Cory shoved it back in his pocket and paused, giving one last glance at the sky. Only a few more hours, and they would be gone, past these mountains and away from this school. The mission didn't matter to him at this point: only the freedom. He turned and headed back into the building, leaving the frozen world behind.

The day continued to drag on at its slow meandering pace through lunchtime. Most of his classes were a blur, and Cory felt little desire to concentrate or acknowledge anyone. But as he made his way toward the gym, a voice finally broke through his thoughts, dragging Cory back to its too-familiar source.

"Hey, didja hear?"

Cory yawned, pausing before he answered. "Hear what?"

"Kibbsty headed to Laguna Beach this morning," Trish began, falling into stride with him. Her green eyes looked eager and excited. "He's been tracking a family around that area for a while. Looks like he's ready to make a move."

"We know who's going?"

"Tray, Zen, and Harris for sure, though he may add in some others if he feels like it. He's coverin' his bases which may seem like overkill for one girl, but it is good practice in case we run into a stronger Strand. If she can fly, Zen will herd her toward Charity, and Tray can catch her there; he's gettin' dropped off ahead of time. Oz and Peta will be watchin' the ground if she stays on foot though. I think the whole thing is odd. He's *forcin'* more and more students to join now, instead of there being a choice at all. I just—"

"Don't think about it. It's none of our business what he does." Trish flinched and rubbed her arm as the air temperature dropped. He paused at a doorway, waiting for a couple of other students to pass by, and gave Trish a cold look. "You will get yourself killed by asking too many questions."

"You'll get yourself killed by not," Trish responded. She brushed a strand of hair behind her ear; the lighter green lock slipped under the darker strands. The moment grew uncomfortably tense and they stared each other down. Yet, after a moment, Trish sighed and began walking again. "Maybe you're right. I'm thinkin' about this too much. I gotta get my head back into school. I just...I see 'em come here, see the growin' tensions. I don' know if I like it."

Cory gave a small grunt. "You think too much and spend too much time in the lab, Trish. They aren't our concern. We live to survive, and if you get soft like this, you're gonna get killed. You got emotions plastered all over your face like makeup."

Trish scowled, "Gee, thanks for puttin' it so delicately. But I don' get out there like the rest of you. I have to keep my ears open to know anything. An' what I hear...troubles me."

"We all get opportunities when we're useful to Kibbsty. Don't make wishes you'll regret later." His icy eyes turned toward her, then away. "What happens will happen. And you're already coming on this trip. So if you ever want to go on more of them, focus on keeping your grades up."

"Gee, like you're one to talk."

"I'm going to class, aren't I?"

"You're just goin' for the fist fights."

They paused at the gym doors, and Cory felt his face pulling into an icy smile. "So what if I am? I have a few scores to settle, and today seems like a good day to do it."

Trish rolled her eyes and entered behind him, then moved toward the lockers where the cloth bandages were. As she wrapped her knuckles, she finally chuckled, and gave the boy a push on the arm. "Don't get too cocky, or someone will make you eat your words."

Cory's eyes gazed ahead, and he breathed through his nose with a visible exhalation of cold air. "Let them try. Today, I really don't feel like taking anyone's crap."

Trish glanced his direction, but said nothing. That was good, because he didn't want her in his way if he lost his temper. He'd rather let it out on a worthwhile target. As he wrapped his arms for class, the memories from the morning finally slipped from his thoughts. Images of power, strength, battle, and triumph filled his mind, and he became the person that he was most comfortable being. He turned to face the center of the gym where the class was gathering, falling into stride with the life he now lived.

The past? None of that mattered now.

This was today, and today he would fight.

CHAPTER THREE

WATER, WIND, AND ELECTRICITY

First a sound, then a feeling, then a pain came to her, until Lilly slipped into wakefulness. She was lying on cold dirt in an unfamiliar alleyway; her feathers, hair, and pajamas were damp and chilled. For a moment, her surroundings confused her, then fear pressed the terrible memories to the surface of her mind. In a staggering blow, her final flight came back, along with images of her descent into this rubble-strewn alleyway, until there she laid, shaken, as the things she had concluded to be nightmares turned back into reality.

Above her, stars littered the sky in a greater number than she had ever seen, and the moon glowed unobstructed, the light in this dark world. A numbing cold bit her feet as she stood and took a few shaky steps forward. Everything was different and new, terrifying and strange. Yet it was what she had to accept existed, regardless of her fears. Memories of the night slipped from immediate thought, and survival instincts took control. Her wings fluttered slightly, weakly working to balance her, while the air cut sharply through her pajamas and bit her exposed arms and face. She moved like a toddler, testing her limbs, only to trip on a piece of rubble and crash to the ground. Her yelp of pain echoed eerily, reminding her of just how alone she was. The last sparks of energy pushed her back to her feet, about to move again, when a voice sent her reeling backward in terror.

"Well, lookie here. Hey Zen! I found me a lost lil' bird!"

"A bird, eh? Looks more like a girl," a second voice answered from a different direction. Eyes darting around in the darkness, Lilly tried to pinpoint where the voices were coming from, and she pressed her back against the wall for security. To her right, a spark flickered, then faded, and a soft chuckle echoed off the buildings.

"I think iss sorta both," the amused voice answered.

"Who's there?" Lilly squeaked.

"Now, now, lass. We didn't mean to startle you. You've got nothin' to be afraid of." It was too dark to see the figure moving forward, but the sound of footsteps alerted her to the approach. One step, two steps, a pause, and then there was silence. In the moon's dim glow, she could barely make out the silhouette of a boy, and she squinted, trying to clarify the image.

"I said, w-who's there?"

"She can't see you, you idiot. You're scaring her."

"Well then, I'll turn on a light." To her bewilderment, the alleyway was suddenly illuminated, leaving the girl stunned and blinking until her eyes adjusted. When the dots left her vision, she was staring at a hand now sparkling with electricity. Shadows danced across a boy's face in front of her, his green eyes occasionally flashing yellow with the light from his palm. Exhaustion prevented confusion from overwhelming Lilly, though fear still had enough strength. "There, now we c'n see each other. M'name's Tray, and that over there's Zen. What's your name?"

"I..." Lilly felt words unwillingly slip forward. "I'm Lilly." She closed her mouth, watching the lights dance in the dim night. The laughter filling the alleyway made her feel cold and trapped, yet she was too tired to move.

"Lilly 'tis. What's a lass like you doin' in a place like this?" Tray set one arm against the wall by her right wing, and looked into her face. "You must be lost to end up here. This is a ghost town, m'dear. Been abandoned for longer'n you been alive." He held out his hand, and suddenly, a bolt of electricity shot down the alley, leaving a trail of light as it passed through a long narrow road. An unhappy scene came into view: a wake of destruction from long ago. Broken windows, damaged walls, and dusty weeds shone briefly, and then faded back into the night. "See? Nothin' but alleys. That's all this town really is...*alleys*." He laughed heartily, the sound reverberating off the walls, and his drawl seemed to fade a bit. He watched her for a moment, as if assessing her reaction. Lilly felt her eyes cast away from him, toward the ground.

"Why are *you* here, if this place is abandoned?" She felt herself whispering, a feeling of apprehension growing in her gut.

Zen chuckled lightly, and Lilly looked back up, watching as he pushed his hand through his hair. Tray's glowing hands revealed the other boy's flame-like hair and startlingly vivid blue eyes as the quieter teen spoke. "No one lives here, but it doesn't mean no one *comes* here, girl. There're still things worth discovering in a town like this. Secrets of the past, buried around. And there're some other folk who come 'round here just to cause trouble. This is our playground. Our clubhouse, if you will. You just happened to stumble into a mutant's den."

"What do you mean?"

"You aren't alone in the world, girl," Tray picked up. "There're people, like us. And this is a place we c'n come and be ourselves. No one minds seein' your wings here. You can be free." His eyes found hers, and something in the dangerous green irises began to pull her in. People like her? Them? There were others? People who were different?

Different.

"People like us?"

"Aye, lass. Like us. I know a whole school, in fact, just for people like you and me. We're not that different, y'know..." The light in his hands flew in an arc into the air, floating from one hand to the other. Tray caught it, his face filled with a strange energetic glee as he let it snake across his hands and arms. He continued speaking, his eyes never leaving the sparks. "Are we so different, Lilly? You got your gifts. I got mine. Yet they're the things we have in common. Our differences make us the same. That's how it is for the people at the school I go to. We're united against those that would call us misfits, outcasts, weird, or strange. Zen an' me, we go there, and you could go there too, y'know..." Lilly listened, but it was all too sudden for her. His smile faded, and he leaned closer. "You could belong for once. Haven't you ever wanted that?"

"Yes, but..." Images from that night flew through her mind. The shadows running across their lawn, the threats of the man from the store, the sounds of her parents defending her. "I don't want that anymore. I wanted to belong, but now, I just want to go home." Slowly, her courage returned, and she began to move away from the boy. "I'm sorry, I...I have to go."

"Go where?" A powerful gust of wind billowed up like a wall in front of her, and she fell backward, crying out in surprise.

"You just got here, lassy. We c'n help you, if you just slow down. Listen—"

"Leave me alone!" Fear caused Lilly's frozen feet to move, but she was yanked back by a jerk on her arm. Terrible laughter filled the alleyway, and she fought back with terror-driven adrenaline. Wind and electricity rippled around her, close enough to send shivers and tingles up her feathers.

"Don' be hasty, love! Where're you gonna go? You don't even know where you are..." With a blinding flash of light, Lilly was thrown back into the wall, stars filling her eyes. "Come on, child. You don' wanna get on our bad side, do you?"

"Go away!" With a burst of panic, Lilly threw her wings open, connecting hard with both forms, throwing them backward. Without giving them a chance to recover, she bolted into the nearest building, rocks tearing into her exposed feet.

"Hey! Get back here, you—" The threat was lost as the walls passed between them, and the terrified girl found herself in a warehouse, diving between boxes. She ran in numb fear, trying to get as much space between them as she could. Outside, the wind howled angrily, then faded, but she could still hear the distant crackle of sparks. Darkness, boxes, crates, shadows, shapes; everything melted into one blur.

Suddenly she faced a dead end, as a burst of electricity exploded behind her. The force threw Lilly to the floor, and a jolt of lightning shattered the lights above her. Glass rained down on her back; she covered her head protectively with her hands.

"You think this is a game, girl? Well, le's play then."

Another bolt came to her right, and she could feel her wings shocked by the tiny tendrils of light that reached her. But she was too frightened to move away. Her mouth was open in a scream as she curled back against the wall, struggling to breathe as tears rolled down her face.

"Help, anyone, please!"

Laughter was all that answered, as Tray advanced. "No one c'n hear you. So why don' you just calm down, an' come with us?"

WHAM!!!

The noise that resounded cracked with the sickening thud of bone on wood, and the last sparkles of electricity illuminated the falling body with a silhouette behind it. The new figure panted, leaning back against the wall, and Lilly's eyes slowly adjusted as he dropped the baseball bat in his hand. "Are you all right?" his voice spoke, but as he took a step toward her, Lilly scuttled away, trembling as tears continued to fall down her face.

"Please... Just, please, leave me alone. Just leave me alone."

Footsteps approached, and Lilly curled away, only to feel a hand tenderly brush a tear off her face. "Hey now, it's okay. I'm not going to hurt you. If I wanted to, wouldn't I have done so already? You poor thing, you must be freezing to death!" From the corner of her eye, she was able to see his face, and somehow, she was comforted by what she saw. His posture was relaxed, his facial expression was soft and unintimidating, and genuine concern filled his features. She began to cry more openly, and felt his hands reach out to comfort her. "Hey, it's okay. I promise I'm not here to hurt you. Just give me a chance to prove it."

Anger brewed abruptly inside her, and Lilly yanked away. "A chance to prove what? That you'll kill, or hurt, or attack me? My parents didn't get a chance!" Her words were hysterical, her body shaking with grief and despair. The boy stayed where he was, watching her with an expression that looked stricken by her anger. "They just came...looking for me. Everyone is chasing me, hunting me, hurting people! Why? What are they doing this?!"

"You're a Strand. These people hunt us. Your gifts are what they're after," he answered softly.

"What gifts? What's a Strand? Us? You don't have wings! You're normal!" She pointed at him accusingly, tears staining her cheeks. The boy quietly responded by holding out an arm, and the tiny tears from her face floated into his palm. She gasped, touching her dry face in disbelief.

"I'm not normal. I'm a Strand, like you; I have my own powers." The tears formed an orb that reflected the little light there was, and he kept his eyes on it as he spoke. "I control water. That is one of my gifts. Your wings are yours. You're one of us, and that is why I am here. To help you, protect you. I'm not like Tray or Zen." He let his hand fall to his side, and the tiny sphere of tears continued to float by itself. The final sparkles of electricity overhead were fading now, and the dim glow outside was only enough to leave his lingering outline. "I just wish I could prove that you can trust me."

"How can I trust you?" Her energy was fading, her body unwillingly dragging her to defeat. She stared at the ground in hopelessness, just waiting for him to turn on her like the others. There was a shuffling noise, and a hand finally touched her shoulder. The kindness of it surprised her.

"The only reason I have for you is that I'm the only one here now. You're in the middle of an abandoned town, miles from all civilization. Everything you knew is gone: friends, home, your life. I've been where you are, and I know what it's like. You're alone, scared, you don't want to trust anyone, but you know you can't do it alone. But chance—or fate, or whatever you believe in—brought me here, and if it hadn't, you would be in a much worse situation. Come with me, and I can give you shelter, give you answers. Please...just don't stay and suffer more."

Slowly Lilly felt herself relaxing, and her final resistance faded. As he knelt next to her, she felt a calming reassurance, a feeling of safety she never thought she'd feel again. Could she trust him, after everything? Or would she rather stay here, and wait for Zen to return or Tray to wake up? Her allayed fears allowed reason to return. "I...I'll go with you," she finally whispered, sealing her fate regardless of the risks.

"Good girl. Now, let's get out of here." He paused and helped her to her feet, stabilizing her while she got her bearings. "My name is Jake, by the way."

"My name is Lilly," she answered timidly, and gave a tiny smile. As they walked around Tray's form, she paused, worried for a second he might be dead.

"He'll be okay," Jake said, gently leading her away. "Angry, but okay. It's best we're not here when he comes to. I left Zen where he won't get out for a while, but if Tray finds him first, the winds around here are going to turn into hurricane season. Just stay close until we get to the safe house. It's not too far."

Lilly nodded, keeping in stride with him as they left the warehouse. When she finally stood at the door, relief flooded her limbs, and she breathed deeply as if she was waking from a dream. The cold night stirred her pajamas, ruffling her wings in a playful way. A deep blue sky welcomed her, glowing with a blanket of stars. Everything felt so different in this moment. Like a giant flower, the abandoned town had closed around her tightly at first, its clutches suffocating her frightened limbs. But now it had opened and let her tread across its petals. Along her back, her wings nestled gently, and for once in her life, she didn't feel the need to worry about their exposure. She felt a quiet safety.

Jake led her through the alleys, this world more familiar to him than her. He had an effortless sense of direction and a tranquil demeanor that helped her stay calm. She felt numb from cold but kept moving, holding to the promise of someplace safe and warm. One step, then another, following the shadowy form in front of her; it was all she needed to do. The dim glow of the moon transformed into the soft light of morning, and Lilly watched her surroundings change, as well. Painted walls reflected colors. Blurred outlines became antique store signs. It was as if everything in this town had frozen where it was, and time gradually ate away at the remains. It was a peaceful decay, a final slumber. Glass glittered in windows and was scattered on the roadside like sprinkles on a cupcake, but even that held a dangerous beauty as Lilly grew more cautious of where she stepped with her bare feet. As careful as she was, the distracting sights caused her to grow clumsy, and she felt a sudden pain in her left foot.

Crying out, Lilly stumbled and fell, hands and knees connecting with rocks. As pain shot through her foot, Lilly curled, trying to reach it, but Jake was at her side, now holding her arm back.

"No, no, no. Don't touch it, let me look," he whispered, taking her ankle tightly in his grip and looking at the cut. Dribbles of blood trailed down her heel, mingling with dirt and grime. "You have a piece of glass in there pretty deep. I'm sorry, I should have noticed you were barefoot."

Lilly winced, gritting her teeth at the pain in her previously numb skin. "I'm sorry, I should have been more careful—"

"You have no reason to apologize. Now just hold still."

She nodded, ignoring her protesting muscles, and watched as Jake held out his palm above her foot. From seemingly nowhere, drops of liquid gathered in his hand, which he then delicately directed over the wound. It felt strange, like the water was crawling against gravity, slipping into the cut with a slight sting, then pushing the glass from her foot with the delicacy of a surgeon. As it gathered back at the surface, the remaining water cleaned the cut before running to the ground. Jake then tore a strip from the bottom of his shirt and wrapped her ankle gently, finalizing his first aid. "There, that'll hold for now. We're just around the corner from the house, and I'll wrap it better there." Before she could thank him, he scooped her off the ground, and began walking with her tucked into his arms bridal style. Face flushing red, Lilly averted her eyes and hugged her arms across her torso. The whole event felt humiliating, and her heart weighed heavy with helplessness. Gratitude drowned out guilt, however, and she refused to look up until the shadow of a building they were entering passed over them.

"Is this it?" Lilly inquired, looking around at the dusty, glass-covered floor. Jake shook his head and set her gently on a countertop.

"No. Well, sort of. Just hang on one second and you'll see." He reached down to the floorboards and grasped the edge of one of the panels, muscles flexing as he yanked upward. With a soft moan, a section rose, revealing stairs heading into the ground. "This used to be a cellar, but we built on it, expanded it under the full building and made it much sturdier. The rest of this house we left alone as a false front. We think this place used to be a schoolhouse. Now it's just our home away from home."

"'Our?'"

"Yeah, the other students and I. A few of us were here today, playing a late game of baseball. I left the bat behind so I had to backtrack, but when I was starting back toward the school I heard the commotion. I don't know if my friends will realize I'm gone right away though. It's pretty early in the morning now..." He lifted her up and carefully carried her down into a small storage room. It looked like an old cellar, cold air naturally settling into the concrete structure, but the door at the back of the landing seemed like an addition.

"Hold on. Can you stand for a second?" Jake asked. Lilly nodded, and he gingerly set her down. With a few strides, he was back up the stairs, and shut the upper door, temporarily creating darkness. His footsteps returned, then the second door opened and a light switched on. "Now we're here."

Lilly limped into the room and exhaled gratefully. A clock ticked on the wall, light bathed two couches in her immediate sight, and a strange sense of calm surrounded her, creating a soft welcome. The room she was in wasn't grand, but the essence it contained reminded her of home. Beyond the mismatched sofas— one a polka-dotted burgundy and the other a clashing shade of orange—she could make out a kitchen, and to the right the wall led straight back into a hallway. Posters decorated where photographs would be, held up with a mixture of duct tape and staples, and a backpack sat half open against a kitchen counter, its surface littered with a few glasses that hadn't made it all the way to the sink. In a way, the slight mess helped her relax. It assured her that there really was 'normal' life flowing through the walls of this place, and she quietly moved to take a seat on the couch.

Footsteps drew Lilly's attention back to the right corner of the house, where she saw Jake approaching, carrying a first-aid kit, two towels, and a bowl of water. He gave her a small smile, and nodded toward her foot. "Let's take a look at that cut now."

Lilly nodded and scooted to make room for him. Jake set his supplies on the coffee table, then lightly lifted her calf onto his knee. "So, how did you end up here anyway?" he asked conversationally, untying the strip of cloth wrapped around her ankle.

"I flew," Lilly replied. She flinched as the warm water engulfed her foot, then again as Jake frowned at her.

"No, like, what happened? Tell me how Tray and Zen ended up chasing you. Talk to me about what happened. The more I know, the more questions I can answer for you." Jake gently pulled away the fabric as the water soaked the dried blood, and he used a fresh towel to further clean it.

Lilly shivered as the images flashed through her mind. Like a videotape, her memory forced her to rewind and relive those terrible moments over and over. Every time she thought back, she saw more, felt more, regretted more. Watching the blood from her foot stain the water red, she felt hindsight similarly taint memories from the days before. She told him about the day on the beach, how the man came to her house and attacked her family, and finally, how she ran away. It was hard to speak about the last few memories without feeling a lump forming in her throat.

"Everything happened so fast. One minute I was listening to him interrogate my parents, the next I was running as fast as I could out of the house. Then those boys came after me. It all just feels unreal, but then the power of those thoughts remind me it's too painful to be a dream." Images spread before her mind's eye, filling her thoughts with 'could haves' and 'should haves' before facing the still reality of 'did.' She let that thought catch hold, forcing her eyes to meet the boy's own. "Jake, tell me the truth. Do you think I'll see my parents again?"

Jake was silent as he secured the bandage and sat back on the coffee table. Finally, his gaze met hers, and it seemed to hold a certain trace of sorrow. "I...can't tell you that. I wish I could. Maybe they escaped too, or maybe he let them go. But there's also the possibility that he didn't, or they fought and were..."

Tears began to build in her eyes, and Lilly looked away, pulling her knees against her chest and wrapping her wings tightly around her like a blanket. An emotional weight crushed her throat and lungs, but before it overwhelmed her, Jake touched her shoulder. "Lilly, I won't lie. It's going to be tough. At first, it's like you're numb to what has happened. Then there will be moments when you feel so much loss, you can't even begin to think of a future. But with time, and healing, you grow stronger. Build a new life, find new hope. Lilly, there are more of us, and we've been through it. We can help you. We can't make your life go back to normal. We can help make a new life for you, one where you can really find out who you are. Even if you've lost your family, we can build a new one. If you give us a chance, we can get you through this."

Part of her should have felt relieved, but Lilly was exhausted to the point that she could only gather melancholy interest. Any promises seemed empty, and she just couldn't be hopeful yet. Jake seemed to sense this, and gave up the monologue before standing and glancing at the clock. "Someone should be here soon, after they realize I still haven't made it back to the school. We should get you some food for now. What do you want? I got some soup, a sandwich..." He went to the kitchen and started sifting through cupboards. "We got bread, we got cheese. We got chicken noodle soup. We have apples! What about apples? Do you like apples?"

Lilly couldn't resist a small smile, "Not in soup, I don't."

Jake laughed and came back, giving a fake frown. "Not what I meant, you smart aleck. Like, to eat." He tossed her the fruit, and Lilly clumsily caught it.

"Yes, I do. Thank you." Her smile faded a bit, and she turned the fruit over, its yellow-tinted skin reminding her of the electricity Tray had used so violently. Touching it slowly, as if to reassure herself it was just an apple, she looked up at Jake. "So...who were those boys, really? And the man. Why are they after 'Strands' like us?"

Uncertainty seemed to move across the boy's face, but it quickly vanished, and Jake focused with unusual concentration on a nearby poster. "Someone else could probably describe it better. If you waited, then—"

"I want to know, Jake." Lilly startled both of them with her earnestness, sitting forward so she was barely on the couch at all. "Please. If you can explain at all, please do. Why did that man come after me?"

Jake was quiet, and his face revealed nothing of his thoughts. He sat back and thought carefully before finally speaking. "Tray and Zen work for a man named Dr. Kibbsty. He is a genetic researcher, and for years he has been studying powers like ours. A long time ago, he found out that the lilac strands we have in our hair were linked with unusual abilities, and since then, he has been tracking down and gathering students for his school, Firestone Institution."

"Wait, Strands. Lilac strands. I didn't realize—you have lilac hair, too?" Lilly glanced at him more closely, but couldn't find the familiar shade of purple. Jake turned his head slightly in response, pushing back some of the longer curls, revealing the slender locks of hair. The two lines of color seemed much less prominent than her own strands.

"It's something that's hard to see unless you're looking for it. It took us a long time to even realize some of us had more lilac than others. But when Kibbsty knew what to look for, it was easier to identify new Strands. In the past few years, his power and numbers have grown, and his methods of obtaining...subjects for his research are growing more and more deadly. You're not the first to suffer because of him, and sadly, you're not going to be the last."

"What exactly is he trying to find out about us?" Lilly questioned.

"Anything, everything," Jake started vaguely, and after a few moments, clarified. "The origin of our gifts, what controls them, what makes us who we are; basically, he is looking for a way to replicate us. As it stands, we know so little about ourselves that it would be building everything from scratch. We know that we all have powers and lilac hair, and there is a link between the two. Originally, this link was all Kibbsty knew." For a moment, a strange look took over Jake's features. It was as if all sight left his eyes, his face seemed drained by a distant grief and unreachable pain. His hair—the color of freshly-turned soil—seemed to shadow his face more deeply, and he looked just over Lilly's shoulder as if slipping off into himself for a moment. Lilly waited for him to continue, but finally spoke when he didn't.

"Jake, how did Dr. Kibbsty find out about us? And how did you find out there were others like you?"

Jake turned toward her and sighed before moving to take a seat on the couch next to her. Slowly he spoke again, bringing Lilly into his story with the rhythm in his voice. "It might be easier to start at the beginning, before any of us knew who and what we were. In those days, the idea of 'powers' or 'superhuman abilities' was something from cartoons and comic books. Our generation had yet to emerge, and the still-dormant abilities hadn't revealed themselves. Maybe a few people had discovered they were different, but those isolated incidents flickered and died in the massive population of the world. No one realized that others had powers, because everyone was trying so hard to hide them. But somewhere, in the core of our existence, there was a stirring, like a burning ember. Every person who discovered their powers made it glow, until the world was just waiting for a spark to ignite the fire. That spark turned out to be a boy named Fin."

CHAPTER FOUR

AN EXTINGUISHED FLAME

"Fin was born on December 3, 1986. Few people ever met him, but those who did described him as caring, energetic, and intelligent. There was something else to him as well; it was like his powers were already a part of him, they just hadn't manifested in a usable form yet. Fire was in his character and his actions."

"I don't get it," Lilly said with a frown; Jake's wordy way of speaking created too many questions in her mind.

"Well, think about it," Jake readjusted himself physically and verbally, trying to simplify what he was saying. "Even before our powers manifest, there's this connection inside us. It's like how for me, every time I'm around water, something stirs, almost *breathes* inside me. Ever since I was a kid, it was like that. Sitting by a pool or a lake made me feel alive. Does it feel like your wings give you a connection with birds, or other winged creatures? When you're around them, do you feel like 'Wow, this is where I'm supposed to be'?" Lilly nodded, and Jake continued. "Fin, like all of us, knew that feeling. He spent the first few years of his life like a normal kid: going to school, learning, playing with friends, waiting for that moment when he would learn what was missing."

"What do you mean 'missing'?" Lilly asked.

"When we're young, we don't know that we're different from others, nor what will happen later in life. All the same, we know there's something we can't quite reach, and we're just waiting for the day when we discover what it is. That's what Fin was waiting for." Lilly slowly understood, and as she thought about it, she felt like she could relate more to this boy. Like her desperate longing to be in the air, maybe Fin had felt a confusing connection with fire. For the first time, the ache she had felt all her life seemed normal.

Jake let her think for a moment before continuing his story. "Fin was eleven when things changed. He was on a camping trip with his mother, not too far west of here, outside of Pierce. Young, bored, and annoyed by a campfire that wouldn't start, his powers caused the wood to ignite. You can imagine the shock this caused. Dr. Allina, his mother, saw this and, after some denial and more flames, she was forced to acknowledge that her son could generate fire. The response was very different for each of them. Fin was excited and wanted to test his powers, but Dr. Allina was frightened by his gifts and worried that it could be something harmful. To ease her mind, she took him to work to see what was—as she presumed—wrong, at a medical clinic that was closed for the weekend."

"She experimented on him?" Lilly interrupted, startled.

Jake shook his head and gave a reassuring smile that bordered on a grimace. "'Experiment' is a strong word for her actions. She took a sample of his blood and ran a few tests on it, looking for some sort of anomaly. No lab-rat type exams, wires, or test tubes though. It was more of a checkup. Dr. Allina was genuinely concerned about her son. How many eleven-year-old boys do you know who could spontaneously start lighting things on fire? Everything was too unreal, too science fiction. Her education told her it wasn't possible, and she wanted to use her medical training to identify the truth, as she was taught to do all through school."

"So for her, running a few tests would be like taking a temperature when you're sick?"

"Exactly. It wasn't something she thought through. To her, running some tests would be like reaching for a thermometer. She just had the tools available to study more about what was happening than a mom who wasn't a doctor." He paused, and that sad look crossed his eyes again. A chill drifted through Lilly even before he continued.

"In a way, you could say her need to understand their situation was their downfall. That day, once she had left, a colleague of hers found out that she had run tests on her son and wanted to know why. When he broke into the security footage and found that the tapes were missing, he became convinced that there was something more to find. He ransacked the office and eventually found a piece of paper that Dr. Allina had ripped up and thrown away. Her notes about the tests were on it, with scrawled remarks about proteins, mutations, and the word 'lilac.' To the average person, they didn't mean much. But for her colleague, it was everything he dreamed of discovering. He had studied human genetics and focused on mutations for years, but that could be the breakthrough he was looking for. So that day, he made plans to kidnap Fin."

"That man. Was he..." Lilly shivered and couldn't even get the name out.

Jake gave her a knowing look and then continued. "Yes. That man was Dr. Kibbsty. Late that night, he staged a break-in at the clinic to draw Dr. Allina away. While she was gone, he snuck into Dr. Allina's house and tried to kidnap Fin. His plan failed horribly when Fin's fear caused the floor between them to ignite, and Dr. Kibbsty tried to defend himself by shooting the boy. Fin died from the wound, and Dr. Kibbsty escaped, leaving no evidence to convict him for his actions."

"That's awful! But if Fin was dead, how come he didn't just...give up?" Lilly implored.

"Anger, mostly. He was angry he had lost a key to his research, and he was determined to try to find that link again. He was the type of scientist who believed this first hint of a new life-form or mutation would just be the start of things for him. Like an iceberg, more would be underneath; Fin, to him, was just the start. Unfortunately, it wouldn't take long for him to find another 'subject,' and he was able to continue his research."

"What about Dr. Allina?"

Jake didn't speak right away, seeming to struggle with composure and his words. The formal narrative he used at first slipped for a moment, and he looked over Lilly's shoulder while he talked. "Dr. Kibbsty got away, and Dr. Allina was heartbroken. Her son was killed because of the power she had discovered, and she was afraid...afraid of what she had started. His desire to understand took a life, her child's life, and at first, she wanted to pull away from medicine altogether. But after a while, she realized that if mutations like her son's were possible, other children like Fin could be in danger. So she made plans for a school—the school I mentioned—that would be a safe haven for others like her son. She called it Charity Academy."

"Those boys talked about a school, too. There are two of them?"

Jake sighed, glaring at a wall to his side. "Dr. Kibbsty also created a school, most likely taking Dr. Allina's idea and trying to twist it. After a few years on the run, he came back to Idaho and built it up in the mountains. He managed to gather a handful of his own students and teachers, and he started working his way to the control he wields now."

"It just seems odd to me," Lilly blurted out, recoiling shyly when she realized she had interrupted. Jake nodded to encourage her to speak. "I mean, I just, I never met anyone like me before, and here you are, with teachers and students and schools, all hidden up here in the mountains. How could you find each other without being *found*?"

Jake put his hands behind his head, reclining on the couch with a thoughtful expression. The clock ticked on the wall, reminding her of the time that had passed since they began speaking. The discomfort and anger faded from his features again, and his voice regained its rhythmic tone. "Students like us, we're drawn to each other through tiny connections. We're attracted to the safety of numbers, but in a way, that creates danger. When we're together, we're stronger, but we're also more noticeable, and the more of us we find, the harder it is to keep everything secret. In the beginning, it wasn't like that. It was a game of hide-and-go seek, a contest to locate someone first. As our numbers grow, it's harder to stay safe and out of harm's way. It's *not* perfect. We find each other, get discovered, cover our tracks, and hide. We've also fought each other, as the opinions of how we should use our powers separate us.

"It's like a civil war is ready to erupt, and the line runs right through this town, this mountain. We've gone on for so long and grown so large in our numbers, it's created tensions that are old for us, new to you. For you, there is so much to decide and take in because this isn't just a new world, it's a battlefield. The sides you choose now, the people you listen to... Every choice is going to decide your future, whether you're ready or not. It's not fair, it's not right, but it's our lives now..." As he finished, he sat for a moment before picking up the towels and bowl from the table. He shut off the conversation, lost in his own thoughts as he moved away. He didn't look back at her, but paused at the edge of the room, turning the bowl slowly in his hands.

"I'm sorry if it confuses you, but with time, I think everything gets better. Try to rest and think, but don't stress about it. I'm going to check and see if we can get to the school safely yet."

With that, he left, and Lilly was alone once more. The emptiness around her was growing more familiar as she curled into the couch, laying her head on the shoulder rest. Lilly gazed at the ceiling, imagining the stars beyond her reach, like the life beyond her touch. The weight of the changes finally registered, and now she just had to look ahead and try to decide where she belonged. Her only comfort was with the quiet boy who had rescued her and whatever safety his presence might bring her.

It had been an hour since the conversation ended, and still nothing had changed, leading Lilly to feel like a rabbit in a fox's den, patiently expecting the end to all her misery. As promising as Charity Academy sounded, Lilly could not see past the tiny house in which she was hiding, gradually growing more claustrophobic. Jake kept promising that his friends would arrive soon, but the longer they stayed, the less his words affected her. Jake had been gone for hours; certainly if help were coming, it would have already arrived.

"Stop thinking about them," Jake scolded her, coming back in the front door from his scouting mission. "We're just waiting a few more minutes, and if no one comes, we're going to and make it to the school by ourselves."

"But, my parents…"

"I promise, we'll try our best to find out what happened to them, but I'm pretty sure their top priority would be keeping you safe." He glanced at her expectantly, and Lilly slowly nodded in agreement. He continued, "I've been looking around, trying to get an idea of the safest way out, and once we slip past Kibbsty's goons, it's a straight line to the school. For now, you need to relax."

"How can I relax, Jake? There is an electric psychopath and a weather manipulator out there ready to tear my wings off!" Lilly whimpered, huddling under her blanket. They had been going on like this for the past hour, but Jake wasn't ready to leave and Lilly wasn't ready to relax.

Jake sighed and sat on the couch, rubbing his forehead with his hands. "I know, it isn't exactly a vacation, but worrying isn't going to help the situation. As scary as their powers seem right now, just remember, they're only Strands like us. We have gifts too."

"I have wings. What am I going to do, tickle them to death with a feather?" Lilly grumbled. Jake's mouth twitched, as if trying to suppress a smile.

"Let's just talk about something else. Is there anything less morbid on your mind?"

Lilly fiddled with her hair a little, and as she touched the lilac streak to the right of her face, it triggered a question. "So, you keep calling us Strands. You said it's because we all have the same little chunk of lilac hair, right?"

Jake nodded, and sat forward to explain. "Being a 'Strand' may refer to the lilac hair we have, but that mutation carries a lot of different things. It is more than just connected with our powers; its physical nature is unique. For one, it's resistant to any damage like dying or perming, and the color is consistent, always this pale, almost pastel purple, regardless of the individual's hair color. And we're pretty sure each 'Strand' has about ten individual strands of lilac hair. That's been pretty consistent. It's like these mutations are controlled by something separate from normal physical attributes. People with curly hair can still have a perfectly straight strand, and people with sun-bleached hair show no change in their strand's color. I think part of the reason it doesn't respond to typical inherited traits is the connection with our powers. The lilac strands act like an indicator of how many powers we have. No one really understands why it happens, but it's like there is a genetic link between the proteins that cause the pigments in our hairs and our abilities. When someone has one ability, they have one lilac strand, and the powers connected to it seem, as far as we know, random.

"Our parents didn't show signs of powers, and it's been hard to trace the gene that causes this. We don't understand what instructions our bodies followed to produce what they did. What makes one person able to control the weather and another only able to make office supplies is a mystery to us, but the variety in our abilities is astounding, even with all the uncertainties. Once you start meeting others like us, you'll be amazed at the wide range of powers everyone has. And yet, everyone is connected by their strands." Jake gave a small chuckle and sighed, rubbing his hand through his hair. "It really is remarkable."

"You said each 'Strand' has a certain amount of lilac hair. What do you mean by—"

Lilly never finished, because at that moment, a bolt of electricity shot through the lights, and plummeted them into an explosive darkness.

CHAPTER FIVE

BLOOD-COVERED HANDS

5 Hours Earlier...

"It's done," spoke the teen, as his arm shifted back into normal flesh. A few stubborn drops of water clung to the edges of the wooden chest by the bed, but nothing would have drawn the eye to the once crimson-stained floor. Everything looked as it had once been, before the terrors of the night swept through this peaceful home. The only things out of place now were the figures standing in the room: a teenage boy as still as a toy soldier and a middle-aged man standing at the window. As the water evaporated, Dr. Kibbsty stood like a sentry, before finally nodding.

"The bodies are taken care of?"

"Yes. All is done."

"Very good. You may return to school with the others. I will follow once I'm sure no evidence remains."

"Understood."

The teenage boy gave a respectful nod before leaving the room, and Kibbsty turned to the closet, his gloved hands resting lightly in his pockets. He stood immobile in an intense vigil; his soundless battle with a long gone foe. No clues or resolutions could be found within this room, only frustrations and failed plans. Time snuck silently by as he gazed at the space where the clothing had been pushed aside, going over the events from that night before finally settling his thoughts into that solitary moment, when his carefully laid plan had slipped from his grasp.

He stood there, the parents helpless at his feet. Defiant to the last moment, they refused to tell where the girl was hidden, with that selfless sacrifice with which he'd grown so disgusted these past few years. All it took was a nod, and Harris struck the father with a metal arm—a blow that would surely have crushed his ribs—leaving them quietly crying at his mercy. It was a sweet satisfaction, the blood from the hunt, leading to the kill. His final taunts, verbally torturing them with threats for their daughter, hissed in their ears before he gave Harris the order to kill.

That was when the first rip in his meticulously stitched plan appeared.

The teen stumbled backwards, as if struck by some invisible force, his arm only halfway to gun form. Though the boy rarely showed any emotion, Kibbsty could see confusion dance across the shadowed face.

"What are you doing?" Kibbsty felt himself yell, whirling in the darkness to face the frozen teen.

The emptiness returned to Harris' face, and he straightened to attention. Even rigid and silent, he stole a small glance to the left, but he didn't seem to see what he was looking for.

"I thought... It was nothing. I apologize for the delay." His speech cleanly ended, and the only noise that followed was the click of his mechanical forearm loading the gun.

"Don't let it happen again. Finish the job."

Two thuds of bullets into flesh answered, one quickly after another. There was no chance to scream or feel pain; they had been spared that much. Perhaps he could have let them live, subdued them until he found the girl, but that would have taken away the satisfaction of reminding his followers the cost of defiance.

Kibbsty growled as he ordered the house to be searched, then grew angrier with each empty room. It was as if the world had swallowed his prey, causing her to vanish without a trace. Now, as he faced the closet, he still didn't understand it. Traces of feathers lingered among the jackets, still warm from body heat. The clothes were pushed to the side, suggesting the girl had hidden among them, but she was gone. This wasn't the first time one of his prospective subjects had escaped; these individuals were elusive by nature, and he had acted accordingly. This girl had seemed much easier, a stranger to the cruelties that could be inflicted on her, yet she still managed to evade their efforts. It was an unfortunate blunder, but one he wouldn't make again.

Dr. Kibbsty turned and looked out the window. The street lamps were dim in the distance, and the night deep and black. He ran a hand through his hair and replaced his hat as he pondered. She couldn't get far. She had wings, but she was also young and sheltered. A scare such as this would have limited the distance that she could have traveled, and his students were already after her. If she was flying, Zen would direct the winds, driving her toward the ghost town where Tray would be waiting. If she tried coming home, Harris would be ready. But something didn't settle right. He couldn't be confident that he had her. Outside the window, the darkness cloaked the city much the same way the lack of information hid this girl. He knew he had to capture her, but her movements were hard to predict under the veil.

As the aged man gritted his teeth, he touched his right arm, then let his fingers linger just above his jacket and the skin underneath. There had been a time when he underestimated a child, and he still had the burn to prove it. Now he wouldn't make the same mistake; it was more than a matter of pride, or even the money he would receive from his research. This girl was a threat now, one that needed to be contained; if someone as fragile as she could evade him, how could he keep fear in the hearts of his followers to ensure their cooperation?

Run where you can, little girl. This battle has just begun.

With a final glance at the blackened night, Kibbsty swept his jacket on and determinedly strode from the room.

He would find her.

"Somethin's wrong."

The statement came with the calmness that tended to accompany unsettling worry. The green-haired girl stood quietly on the roof's edge, gazing at the starry night above her. The silver-haired boy leaned against the chimney beside her, like a sculpture carved into the building; he didn't move or seem to acknowledge what she had said. It didn't bother her; she was long used to his stoic disconnect with trouble.

"Cory, can't you sense it? Somethin's happenin'. Do you think we should—"

"He hasn't called us; he doesn't need us. We have our job, Trish. You know that."

"Yeah, but...I can just feel it. The winds are unsettled, there're flickers of light in the distance; Tray and Zen are fightin' somethin'. It shouldn' be like that."

"Let it go, Trish."

The edge of the words felt physically cold, and Trish sighed, forcing away her anxiety. It had been nearly two weeks since they moved into this school, but she still felt on edge. Compared to Firestone, it could have been paradise, but maybe that was what unsettled her. She was used to the cold floors, the bare walls, and the candles flickering in the corridors late at night. A haunted house atmosphere was all she had known for the past few years, and now something so warm and cozy just didn't feel right. In fact, it felt more dangerous than ever. Kibbsty always had reasons for his missions, though. There was always someone to collect, something to discover, some upper hand to gain in their continuous war against whoever stood in the way. Having a few double agents in place at Charity just seemed like a nice backup plan back then. Now it seemed their mission would be more important than ever. They couldn't risk making a mistake.

"We should check in soon."

"I'm heading out in the morning to meet with Kibbsty." Cory turned toward her, his expression eerily calm. "But the rest of you need to keep it together. If you're so worried about tonight going badly, then you better make sure we're not the next to mess things up. You need to keep our cover here. I won't be gone long but..." He gave her a sharp glare, and she returned it irritably.

"We'll do our part, but when somethin' goes wrong, it's all of our problems. You need to realize that."

"I carry my own weight. Tray should just learn to handle his better." Without another word, he turned and slipped back down the building on a staircase of ice. His abruptness could be insulting to those that didn't know him, but it was all about how one read it. Cory didn't like to waste words or time. Part of Trish admired him for that; the other part wanted to strangle him for it. Groaning, Trish rubbed her face in her hands and tried to take in everything that was happening. It was too much for her. Maybe Cory was right. She just needed to learn to be a better villain, or she wouldn't survive.

Trish breathed in the night air and sought that quiet place inside her, where the conduits of her powers connected. She let the energy flow into her hands until they glowed with tiny orbs of light, then released them, throwing the spheres into the night. They popped loudly, spinning in a careless freefall toward the earth before erupting into sparks and trailing into the grass. It was strangely calming. For a few moments, she almost forgot the trepidation that had touched her, and then she felt the wind tug the long hair on the right side of her face, as if trying to tell her the tale of what was happening beyond this rooftop. Surrendering her momentary relief, Trish crept back toward her own end of the building, but not without one final glance at the foreboding flashes of light in the distance.

CHAPTER SIX

A SECOND GIFT

"Lilly, we have to leave, now!"

Confusion and pain mingled together, and Lilly felt disconnected as she tried to move. Dots flashed across her stunned eyes, and her mind couldn't register where she was sitting or what was happening. Explosions, electricity, and the scream of wind became clues swirling in her mind. It was as if the air around her was alive, threatening to drag her from the glass-littered couch. She tried to stand and follow Jake's voice, but another explosion knocked her from her feet; her fall was broken by a strong hand on her arm.

"There's a back exit, but we have to hurry! This building isn't built to stand up to this kind of abuse!"

Lilly nodded to the darkness, and Jake pulled her through the house as sparks raced like veins across the ceiling. The boards creaked and groaned as the aged wood struggled to stay in place. Lilly saw light up ahead, and it brought her hope—until she saw the two figures standing in the sunbeams.

"Lovely little burrow you found here. It certainly makes our job easier." Tray's face was haunting, features sharpened with shadows and littered with bruises from their previous encounter. Electricity rolled down his shoulders to his hands, cracking with anger and rage. While Zen's face seemed almost amused by the whole event, Tray was ready for revenge.

Everything happened at once—a gust of wind hit Lilly from behind, slamming her into the floor, and the walls erupted with an angry gush of water that crashed through the hallway. Electricity shot through the air, as bright and blinding as bolts of lightning, shattering walls and lighting fires that were quickly extinguished by the water that came behind it. Lilly's senses were overwhelmed: smoke in her throat, dirt on her tongue, and debris in her eyes. All the while, three figures engaged in an elemental battle, destroying the building around them.

Lilly had never seen a fight of this proportion. Water snaked around Zen's ankles, threatening to drag him down as a bolt of electricity sent Jake diving behind the remains of the couch. Wind threw glasses from the cupboards, causing Lilly to jump out of the way, and debris from the ceiling drove her back into a corner. While Lilly's actions were motivated by fear, the three boys moved with soldier-like experience. From tiny bullet-like projectiles of water or electricity to strategic hurling of picture frames and utensils, this chaos was intimidatingly controlled.

"You're brave with your powers, aren't you, punk?" Tray snarled from the hallway, shattering the clock with a coil of light.

"About as brave as you are, Sparky!" spat Jake, flattening him with a wave of water.

Angry and sputtering, Tray staggered, his long legs tense with effort. Instead of readying another attack during his recovery, he moved in a slow, purposeful circle around Jake, his hands down by his sides. "How 'bout we level the field, eh?" Jake watched him, water returning to his side and hovering threateningly in the air. "I c'n fight just fine without my powers. What about you?" Tray's voice ended with a startling silence as electricity vanished and water fell, uncontrolled, to the ground. Taking the opportunity, Zen slowly rose back to his feet, shaking water from his hair and chuckling slightly. Jake stood frozen, eyes staring blindly forward. Whatever Tray had done left him struggling in frustration for abilities he couldn't grasp. From her corner of the room, Lilly struggled with the confusing information. The wind still swirled around Zen, but Jake and Tray both stood powerless. *Level the playing field*, Tray had said. The playing field obviously was only between two opponents.

"That's playing dirty," Jake hissed, hands clenching into fists as he backed a couple steps away.

"That's what separates you an' me. *You* think it's playin' dirty. *I* think it's just survival of the *fittest!*" Tray sent a punch at Jake's jaw and then dove to the side, allowing Zen's wind to tear apart a segment of wall and hurl it at Jake. The plaster-laden drywall caught him across the shoulder and he grunted in pain, falling against the couch and scrambling to move. With a sneer of victory on his face, Tray moved closer, brutally kicking his rival in the ribs and forcing him to the ground. Lilly struggled to her feet, desperate to stop the attack, but her way was blocked by Zen's storm.

"So you've taken to picking on girls and beating up the blind?" Jake kept moving as he spoke, sending a sweeping kick into Tray's shins that knocked the Irish boy to the floor. He taunted them angrily, but with an element of fear in his voice; Zen was already advancing on him, looking calm and unimpressed by his words.

"We use our strengths to our advantage, regardless of who stands in our way," Zen shrugged, retaliating for his companion by blasting Jake back into the wall. "You're wasting your breath. If you knew what was good for you, you'd shut up and stay down." The threat was followed by a sharp punch to Jake's stomach.

Lilly flinched in empathy, but kept herself from speaking out as she carefully approached the wind mutant from behind. Zen raised his hand one more time, compressing air above his head like a weapon, but before he could strike, Lilly swung at him with a broken board—and missed.

The result was chaos.

The board glanced off of Zen's shoulder, knocking his attack sideways. It careened through the front wall and sent a terrible crack through the ceiling. Zen's powers created a blast of anger that flattened Lilly painfully onto the ground, but the wind was drowned out by the building's groans of distress. Zen glanced in shock at the ceiling, then made a break for the door as the building came crashing down around them.

"Did you hear something?"

A group of students sat by the edge of a glistening fountain, the trickle of water creating a peaceful hum as they focused on homework. At the question, a redhead looked up, pushing her hair behind her ear. "What's that, Tami?"

"I heard a crash. Well, more like a *fwump*. Or maybe a *boom*." Tami crinkled her nose in frustration, struggling to hear the sound again. The students around her lost interest and looked back down at their papers.

"You're always hearing *something*," muttered one of the boys under his breath, but the redhead hushed him.

"It could be something important! Where did you hear it?"

Tami stood and turned slowly, pointing finally into the trees. "A few miles that way. The ghost town, I'm sure of it. Is Jake back yet?"

"I haven't seen him, but Caleb said he went back for his bat. They were all out playing midnight baseball."

"He should've been back by now, though. He's usually pretty good at checking back in if he's detained." The boy who muttered the first time shrugged, remaining uninterested, but the redheaded girl stood and glanced worriedly at the trees. "Do you think someone should see what's going on? Just to be safe?"

"I'm sure everything is fine..."

"Humor me."

"I can have a go at it." A teen with a blue sweater spoke up, drawing the girls' attention. He set his books down and stood, letting himself into the conversation. "I can check on it, I mean."

"Thanks, Wyvr, that would help me feel better. You sure you don't mind?"

"No worries. I need to get some air anyway." Wyvr stretched his arms with emphasis.

The redhead looked concerned, but sighed and finally gave in. "Stay in contact with your brother, okay? If something is wrong, we don't want more people involved."

Wyvr gave a small smile and winked. "Don't worry so much, Meg. I'm sure everything is fine." With that, the boyish grin faded into a peregrine falcon's rigid expression, and with a final caw, the now-bird-of-prey quickly disappeared into the trees. Meg, meanwhile, nibbled nervously on a strand of hair, the dark color glimmering like blood on her lips in the morning sun.

When Lilly awoke, it took her a moment to realize that she was conscious. Everything around her was dark, and her body felt disconnected from her thoughts. A fuzzy, dull sensation of pain lurked on the corners of her mind, and as she approached awareness the pain intensified. Her wings felt like they were covered with thousands of white-hot needles, and her body felt crushed by weight on top of her. Everything circled around a realization she couldn't quite grasp—a math problem that she knew she could solve if she wasn't missing one variable. She didn't understand why she couldn't move, or why it hurt to breathe. Then the dirt around her caused a cough to roll out of her lips, and she nearly chocked when her chest didn't have room to expand for air afterward. Confusion slowly slipped to the back of her mind, and fear started to take its place. As Lilly tried to move and break free of the rubble around her, she subconsciously knew what had happened.

She was buried alive.

"Jake?! Jake! Someone, anyone!"

Dirt filled her mouth, and she had another coughing fit as it took its toll. Each reverberating gasp for air further damaged her broken body. Lilly attempted to struggle against the debris that held her, but no amount of fighting seemed to allow her to move more than a few inches.

<Stay calm. The more you struggle, the less air you're going to have.>

Lilly didn't recognize the voice, nor did she understand where she was hearing it. Her mind grew fuzzy again.

Help...someone...

<Help is coming. Try to relax.>

Darkness took over Lilly's mind, alongside the voice trying to calm her. In her last moments of clarity, she wondered who had been talking, and how they managed to speak inside her head.

The shelter from the night before was unrecognizable as Jake dug himself out from the debris. Boards, glass, and metal folded atop themselves like a poorly stacked deck of cards, with everything from bricks to glass demolished beyond recovery. Miraculously, Jake came out mostly unharmed, using his powers to protect himself from the worst of it. As he looked from side to side, however, he could not find the girl that had unwittingly instigated the battle.

"Lilly! Lilly, where are you?"

He lifted boards with his water and searched with thermal vision to locate the girl. Near the middle of the building he found her, a tiny pulse of life in an empty void, flickering back at him. Guilt swam in his stomach as he rummaged through the debris; he felt like a failure for letting this happen. She was in his care right now. He was supposed to keep her safe, but as time went by and the heat got dimmer, he knew how poorly he had done.

<Jake! Jake, what happened?>

The voice entered Jake's mind telepathically, and he glanced up as a peregrine falcon fluttered to rest in front of him. With a light hop, it found a solid place to perch before shifting back into a teen and standing warily on the rubble.

Jake leaned back on his heels and kept lifting boards while he spoke. "I left my bat back in the empty lot last night. When I went to get it, I heard a bunch of yelling and found this girl being chased by Tray and Zen. I managed to help—" he grunted as he lifted a particularly large piece of drywall, and Wyvr quickly moved to give him a hand "—but it was too hard getting her back in the shape she was in, especially at night. We were going to wait until a little later this morning, but then those idiots attacked us. Everything is a little fuzzy after that..."

"Where are Tray and Zen now?"

"No idea. I don't see them here, but I've seen them worm their way out of worse before. Can you check on Lilly with your telepathy? Just to make sure she's okay?"

"I can try, but I won't be able to help you dig while I'm using telepathy. Doesn't work when I'm a human."

"Making sure she's not panicking is going to be more helpful right now. I can use my powers to dig, but from what I can feel with my powers, she is a long way down. She needs to stay calm and save whatever air she has."

Wyvr nodded his head and moved out of the way before returning to bird form. While the falcon concentrated, Jake continued to lift more of the larger objects with water pressure. The body heat was still dim, but they were getting closer. Object by object, rubble was moved aside with care. It all looked the same to Jake after a while: supports, bricks, aged concrete smashed to pieces. With increasing amounts of effort, Jake continued to condense the water clinging to the porous objects and move on; eventually he was forced to lift the last few pieces by hand. Wyvr reappeared at his side, grabbing and lifting boards, together bridging the final gap. "I lost her; she kept drifting in and out of consciousness." He cut his sentence short, and Jake saw the fear on his companion's face. They needed to get to her soon, or it would be too late.

Their pace crawled along, but finally they saw a feather poking out from the dirt, then handfuls more. They carefully uncovered her slim figure, and Jake tried not to focus on the damage to her skin. Blood lingered around her, and as they lifted her, he could feel its sticky texture on his hands.

"Lilly! Lilly, can you hear me?"

Voices. Voices came to her ears again, from somewhere far away. It was a place Lilly didn't want to return to, but was unwillingly dragged toward. She once again felt dizzy. Drained. Things didn't register in her mind properly, like a scratched CD jumping forward in the song repeatedly.

"Lilly, come on, girl! Hang in there."

Words. Words were so useless. Pointless. Did they make the pain go away? Maybe they could make the pain sound like nothing, but no word really healed; only action could do that. She laid still, her heart fighting to stabilize its fluttering rhythm. She tried to piece together what she was hearing and forced herself to listen. She needed to move. It was time to wake up. But she was numbed by the pain she felt, and wanted nothing more than for it to go away. Go away. Just go away. Her scattered thoughts struggled for clarity, fighting against the fog. Then finally a voice in the back of her mind made its way through.

When one longs for healing, one must wish for it. The mental battle is the first step. You can't heal unless you want it. She could still hear Jake's quiet whispers and confused mutterings, her own wordless doubt, but then…

Something happened.

A strange sensation began at the tips of her wings and slowly glided through her veins, through each damaged feather and down her back. It crept along her ribs and spine, down to her toes, and out to the tips of her fingers. It slithered along her head, and finally zipped to the very end of her lilac strands. Her eyes shot open as the feeling took over, like being dropped in a hot bath, or sinking to the bottom of a sandy ocean floor. It was absolute peace and quiet, and her eyes slowly closed again as she drifted into the gentle rhythm of the manifestation. The sensation was like smelling a silent night or seeing whispers; she was experiencing something that couldn't exist and was being humbled into numbness. The world faded from view, and soft healing overtook her weak body. Suddenly, it was over, and her eyes fluttered open.

"Li...Lilly?" Jake whispered, and she sat up, holding a hand delicately to her head. She gazed dizzily into his face and looked at her undamaged skin, confusion continuing to grow. Around her, the chaos-struck building painted a scene where her memories struggled for information. On her arms, blood was still dried on her skin, but the injuries had vanished. While she tried to process it, Jake stared, blinking as if he couldn't believe what he saw. "You're...okay! Lilly, you're a Second Strand! You can heal!"

Lilly felt bewildered as she pulled one wing next to her face, then the other, finding every feather in perfect order. It should not have been possible, after the pain she felt. She looked up at Jake as he came closer, beginning to shake. "I can heal myself? But why all of a sudden? I've never been able to heal like that before!"

Jake shook his head, putting his hand behind his neck. A boy next to him spoke up instead, one Lilly hadn't met before. He wore a blue sweater with the name 'Wyvr' embroidered on the right side of his chest. "Maybe that gift hadn't manifested yet. Some of them come with puberty, or are from birth, while others only reveal themselves in frightening or dire situations. But yours could just be dormant and only come when needed and called on. Did you want to heal?"

Lilly was baffled. "Of course I did! That hurt like heck!"

Wyvr laughed, relaxing enough to give a natural shake of his head, and reached to help her step out of the debris. "I'm sorry, mate. Stupid question. No use breaking our brains on it now. One thing's clear—you're not a normal Strand; you're a Second."

"A Second? I...I don't understand."

Jake chewed his lip for a second, collecting himself before answering her question. "Second Strands are like regular Strands, but they have a second batch of lilac hair that connects with their new ability. Unlike everyone else though, Second Strands also have a glitch. Tray can control electricity, and he can suppress a Strand's powers. His glitch is that he can't use both abilities at the same time. Or there is me, for example: I can control water, and can see just about anything. But my weakness is that without my powers, I'm blind."

"You're blind?" Lilly interrupted, then quickly regretted it and started to apologize. Jake cut her off.

"Don't be sorry; it's not like I act blind. My powers allow me to see in everything from thermal vision to x-ray, but my normal vision, which would allow me to see colors and shapes as you do, is gone. So in a way, I'm still 'blind,' but my powers sort of substitute for what I can't see. A lot of our powers are like that; they give and take. I think it's the way the body handles the changes they're put through. There is only so far it can be altered before it becomes too unstable to function. That's why you'll only see up to two strands: the body just breaks down and can't handle more."

The concise statement sent a chill through Lilly, and she could hardly believe what she heard. "You mean there are no Third Strands? Maybe you just never met one," she struggled to speak.

Jake seemed oblivious to her discomfort. "Well, it's because of the 'glitches' you start seeing in the Second Strands. If someone was born with a third strand, then judging from what Dr. Allina has gathered, that person would experience a total internal breakdown. It's like everything from the microscopic level up would start falling apart, because the strain of what they should be and what they've become would grow to be too much. But the malfunction that occurs between our mutation and 'normal' genetics is exactly what has stumped Dr. Kibbsty so far. He's trying to adapt powers to people who don't have them naturally, and the process of trying to place these abilities in normal humans is out of his reach because their bodies cannot cope with the changes. The lack of living Third Strands has proved to be a problem."

"But, I…never mind." This didn't seem like the time or the place to argue about it, so Lilly let go of her questions and focused on getting out of this ghost town instead. She missed the second glance Jake gave her lilac hair though, his shared concern vanishing in the silence that followed.

The new arrival hung back and put his hands in his sweater pockets as they slipped into the alleyway. Their safe house, once one of the few standing figures, was now even worse than the ruins of the neighboring structures. After they moved a few steps farther, it blended into the endless piles of debris that would have long ago been removed in another town. Through the skeleton of the exteriors, Lilly could see the half-collapsed remains of fragile-looking supports and a thick layer of rubble unevenly scattered across the ground. Enlivened by her healing and filled with curiosity, Lilly paused at one of the larger buildings and gazed through it for a moment. Maybe she wouldn't question Jake about her strands, but it didn't stop her from wondering about their surroundings.

"Why do they leave condemned buildings up like this? The one we were in, these ones here... It just seems dangerous, even without turning them into battle fronts," she whispered, staring into the ghostly structure.

Jake focused on where she was peering for a moment, as if he was analyzing the view. "This town is a ghost town. All of the buildings are like this, and no one is around to demolish them—no reason to rebuild. I've heard the state just wants it left like this for now. Gradually, people just moved away and forgot. Who would want to live here? Nearest town is Pierce, which is a half hour's drive minimum from here, going west."

"Where is 'here?'" Lilly asked, walking alongside him again.

"Um, well..."

"It's at the base of Snowy Summit and Weitas Butte, in the Rocky Mountains," the other boy spoke up.

"Montana?"

"Idaho. Close to the Montana border, though." They passed another dilapidated structure, a building with the windows blown out and what looked like rusted bird cages fallen on the floor inside. Lilly's wings gave a flutter, and she hurried past.

"Idaho?" she said, making a small face.

Jake chuckled. "Yeah, Northeast Idaho. Pierce is six hours from Boise, if you know where that is."

Lilly nodded and scurried across a patch of smoother dirt, walking more carefully along the rocks, with her bare feet complaining all the way. The alley transitioned into a path for a short bit, then they turned a second corner, and it was back to rubble and dirt. What was strange was, in many ways, Tray had been right. This town *was* practically alleys.

"So, where is the other school? Firestone?"

"Southeast of here, a few miles off of the Montana border and in the middle of the Rockies. On Bad Luck Mountain, of all places."

Lilly laughed. "Now you have to be making that up."

"Nope," Wyvr grinned. "Look on a map sometime if you don't believe me. Or even read up some history. That's where Lewis and Clark really ran into some 'bad luck.' Almost didn't make it."

"Huh. Still, that seems a bit too fictional to me."

"Says the girl with the angel wings," Jake winked.

They weaved their way through the buildings and the undergrowth; Lilly's calves soon burned with pain and her feet ached in misery. From one street to the next, Jake navigated like an expert, and she delicately followed. Each building was unique—some looked like houses, one resembled a church. Slowly, forestry closed in around them, and the going grew a bit slower, with more hazards to avoid stepping on.

"Hang in there...not much farther."

This sparked a tiny flame of energy through her, enough to get her through the foliage. Before she knew it, they had reached the edge of the trees, and a building came into view. "There it is, Lilly. Charity Academy."

Some things we never forget, and for Lilly, this was one of them. To her, a girl who had never seen a normal school, let alone something of this scale, it was stunning. It sat perched like a brown eagle, with huge wings of windows and walls reaching to the sides, the entrance an elegant head in the middle. The walls were a soft tan and the roof a deep brown. The grounds weaved around the school, featuring gardens to the distant right, a glittering lake behind the school in the east, and in front of her, an elegant fountain encircled by a ring of grass. Flower beds, rose gardens, and splashes of color were everywhere. It was like one of the paintings she so admired had come to life. Despite that, the school only held her gaze for a minute, as other things captivated her even more: the *students*.

They were scattered across her field of vision, and they were all *like her*! A group of boys played poker under a tree, until one boy shoved the others and somehow switched all their positions, as if they had been shuffled like a giant deck of cards. By the fountain, a different boy laughed at the blue-eyed girl next to him as she frantically tried to shield herself from water exploding from her drawing pad. Yet another boy spat a ball of fire at a squirrel, then laughed before transforming into a green lizard and quickly scurrying away from the chattering animal. Lilly watched them disappear, mouth open slightly with awe and fascination. It couldn't be real.

"Hey, look out!"

Lilly's attention was yanked back to the path, where she saw a girl in the distance, frantically waving her arms in her direction. Lilly's mouth curled downward in a confused 'O,' and she turned back to the path, when she heard a rumbling noise. The next moment, she was forced to dive into the grass, narrowly avoiding being hit by a boy on a skateboard.

"Whoa!" She looked up in time to see the teen fall, his skin flashing as a covering of metal scales appeared, clanging loudly against the rocks. It mingled with the sound of splintering wood, and the boy let out a loud moan as he crawled off the remains of the skateboard. "Aw, man!"

"Caleb, you could have killed her!" The boy made a face as footsteps raced up, and someone spoke behind Lilly. "Hey, are you okay?"

Brushing the grass from her pants, Lilly turned to face the girl that had saved her neck. Her two male companions helped her to her feet and glared at the skateboarder. "Yeah, I'm fine," Lilly said dizzily, holding her arms and wings out to reassure the spectators.

Jake focused on the other girl. "What in the world happened, Katie?"

"'Kat' works, Jake. I hate being called 'Katie.'" The girl pushed her glasses up her nose, and her short black hair fell flat again. She glared for a moment in the direction of the skateboarder and huffed. "Caleb was being himself and nearly ran your friend here over. I'm just glad this time I was looking out for someone in danger of his antics."

"What antics? I'm a good skateboarder!" Caleb protested, despite the angry gazes. Kat stuck her tongue out and he frowned more deeply. "And that board was custom! Do you know how hard it was to get that deck?"

"Caleb, you really need to grow up sometimes," Kat snarled.

"Make me, *Katie!*"

"I would, if I thought it was possible!"

"Yeah? When have you ever tried acting like anything less than a know-it-all?"

"Well I know *something*, unlike you!"

"Yeah, well let's hear what you know about skateboards and maybe I'll be impressed!"

"You're riding around on a piece of wood with wheels on it!"

Lilly managed to suppress a small laugh as Jake slowly directed her away from the two arguing teenagers. They snuck around the broken skateboard and resumed their walk without further incident. Following the path, they took the fork to the right around the fountain as smells of flowers and water drifted to Lilly's nose. Noises came to her ears from various groups, the loudest from the poker game, its dispute still billowing. Somehow, these little spats fascinated her. Even when the people around her were bickering, Lilly felt drawn to them. It was a world they had here, just like the outside one, but with an added dimension: one of powers. The things they were doing were so natural to them. Everything sounded so strange, the little moments revealing sound bites of their world.

"You're cheating, Will!"

"Am not!" argued a boy with red-brown hair. Cards were scattered everywhere.

"Your eyes are silver! You seriously think you can fool me?"

"I don't know, is it working?"

A sharp whistle interrupted them, and the two boys yelped and jumped up with what looked like flames igniting from the cards they were holding. Both yelled angrily in unison at a skinnier participant, "Olly!"

"It wasn't me! Tag has my powers!"

"Tag, knock it off!" Jake yelled over his shoulder.

Wyvr chuckled, following Lilly's gaze. "I promise you'll get used to it. Well, most of it." He gave her a grin as they stepped through the door, leaving the chaos behind.

Stepping under the main archway, Lilly let out a tiny squeak as her toes hit the cold tile floor. The relief on her aching feet was only temporary, as the cold eventually forced her to scuttle faster across it. Jake smiled and hurried to keep up until the flooring shifted to a stiff, brushy carpet at the end of the foyer. From there she let him lead her again down each corridor, and she found herself relaxing. Her wings were quietly folded on her back, and even in her tattered pajamas, she felt rather at home. It was peaceful—safe.

Finally, Jake stopped in front of a door and gently knocked on it. Lilly's ears perked toward the solid sound that emitted from it. Like everything here, it was made to last, built solid and strong against whatever would come. The door opened before her, and Lilly found herself looking at the woman who made it all possible.

"This is Lilly, Dr. Allina. Lilly, this is the woman who founded Charity Academy."

Dr. Allina seemed to have aged out of her thirties (and possibly forties), but she still had a glimmer of the young lady that she had once been. Her hair was short and curled, with a mix of blonde and red framing her slim face. Her expression was worn, and the life beneath the features seemed stretched with work and worry. But her eyes still held her together. As they fell upon Lilly, they seemed to spark, and the vibrant blue color leapt to life. The face, the hair—everything seemed to jump to attention as she saw the girl standing on the doorstep, and a glowing smile flowed across her face. "Nice to meet you, Lilly." Dr. Allina said, her maternal demeanor warming the tired youth.

Lilly blushed and suddenly felt embarrassed to meet someone so important in such a state as she was. Her feet curled under her pajamas and her wings shifted, hoping to hide the dirt on her pajama bottoms. Much to her surprise, Dr. Allina quickly motioned for them to come in, taking the most interest in Lilly.

"Before I hear anything, we should get you into something better than your pajamas, dear. I imagine you would like to clean up, as well?" Lilly just blinked her eyes, as if in doing that everything would suddenly become clearer, but she still struggled to keep up with Dr. Allina's motherly actions. Wyvr slipped out in the bustle, leaving her and Jake behind, and the doctor started shuffling about the room before turning and taking a good hard look at Lilly. "You look a little smaller than Meg, so maybe she has some old clothes you can have. That way you can fix them to be more comfortable. Jake?"

Jake nodded and he, too, disappeared through the door. Lilly just watched him go, slowly turning in a spot on the carpet. Her thoughts became slow and confused, and she felt out of place. Everyone had welcomed her like she had been there all along, and when anyone was that friendly, Lilly always felt a bit squeamish. The large room seemed to cave in around her, like huge jaws closing, and Lilly squirmed a bit. Thankfully, Dr. Allina left no more time for pondering. She bustled over, smiling at Lilly, and handed the girl a stack of towels of different sizes. "There's a bathroom in there, and you can take a shower or a bath if you want. I know this is probably sudden to you, but you can relax now. You're a guest, so don't be afraid to ask for anything. I'll set the clothes inside the door for you when Jake brings them back, but for now, you just make yourself at home."

Lilly nodded, and Dr. Allina gave her a gentle shove toward the bathroom. Lilly started forward, as if propelled magnetically, and when she finally stepped through the door, she let herself drift in the solitude of a quiet bath.

Free of her awkward outfit and scrubbed clean in warm water, she let her wings fan out to both sides, feathers damp but clean. With her face gently resting on the porcelain and her eyes closed, she thought back on the day. It seemed like a dream. Maybe she was really home, and would wake up in her own bed in the morning. Maybe she would just find that she fell asleep during her mother's lesson again, and would get a sound chiding in the morning. Maybe—

No, she sighed. Those were all the same excuses she used when she found out that she was growing wings, nine years ago. She soon realized that they were real, just as she was learning now: it was too painful to be a dream. Sinking into the water, she curled her wings in. So, if it was all really happening, did it tell her what she had to do? Did it tell her where to go? No. Lilly was still alone, still confused, and mostly, still terrified of the world. Carefree thoughts were beyond her, and there was the heavy weight of all the fear dragging her down. The more she let herself think, the more it pressed against her heart.

"Why give a child the wings to fly, only to chain her to the ground?" Lilly let out a deep exhale and turned on the hot water, sinking into the turmoil that had become her life.

CHAPTER SEVEN

NEWS LIKE WILDFIRE

Jake paused at the door of the stairwell, anxiously tapping his foot as he waited. After catching August at the entrance to the girls' dorms, she asked him to wait a moment then went inside to warn the other girls of his presence. He felt jittery and impatient as he listened to the murmurs on the other side of the door. He couldn't help it, though; he was eager to catch up with his friends, and since Dr. Allina had sent him to get clothes for Lilly, it all worked out nicely.

"Jake? All clear!" came the sound of August's mellow voice, and she waved him through the common room with a slight smile. A thank you, a few stairs, and a couple turns later, he was at room 201 where his red-haired friend waited with a puzzled expression.

"Jake, what are you doing here?"

A second face appeared, and Kat shoved her way forward. "It's about that new girl, isn't it? I knew it! I was just telling Meg what happened outside."

Jake nodded. "Dr. Allina sent me to see if you have any clothes you've grown out of. They're for a girl named Lilly, and yes, she's the 'new girl' you met earlier."

Meg's expression grew serious, concern showing through. "Why didn't Dr. Allina just send someone else up? Oh..." Her voice dropped to a whisper. "Was it one of *those* cases?"

They stepped inside the room as Jake quietly explained. "She's had a rough week. Got tracked down by Kibbsty, house got attacked, Tray and Zen on her trail, and I barely managed to help her in time. I was out with the guys playing baseball, and we were on our way back when I realized I left my bat at the lot. I told them to go ahead, and I would run back and get it. They knew that if I ran into trouble, I'd just take cover in the house by Cherry Street, so they headed back here." As Jake talked, Meg rummaged through her closet and Kat listened, perched on the edge of her bed. "I got to the lot without trouble, but I could sense something was up; Tray and his goons had been running around the town a lot, after all. Then I heard Lilly scream from a warehouse close by. I got there in time, but she was still pretty shook up. I convinced her to come with me to the safe house, but it was too dangerous to come all the way alone. That's why we didn't get here until this morning."

"So he attacked her home? How did he find her?" Meg asked, dropping a couple shirts on her bed and looking up with curiosity.

"She was a pretty sheltered kid, home schooled, but when she was buying hair dye at the store he ran into her. Her family left town, but Kibbsty didn't give up and last night he went to her house and broke in, looking for her. Lilly's parents refused to cooperate, and when Kibbsty instructed his minions to have them killed, Lilly ran for it. Tray found her in the alley, but she got away. Then I brought her here."

"Poor kid," whispered Meg, messing with the jeans she was checking for size. Kat grimaced with agreement.

"You should have seen her, Meg. I'm not sure how she's still keeping it together. Her pajamas were torn up, still covered in dried blood, Caleb nearly ran her over! It would have been a nasty crash if his metal skull hit those wings. Speaking of wings, we'll have to sew Velcro on the back of those shirts or cut holes in them or something. The way her wings attach to her shoulderblades would make it a mess to get them through." Kat pointed, and Meg nodded, going back to the closet. Her voice still carried from around the corner.

"Why do you think Kibbsty put that much work into getting her? Usually he doesn't seem to make such a mess chasing people down."

Jake shrugged, leaning on the door frame. "Funding, or a client. He always has a new reason to justify what he does. Remember Roni? He was annoyed that she got away and he broke in here twice trying to get her. Or maybe he thinks Lilly will be a valuable aspect to his research. You don't know with him. That man is as twisted as twine... Whatever he wants with her, you can be sure she wouldn't be interested."

Meg sighed, heaved her sewing machine onto the bed, and grabbed the end table. "I don't like that man; ever since I came to this school, all he's been is trouble. I mean, I don't think I'll ever get used to how...*sick*...he is." She spat, fingers clenching the wood and mouth twitching angrily. From Jake's limited vision, all he could see was the shape of her mouth in a growl, and her curls of hair falling heavily over her face. "I mean, how long will we have to be out there playing superhero, trying to save the rest of us from his hands? He only gets students for that school of his through murder and deceit." She sighed again and picked up her sewing machine, setting it on the table and plugging in the cord. As she turned it on, Jake moved over to her and slipped an arm over her shoulders. If his thermal vision had been active, he would have seen the flush of color cross her cheeks.

"Hey, it'll be okay. You know, the three of us have been here longer than anyone, and if there's one thing we know, it's that Kibbsty's just a man. He may be evil and powerful, but that doesn't mean he'll win. We may have dealt with him longer than most people, but that doesn't mean we put up with it for nothing. One day, we'll be able to really do something. For now, we just have to hang on and protect those who need us. Like this new girl."

"But how long, Jake? Every time another student comes, I get more excited, but at the same time more afraid. It's like I'm watching a line being drawn down the middle of my world, and the people on his side should belong on ours. With every student we save, I wonder how many he's gained." She shook her head and slowly cut into the fabric of the shirt.

"It may seem that way, but when you think about it, those kids over there aren't that different from us. We're connected, one way or another. Someday they'll realize it."

As Meg quietly worked with the fabric, Jake wondered if she had even been listening to him. He got up and moved to the window, looking out into the trees. The sun was high in the sky now, and it would soon be heading back down the other way. As he looked at the clouds, he could see small birds flitting in and out of them, flying free and happy in the air. That was what Lilly had been—free and happy. Then all this had crashed on her. As much as he hated to admit it, he could empathize with Meg's frustration. He had seen how scared Lilly was, the terror in her face, and the anger that something like that had just happened to her. He sighed and walked back over, watching Meg stitch Velcro expertly into the shirt. Before long, he was waving goodbye to them and moving quickly toward Dr. Allina's room, but the feelings Meg had surfaced in him wouldn't go away.

How much longer would this go on before they finally got rid of Kibbsty and his murderous ways? When would it end?

They were battling a silent battle here, one where they didn't even know the rules. All they could do was protect those they could, and hope a resolution would arrive soon.

CHAPTER EIGHT

UNBURIED

The sun was surrounded by clouds as Zen crouched on the edge of the rooftop, nursing his bruised leg. Next to him, Tray wrapped various cuts on his arms, the unfortunate aftermath of their failed assault. They had managed to crawl out of the rubble before either of the other students, but neither teen was strong enough to do more than move to higher ground and rest. Now that their prey had slipped away, they would have to face the consequences, but the whole experience had been humiliating enough to begin with.

"We should've just finished 'em off."

"Kibbsty needed her alive. If we tried anything else today, we could have lost her for good. It was a tactical retreat."

"Tactical retreat my arse! How could they beat us? We have twice the trainin' they do!" Electricity flickered around Tray's hands, but Zen kept a calm voice, staring vacantly into the air.

"Sometimes, training loses to the hand of luck. This time, they win. Next time fate may deal different cards."

Tray glared at his companion irritably and tightened his final bandage. The wind master was annoyingly 'Zen,' well-suited to his name. Tray was used to being the best, being counted on. His pride was hurt worse than his body as they moved along the roofs, going toward their meeting point.

"I called Jonathan and Oz. They should be here soon with our ride."

Tray snorted and shoved his hands into his pockets. "Gee, you know how I just *love* ridin' in someone else's tattoo."

"It's a nice vehicle. The artist did a good job."

"Still weird. Don't you ever get freaked out by other people's powers?"

Zen blinked once and then gave a little shrug. "Not really. Some people can animate tattoos, some can animate the wind. It's all a little messed up in the end."

Giving up conversation, Tray dropped to the ground below them and kicked at a few pipes for a moment. With each jab of pain, he felt his frustration fading and was able to release the electricity from his body. In the distance, he could hear tires on dirt, and he moved to meet his team.

The vehicle was a black monster of a four wheeler, with the two front wheels stretched out in front, and the two back ones heavy duty, rising above the cab of the car. Sleek black paint glimmered in the sunshine, but to Tray, it still looked fake: if one looked closely enough, everything looked like ink and had a scratchy nature to it, just like a tattoo. The master of the vehicle reclined in the passenger seat, eyes closed in concentration.

"I take it there were complications," Jonathan said, climbing out of the driver's seat. Tray avoided eye contact. Jonathan was someone he didn't enjoy spending time with.

"Some of the Charity twerps got in the way. Kibbsty may have to use plan B at this point, unless he wants her dead."

Jonathan grinned in a slightly twisted way. "Not a bad option. I'd enjoy eliminating a few of those losers."

Tray grunted and climbed in the back seat, and Zen slipped in behind him. The vehicle started rolling moments later, and Tray stared out the window, watching the countryside roll past. Internally, he was still irritated, but for now he had to just ignore those feelings. It was time to regroup and reassess their situation. Later, they would get back at that troublesome brat.

CHAPTER NINE

CHARITY ACADEMY

Lilly was not born with wings, but she could not remember a time without them. Somewhere in the back of her mind rested traces of memories from when they appeared: long nights spent awake with a fever, or curled up with intense growing pains. Lilly's parents did their best to help her through the ordeal, and she never truly understood what it took to keep her mutation a secret— at least, not at first. Those memories now seemed much more vivid and important as she focused on their details, hoping never to forget them.

Lilly was three when the nubs of flesh first appeared at the base of each shoulder blade. Nestled inside the bone, the small wings were unrecognizable at first, the bones and feathers growing in slowly and taking her worried parents by surprise. Lilly's mother, a veterinarian, soon recognized the appendages for what they were and couldn't believe that wings were growing on her child. Already health conscious and protective of their daughter, the Douglas' resisted taking her to the doctor and chose to use homeopathic medicine to ease her growing pains. They home schooled Lilly, hiding her from prying eyes while they sought a solution on their own. In the end, the only answer they came up with was to just keep everything a secret.

Lilly never expected those years to matter so much, but she found herself focusing on details of her parents almost desperately, especially the memories of their lives before they left California.

Mr. Douglas was a police officer who dealt more with paperwork than he spent time in the field. He was a quiet man, well-built, with wide shoulders, a soft face, and no desire to hurt anyone. Rather, he was more of a wall—existing to protect those around him; the police force considered him passive and less suited for conflict. Memories of Mr. Douglas rarely involved his job. When he came home, his attention was for his family, and a stack of papers could wait when there was a game to be played. Lilly recognized his protection, but saw more of his care throughout her childhood. He was the figure in the doorway that turned the lights out before she went to sleep. His silhouette meant security.

Mrs. Douglas, by contrast, was slim, pretty, and down to earth. She never wore makeup and she spent much of her time at home in the garden. He was a rock, and she was the air, a carefree spirit that drifted from room to room. At work, she spent much of her time tending to animals in the recovery ward. She was quiet and had a calming effect on both people and animals. Lilly saw her as a guiding light. She was the voice in the mornings hat woke her with excitement for a new day.

Things seemed simpler back then—back before she started to question what was going on, before her wings were fully developed, though she still faced challenges from time to time. Her twelve-foot wing span was hard to contain within a jacket or long coat, and it took months to learn how to curl her muscles and bones into that painfully awkward position, her feathers tangled together. She got through that however, and she could get through the trials she now faced. Some problems were large, like adjusting to a new home, while others were as simple as drying feathers.

As Lilly stood there at a new school, wings drenched with water, she remembered how troublesome it had always been to dry her wings. It had been easier when she was younger, but with fully-grown feathers and downy plumage added to the mix, her wings had to be carefully preened by hand. She took a seat and ran a towel across her wings—one curled along her back while the other stretched out toward the tub—processing her emotions about the whole situation. She missed that old lifestyle; her parents were always there for her, and she never realized how hard it would be without them. Every damp feather she couldn't reach and every elusive memory served as a painful reminder of things that could never be.

On the counter, Lilly found some clothes, and she smiled when she saw the Velcro sewn on the back. Somehow, even when things were chaotic, she took heart in these little things that proved someone was still watching over her. She wriggled into the new outfit, her wet feathers leaving damp spots on the shirt, and the clothing fit surprisingly well. That cheered her up. Without the dirt on her skin and the tattered clothing, she felt more at home, and more able to focus on the present, not the past. The mist had vanished from the edges of the mirror by the time Lilly was done drying her hair, disappearing with the last of her thoughts, and with a final shake, she ventured beyond the bathroom door, forcing herself to face what was on the other side.

When she reentered Dr. Allina's office, she was surprised to find Jake and the older woman waiting for her. She worried that she might have thoughtlessly taken too long, but Dr. Allina's warm smile stopped her. "There, now, isn't that better? We'll have to get you some shoes still, but at least now you can feel more at ease. Take a seat, dear."

Lilly bobbed her head meekly and sat so lightly on her chair, she thought she might be perching. Her heart still had a whisper of adrenaline pounding through it, but her noticeable fear of further assault gradually dissipated. She was safe here; she didn't have to be afraid.

"Thank you. I hope I'm not a bother," Lilly whispered, but her faint start of an apology was interrupted.

"Not at all. I just hope you realize that you're safe now, and while you're in our care, we will do whatever we can to help you adjust and feel comfortable. As far as I'm concerned, Charity Academy can be your home, as long as you want it. This is more than a shelter: it's a place where you can grow and explore your abilities, and be among people who understand you and your differences. You can try to attend classes and try to find some form of normalcy, but I'm not forcing you to stay. After a couple days, tell me what you think."

Lilly nodded and tried to give a little smile. "That's more than I could ever ask from you. Thank you," she whispered, pulling her wings around her like a protective blanket. Cuddled in the still-moist feathers, she somehow felt safer. Dr. Allina was nice, but she was no mother, and no one could replace the care that she had grown up with. Lilly still felt alone.

Dr. Allina nodded her head toward Jake, and the older boy got up. "Jake, show Lilly to her room. Lilly, for now we'll let you stay in one of the guest rooms down the hall. If you need anything, you can always come to my office to find me, but just take it easy for a little bit. Once you settle in, if you feel you're up to it we can move you to the girls' dorm with your peers. I know Meg and Kat would be more than happy to have another roommate." She smiled encouragingly, and Lilly nodded, pulse flickering faster and then more slowly in her throat. There were too many things that weren't being said in this conversation. What about her parents? Would they try to get ahold of them? Why wasn't she trying? The doubt and fear swelled, but she forced herself to stand and follow Jake toward the door.

"I hope you enjoy it here, Lilly." The last statement was spoken with a tone that Lilly registered as sad; it was more of a wish than a promise. There was still much for her to work through before she could really enjoy herself. Lilly whispered a final thank you and followed Jake out into the hallway, the door closing with an echoing click. Her bare feet slowly shuffled on the carpet as Jake led her to her room.

The hall from Dr. Allina's office to the guest wing felt longer with the silence the teens walked in. Exhaustion had spread through both of them, and Lilly felt stress weighing down on her. When they reached the door, she paused and glanced timidly at Jake. He gave a reassuring smile and dipped his head down the hallway. "There are plenty of teachers close by, and any of them can help you if you need it. Try to get some rest." She wasn't sure there was much else to say, and slowly pushed open the door.

"Thank you... For everything," she whispered. He gave her one last smile before turning away, leaving her to make the last step of the journey by herself.

The room was sparse, furnished with the basic necessities: a bed, dresser, and a night stand. The walls were pale blue, but lacked decorations like she was accustomed to in her own room.

There were no photos, no artwork, nothing to make it appeal to one visitor or the other. The down comforter was soft as she crawled onto it, but the pillows felt cold as she curled up and hugged one to her chest. Everything here felt safe, clean. But not lived in, not alive. She wanted her parents to find her, and wanted things to go back to the way they were. But it seemed more impossible the longer she was away.

There were words she couldn't focus on, things she couldn't accept. The yells outside the closet door were being buried, the fear pushed aside. Her parents escaped. They had to have. She held onto the hope that they were alright, and this would only be temporary. She'd go to classes, learn new things, and have something to share with them when they were reunited. Her parents were the strongest people she knew. She might have had the wings, but they were her superheroes, and it seemed impossible anything could take them away.

Curling under the covers and falling into an exhausted sleep, she held onto that hope. If she had escaped, so could they. She would be brave until they returned.

The door let out a creak as Lilly crossed the threshold, and the noise echoed through the empty room. There was a lingering smell of smoke and crackling of flames to greet her as she moved into the common area, and she tried not to feel nervous as she looked around.

The common room was set up in a simple manner: there was a cream-colored couch facing a fireplace, matching chairs scattered across the floor, and a small window seat nestled in the corner accompanied by a table. The walls were dark beige, and the carpet was faded but cared for. All in all, this area had a serene, lived-in quality to it. Lilly was already feeling relaxed in the atmosphere.

There were stains and a few rips in the upholstery, but they had been mended and cleaned well. End tables had school books and other belongings left out on them, and while the area was empty, it was clear people used the space. Compared to the empty room she spent the past few days in, any clutter was a relief.

Lilly could hear voices from above, but they were distant and quiet thanks to the well-insulated ceiling. As she drifted toward the stairwell, it was impossible to process what she was thinking. She'd had time by herself, but eventually felt secluded by the guest room. It was lonely, and even though fear still clawed at the back of her mind she was desperate for something to keep her mind off what had happened. Jake had gone back to look for her parents, like he had promised, but the house was empty when he got there. Dr. Allina said she would keep looking, but waiting around was only making Lilly more nervous. So now, she was finally moving in with a few of the other girls, and the transition was both welcomed and feared.

Reaching the room, Lilly gently knocked, nervously anticipating meeting her new roommates. As soon as the door opened, however, her fears dissipated by the welcoming smiles on the other side.

"Hey, Jake said you're going to bunk with us," the redhead smiled warmly, and she quickly ushered Lilly into the room. "You've met Kat, and I'm Meg. How have you been doing?"

"Okay, I guess." Lonely? Confused? Sad? Uncertain? She couldn't vocalize the twist in her stomach that could have answered Meg's question. The understanding gaze back assured her that was all right though. "Are you guys sure it's okay that Dr. Allina wants me to share a room with you?" Lilly held her small armful of new clothes tighter, relaxing only when Meg beamed widely.

"Of course it's okay! We'll try not to scare you away, though. And we can even show you around later once you get settled in. The girl's dorm is pretty quiet right now, but you should see the common room after lunch. It always gets a little crazy then." As Meg spoke, Lilly took a moment to glance around the room. It was simple, with four beds, two on each side. One side screamed 'occupied,' both beds with sheets strewn and personal objects scattered about, while the other two beds were trim and neat, awaiting occupants. A large bay window was situated at the end of the room, adorned with soft blue curtains that hung down in delicate waves. Lilly stepped in and trained her eyes to look out the window. When she did, she hypnotically moved closer, her mouth hanging open gently at the awe-inspiring sight.

The sun was slowly fading in the sky, just out of view on the other side of the building, but from their room, Lilly could still see its waning light, coloring the trees with a golden hue. It streaked through the leaves and glided across a lake far to the north, where it slowly settled, crystallizing and glittering across the grass. Cherry blossom trees grew to the far right, and their tiny pink flowers floated like snow onto a cobblestone path, and the more exotic trees stood out against the backdrop of natural forestry. Lilly leaned closer and saw the iron-barred fence in the far distance, gently enclosing the school from the outside world into a misty veil of nighttime shadows. Teenage couples and groups of friends dotted the wide landscape, a few teens even playing soccer on the field, enclosed in the shelter. She could almost imagine getting used to a view like that: a painting right outside her window.

"You like it?" Meg whispered, and Lilly jumped, caught daydreaming. She blushed self-consciously.

"It's absolutely perfect. I can't even begin to describe how it makes me feel," she whispered honestly, then sighed, turning around again and spreading her wings as she breathed in her surroundings. "This school, it's a blessing—more than you know. My wings are out, and no one cares. I came with nothing, and I've been given everything. It's unbelievable, but it's more magical that way." She turned around and smiled at the two girls, who stared at her, clearly surprised by her poetic choice of words. "Sorry, got carried away," she giggled. The sensation of laughter made her relax, and after the week she'd had, she hadn't thought she would feel that way again.

Kat laughed, rolling her eyes at Meg. "Trust me, I'm used to it. You should listen to *this* one ramble. But we know what you mean; lots of the kids here feel that way. Some of us have had normal lives, but a lot of us have lost a lot because of who we are."

Meg nodded, smiling warmly at Lilly. "You'll soon understand that everyone here has a story, and we're all family; that *includes* you. Don't be shy to approach any of us if you need something, or have questions. You're one of us now, and we want to help make the transition easier," she said kindly, and Lilly tried to feel relieved. Part of her still felt nervous of the group mentality, but when it came from Meg, it felt welcoming instead of frightening.

Lilly smiled shyly and stared at her feet. "Thanks for accepting me."

Kat laughed, forcing Lilly to glance up as the girl flopped on what seemed to be her bed, the sloppier of the two. "Thanks for putting up with *us*! You know, I was starting to think that Dr. Allina was afraid to let anyone bunk with us! We've been in need of a new buddy, and she ignored our requests until now. You'd think that we were troublemakers or something!"

Meg slugged Kat playfully and sat on her own bed. "Kat here is a troublemaker when she wants to be. It's all because of her 'gift.' She can sense danger when she's looking out for it, so she never gets caught." Meg shook her head, and Lilly blinked her soft brown eyes, clearing away her confusion. She remembered Kat's conversation with Jake, and things made a bit more sense now.

"I get it. So you have to be *looking* for danger to sense it?"

Kat sighed, though it seemed more like a huff. "Yes. It's a stupid little problem I have, but what's a gift without a weakness?" She shrugged and flopped onto her belly, leaning over the edge of her bed to fish for something. Meg made a face at her and opened the closet behind the other spare bed.

"You're getting out that stupid computer? We have a new roommate, Kat! Sorry about her manners—do those clothes fit okay? I forgot to ask." Meg looked back from the closet hopefully, and Lilly smiled.

"Yes, thank you. Perfect fit," she nodded, and Meg let out a breath of relief.

"That's good! I already got you some pajamas together, knowing you probably needed some new ones. I hope they work out." The redhead reemerged, holding out a small pile of clothing.

Lilly took the soft lilac pajamas, unable to hide her appreciation. She slowly fingered the stitched Velcro straps and smiled up at Meg. "Thank you... They're perfect." Running her fingers across the soft fabric, the word rang in her mind. She thought of the grounds with the breathtaking trees, and the lake with the ocean-like gleam. The students with powers like her, and there were new friends she was getting to meet and spend time with. She thought of her roommates and the hope of finding a new life here. The burst of happiness dwindled, the giggles transitioning to polite silence.

"Everything here is perfect."

She couldn't keep a lingering tear from running down her face at the shadowy grief still trapped in her heart.

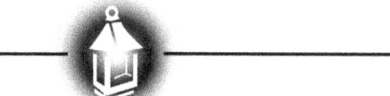

Sighing and pulling her cheek from the cold glass of the window, Dr. Allina rubbed her tired eyes and turned back to Jake. The teen looked equally exhausted, his expression matching her own internal turmoil, the stress growing as their conversation continued. "This is disturbing news, Jake. Dr. Kibbsty isn't usually so persistent to get one child. He's acting desperate to recruit students." She knew it didn't bode well for her school either way, but she hesitated to admit it, even to the boy whom she regarded as a personal confidant.

Jake seemed to sense her fears. "It's getting more dangerous. The way he's been hunting students lately is more deadly and harder to predict. It's more than just clever persuasion—he's jumping to attacking Strands now and using fear to manipulate them. The way they had Lilly cornered is an image I can never forget, and then when the house caved in, I…I let her down. She got hurt, and if she didn't heal—"

"She is here now, Jake. And she's safe. That's all that matters," Dr. Allina said. She moved to her desk chair and took a seat, watching the teen as he fidgeted.

"It feels like nothing we do is going to be good enough. This is another close call, and I can't feel satisfied with how it ended. I don't know how to smile and reassure her that things will get better when I don't know if they will." He stared at his hands, and Dr. Allina sighed.

"That isn't your responsibility, Jake. You already take on too much. You're a student here with all your peers. Focus on school, and I'll figure out the rest." She offered a motherly smile, trying to catch his eye and reassure him. He didn't look up.

"But that's not all," he continued slowly. "I'm worried because... There is something I have to tell you about Lilly. She..." The teen's voice stalled. Dr. Allina waited patiently as he collected himself, her hands folded lightly in her lap. She looked at the pale color in her student's face; he had never seemed uncomfortable sharing information with her before. She felt goose bumps growing on her arms as she waited, then listened closely as he started to speak.

"Dr. Allina, Lilly doesn't have one strand of lilac hair, or two. She has three."

The doctor's spine tingled. Her mouth could hardly form the words she wanted to say, and she shifted in her chair.

"But Jake, that's—"

"Impossible? That's what I thought. But when her healing began, I got a good look at her strands. It was like they were glowing, and I swear, I counted three separate chunks. I was going to ask Wyvr if he saw, but he was looking away... I thought maybe it was a glitch because of her second gift, but none of *us* have glitches like that. Could a third strand be a glitch?" Jake asked, his brow wrinkled with confusion.

Dr. Allina rubbed her forehead, feeling even more drained than when the conversation had started. "I don't know, Jake. I've never seen a glitch appear as an extra strand before."

"And that's not all."

Not all? What more could there possibly be? thought Dr. Allina.

Jake shifted as he looked at the table with quiet eyes. "When her second gift manifested, she told me that it had never happened before, so that had to be the first time when I saw it. But all glitches arrive *after* the student gets their final gift. If she was a Second Strand, her glitch would have shown up when her powers did. But if she's a Third, that means when her third gift arrives, she could still…"

"Hope for the better," Dr. Allina interrupted his thoughts. "I'd rather not consider the alternative. It could be a fluke, like you said."

"But what if she's really a Third Strand? None of them survived this long. The ones we knew of were just babies. You always suspected the glitch was accelerated with Third Strands. Do you realize what that would mean?" Jakes eyes suddenly held fear, and Dr. Allina realized it too, her own face going pale.

"It would mean something could be keeping it at bay. If Dr. Kibbsty ever got ahold of her, information like that could further his research. This is grave news. What can we do but protect her? Whether or not she's a Third Strand, Dr. Kibbsty is looking for her. We need to have her close and keep her safe."

Jake nodded and let out an angry sigh. Dr. Allina looked at him in surprise as he twirled around in his chair, putting his hands behind his head. "I just don't get it. It's so weird. I mean, when I found her, she was scared, but she wasn't too scared to let me help. She was terrified, but she didn't know anything else to do. Everything is different to her, and she's been so sheltered from all of this. And just look at her now! She's lost her family, her home…everything! And yet, unlike all the other students here, she still has the strength to smile, and she has the will to trust. Why does Dr. Kibbsty have to want her?!"

Dr. Allina sighed. "Maybe he thinks she was sheltered for a reason. Or maybe he just wants to study her wings. We don't know his mind, but we do know that whatever happens, Lilly's here now, and she's alive."

"But for how long? How long can these walls protect her? How long can these students stay here unnoticed? How long will we be able to hide?" Jake whispered, letting out a deep breath.

"I don't know, Jake. For now, we just need to look out for Lilly and deal with this as it comes."

Jake nodded and slowly got up from his chair, his body slumped in resignation as he moved toward the door. "Third Strand or not: I'm not going to let Kibbsty take her like he took Fin. I promise you that."

Dr. Allina smiled sadly and nodded as he left. "We can only try, Jake."

CHAPTER TEN

RETURNING EMPTY-HANDED

Tray's heart festered with dismay and anger as he stalked through the empty hallway. The lengthy drive back to Firestone kept him silently stewing, and now his irritation was at its worst. Oz had teased him relentlessly—releasing the snake tattoo from his calf, then letting it loose during the drive—and Tray found himself trying not to squirm when he found the inky creature curled around his legs. Despite that, once they arrived at the school they respected the sensation of concern that resonated through them. The joking had ended, and now fear was filling their bodies.

As they parted ways, Tray started the slow march back to check in with their leader. It was both a blessing and a curse to speak to the man alone. On one hand, if anything unfortunate occurred, his humiliation would be private. On the other, it left him the lone target of any wrath from Kibbsty, which was almost certain at this point. Failure would come back to haunt them, Tray just wasn't sure how.

It was a looming threat that hung over their heads every time they came back empty-handed. Kibbsty may have been an ordinary man among young and powerful mutants, but the control he had on their lives was insurmountable. Parents, siblings, friends—with a single word, he could change or end their lives in an instant. Some people got lucky, like this girl's parents: death was quick and final for them. Some weren't so lucky, and a wrong move meant pain and suffering for those that mattered most to them. It was enough to make him move faster toward a conversation he dreaded.

Only obedience would protect them.

Laughter echoed down one of the hallways, glancing off the obsidian walls and rattling in Tray's ears. Hissing, he turned to the figure seated at the end of the hall, who was idly forming little icicle darts and throwing them into the wall with a spray of icy splinters.

"Well, well, well, Tray. You've been *outwitted* again. Don't you think Kibbsty will be horribly disappointed with you, his 'pet?'"

"Shut up, Cory! Like you've been doin' any better on *your* mission! You're just sitting around while we do all the work. We have ourselves another Second Strand, and this one, this one's different. The lass, she's got somethin' those other idiots don't have. I can feel it when she's around; her powers are harder t' register and understand." Tray leaned against the wall, rubbing his chin in thought. Cory's laughter echoed through the commons once more, along with the *swish* and *shatter* of another icicle dissolving into fragments.

"Different? They're all the same, Tray, at least to Kibbsty. You get one, you're rewarded. You lose one..." *Swish, shatter.* "You know the drill."

The Irish teen suppressed a flinch in reaction to a frozen dart that barely grazed his cheek. With irritation in his expression and electricity crawling across his fingertips, he flicked off the icy flakes that hit him and exhaled strongly through his nose. "Well you haven't got any further, have you? I don't see you paradin' her here. You should be just as prepared as I am t' face him. It's not gonna be a pleasant day for either of us," he grumbled. Cory just looked amused.

The ice mutant leaned forward, and his mass of silver-blond hair fell over his eyes in perfectly straight chunks. Tray hated being around his classmate; something about his eyes seemed empty and terrifying. It gave him chills, and not just from the other boy's powers; Cory seemed frozen from the inside out.

"I didn't let the girl get away. Kinda takes the heat off me, once he's busy being angry with you. So you say she's different.

Do you really think Kibbsty will care, if she's not here as proof?" It was a rhetorical question, one they both knew the answer to. Tray just spat and rubbed his charged hands, still burning with the pain of his defeat. He glared angrily at the melting ice shards that littered the ground.

"She may've made a fool of me, Cory, but I'll get her back. I will!"

Laughter interrupted the '*swish-shatter*' rhythm of Cory's game of darts as he turned back toward the wall. The mutant's shoulders shook wildly with his amusement.

"I'm sure you will, Tray. I'm sure you will."

CHAPTER ELEVEN

WINGS TO FLY

The sun was barely rising when Lilly crawled out of bed. Even after the stressful day before, she couldn't let sleep stop her from moving her restless legs to the window. Sitting down on the cushioned seat, she pulled up her knees and set her chin lightly on them. The grounds were quiet, and the sun's bright light forced the last night owls to drift and hide. Somehow, this little patch of the world felt untouched by the frightening experiences she had fallen into. It was almost like she was back home—once again enclosed by the walls of a building and protected by the people around her. Safe—that was the only way to describe it. She felt safe.

She heard stirring behind her and turned, watching as her friends started to wake up. The morning light moved its way through the window and reflected off Meg's bright red mane of hair, the locks displaying an array of colors. Lilly momentarily hunted for a hint of lilac, but couldn't find the strands that were part of their connection. As the redhead sat up, she seemed surprised to find Lilly awake.

"Hey, girl. You been up long?" She yawned sleepily, brushing her tangled hair out of her face. Lilly shrugged.

"Not long. Just wanted to watch the sunrise," she quietly remarked. Meg nodded and made her way to the closet.

"Well, hopefully you weren't waiting too long. I'm not used to rooming with an early riser. Kat is nearly impossible to wake up." She chuckled, and the dark-haired girl seemed to sense the conversation as she burrowed deeper under the covers. Meg shook her head. "How about we pick out some clothes for you? I'm sorry all we have are hand-me-downs, but at least they fit, right?"

Lilly got up and moved to stand next to her friend. Peering into the closet, she watched Meg sift through all the clothes before she finally pulled out a shirt and a pair of capris. "How's this?" Lilly looked at the brown, velvety fabric of the pants, with a ribbon dangling to the side. The shirt was a nice shade of tan, and the styles complemented each other. Lilly nodded her approval, and Meg handed her the capris, taking the shirt and moving back to her bed. "Let's get it fixed up for you, then."

Before long, Lilly was sitting comfortably in a new outfit, and she and Meg were sorting through shoes. Lilly had grown fond of the older girl; something about the way she carried herself and acted felt reassuring. For a girl whose only companions had been her parents, the friendship that was forming was new, but welcomed. The redhead was more than willing to distract Lilly from her own painful experiences; she let the attention turn to questions about herself.

Meg could shape shift, but as with many Strands, she had her own weakness: she couldn't pick what she changed into. Lilly listened to the funny stories about her turning into all the wrong things at the wrong times, like an elephant when she was trying to become an eagle, and Meg left Lilly sobbing with laughter as they hunted through the closet. She finally pulled out a pretty brown pair of flats with soft, white rabbit fur on the edges. As she slid her feet into a pair of shoes for the first time since her escape, Lilly didn't feel so alone.

Lilly slipped the greasy bacon into her mouth, savoring the flavor and oblivious to how unhealthy it might be. The fact that her orange juice wasn't freshly squeezed or the cereal was a sugary mess didn't matter; any petty worry was beyond her right now.

Everything was just the way it should be. Today, she wouldn't let herself miss home, she wouldn't miss her mother's cooking, and she wouldn't miss the smell of her father's coffee. She would just enjoy the moment and try to find a new normal for her life.

At least, that was her goal. It was hard to rid herself of that tight sensation of sorrow that filled her throat as she tried to eat. When she started to feel happy, grief forced its way into her lungs and pressed against her chest. She was ready for another distraction. Maybe then she could push aside the memories prowling in the back of her mind.

"Coming, Lilly?"

Lilly looked up in surprise as Meg came over to her side. The redhead looked expectant, and the younger girl stood, setting her napkin on the table. "I guess. Where to?"

"Flying lessons. I know you're still getting settled in, but I thought it might be a good distraction." She smiled warmly, and Lilly returned the expression, feeling grateful for the offer. Leaving behind the remnants of her breakfast, they left through one of the side doors and made their way across the grounds to the center of the field.

The smell of water drifted over from the lake, and the scent of the trees, as beautiful as their appearance, met her nose for the first time. Light and airy, the sweet arboreal aroma mingled with those of grass and water, something far different from and more enjoyable than the smells of the cities she had lived in. A couple of other students came into view, and Lilly scanned the group for familiar faces. She hadn't met any of these students before, but she was eager to be introduced, and Meg was more than happy to oblige. Sethian, who went by Seth, was gifted with telekinesis, which enabled him to lift his own body off the ground and fly. Michaela could transform into a strange mutant bird, with fur a wild magenta like gaseous iodine and intimidating red eyes. Kent was the last student, who could fly like a typical superhero. Surrounded by students with similar abilities, Lilly had a feeling of belonging. These students may not have wings exactly like hers, but they knew what it was like to fly, and knew how she felt being in the air.

Before long, the teacher came into view, a tall man with an academic flair called Professor Wagner. He had dark hair, glasses, and a slender build, but it fit him rather than making him look lanky. As he approached, he turned to Lilly with a welcoming expression, one hand resting on his shoulder bag. "Ah yes, Miss Douglas. Lilly, right? Dr. Allina mentioned you. Welcome to the chaos, I mean, class!" He paused for a moment, giving her a quick look over as if assessing her potential, then quickly reached into his bag. "Before I forget, I have your schedule..." He stopped, his face disappearing inside the brown case before he pulled out a rather crumpled paper that he handed to Lilly. Straightening his jacket, the professor turned to the rest of his students. Lilly thought she heard more footsteps behind her, but didn't get a chance to turn. The professor was speaking again.

"Today we'll be working on the takeoff. It is one of the most important skills you can master, being essential to your exit plan in any dire situation. Last week, we gave a few test runs, and there was some difficulty, wasn't there, Kent?" The students laughed and nodded, and the professor smiled as the boy in question toed the ground. "Much like that, I'm going to ask each of you to demonstrate your takeoff skills. We'll time you on how fast you can get into the air and then try to improve on that. The pressure of having others watch you is only a fraction of what you'd face in a real life situation, so don't be afraid if you don't succeed at first. Instead, commit yourselves to improving. Now, any volunteers?" Not a hand was raised, nor was there any hint that one would be. The professor seemed undeterred, however. He turned, and Lilly got a chance to face the students he addressed. She couldn't help but do a double take. "Wyvr, Dryk, since you two felt the need to show up late, you can start first."

It was Wyvr. But there were *two* of him. Standing beside the teen in the familiar blue sweater was his twin, almost indistinguishable beyond the green color of his sweater and the name embroidered on it. The two boys glanced at each other and then back at the professor, giving laid back shrugs as they stepped away from the group. Their movements were uncannily similar, acting as if they were reflections rather than individuals. Without warning, they transformed into twin peregrine falcons and took to the skies, one blur of feathers after the other. The feat was impressive, and Lilly was almost envious of their demonstration, and she wasn't sure how own flight would compare. Their elegant loop-de-loops and complicated flight patterns made her feel intimidated. She couldn't relate to that level of flying.

Eventually, the teens landed with a seamless transition into human forms, resisting smirks as they took their places in the group. Lilly felt a flip-flop in her stomach and her heart began to race. She always felt excited before she went flying, but today another emotion set in. As Professor Wagner turned to her, her mind spun at the words he was saying, "Lilly, would you like to try?"

It seemed like a dream as she stepped away, shaking her head, "I don't think so." The words drifted from her mouth in a daze. She felt foggy, dizzy. He smiled and turned to another student, seemingly unbothered by her rejection. But the guilt struck inside her with stinging force. Memories of her escape made her wings feel too heavy to manage. She felt afraid. She had ran and hidden. Here she was trying to have fun, start school, when she should have stayed with her parents. Flying didn't feel like the same escape she sought before. It had a new guilt in it she couldn't cope with.

"You okay, Lilly?" Meg asked softly, putting an arm on her shoulder. Lilly shook her head to the side softly. She really wasn't sure how she felt now.

Class continued at a crawling pace, and Professor Wagner worked individually with each student, evaluating their techniques and giving feedback. While he taught, Lilly and her peers watched and occasionally chatted in the background, Meg spending much of the time trying to change into something sky-worthy. The break gave Lilly time to unwind, and her rush of panic faded until she felt more relaxed. By the time they were released for a little free time, Lilly was able to take to the air with her fellow students. The rush of flight melted her concerns and she tried to just breathe.

Coward! a voice whispered in the back of her mind. She felt her wings catch a pocket of air, pushing her lower and making her stomach turn more. *You don't care what happened to them!* Guilt drifted down her wing tips and made them tremble. She squeezed her eyes shut and tried to suppress those thoughts. *Why worry about school? What about your family?*

What had she done?

<You look a little stressed,> a voice interrupted her thoughts. Wing beats fluttered nearby and she turned to glance at the falcon.

"I just…it's been a long week. It's hard to try relaxing…" she stammered. The falcon gave a twitter of understanding.

<Well, try to take it easy. I'm sure Dr. Allina will understand if you don't want to come to classes right now. We all go through it, even Dryk 'n me. Sometimes, classes are a nice distraction. But sometimes it's nice to have space, too.> He gave a dip of his head which made up for the fact he couldn't smile, and Lilly gave a small nod of appreciation.

Their conversation was shattered by a roar of thunder.

The rain came down with sudden force, jumping from drops to cascades in a few moments. Lilly flinched in surprise as she felt rain pounding on her face, and shook the water from her eyes. Damp as her feathers were, she quickly landed and moved to where the professor was waving them in. He shook his soggy hair with a bewildered expression, and tried hopelessly to find a dry article of clothing to wipe his glasses on. "I don't understand it! Mike predicted clear skies! He's never failed before! I guess we'll cut the lesson short today. Where's Megan?"

Lilly looked around, trying to see through the pouring rain. She brushed her wet hair out of her eyes and shielded them as she searched further. The faces of the other five teens stared back, and a flash of lightning showed that Meg was nowhere in their group. Lilly quickly spoke up, stepping forward. "I'll go find her!" She almost had to yell for her words to be heard, then flapped her wings to shake loose the water. She waited for the professor to nod softly, still struggling with his glasses, then quickly leapt into the sky.

The wind and rain crashed against her, threatening to throw her back, but her strong wing muscles lifted her into the sky. Every raindrop felt like a needle piercing her skin, and every gust of wind was like a hurricane whipping her around. She wasn't sure if she was making any forward progress, it was just an endless fight against the elements as she struggled to see through the storm, straining her eyes to look for Meg. Her wings felt like lead, a feeling that was echoed internally when she realized Meg could be in any form: a sparrow, a bug or something else entirely.

"MEG!!! MEG!!!" she called out, turning a circle in the air feebly and looking around; fear had set in. Then she heard her.

<Lilly! Lilly, I'm here! I...I can't get to you! Lilly—Help!>

Meg's voice echoed in her mind, and Lilly spun in the air, looking around frantically. Without an audible sound to guide her, she was still searching blindly. *Why is there so much water?* she thought to herself. There was no break in the darkness, and the thunder boomed around her. She felt so alone and so afraid for her friend, and it didn't change when she finally saw her: a tiny bluebird, being thrashed around in the air. Her eyes locked onto the tiny form, and Lilly took a deep breath.

"Hang on, Meg!" Lilly yelled as she thrust everything she had against the storm. She felt herself quickly moving forward, but as she did, a gust of wind ripped into both of them, sending them tumbling across the sky. Cartwheeling and besieged by the storm, Lilly barely righted herself, sneezing away the water that got in her nose. She lost sight of Meg's tiny form in the process, looking around quickly until she noticed the blur of blue plummeting to the ground.

"MEG!!!"

The world seemed to freeze; the lightning's flash became a nightlight illuminating the sky. The rain hovered like tiny beads on strings as Lilly saw the ground, once so far away, now all too close. The emotional struggle she faced earlier collided with her fear in that moment. She abandoned her parents, but she wouldn't abandon her friend.

Lilly dove after her crumpled friend; she focused, pulling her wings as far in as they would go. She passed the raindrops and the lightning bolt, free falling after Meg as fast as she could. She barely felt her stomach jump into her feet and didn't notice the prickles of ice cold pain as the wind ate at the droplets of water on her face. She wanted to go faster, only faster—just fast enough to catch the bluebird in front of her.

Abruptly, she felt her fingers touch Meg. Surging forward one more time, she slipped her fingers under the mass of feathers and scooped her up, letting out a tiny gasp as the ground rapidly appeared in front of her. Pulling up as fast as she could, she barely missed the ground; the tips of her feathers brushed the mud. It seemed she would hold her flight, until a sudden flash of lightning blinded her. Screaming and pulling Meg protectively against her, Lilly covered her face with her wings in a panicked burst of energy. As she clipped the edge of a lightning bolt, a touch of electricity shot through her soaked form. Beads of static jolted her wings, and she felt tickles of electricity shock her. Once she was through the jolt, her mind belatedly screamed at her to open her wings again; instead, she hit the ground hard.

Mud and water exploded around her, along with a shattering burst of pain, and she curled into a ball as she kept gaining momentum. Cold fear hit her stomach as she tumbled down a hill, rolling head over heels and finally colliding with a tree. When she stopped, Lilly felt the rain still pounding her cocoon of broken wings, and her tear-soaked eyes slowly opened as she panted with pain. They were on the ground, but gravity hadn't let them down easily. Lilly's body wailed with agony, but she forced her wings to open and gently set the bluebird on the ground. As soon as she did, Meg returned to human form, sobbing openly.

"Lilly! I'm so sorry, I couldn't change back! If I did, I could have turned into anything and would have fallen right out of the sky for sure! But it happened anyway, and, oh Lilly, you're hurt!" Meg sobbed, kneeling down and softly reaching out to touch Lilly's damaged wings. Lilly tried to smile to her sister-like friend, but she grimaced instead; she felt so tiny and lifeless. She felt even smaller as Meg gently reached under her, lifting her from the ground into her arms like an armful of feathers, and as quickly as she dared, she struggled to get Lilly up the hill.

Lilly's head swam as Meg tried to help, and she struggled to convince her body to heal itself. She felt her powers flicker, trying to turn on, but the cold and wet wouldn't allow them to work. She was too weak to heal herself and too cold to warm her body. There was the pain lapping at the edges of her mind, shock the only thing preventing the full agony from hitting. Lilly shivered, leaning against her friend. She heard someone call out to Meg, the response indistinguishable, and soon they were hurrying across the field back toward the school.

Another voice joined the group, the murmurs adding to the white noise in her ears and mingling with the splashes of rain on her upturned face. Movements were blurry in the corner of her eyes, and people were nothing but watercolors. Soaked to the bone, the icy water pulled her into a sensation of murkiness that dulled the sting of reality. Eventually, the sensation of numbness took over as her mind drifted beyond the chaotic moment.

Her breathing grew quiet and peaceful. Senses mingled, and she focused on the calm growing inside her. A soft pulsing like an ocean's beat and the roar of distant waves filled her body—a gentle rhyme, a little song, flowing through her broken wings. Suddenly her eyes snapped open, and she let the healing take control, her brown eyes staring into a place beyond her understanding. Slowly her body mended, repairing the damage of the day and whispering tiny soothing thoughts to her. It traced through the wings she had used as a cocoon and repaired the cracked structure. Then it bid her farewell quietly, and she let out a sigh as the healing left her both revived and drained.

Lilly shook her head, as if waking from a dream. Meg looked down at her, pale as fresh linens, as Lilly slowly sat up, trying to give a comforting smile. "As far as today's landings go, I think that was the worst," she joked, sentence ending with a timid shake. Meg just blinked, so Lilly awkwardly set her wet feet on the ground and stretched her wings to avoid returning her gaze. She felt tired, but the pain was gone. Her discomfort was only emotional, until a quick glance revealed her classmates staring at her. Lilly's face turned rosy, and she curled her wings in, wanting to hide in her feathers.

Meg stammered, breaking the silence. "You're... You're a Second Strand? Why didn't you tell me?" she wheezed, sinking into a chair. Lilly awkwardly looked away. Her nose was filled with clean smells like a hospital, mingled with the varying aromas of wet teens. The puddles she saw as she stared at the ground weren't large, but continued growing the longer they stood there. She refused to raise her head until Seth laughed and crossed his arms.

"'Healing Factor' is not exactly on your list of top personal attributes, Meg. When people hear you have that power it kinda goes with the assumption you're invincible. I mean, it's kinda like 'Oh, you can heal? Can I stab you with a fork and watch?' Nothing against you, that is," Seth nodded at Lilly.

"It's okay," she mumbled, giving Seth a grateful smile before shrugging at the others. "Healing is still new to me. I guess I can't really predict whether or not I'll be able to," she whispered.

Meg rubbed her head and sighed. "Well, it's over now. We might as well get cleaned up while we're in here. Right, Ms. Meek?" Meg looked toward the nurse, who had been quiet up to this point. The older woman responded by tossing them all towels, shaking her head.

The other kids were dry relatively quickly—thanks to the help of a couple of blow-dryers—but Lilly was left long after the others were gone trying to make herself presentable. Battling through layer after layer of feathers she tried not to get impatient, and Ms. Meek helped make the task easier by adding an extra pair of hands.

She didn't expect to feel so grateful for this, but having someone carefully dry a feather meant the world right then. When she first arrived at this school, she felt lonesome, and perhaps part of that was still true. Yet she was growing to find comfort in the people around her, whether they were relieving an awkward situation or just helping her dry her wings. With the remaining effects of the warmth tickling her wings, and the momentary fear from her crash subsiding, Lilly finally pulled out her soggy schedule and started hunting for her second class, which was well underway.

CHAPTER TWELVE

THE LETTER

The room was filled with the hum of machines when Lilly let her mind wander. Her third period Home Ec class was filled with students focusing on their projects, and the teacher wandered between the rows periodically. Second period Biology had been rather uneventful, as Lilly had missed most of the lecture, but at least the sewing assignment they were given now was something familiar, and Lilly had no trouble jumping in with the rest of her peers.

It felt strange, in a way, sitting in a class with other kids her age, learning something her mother had taught her as a child. Cooking, cleaning, housework: these things were familiar, but seemed misplaced. School, in her eyes, was in her math book or her English assignment; if her parents told her to do the dishes, she didn't expect a grade. As days wore on, she was beginning to find a new 'normal.' This normal included the fire-spitting boy in the front row, and the girl who could repair damage to clothing. It included lessons on science as well as flying, and for the first time, there were friends; that alone made everything feel like a dream.

"How's your project going?" Meg's voice spoke up, pulling her from her thoughts. Lilly smiled slightly and turned, letting up the pedal to stop the machine.

"Just finished." Lilly lifted the foot holding down the fabric and held the pillow case she had been creating out for them to see.

Kat leaned closer and pointed to a tiny down feather that was stuck on the underside, crinkling her nose.

"Is that part of the pattern, or did you try sewing a chicken on and it got away?" Lilly hastily removed the offending object, wriggling the pale barbs from the threads and then flicking it at her companion. Kat laughed and turned back to her own haphazard sewing, the lines wayward and jagged compared to Lilly's steady execution. "Alright, I'm sorry! It looks better than mine, so I can't bug you too much. I just get so nervous using one of these things! I'm always afraid I'll sew my shirt to it or something, and you're not helping!"

Lilly folded her wings more delicately along her back and shrugged her shoulders sheepishly. Meg ruffled the hair on her head affectionately and stuck her tongue out at Kat. "Hey, at least they're only the down feathers. If she sews her wings to it you can worry."

Kat's face flashed into a horrified expression that forced a smile from Lilly, then pushed her glasses up her nose and went back to her pillowcase. "Not even funny guys… Give me a sewing machine and who knows *what* damage I can cause." The chuckles quieted and Lilly looked down at her delicately stitched case, fingered the design she had sewn in. She felt depressed, and looked out the window of the classroom in a melancholy way. The sunlight dancing on the hills was like a breath of fresh air, and she closed her eyes, absorbing it. She took in the ray of light and used it to keep her afloat. It took all the strength she had to keep herself from falling apart some days, but she managed; being here and trying to get through an ordinary school, she missed her parents in a painful way. It wasn't like she could fly home and return her life to normal. That was beyond reach now, and she knew nothing would change that.

"Thinking about home?" Kat whispered next to her, and Lilly turned to her friend, sighing.

"Yeah. How can I not? I don't know if there's even a home left to go back to, and I'm afraid to try and find out. Kat, where are your parents?" Lilly whispered.

Kat's eyes looked distant, and she turned to look out the window, slowly turning over the thread in her hands. "I guess you could say I know where they are, but I wish I didn't. When I was seven, my mom fell into a coma, and my powers warned me there was a danger of her never waking up. When I told my dad, he went ballistic, and he started trying to figure out a way to stop it from happening. The future is a very dangerous thing to try and change or predict, and he went mad over it. Then, a couple years ago, when he tried to turn me over to some science company to keep Mom on life support, I ran. I've been here ever since."

A feeling of commiseration encompassed Lilly, and she nodded as she took in the details. To her left, Meg's expression matched Kat's, and she couldn't help but wonder if Meg had experienced something similar. It was like the school was built with similar stories, some worse than others, but they were all trying to find a new future together. Her hand touched Kat's shoulder reassuringly, then she turned back to her work, letting her thoughts wander. Slowly feeding the thread back into the needle, she looked deeply at the metal point, as if looking into her own memories. Her recent experiences may have been dark, but at least she had a good childhood until then. Before this, she was sheltered from the pain her friends had experienced. Someone had helped them then, and they were helping her now. Together they were all building a new normal.

When the bell finally rang, Lilly picked up her schedule and pillowcase, and left behind the rest of the students, still feeling lost and dazed. As she followed the other kids toward the lunchroom she felt overwhelmed by so many people. Everything felt strange and unfamiliar, and she was becoming claustrophobic. Nervously, she retreated a few steps before backtracking altogether. She needed air, not lunch, so she made her way back to the dorms.

Opening the door to the common room and hurrying over to the window, she slowed and climbed onto the seat. The rubbery fabric felt cool under her knees, chilled without the sun's heat. Shivering, she looked through the clean glass and found herself staring longingly into the sky. The sun had climbed toward the top of the school, so the light was only partial and the warmth fading. It was enough, though. She already felt calmer.

Unlatching the pane, Lilly slipped her fingers into the framing and pushed it open with a squeak. Making a face at the seemingly thunderous effect on the silent room, she leaned out to breathe in the air. A cool breeze met her, coming from the lake in the distance, and there was laughter echoing through the little valley as students wandered on their lunch break. Lilly kept watch there in the window sill, spreading her wings as she breathed in greedily. The air filled her body like a refreshing spring; there was no fear of the future, no thoughts of the present. She was just somewhere she could sort out her thoughts and problems. It filled her better than any lunch, into the void where her family used to be.

It wasn't that she disliked her new friends or school. She just didn't know if she was ready for it all yet. It would take time for the pain to fade away and for her to accept what was happening. She wasn't accustomed to change, and new things terrified her. Just walking out the front door had been a journey, and here she was in a building trying to accept all these kids with magical abilities. It was the growing pains from childhood all over again, but she was alone facing them.

The clock ticked on the wall, and her thoughts continued in a directionless stream. Figures moved from one end of the grounds to another, disappearing indoors and fading from sight. Lilly didn't think much of it at first, until her solitude was interrupted by the sound of talking and laughter. Like sand being buffeted by the wind, her thoughts scattered as she watched girls returned from lunch in small groups, settling into the common room without paying much attention to the feathered girl perched in the window. For a moment, she felt almost invisible, until she was spotted by Meg and her two roommates came over.

"There you are! We were wondering why you never showed up to lunch. Are you feeling okay?" Meg said with concern, taking a seat to one side of her. Kat started to move for the other side before pausing and jabbing the pillow before she sat. Lilly tilted her head slightly in confusion and Kat gave a shrug of her shoulders.

"There's a girl named Tara who can turn into pillows. She has a bad habit of putting herself where she doesn't belong to pick up on gossip. You'll learn to check all the pillows in a room when you need to have a private conversation. Although with powers like enhanced hearing, that's still hard. You'd think Dr. Allina would find some way to block nosy powers like that. She probably ran out of resources keeping this place hidden, and even that security is flawed. Once someone is invited in it breaks the illusion Emre made..."

Lilly nodded dumbly and sat back, tracing the soft fabric that covered the table while Kat continued rambling about the school's security measures. For a while, she just enjoyed herself, listening to the teenagers' conversations, then, as she scooted back toward the window, something rustled under her thigh.

Confused, Lilly turned and found a small envelope sitting in the corner. Her heart stopped when she realized it was addressed to her.

"Lilly, what is it? You look a little pale." Meg scooted closer, glancing at the envelope. Lilly felt her heart pounding, and she clutched the paper in apprehension. She recognized the writing on the front. She had seen that same handwriting on letters before her parents moved their family. It could only be from one person, a dark shadow that haunted her life.

Before anyone could stop her, Lilly ripped the envelope in half, then proceeded to tear it again. She didn't want to know what it said; she didn't want to see another letter from that man. To her surprise, something fell from the fibers with a clatter, and Lilly looked down to see a pair of rings hit the ground. One was a delicate band with an inlaid diamond, the other was a thicker ring designed for a man. She dropped the paper and recoiled in fear. She would recognize those rings anywhere. They were her parents' wedding rings, and there were traces of dried blood on the metal.

"Oh my God..." Kat gasped, but Lilly barely heard her. All she could hear was her own scream of fear as she backed away from the table. Girls panicked around them, startled by her yells, but Lilly didn't notice. Her mind was filled with memories of the night of her escape, punctuated by the almost certain death of her parents.

There was no home to go back to now. Home was gone.

"Dr. Allina!" Jake pounded on the solid oak door as soon as the bell released him; with his last class over, he could express his frustrations. After overhearing Meg talking to another girl about what had happened in the dorms, he couldn't contain his haste. What he heard had made him panic, and he needed to talk to Dr. Allina as soon as possible.

The handle turned and Jake jumped through the doorway, quickly shutting it and startling the woman before him. Her expression made him pause momentarily, forgetting what he was about to say. She looked exhausted, hair greying and face showing evidence of sleepless nights. When she took him in all those years ago, she was a woman of youth and a woman with dreams; now she was a lady of work and a woman of worry. Those surprised eyes staring back seemed to sigh and prepare for the weight of his words, and for once, Jake felt guilty to drop them on her, and wished it wasn't necessary.

"What is it, Jake?" the doctor asked, taking off her reading glasses and cleaning them on her shirt before tucking them in a pocket. Jake let out a frustrated puff of air and shoved his hands in his pockets.

"I guess you haven't heard what happened. Lilly got a letter, and it had her parents' wedding rings in it. They... They were covered in blood," Jake said quickly, and watched the doctor's reaction. She moved slowly, trying to suppress the chills he knew the news gave her.

"I don't know how such a letter got here, but it's a threat we can't ignore. He's pointing out our weaknesses," she frowned, and sank into her chair, rubbing her head. Jake grumbled.

"Lilly hasn't left her room since lunch, and half of the girls are too upset to leave the commons," Jake whispered; Dr. Allina sighed, gripping the chair tightly and leaning back into it. The boy didn't wait for a reply, and just paced the room, digging his heels into the carpet as he stalked in circles. "This is madness! I'm sorry,
102

but it's true! Dr. Kibbsty is turning into a madman! The storm I could have considered a coincidence, but this letter is out of the question! Someone is definitely trying to harm her!"

The doctor shifted in the chair, rubbed her forehead without a word, and let out a tiny breath. She looked aged, as if the news had taken the life out of her. "Jake, I think your guesses are right, but there's no way we can fight back right now. All we can do is try to make this as easy as possible on Lilly. We have to relax; we can't fight with people who aren't here."

"But we have to fight something!" Jake yelled back, letting his fist fall heavily on the table with a thud. Pain simmered powerfully, but he wouldn't let himself wince.

Dr. Allina looked at him and spoke sternly, "Jake, you let your emotions get in the way too much. This is about what's best for *all* of us at the moment. We can't do anything yet! We need to consider this until we know more, and I'd like it if you left my furniture out of this!"

The anger faded from his brown eyes, and he sank into a chair. "You're right, but sometimes, I wish you weren't."

Both sat in silence, then let out long sighs as they tried to come to terms with what was happening. They faced an enemy that was attacking them slowly, but purposefully. It was all they could do to keep everyone safe from the coming danger. With every day, that task was looking more and more impossible.

CHAPTER THIRTEEN

A DISTANT STORM

"I don't know what he was thinking," Tara spoke as she moved into the room, her eyes squinting angrily as she tossed her backpack on the couch. "That was like shooting a bullet into a beehive. All he did was agitate them!" A chuckle resounded as she faced the figure lurking in the shadows. Light trailed up his arms and illuminated the Irish teen's face and his yellow-green eyes. An angry red cut stood out against his pale complexion, and Tara tried not to stare at the line that went from his temple to his chin. As if challenging her to say something, he tilted his face to let a line of electricity crawl parallel with the mark, but Tara knew better. She looked away again.

"You c'n always tell him what you think," spoke the boy darkly. "I'm sure he'd love to correct your...opinion." The long-legged teen slipped to his feet and made a slow circle around the girl as he moved toward the door. Her fists clenched and unclenched, and she hissed under her breath.

"You know well enough what would happen if I did. What am I supposed to say? He was hoping he could just scare her into running home, but now she's realizing there is no home to go back to! Try and tell him that? Suicide. I'm not on his good side!"

The two different shades of green eyes met, the darker green gradually filling with fear, and the yellow-tinted irises flickering with delight. After his latest failure with Kibbsty, Tray seemed all too eager for someone else to fall after him. "None of us are really on his good side, love. And the lass isn't stirring out of there easily. If he's always gonna punish us for failin' to capture her, the whole school may as well get ready. Face it, there's somethin' different about that brat. She's not like the rest of us. If he underestimates her, then Kibbsty may've met his match," he whispered audaciously.

Tara blinked and took a small step backward. "You can't mean that," she stammered quietly.

Tray shrugged. "So wha' if I do? I've been with Kibbsty for a long time, an' I've never seen him so angry. He's takin' it personal. Perhaps she wasn' such a big deal to begin with. But she's a mouse loose in the house. So he's settin' mouse traps."

Tara rolled her eyes at his analogy, but felt calmer. Glancing at the watch on her wrist, she fidgeted and tried not to think about her pending meeting with Kibbsty. After this, she would have to sneak back to Charity and hope no one noticed her disappearance. It was risky, but Kibbsty always did like to play on the edge. "Where are the others?"

"They're already with the boss. Doing a briefin' about that trip later this year."

"The one to China?"

"Yeah. You goin'?"

"I want to. You?"

The boy shook his head and gave an unconcerned tip of his shoulders. "Nah. Kibbsty asked me an' some o' the others to stay and look after things here wit' him. Someone's gotta fix his problem with the girl."

Tara pushed her glasses up and muttered to herself. "Well good luck fixing that mess... Cory staying too?"

Tray's voice bordered on a growl as he spat the word, "Unfortunately."

"You don't like him?"

Tray sneered. "I don't even like you, darlin'. It's not a matter of likin'. He just gets under my skin. We don't exactly see eye to eye," he muttered, electricity flickering dangerously close to the girl's face again. She forced herself not to flinch, then put her hands behind her head and let her eyes flicker closed.

"Well, it's better than being in that school. I hate it there. Everyone is so kind and bubbly and... Happy. It's disgusting."

"I c'n imagine." An awkward silence took over for a moment as both teens stared at the empty wall; neither moved until Tray continued. "Wha's the homework like?"

"Easy, surprisingly. They even give you free days to just goof off with your powers. It's like mutant kindergarten without the snack time."

Tray gave a snarky chuckle as the image crossed his mind. Then the silence returned, and the seconds ticked by.

Tara let her head drop a little, energy fading as she sighed. "So what's the next plan?"

"We'll just have to wait an' see. Plans don't just pop out of the air, y'know."

"Don't they? Rock was saying something about just busting in and grabbing her. I think it could work, but Kibbsty'd have to approve it."

"You want to break into their little home and grab one o' their own? That seems like it'd be askin' for trouble."

"They're more passive than we are." Tara twirled her bangs and laughed, the sound echoing in the room eerily. "We have like, drills and protocols about that type of stuff. No one is allowed to fight intruders, only defend themselves. 'Stay safe, don't get hurt.'"

"Well, we'll see how well that works against our 'shoot first, ask questions later' policy."

Silence.

Tara got back to her feet and brushed the dirt off her pants. "I have to go back to the school after I check in, but I think those of us who are over there can get a plan B together. As much as you don't like Cory, he's good at thinking on the spot. If you got over your ego and stopped sulking maybe you'd see the value in working together."

"That so?" Tara glared and he returned the expression, leaning forward and staring her down. "I was movin' up Kibbsty's good list, then that little brat comes along, and undermines everything I worked for. Of course I'm going to act upset, or angry, or whatever you think I'm doing! And Cory just saunters through like it's nothing. I'm sick of it." Tray's words slurred and shortened, his Irish accent becoming thick and heavy with his temper. Tara sighed and closed her eyes.

"Whatever, Sparky. You're barking up the wrong tree. Just... I don't know. Loosen up a little. Both of us need to. There's no point in arguing amongst ourselves. We just need to relax and focus our energies on getting back at that girl."

"Whatever." Tray turned his back on her and continued to glare at the wall. "Enjoy your talk with Kibbsty."

Tara stopped trying to force the conversation and admitted defeat. With a sigh, she started the long walk down the hallway toward their leader's office. There was no comfort to be found in the conversation with Tray, it was nothing more than water cooler gossip to pass the time between projects. They weren't really friends, not really peers, almost like shadows passing in the nighttime, mingling for a moment, then wandering their separate ways. It was a lonely existence.

The pillow under his head could have been a brick for all Cory tossed and turned; it was impossible to relax on something so comfortable. After years at Firestone with minimalistic living, the homey atmosphere of Charity was suffocating. It was one thing to have trouble sleeping here, but what bothered him the most was the way it made him feel. Trying to go through the motions here was chipping away at him. He once was a solid wall of ice, and now areas were becoming melted and raw.

Rolling over and breathing deeply, Cory tried to focus on clearing his mind and getting some sleep. On the other end of the room, one of the other boys grumbled, and outside the window the wind rattled the pane. After hearing Lilly's response to the letter Kibbsty had sent, he should have been smug. Yet, that raw area in his gut was revealing something else: remorse. Even from the hallway outside the dorms, the scream had carried to where he was walking. At Firestone, such a noise wouldn't have sounded so strange, but here at Charity, which took such care to maintain a feeling of safety, it caught him off guard. It forced him to consider what they were here for, and that was something he had never intended to do.

The air around his bed dropped a few degrees as Cory pushed the covers off. He shut his eyes and tried to focus, straining to repair the chips in his mental walls. But images drifted through his mind as sleep pushed its way forward. He saw blue eyes and golden locks of blonde hair. He wished she was smiling, but all he could remember was a frown.

"Cory, stop! Dad told you not to mess with his tools. You're going to get in trouble!" The young girl scowled, and the silver-haired boy scoffed over his shoulder.

"You're such a baby, Carla. Dad's not here to stop me, is he? Don't be such a scaredy cat."

"Dad told you no!"

"Scaredy cat! Always doing what daddy tells you. Always afraid of getting in trouble. Not me. I do what I want to." He swung the hammer at the block of wood he was tinkering with and missed, slamming it into a level that was laying nearby. There was a pop as the plastic broke, and liquid slowly dripped from the crack. Before he could react, Carla took off running, yelling at the top of her lungs for their mom. Cory quickly shoved the level under the workbench and took after her, loudly denying her reports.

Cory rolled over and shook his head, dispersing the memory. There was still the image of that frown in his mind, disapproving of what he'd done. He could imagine her hovering over his shoulder, reminding him that he knew better. She would have hated to see him hurting people like this. She would have hated to see the person he had become.

Some things never changed as he blocked out the guilt and went to sleep. She was frowning in his memory, but he was used to pretending he didn't care.

CHAPTER FOURTEEN

COMPUTERS AND FEVERS

The letter marked the tipping point that obliterated what remained of Lilly's past, a shift that forced her to look forward. Fear took over where hope once was, and there was nothing to do but let go of her old life. It seemed easy enough in theory, and she had moments where she felt she'd be okay. Then the frightening images from that day followed her into her dreams, and left her continuously shaken.

Morning came though, and broke the cycle with the soft chirping of birds; the sun's warmth somehow found Lilly in her bed and reminded her to persevere. Dwelling on what had happened would only cause more pain, so she did the only thing she could and put it behind her. Finally ready to try her B day schedule, she studied the list of classes before gathering her clothes and moving to the bathroom to get ready.

The hot steam from the shower helped clear her mind, and drying her wings gave her time to collect herself. It took almost an hour before she returned to her room, dressed and ready for class. Little had changed since her departure, however, and one of her roommates was slumped under the covers and the other lay awkwardly over the edge of the bed. Confused, the younger girl moved to her roommate's side, gently nudging the redhead on the shoulder.

"Meg... Meg, aren't you going to class?" Lilly whispered, and slowly pulled the covers back. Meg's expression said enough, as she dizzily looked for a clock and put her hand up to her forehead.

"I... I feel awful, Lilly. I'm sorry, I don't think I'm gonna make it to class, Hun," she whispered, her face flushed with discomfort. Lilly set the back of her hand against her friend's forehead, brushing the hair out of the way. The younger girl's face wrinkled with worry; Meg was burning with a fever.

"Should I get the nurse?"

Meg pulled the covers up to her nose and looked away. "I don't want you to... But I think it would be best. It looks like Kat's got it, too. I'm so sorry, Lilly. We wanted to make sure you were settled in all right and—"

Lilly hushed her, tapping her chin like her mother always had when she wanted to lovingly correct her. "Don't apologize to me, I'll be okay. And as long as I get help, so will you." Without waiting for further protest, Lilly took off through the school, trying to navigate back to the nurse's office. Several wrong hallways, some shy stammering, and a quick response later, Meg and Kat were being diagnosed.

"Are they going to be okay?" Lilly whispered, doing her best to peer around the older woman as she struggled to see what was going on. She was just under five feet, and even though the nurse was almost as short as she was, her view was blocked by a fluffy bun.

The understanding adult ignored her concern at first, then Ms. Meeks turned to her and put her thermometer away. "They'll be just fine, Lilly. Just a bit of fever, is all. Meg's been battling a cold on and off, and Kat's always catching anything that's floating about. I'm surprised you're not under the weather, too."

Lilly flushed and toed the ground awkwardly, uncomfortable having the attention back on her. "I guess I just have a good immune system."

Ms. Meeks laughed warmly, "Yes, but you have a gift for healing, don't you? Well, they're probably not about to be going to class today, but I'll look out for them. But you, you should be heading along now." With a gentle shove, Lilly was shooed out of the room and was soon staring at the woodwork of their door.

Purpose fading, she felt a flicker of sadness well in her gut, then she pushed it away and returned to the only routine she knew.

Making her way through the halls, she fumbled with the worn schedule in her hands. The room numbers were smudged, but she managed to get to first period without many problems. A bell pinged overhead as Lilly stepped into the classroom, and she heard a 'tsk' from behind her as the door closed. A rather ruffled looking teacher was sitting behind the desk to her left, and he waved her toward a computer along the back wall. "Cutting it a little close, Miss Douglas, aren't we?" The teacher took a moment to look down at his clipboard, and sighed. "But we're all a little slow today, it seems. Seeing as you're new, I'll let it slide. You can have computer number four." When Lilly looked lost, he pointed a stiff finger to a computer, and she quickly sat down, flushing.

To her surprise, there was a snicker from beside her, and she turned to see Jake smiling back at her. If it was possible, Lilly turned even redder, and covered her face with the tips of her wings, hiding behind the shield. Jake just shook his head and turned back to his computer, whispering from the side of his mouth. "In trouble already, Lilly?"

After the week she'd had, the comment felt mean, until she saw the gentle smile that accompanied it. He wasn't trying to make her feel worse, just joke and relieve some of the tension. His kindness made her that much more nervous though, and she turned to her computer, trying to remember which button would turn it on. "Meg and Kat were feeling under the weather, and I got lost trying to find the nurse, and I..." she trailed off. Jake look up quickly at the teacher, and then back to his computer.

"Don't stress so much, we understand what you're going through. Just try to relax. Mr. Ralf can be a bit snippy, but he's a great guy; as long as you respect him and listen, he won't give you trouble. You'll get the hang of things soon enough." He turned to see what she was doing, and raised an eyebrow as she wrung her hands in confusion. "Need help?" he asked slowly, and Lilly let out a flustered whimper.

"Uh, yeah... What button turns it on?"

This was going to be a *long* class.

Shifting her weight so she didn't drop the plate balanced in the crook of her wing, Lilly struggled to open the door to the room. Her hand slid along the wood paneling until she found the knob, then the lock moved and she quietly crept inside. Meg and Kat were still asleep, so she set the food on each of their bedside tables with their cups, glad to uncurl her cramped wings. Carrying food for the three of them from the kitchen wasn't an easy job, but it kept her busy and her mind from wandering.

Lilly sighed and took her own plate to her bed, wings trailing down toward the ground before she sank into the mattress. Computers had been a tough class, but after some awkward explaining, the teacher had allowed Jake to help teach her the basics of operating the technology. In her home in Wittier, they never owned a computer, and Mr. Douglas answered all of his e-mails from work to avoid bringing that influence into their household. She knew how to type on a typewriter and had seen similar computer models on one of their rare shopping trips, but she'd never had the opportunity to sit and work on one. It took patience to run through the most basic operations, but Lilly was a quick learner and soon she was able to work in their typing test without causing any major mishaps.

Lilly sighed and sat up, musing over it more as she picked a biscuit off her plate. In a way, Jake had saved her twice thus far, and she hardly knew him. She didn't really know what she thought of the boy, having rarely been around men other than her father. They made her almost as nervous as technology. Lilly let out her breath again and turned back to the rest of her food. She wondered if time would fix that, too.

Her thoughts were interrupted when mumbling came from Kat's bed, and Lilly slowly turned an ear to listen. At first she thought the dark-haired girl was talking to her, but the words were jumbled and didn't make sense. Politely, Lilly started to ignore the feverish rambling, then Kat went quiet and she turned over with a feverish whisper.

"Lilly... Lilly!" she gasped, her voice ragged. A chill went down Lilly's spine, and she put her food on the bed, uncertain how to respond.

"Kat? What is it?" she asked, slowly getting up. Kat rolled her head to where Lilly was, but didn't open her eyes. She sneezed, and slowly started whispering in a haunting way.

"I... Lilly, whatever happens, stay hidden; stay safe. Don't ask questions, just listen. Please, trust, and stay hidden..." Kat's voice sounded raspy, and transitioned into a fit of coughing. Lilly rushed over, but Kat had already sunk into a deep slumber.

Confused and alone, Lilly slowly turned in a circle. Her meal stayed on the bed forgotten, and another concern was added to the already heavy burden on her shoulders. She stared out the window and whispered a soft prayer for some sort of guidance to get her through this. A sparrow sat on a nearby tree and gazed back at her solemnly. It didn't respond, but its dark eyes had a comforting expression that stayed with her until she turned to find her next class.

CHAPTER FIFTEEN

RAIN OF CONSEQUENCES

Sitting in English after lunch, Lilly pondered Kat's warning. She knew her friend had been sick and feverish, so it was hard to decide whether it was concerning or not. Supposedly, Kat could only predict danger when she was looking for it, so it didn't seem likely the warning was real. But Lilly also didn't know what happened when Strands got sick, so it could very well have been a side effect. In the end, she decided to go with the flow. When the time came, Lilly knew she'd discover if it was a valid warning or just the mad ranting of a sick girl's mind. She just wished she could shake her apprehension until then.

"Is this spot open?"

The question interrupted Lilly's ponderings, and she looked up in surprise; a girl stood over her, eyes focused on the seat to Lilly's right. Lilly nodded, motioning to the chair, and the stranger smiled in response. "Thanks. I'm Karen, by the way. Karen Evenhow." She pushed her light, almost cream hair, from her eyes, and Lilly tried not to stare: Karen's irises were a stunning lavender color.

"I'm Lilly Douglas. Nice to meet you. Your eyes…" Lilly stumbled to find a phrase to describe her admiration, while Karen laughed and blushed a little.

"They're a little different, aren't they? I've always loved the color, and it's great to be able to display it. Mom always had me wear contacts so I didn't draw attention to them when I was younger, but it's great to just be myself here. I bet you know what that's like, because of your wings." Karen settled into her seat, her books in a neat pile on the table in front of her.

Lilly nodded with a smile, pushing her own pencil across her notebook and watching it roll back slowly. "I...I guess I understand. I could fold them up enough to walk around outside, but it was never comfortable and I thought I looked ridiculous. I didn't think I could do anything other than that though. Now, I can sort of say being 'myself' feels a lot nicer." She stared at the desk for a moment, feeling a bit shy, then she turned back and felt a question escape her lips. "So is the color of your eyes your Strand?"

Karen's laughter startled her, but her smile was genuine and wide. "Oh, I hope not! I'd feel a bit left out if my eyes were purple while everyone else is doing things like flying! Actually, I can—" Suddenly, the teacher tapped on the chalkboard, and Karen quickly shut her mouth. Class had begun, and it seemed their conversation would have to be delayed. Although Lilly was curious, she was respectful of adults and smiled to Karen meekly, hoping to continue the conversation later.

English was tedious at best, and Lilly's mind soon abandoned other distractions in an effort to keep up. Their review on grammar and language usage was intense in preparation for midterms, and the information overwhelmed her exhausted mind. Her pencil scratching soon slowed, her eyelids flickered, and she felt the unmistakable sensation of sleep taking hold. After such a restless night, she could find little energy to fight it. Her heartbeat became a gentle rhythm she listened to, and she was about to drift into unconsciousness when she heard a loud rumble, and something crashed through the wall.

Kids leapt to their feet, and the teacher jumped forward to get everyone clear of the rubble. A large boulder was laying inches from his desk, and as she watched, Lilly saw trails of electricity following it in. The calls of their instructor were drowned in fearful chattering, and Lilly couldn't make out what was being said. She backed away from the damage fearfully, wide awake with growing anxiety, before Karen quickly grabbed her hand and pulled her under a desk. "Karen, what's going on? What—"

"SHHH!!! Lilly, listen to me. Don't ask questions, just look at me!" Karen's voice was hushed and she was staring so intently, Lilly stopped talking and backed into the edge of the table. She started to look away, but Karen grabbed her chin and pulled her face around to look at her. Those lavender eyes were burning with a fire that Lilly was terrified of, and she felt herself trembling. "Lilly, please. You were the last person they were after, if they're here for anyone, it would be you. Just please, let me help," Karen begged, but Lilly was so frightened she didn't know what to do.

Lilly, whatever happens, stay hidden; stay safe. Don't ask questions, and just listen. Please, trust, and stay hidden. Kat's voice echoed in her mind, and Lilly shivered. *Don't ask questions...* Slowly, Lilly let out her breath and looked into Karen's pleading eyes. Immediately, the lavender-eyed girl let go of her face and stared back at Lilly, holding her hands tightly now, each wrist clenched in her grasp.

"Lilly, look deeply into my eyes, and just let your eyes go out of focus. Don't think about the noise, don't think about class. Focus on me and don't let go." Lilly forced herself to slow her breathing until it was even, ever staring into Karen's eyes. There were noises outside their room, talking and footsteps, but Lilly pushed it all away. Suddenly, the pinks and lilacs seemed to mix and the colors danced together. Lilly's eyes widened, but she never took them away. She stared deeper, drawn in and mesmerized until finally everything winked out of sight. Startled, Lilly tried to look for Karen's eyes, then her face, but she was gone.

"Shhh. It's okay," whispered a voice, and there was a squeeze on Lilly's wrist. Panic surfaced in Lilly's mind before she realized that Karen *was* there, Lilly just couldn't see her. Finally, it all made sense: Karen could turn invisible. Something about her eyes must control the change, and Lilly glanced down expectantly. She could see the ground under them both, and not even a shadow to indicate where they were sitting. There was no time to wonder, because the door started rattling. The kids in the class let out terrified mutterings, and Lilly felt Karen tremble as the two girls huddled in the darkness unseen; she still felt exposed. As the door suddenly gave way and opened inward, the world seemed to stand still for a terrifying moment as two figures stepped into the classroom. Lilly's breath rattled in her chest but she bit her tongue to keep from crying out. One figure was taller and stockier than the other, while the second seemed to sneer under the ski mask he wore. Both proceeded into the room with relaxed movements, and Lilly had a feeling that attacking them would be useless. Even the teacher was restraining himself in front of his students, not acting against the intruders.

"Check under the desks; we don't have a schedule, but this should be the place, if the bloomin' information's correct." The voice that spoke sounded familiar, and his companion nodded. Lilly let out a tiny squeak as the first intruder grew even bulkier and lifted up the desk next to her like it was a stick. The two girls backed away, staring up at the intruder with frightened eyes, but he only dropped it with a rough thud back where it had been. The second desk he lifted sent papers flying everywhere, and Lilly tasted blood on her tongue as her teeth clenched tighter. Her breath seemed loud as each step brought the invaders closer, and Lilly, who had lived in hiding her entire life, felt exposed in this new place she knew nothing of. Where was the closest exit, what were they supposed to do? She didn't know! She just didn't...

She glanced at the other students, hoping for some sign from them. One of the bigger boys was standing protectively in front of some girls, arms bulky and intimidating. Another girl was curled in a cocoon of plants, and Seth from flying lessons was trying to comfort her while other students were trying to calm another student whose tears were burning the floor like acid. No one was making any move to stop the strangers. They were just watching intently, waiting for the intruders to do something.

"I don' see her. Do we hafta check *all* of 'em?" The bigger person asked, his accent slurred, and she heard an angry hiss. A bolt of electricity shot from the hands of the second person, shocking the former angrily.

"You big buffoon! Of course we do! You'll take orders from me and find the lass, or it'll be your head on the choppin' block!" It was Tray; Lilly was sure of it now. The other must also be a student from Dr. Kibbsty's place, and they were here looking for someone. Or maybe someone had something they wanted? Karen trembled as the strangers drew nearer, and Lilly curled in fear as the intruders stopped at the desk.

There was a great rumbling: the sound of papers and books falling to the ground as the huge teen lifted the desk high into the air, and Lilly's eyes followed it up, widening as she sat in the open. Even though she knew she couldn't be seen, she felt as if everyone was looking at her. Her mind was screaming for her to run, and she struggled to resist that order. Like a bird waiting for a hunter to send the dogs at her, she knew if she flew, she would only meet the bullet from his gun. So she sat in utmost fear, hoping that she would stay safe and Karen would, too. Thankfully, the desk was returned to its original position and the two moved on to check the rest of the students. Lilly couldn't help but let out a sigh of relief, her wings uncurling from their rigid position. To her horror, the action released a tiny down feather, and she watched as it seemed to melt into the air and fell exposed on the open floor, visible.

Before she could grab for it, Tray glanced their direction and his eyes snapped toward the feather. Hurrying over, he snatched it up and looked around frantically to find where his prey was hiding. Before he could pinpoint the source, Lilly's panic won over her control. With one huge tremble, she shot from under the desk, let go of Karen's hand, and tumbled through the hole in the wall. *Coward.* She was running again, choosing to save herself when danger was at hand. Lilly struggled to see through the glimmer of tears. *Escape.* Her mind screamed, and it was the same flight that had driven her from her parent's house. No reason, no direction, just one mission: survive.

The next thing she knew, she was cowering in a large tree, sobbing tears of guilt. Lilly shivered in fear as the wind seemed to howl to life, ripping into the tree's branches and nearly knocking her out as it burst to life. Clinging to the bark, she tried to stay as still as possible, and kept her wings folded across her body protectively. Then she waited.

It felt like she would be waiting for eternity.

Every minute seemed like five as her stomach turned with fear. The wind became a roaring gust that bit into her skin, numbing her arms, and rain came for the second time that week, lashing out at her. *What did I do?* She struggled with the choice she had made, the spineless instinct to flee. In the sheltered nook of the tree, she curled up in a little ball, trying to shield herself from the storm. But after a bit, even that couldn't keep the fury away.

Tears hit the bark, washed away in the squall, and the wind cut at every drop of water on her skin, leaving her miserable and chilled. Somehow, the weather's punishment felt like a repercussion for her choice to hide. Kat's warning played in her head, and she sniffled, wishing she had stayed with her friends, and listened to the advice. Would she have been safe? Would Karen have kept her hidden? Were her friends okay once she left? The turmoil of thoughts continued to play in her mind like a broken record, until finally they followed her into a restless slumber.

"Found her outside in a tree. Half frozen, she was!"

"Very well, Albert. Thank you."

Dr. Allina watched as Ms. Meeks took Lilly's temperature, then gently shooed the groundskeeper, Albert, from the room. She had to admit, Lilly looked bad. There had been another thunderstorm that day, and Lilly had been outside for the majority of it. No one had a chance to find her while the school was being searched by the intruders, and in the turmoil that followed it had been just as difficult to look. She was soaked to the bone, and it didn't look like her healing was working at this point. Though they hadn't captured Lilly, the teens had still managed to hurt her in their attempt.

"Well, she seems to be in decent condition, despite her appearance. She's lucky she has such a high immune system. She's got a mild cold, but apart from being exhausted, she should be fine. The damage doesn't look lasting." The nurse wiped her thermometer on her apron, and smiled. "She's a tough girl."

Dr. Allina sighed. "Tough isn't necessarily the word I would have thought of. She always seems so fragile to me, although her emotional strength is a gift of its own. It's a wonder how she got out of the room without being seen. We're still getting the story together."

Ms. Meeks nodded. "It is a mystery, but not one I can spend time considering now. There are other matters to deal with; the students are all quite hysterical. Tina got startled during the break-in and accidently turned Karanie into a mouse, then one of Joanna's cats took after her. Who knows what else happened in the meantime."

As the nurse hurried off, Dr. Allina went to Lilly's side, and watched the gentle breathing of the frail girl. Even with every blanket available tucked around her body and wings, she seemed pale, cold, and broken. The doctor knew that this school was starting to fall apart, thanks to Dr. Kibbsty's mayhem. This used to be a peaceful place, full of spirit and hope, and now it was a place of fear and distress. As the founder, Dr. Allina wanted to do so much to help these children. But maybe, maybe her expectations were too high.

Lilly stirred and Dr. Allina looked hopeful, but it seemed to be only a bad spout of dreams because she slipped off again. The older woman frowned and sat by her side, continuing her thoughts. This girl—whom no one had much chance to get to know—had managed to gain quick friendship and attention from her peers. Maybe it was the beauty of her wings, or the innocence in her face. Maybe it was that she was so untouched by the world, having grown up so sheltered, and now so exposed. Maybe it was because of that, that people wanted to protect her, to shield her from all that might spoil her guiltless eyes. Lilly clung with childlike faith to hope, and seemed to drink up words of wisdom from anyone older. She was so curious of this new world she had found, yet so naïve. She was so interested in new things, and could pick up new subjects the first time they were introduced. Oh, these were things that Dr. Kibbsty would find no interest in, but made her so appealing to everyone else. If he had some plan, it could be nothing good for such a delicate child.

Dr. Allina knew that her student and almost-son, Jake, was frustrated more than any of the others. The more he got to know Lilly, the more concerned he was Kibbsty would take her away. Jake had lost someone once, and that wound had never fully healed. Though no one knew it, Fin had saved Jake from his own demons and helped Jake become the person he was today. Fin had been the one who was so innocent, and Jake so brash. Those boys were opposite forces, tightly connected to each other; one had a fiery spirit, but watery powers, while the other had gentle, kind mannerisms and a flaming inferno in his control. Years ago they had been torn apart, and Jake was left to deal with his loss. Fin had been much like Lilly: full of life, willing to trust, and filled with hope. They lost that spirit once. No one wanted to face that again.

Jake carried the burden of the fire Strand's death throughout his life and was never the same. He always seemed to wish he had been taken instead, although he knew it had been out of his control. But he made sure it didn't happen again. He fought tooth and nail for every student in this school, to keep another one from being taken; for some reason, he was fighting increasingly hard for Lilly.

"And why shouldn't he?" whispered Dr. Allina, her fist clenching and unclenching. "She deserves the chance that Dr. Kibbsty's tried to take away."

Slowly getting up and tucking the blankets under the sleeping child's chin, she tried not to be discouraged by her own fears and maintain the level of determination she saw in the teens. Her weary mind found it hard to keep faith, however, when the pain of the past still lingered in her heart.

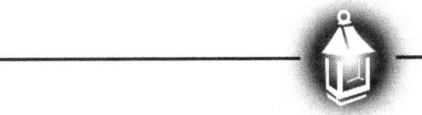

Although frightened and in shock from the attack, Lilly rebounded well. She rested for the remainder of the day in the infirmary, gathered her strength, and then went back to her classes as if nothing had happened. Inwardly, she was still troubled by it all—the way the students acted, the ease with which the villains had entered the school, and the uncanny calmness that let everyone return to daily life—but when she tried to ask questions there was a general surrender to this behavior. The school policy was against offensive action. As long as no one was hurt, it didn't matter.

Buildings could be replaced but students couldn't, so trying to stand up and stop incidents like these created more danger. Her friends understood Lilly's fears and stress settling in, but they also taught her the same things they had learned. This school was about adapting and trying to survive in a world that wasn't safe. Nothing they did would take away that danger, but they could learn the means to survive it.

Though the memory of the attack had faded, excitement in the school wasn't in short supply. Classes picked up their pace and Lilly found herself joining any clubs she could find. She wanted to know it all, to experience it all, and the busy pace helped ease the sting of her loss. The classes she took became an escape, and everything from Home Ec to Band let her rebuild her life and explore new things. Her recovery and optimism were uplifting no matter where she went, and even her laughter at her clumsy attempts at flute drew the attention of her peers.

And one person in particular.

Everyone had left Band that day, but Jake remained, slowly fingering the strings of his guitar. He moved mechanically, but no noise came. He was still staring at Lilly's seat, and her face was stuck in his mind. As he strummed his instrument, he let out a slow sigh and shook his head. "What is wrong with me?" he whispered, his mind spinning with the feelings he was facing. For some reason, he couldn't stop thinking about Lilly. This girl he had found on the streets, terrified and abandoned, and taken to this place of shelter, had blossomed in front of him. More than wanting to protect her, he wanted to get to know her. He was seeing her as a girl now, and was confused by what he felt.

As he left for lunch he could feel his ears turning red with embarrassment. What was happening to him? Why did he care so much about her? Jake didn't randomly crush on a girl out of nowhere, especially one he brought to the school. Many of them had crushes on him, so he had options. So why Lilly?

He knew, as much as he tried to lie to himself, that Lilly was special. No, she was amazing, and no one in their right mind could look at her and see just another girl. The purity she had... She was one of a kind. He couldn't let her slip past without trying to connect with her. Still, he didn't need a girl right now, especially with all the responsibility Dr. Allina trusted him with. He helped organize files, arrange class schedules, and get students settled in. Dating a classmate here would feel like dating a client. They trusted him to protect them, not to try to take them out to lunch. He'd just have to get over her. Besides, if she was a Third Strand... She might not be around long. If he started to care, she would be taken away, and he didn't want that. He wanted her to live the life she was granted and enjoy the gifts that she was blessed with. He didn't want to complicate things.

Jake turned into the cafeteria and made up his mind. He didn't care how deep his feelings were. For now, he was just going to make sure she got the chance she deserved, as Dr. Allina had said. All other emotions had to be set aside, for both of their sakes.

CHAPTER SIXTEEN

CHASING DREAMS

The sunlight's twinkle was fading from the window, chased into nighttime by the shadows engulfing the sun, and the moon was just a silver smudge, soon to brighten as dusk rose. Another day was lost and the school's work load was increasing, but the busy pace at least took away from life's other dramas. It was the slower moments that hurt the most, and in silence Lilly felt her thoughts drifting toward darker times. Today, before the weight of sadness could build, Kat let out a little laugh and drew her attention.

The grin beneath her glasses and black hair was surprising; for once it didn't have that sneer of mischief. Lilly felt taken aback by the expression and set her notebook down as Kat spoke. "You know, I'm kind of glad there are only three of us."

Meg's face filled with surprise, and her hair swished over her shoulder. "Why?"

"Well," Kat leaned back, putting her arms behind her head as she looked up at the ceiling, "if we had another roommate, we wouldn't have as much fun. I mean, I feel like the three of us have a good connection. You're nice, I'm fun, and Lilly's grounded. So when we need to have adventure, I can have control, when we need to be thoughtful, you can take over. Then when we need to work, Lilly is in charge. We're just different enough to keep each other straight, and alike enough not to hate each other. I like it." She sighed, smiling to herself.

Lilly was surprised to hear Kat say that, and Meg made her opinion known with a toss of a pillow. After considering it, Lilly felt herself inclined to agree in the end. "I enjoy hanging out with you guys. It's almost like we're...sisters."

Meg beamed, ducking as Kat returned her throw. "I know how you feel, and I hope it stays that way. You know how the future seems to change things? You want to stay with the people you care about forever, and then turn to find they're gone. I want us to be friends no matter what," she sighed dreamily, and the others seemed to be just as lost in the thought. But Lilly's attention had caught on that one sentence: *the future seems to change things.* What would happen with their future? This school was here now, guiding them and helping them, but after?

Abruptly, she voiced her thought. "Meg... Kat... Is there any real future beyond this school?" she whispered, and curled her wings around her as she rolled onto her stomach. Both girls were looking at her now, and they seemed lost without answers.

"Well, I can't say that anyone knows; I mean, there's Professor Wagner and maybe two other teacher with strands, but they're all really young, not much older than us. That's why Dr. Allina made this school, because we're a new beginning. She's helping us learn to live normally, but from there... I think it's still getting worked out," Meg admitted softly, and Kat nodded.

"It's estimated that only about one out of every million kids has a strand, and almost all reside in the US. It's like it's all localized here. It's fairly common for siblings to have strands, and some cities have more strands than others, but still our numbers are pretty low. That makes it our problem, I guess. We're learning to adapt, and eventually we might blend into society if we go underground."

"So it's all a lie then? Wherever we go, we'll still be hiding," Lilly whispered, her heart starting to ache deep inside her.

Meg sighed. "It sucks, but there's nothing we can do right now. We're the first to walk this path, and from here, we decide our future. Maybe someday answers will be ready, but right now, they just aren't. I wish we could help you understand, because we've all gone through that longing to be out in the open. It's hard to change what we barely understand."

Lilly buried her face in the sheets in exasperation. "But if we're the first, why hide? So others can hide too? Why did we have to be the first ones? I just don't understand."

"Lilly, someday the world will know, but we're not ready yet. *They're* not ready yet. Do you want to be pried and poked at like a freak, or have the world despise you because you're different? It's for our protection. Until the world's ready, we stay hidden. We just have to wait."

Lilly looked at her blanket, tears stinging her eyes. She shook her head slowly, looking pitifully at her friends. "But I don't want to hide again. I've hidden my whole life. I want to be out there and fly wherever I want to. I want to go to stores and to shop for clothes, without having my wings cramped by my sides. I want to sit on the boardwalk and talk to people without them caring that I'm different. I want to be accepted! Why is the world so bitter toward those who are different?" she asked.

Kat shrugged. "Because the world is afraid. The world doesn't know how to react. The world doesn't have all the books and stories and knowledge to tell them what to do. The world fears change, Lilly, and you can't alter their minds. It's cold out there, it's bitter, but it's human. We have to learn to live in it. Not everyone in the world is going to hate us, some might accept us. But there are always risks. They could cage us, study us, treat us worse than animals. Heck, my *dad* almost sold me to people like that. I don't even want to think of what could have happened, or what has happened to other Strands. Even if they don't treat us like freaks, just think of all those people out there who are already trying to fit in. The world is full of stereotypes and discrimination. At least we don't have to be a part of that. That alone should be a blessing."

Lilly let those words sink in and felt her thoughts shifting in her head. She searched for answers, but she only came up with sour anger. She wanted to fit in, wanted to get away from all the pain. That possibility seemed to be diminishing. "Meg... Kat... Are you afraid of the future?" she asked, looking up at them with wet eyes. An honest answer was all she needed, it was all she wanted. Meg looked surprised and turned to Kat before she replied.

"Well, I think I am, in a way. I'm afraid to have to go out there where the world isn't understanding, where things will be hard to get used to, but I've learned not to dwell in it. Sure, I don't want to be out there in it, but I've gotten used to the idea. What the future brings, it brings, and I've learned to accept that."

"Kat?" Lilly turned to the other girl.

"I guess I do... I fear it because *my* future's the only one I can't really see. My gift grants me the ability to look out for others, but I want someone to look out for me. The future is such a wildly changing thing. I mean, I can sense danger, but I don't know if it'll come around or not. Even for other people. When my mom was sick, I could sense things getting worse, or better, but long-term, I didn't know what would happen. Uncertainty is a scary thing."

Nodding, Lilly sat up and looked out the window at the sunset and felt a tear trickle down her face. Tucking one leg under the other, Lilly picked up her paper and pencil again, and the other girls went back to their work. She tried to focus but couldn't seem to keep her mind on anything. She found herself sketching, and her eyes welled up with tears as a shape came into view. She saw her mother's gentle eyes take shape, her pretty nose, freckled cheeks, and frazzled hair. The love in her eyes made Lilly's heart long, and she rubbed her eyes. Ms. Meeks and Dr. Allina were great at playing mom, but it wasn't good enough. Lilly wanted her mother; she wanted to see her parents again.

Her parents would know what to do. They would guide her and help her out, teach her how to be strong. They would tell her that whatever happened, they loved her; they would tell her it would be okay, and she would hold on for just a little longer. Leaning back in bed, Lilly stared at the ceiling, the tears rolling like rivers down her face. She didn't know what to do anymore; her life was cloudy, and she couldn't see the future.

CHAPTER SEVENTEEN

THE BONFIRE

It was lunchtime, and Lilly was the last person at their table, finishing her food before her English class that afternoon. She had her school book open and was taking notes on the last few pages of their assigned reading; the rest of her friends had already left for class, giving her a few minutes to think without the constant talking.

School had been hard to adjust to, and the presence of other students was another hurdle. Studying when she was home schooled had been easier: there was no one to avoid, and she never had to fight to find a silent room. She missed the quiet time she needed to study, and—as much as she loved Meg and Kat—having roommates afforded little privacy. Even at lunch, there were constant distractions that made studying difficult. She hadn't expected so many problems just from the presence of other people, but day by day, the rowdy teens tested her patience and she began to wonder why she had wanted this lifestyle so much. Homesickness turned in her stomach as she thumbed the thin pages of the textbook. She wished it were a Saturday so at least she could find some way to escape for the day.

The traffic in the cafeteria was steady, so Lilly didn't take note of the footsteps approaching. The only sign of trouble was the almost unnoticeable chill on her neck before something cold slipped down her back and interrupted her peaceful lunch. With a cry she jumped from her seat, hand struggling to catch the sliver of ice. It clattered onto her seat seconds later, but by then several nearby figures were chuckling with amusement. The culprit was hidden somewhere among the other diners, so Lilly couldn't pinpoint who had played the joke on her. She let her annoyance pass, packing up as she tried not to let it bother her.

But that was just the start of her trouble.

Leaving the lunchroom, the behavior continued as students pushed and shoved around her on their way out to the fields. She willed herself to be patient, until a particularly strong push sent her flat on her face and she flinched in pain. Laughter resounded around her, deepening the rush of color to her face, and her resolve began to crack. "What is wrong with everyone?" she whimpered, pushing herself back to her feet and hugging her arms to her chest. No one seemed to show concern over the hostile actions toward her, and she wondered if it was just her imagination that the students seemed unnaturally mean. She wished Meg and Kat were there, uncertain how to deal with her peers. She wished it even more when she saw a group of boys coming toward her, expressions filling her with dread.

"Hey, look, its Big Bird!" A call rang out, and the color on Lilly's cheeks deepened while she willed herself to keep walking. On either side, teens appeared, and they sneered down at her. "Look, I bet I could use one of these to write with! I don't need to use a pen anymore!" Lilly yelped and whirled angrily as a boy plucked one of her feathers, curling her wings in with surprise.

"Leave me alone!" she cried, trying to maintain a stiff upper lip. The boys laughed, chortling together with amusement. One boy crossed his arms.

"Aw, look, the little baby's sad. She doesn't like us making fun of her widdle wings," he taunted, and Lilly hissed.

"Can't you think of anything better to do?" She felt fire igniting in her gut, her timid nature melting under the sudden anger. It was an unusual feeling, but it started in her chest and was stoked by their behavior. The boys just laughed, and a couple of girls came over to join in.

"I think you're hittin' a nerve or two. Maybe you can make her snap." An explosion of energy popped by Lilly's feet, and she scrambled to get out of the way, but more followed. The laughter and the explosions scattered her nerves and sent her into a panicked flight. A few feet above the ground she slammed into something solid and crashed back to the earth. Invisible walls, explosions, ice, pushing; everything from that morning collided at once. Falling in a heap to the ground, she threw open her wings, knocking bystanders onto their backs. To her surprise, everyone froze.

She readied herself for more trouble, but a look passed across their faces before the teens dispersed. Watching them go, Lilly turned with ruffled feathers and tried to clear her mind by flying toward the roof. She tried not to be concerned by what had happened, especially the last glance she had seen them exchange: it was a mischievous, knowing look. She doubted that would be the end of her problems. The air had a cold nip as if to confirm her suspicions.

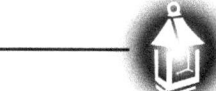

The afternoon went by uneventfully, and the brutal bullying soon felt imagined. Lilly explored the grounds, wandering to the lake and trying to forget the stress completely. It took several hours to stop shaking after the lunchtime fiasco, and as nighttime started to fall she still felt skittish and uncertain. The progress she had made adjusting to school was taking a serious step backward, and it was clear by the way she froze when a female voice called out to her.

"Lilly! Where are you going? You're going to miss all the fun!"

Lilly turned and scrutinized the speaker, who had bright green hair in an ear-length swish on one side, curling around to a buzz on the other. She seemed incredibly familiar, but Lilly couldn't place her face, so she was hesitant to speak. "Uh, what fun?" she asked slowly, her wings opening and closing with a confused pat.

The girl let out a laugh as a few more students approached and joined the conversation. "Why, the bonfire of course! Don' tell me

Kat didn' tell you! Oh, you've *got* to come! No teachers, no adults! You can' miss this! Kat, tell her!"

Things felt disorienting as Kat stepped out from amongst the girls and waved them back. "Cool it, guys. Sorry, Lilly, Trish can be pushy, but you really should join us! Have a little fun." She looked like herself, but something felt wrong with the way she was speaking.

You're being paranoid. She silenced those doubts and forced herself to surrender with a sigh. "I... I guess I could come..." she said, and let out a yelp as she was grabbed by a girl on either side and propelled forward. Dragging her feet, she felt herself moving in the direction she secretly wanted to run from.

It's just a bonfire, right? How bad can it be?

They walked into the forest, the girls talking and laughing as they went. Conversations transitioned from classes to boys, then to parties, but Lilly tuned it out. Around her, the claw-like hands of the forest towered, the static plant-life just looking for a chance to grab her. Timidly, she cringed under it, but as soon as she saw they were heading toward the fire in the distance, her courage vanished completely. Like a puppet, her legs carried her, pulling her toward the voices and the dancing light. As she broke the barrier and into the circle, her doubts were strengthened by revelations that froze her in place.

She had seen the green-haired girl another time that day. Just like she had seen the other students here at this bonfire. They were the ones who had teased her that morning; they were people she didn't want to be around. She started recognizing faces as kids danced around the fire's edge. Powers mingled and tangled in the firelight, but slowly she connected them with their owner's silhouettes. They laughed and played, explosions mingling with music and flames circling dangerously close to trees. It was like a huge zoo; a zoo of super-powered kids. She felt less like an attendee and more like an appetizer.

Lilly backed up, ready to make her escape, when a hand gripped a chunk of her hair and pain sent stars across her vision. She opened her mouth to yell, but the air in her lungs went cold. It was like an invisible hand squeezing her insides, stealing her breath and making her legs buckle. Falling to her knees, she looked up into icy blue eyes, the figure sneering down at her. "For someone who looks like an angel, you've sure been causing enough hell. Someone should teach you to chill." His laughter was all she heard as everything went dark.

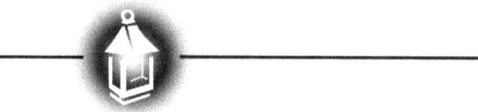

Pain throbbed through Lilly's skull, and she could feel a lump slowly forming against her scalp. Her powers took effect, healing the wound, but it didn't clear the memory of the injury. Her brain was still forming a splitting headache, and her stress was only making it grow faster. She started to squirm, but someone snarled at her, "Don't think about tryin' anythin'. You ain't goin' nowhere."

Lilly's eyes snapped open and she found herself in an unfamiliar room. There were walls made of black stone, high ceilings, and more equipment than she'd ever seen in one room. Computers from different eras were placed together like one supercomputer, and filing cabinets lined the walls. Tray had one of her arms in a vice-like grip and Dr. Kibbsty held the other one, trying to strap it down. To his right, a pan sat waiting with a tiny syringe on it.

"No," whispered Lilly, and she pulled back in reflex. With blind fear she thrashed ferociously, sending the pan flying. Her fist flung out, and she heard a sharp crack as it connected with Tray's jaw, sending him staggering back. At the same time, her wing knocked into Kibbsty, and he slammed into a table, head giving a resounding thud. Lilly had never hurt anyone before, but she knew she didn't care right then. Her mind was set on escape and Lilly ran, once more fleeing from these unrelenting villains.

Without screaming or yelling, Lilly raced through the building, eyes darting for any exit. She shot down the halls, wings tightly against her side and her own terror chasing her like a wild beast; it raced alongside her, biting her heels, and it screamed in her head over the wailing of an alarm in the corridors. Someone tried to stop her, and she threw them out of the way. She couldn't stop! She wouldn't let anyone get her; not this time.

Down a corridor and through a hall, she found herself at a dead end. Panting with exhaustion, her lungs starting to burn, she tried to think of something to do. Then she saw her escape—a window—and ran toward it, desperate to reach freedom. She never made it, as something ropelike lashed around her leg and dragged her to the ground.

"Let me go. Let me GO!!!" Her screams echoed through the building as she threw her body against the bindings. It only made things worse. The ropes tightened to the point she couldn't breathe, feeling her lungs and sides being crushed by the pressure. Finally, she was forced to fall limp, and the pressure only lessened enough for her to maintain consciousness.

"That's more like it. She's a feisty one, isn't she?" someone asked. A laugh Lilly recognized answered.

"Problematic, but not necessarily feisty. We'll work it out of her though, won't we?" Cory reached down and jabbed Lilly in the forehead, a frightening sneer on his face. Lilly stared at them with timid eyes, and her terror was her only companion. Her face felt cold, both from the lack of blood and the teenager's powers. Yet she could do nothing to warm herself. As she was hauled painfully back down the hallway, all she could do was pray she'd somehow escape this, and focused on healing her battered body. This wasn't over yet, she was sure of it, but she had a feeling it was coming close to an end.

Slowly, they reentered the room, and Lilly couldn't help but shudder. Hatred was written on the faces of the two people already there; Dr. Kibbsty displayed bitter annoyance and had a deep gash on his forehead, and Tray wore a vengeful glare with a curled bloody lip. Throwing her face-down into the tile, she let out a whimper and forced herself to stay calm. One of them grabbed her hair and pulled her head up while Tray glared down at her.

"You're going to regret making things worse on yourself, lass. You can be sure of that."

Suddenly the ropes dropped from around her, and Lilly tried to run, but a blow hit her stomach and sent her backward into a table, leaving her gasping for breath. She threw open her wings to catch herself, but it seemed that was what they had been waiting for. The bindings returned, tightening her splayed wings against the board, and Lilly was left squirming helplessly. A leather strap locked into place around her arms, and only her head was free.

"Now, le's see how much spunk ye got left when all is taken from you. We can start with your powers." Laughter roared around her, and something was shoved around her neck that locked into place. Lilly snapped at the hand, only to face retaliation in a slap across the face, the force cutting her cheek against her teeth. Tasting blood, she tried to heal the wound, but felt blocked.

Nothing happened.

She couldn't use her powers.

Her eyes widened, but she tried to stay calm regardless of the fear that was building within her. Her powers were still new, so maybe it was just a coincidence. Tray grinned wickedly, however, signaling that this was only the beginning. She felt someone wrench her wing to the side, pin it down, and heard the clip of scissors. Realization dawned with horrifying clarity. She let out a yell and tried to pull away, but it was too late. There were too many people here, too many bindings. Lilly struggled against all of it, and great tears rolled down her face. She screamed and yelled and wailed, not bothering to hide her distress anymore. They had just done the unthinkable; they had deprived her of her very life and spirit.

They had clipped her wings.

CHAPTER EIGHTEEN

A CHASE IN CHINA

"I hate this place," muttered Xzin, glaring viciously at a passerby. The streets were narrow, leaving only a small walkway for people to pass through, and strangers pressed so tightly it was hard for the group to stay together. The small space was heavy with the thick aroma that clung to unwashed bodies, and it seemed to coat the back of his mouth, forcing a grimace he couldn't remove from his face. A black-haired girl looked back, hair swishing from one side of her face to the other, a chunk of red at the bottom of her hair showing out brightly against her black tank top.

"Xzin, you're from China. How can you hate it?" Cherry asked in surprise. The Asian boy snarled, glaring down strangers on either side.

"Just because I grew up here doesn't mean I have to like it. Besides, it's a big country. That's like saying it's odd you don't like North Dakota just because you live in the US," Xzin grumbled. His companion sighed and stumbled backward as someone rushed by. The growl grew louder, and Cherry glared back, moving away from him with a flick of her hair.

"Don't give me that," she snapped, attracting the attention of the girl leading the way. Dark eyes sharpened irritably and Cherry side-stepped with a nervous flinch.

"*Vámanos*. Stop wasting time arguing."

Xzin reluctantly listened to the girl and went silent. Cherry made a face, then glanced back to the rest of their group. Two silver-haired teens were behind them, as well as a boy with black hair and a scruffy unshaved look. The latter, Harris, crossed his arms and sighed.

"Hey Pilar, how come Kibbsty didn't make Tray come? This would have been so much easier with that brat along."

The girl in the lead sighed. "How'm I supposed to know? Why does Kibbsty do anything?" Her heavy Spanish accent accentuated the annoyance in her voice. She looked ahead, then turned left into a less crowded alleyway. The five behind her followed along, Xzin repeatedly shooting dark looks at anyone who glanced at him wrong, before they slowed to a tense stop.

"They're close."

Cherry moved forward first, and in the blink of an eye, her hair shortened and the red bottoms melted upward before changing to a softer shade of crimson. Evenly cut hair transformed to layers before her face took on fair Asian features, with smaller eyes and a beautiful complexion. She grew taller and lankier, with a thin body and long legs. She moved quietly and quickly, then paused next to Harris. "You'll take care of his sister?" she hissed. "I swear if she sees us and uses her powers—"

"*Silencio.*"

The group obediently grew silent and Pilar started moving again, darting into an alley and then jumping gracefully up, catching the corner of a roof. She gripped the edge of the tiling, swung her legs up and scaled onto it like a spider using pure muscle to carry her. She turned around and held out a hand, helping Xzin next to her while the silver-haired boy jumped up after them, aided by his sister. It was a matter of moments before the three of them were settled and Pilar turned back to the remaining teens on the ground. "Harris, remember, your job is to draw her out and distract her long enough for us to strike. Cherry, get in there and pretend to be the boy's sister just long enough for us to take care of her. Remember, they can't suspect anything!" She spoke in careful English so no one could question her orders "Mar, you need to get that collar on as quickly as possible, right when Xzin gives the signal!" The silver-haired girl nodded in acknowledgement, then disappeared in a blur. The remaining figures on the ground split up, and Pilar waved to the boys by her side. "You two, *ven conmigo.*"

The Spaniard girl and Xzin moved along the roof, before Pilar paused and flattened carefully against it. The tiles were thin and patchy, and where Pilar stopped was particularly worn, gaps in the tiling enabling the teens to see inside. She waved a hand at Xzin and he knelt close, eyes carefully watching the inside of the building. Below, they could barely see the tops of two heads, one with hair the same color and style that Cherry had mimicked, the other a dark and wispy black. It looked like they had been in the middle of a conversation when the girl stood up in response to a knock on the door. Pilar listened closely and could hear the girl say something in Chinese before she started moving toward the door. They would only have a moment to act; otherwise, they would be at the mercy of this girl's powers.

Thall was already moving, carefully walking along the fragile pieces of roof, then finding the best spot to watch. Down on the ground, the other teens were prepared for the approaching footsteps. Harris stood flat against the wall and Mar a short distance away, waiting for the signal. Cherry was just behind her, crouched and ready to execute the plan. They would have to act as a team, and if any of them messed up, it would be over as quickly as it had started. It seemed like they stood for an hour before the door finally opened, and they struck.

The girl didn't even have time to look surprised when there was a small thud and a tiny dart appeared deep in her arm. As her eyes started to knit with anger, Harris yanked her out of the doorway and Mar moved Cherry into position with a blur of movement. It all happened within milliseconds, but it was only the first stage. There was no time to pause as the rest fell into place.

Harris stunned the struggling girl with a blow to the head, holding her easily with his mechanical arm. Xzin quickly jumped down from the roof and grabbed her chin, forcing her to look into his eyes. The single loathing look he got was all it took to get into her mind and look quickly through her memories. Finding what he needed, he hurried to Cherry and shadowed the action, planting the temporary images in the shifter's mind. With that done, he returned to Mar and was boosted back onto the roof where Thall and Pilar were still watching the house.

"Here," he called, pointing to a loose door built into the roof. What once was an emergency escape was now an easy entrance. Xzin and Pilar lifted it easily, and when they blinked, Thall was already going to work. Effortlessly, he dropped into the room below, powers of stealth making his motions virtually undetectable. He crept forward as voices speaking Chinese hissed in the air between the boy and Cherry. Any second and he could realize what had just happened. Unwilling to risk waiting too long and losing the boy, Thall reached behind him, and touched his shoulder with a gloveless left hand. The boy froze, eyes wide with shock as the paralysis set in. The teen behind him smirked in victory.

"Okay, let's move!" Cherry called out, and immediately the other four joined them in the little house. Pilar, Harris and Xzin tied up their captives, snapped on their inhibitor collars, and set them on the pitiful couch the room contained. The siblings were drastically different in some ways, and near identical in others. Slumped against his sister, the boy looked frail and brittle, with black hair that was long and perfectly straight. It was layered, with the hair on the back of his neck in a V an inch down his back and the hair above his ears coming down just short of his chin. His face matched his sister's though, with that fair, delicate look and the same olive skin tone. The boy was even slimmer than his sister, with long limbs, but he seemed small despite them. As he stirred, his eyes fluttered, revealing deep brown eyes that were so dark, they looked black. The instant he saw them, he glanced quickly at his sister and fear flickered across his face.

"Xzin, he's awake."

The boy said something in Chinese, his voice deeper than expected from someone who looked so fragile. As Xzin moved forward, the kid looked him from head to toe and promptly shut his mouth.

"Nuo..." Xzin said, his voice sounding different as he dropped into Chinese, traditionally speaking the last name first. The boy's eyes narrowed, and he hissed back. Xzin listlessly translated. "He asks who we are, how we know him." Xzin rattled back in a dark tone, then continued. "I told him we're from a place called Firestone, their new home." He gave a wicked smile, laughing as the boy started sputtering angrily back. "He just used some colorful Chinese at us, guys. I don't think he realizes who he's messing with."

The Spaniard grinned and took a step forward, and her teeth glittered menacingly. "I can enlighten him." She watched the girl stirring out of the corner of her eye, but kept her focus on the boy. She pulled out a small object and smiled, holding it up casually. "I have the antidote, so I can let 'im pain a little, then stop it before it kills 'im."

Harris let his arm transition back to its mechanical form, and grabbed the boy by his shirt front. The young teen let out a fresh stream of Chinese. "I say we take Pilar's cue. These brats gotta learn same way we did."

Xzin thought for a moment, then signaled Pilar and Harris with the slightest shake of his head. Harris shrugged and tossed the boy onto the couch again and Pilar put away the syringe. Once the boy stopped sputtering in hatred, Xzin knelt in front of him and began to speak.

"Harris. Got a translator in you?" Cherry muttered, flicking her hair back to its normal black and red. Harris quickly transformed a section of his right arm and pushed a couple of buttons on the metal panel that appeared. Then a low translation hummed with the same voices of Xzin and Nuo.

"You still haven't answered any of my questions!" sputtered Nuo.

"That's because you don't need any answers. Listen, the easiest thing to do would be to go with it. Fighting is pointless. We all know it isn't your ideal way of doing things, but you got picked out, and now you need to deal," snarled Xzin.

"Just wait until Hayachi wakes," Nuo said viciously. "She'll paint the walls with your blood."

Xzin gave a dark laugh and nodded at the crimson-haired girl who was still trying to wake up. "Oh, will she? Tell me, have you tried using your powers yet, Nuo?" Xzin watched with relish as a look of knowing disbelief crossed the boy's face.

Nuo looked down at his legs, staring at a patch on his faded jeans. "Yes."

"And I bet you anything, your dear sister tried too," Xzin gloated. "Trust me. Hayachi isn't going to be repainting this room anytime soon. And you aren't in control anymore. We know your powers."

"Liar." The ferocity in Nuo's voice made his face darken, and the Chinese was spat out with twice as much force as the translation. Xzin laughed.

"Hayachi, your sister, can control blood, but only to an extent. She can't pull it out of someone unless they have a wound, although she can cause blood clots, cardiac arrest, and cause it to pull so painfully against the body that the person has to move with it or suffer agony."

Nuo refused to respond, but he was visibly shaken. Xzin pointed a finger at him. "And your name may be Nuo, but it's not Nuo Ya Xue, is it? That's hers. You took it when she changed her name to Hayachi."

"We did it to protect me," whispered Nuo. "When I got my powers, people were afraid. Because I controlled their emotions. Hayachi didn't use her powers unless provoked, so no one really hated her. But they wanted me."

"And when you got sick, she got scared. And put her name down as you."

"Yes."

"And you just kept it?"

Nuo's timidity left his voice and his anger grew, eyes slitted and fierce. "When my sister gave me her name, she turned into someone else. Ya Xue died that day, and I carry her name in memory. Hayachi... Sh-she..."

Xzin chuckled softly. "She started using her powers against people."

Nuo's voice trembled. "She had to pay the medical bills. Mom and Dad died in an earthquake when we were young. She had no way of paying for my treatment. I told her not to, that someone would catch on!"

Xzin took a step forward and spoke so low, the translator barely picked it up. "Well guess what, 'Nuo Ya Xue?' Someone has." He took a step back and faced the others gathered around. He gave a brisk nod to Harris and finally spoke in English. "Wake up his sister. Let's see if we can get them to come willingly."

"As in blackmail? Or persuasion?" Cherry smiled. Xzin gave a soft chuckle.

"A bit of both. The boy needs the medical help Kibbsty can offer. The girl can't afford it and we can offer that help. But it's also a double-edged sword. If she refuses to come willingly, we make them come and they won't get any help."

"Beyond what will keep him alive, *verdad?*" Pilar added. Xzin nodded.

At this point, they were interrupted by a loud string of Chinese, a harsh female voice like sugar mixed with lemon. Thall chuckled slightly, and he and his twin exchanged knowing looks.

"Hayachi," Nuo whispered softly. His sister responded with a quieter, questioning slur. Nuo shot a dirty look at the Firestone students before responding in a hasty tone.

"We can explain ourselves, you know," Cherry snapped at the boy, momentarily forgetting they spoke in Chinese. Nuo seemed to get the point and quieted. Hayachi glowered.

"Leave us alone."

Harris looked slightly taken aback by the English, and Pilar narrowed her eyes, the accent so thick it was hard for her to understand. Xzin stepped forward, and Harris brought the translator up again quickly.

"That's not an option now, Hayachi, as I'm sure you realize. Why don't you listen to our proposal before you turn it down?" Xzin asked in a falsely sweet tone.

"It's probably nothing new," Hayachi grumbled. She glared at them from under her ruffled red hair, lips in a thin line. "You want me to work for you, I bet. Do your dirty work?"

Xzin laughed. "Smart girl, but a little off. We work for a man called Dr. Kibbsty. Very skilled, with lots of equipment at his disposal. Better yet, he's familiar with *our* kind."

The girl scoffed. "'*Our*' kind? What makes you think you're anything like me?" she spat.

Xzin chuckled. "We all have powers, gifts." At this cue, Mar disappeared in a blur and reappeared by Hayachi's shoulder, causing both siblings to cry out in surprise. Cherry shifted into a duplicate of Nuo, who stared as Xzin continued. "We also have lilac hairs like you." He laughed at Hayachi's reaction to this statement. She looked shaken.

"How did you—But why did you tie us up?" She was swaying, but it was clear she didn't trust them. That would have been stupid, considering they had just been taken captive in their own home.

"We know what type of powers you have. You'd send us into cardiac arrest before we could make an offer," Xzin laughed.

Hayachi muttered, "I would have been making a good choice if I had." Finally, she sighed. "But I would have missed out on your 'offer,' wouldn't I?" She gave a hesitant glance at her brother, and then her face hardened. Nuo gave a worried whisper, but she shushed him and spoke in a serious tone.

"Could this 'Dr. Kibbsty' help my brother?" she asked slowly.

To answer, Xzin waved a hand to Pilar. She stepped forward, leaned close to Hayachi's ear, and chuckled softly. Before Hayachi could react, Pilar bit her; holding a hand tightly over the girl's mouth to muffle the surprised scream, the Spaniard calmly waited as the poison spread. Hayachi thrashed in pain, clawing weakly at the hands holding her in desperation. Nuo was crying out in Chinese, the translator not picking up half the words, most just sounds of terror. Through it all, Pilar remained calm and watched carefully, then she finally inserted the needle into Hayachi's skin, giving the much-needed antidote. Gradually, Hayachi stopped squirming, but the fear stayed in her face, resolve visibly shaken. Pilar moved away with a smug glint in her eyes, while the siblings huddled together.

"W-why?" the girl gasped, breathing heavily, body still recovering. Xzin laughed.

"You asked if Kibbsty could help your brother. That was my answer. Pilar's venom is one of the deadliest poisons in the world. Lucky for us, she can control how deadly. If she had wanted to, she could have killed you. In a way, our boss saved your life. Kibbsty created a medicine to counteract Pilar's venom. He is a brilliant scientist, and he has sources that can do more for your brother than anything you can afford." Xzin pointed at Nuo and spoke with power he rarely held in his voice. "You would be wise to take advantage of this offer. You're coming one way or the other. Don't lose the benefits you can gain by making the right choice."

Xzin took a step back, clearly nearing the end of his proposal, and put his hands casually in his pockets. "Your choice, there's nothing more to it. Yes or no?"

The bitterness in Nuo's face sharply contrasted the cool emptiness that replaced fatigue on Hayachi's. She hissed softly, but it was through her teeth and ended quickly. Then, amidst quiet protests from her brother, she answered.

"Yes."

CHAPTER NINETEEN

OF PAIN AND HEALING

It felt like Lilly's heart had torn in two as she sat in the cold cell she'd been thrown in. Everything was gone; she was alone, she was miserable, and she was heartbroken. Looking down at her wings, she felt like Dr. Kibbsty had done more than clip her feathers. They'd deprived her of flight, taken away her means of escape, and chained her to the earth she feared. She had repaired damage to her feathers before, but she wasn't sure if she could regrow when they had been clipped. The fear that accompanied that uncertainty crippled all other thoughts. She could only sit there and let her heart bleed away.

With a scream, she threw her body into the metal bars of the cell again and again, but all it did was gave her a bitter pain in her shoulder to match that in her mind. Throwing open her wings, she tried to fly and lift herself up even an inch, but found herself standing helplessly on the concrete. In more than one way, she was trapped here. The truth was too terrifying to accept.

Lilly sobbed and fell into a ball at the base of the wall. She couldn't believe her life had fallen so far in such a short time. It seemed like it wasn't that long ago that she was sitting at the table with her mom, playing cards or board games. She longed to feel the soft sheets of her bed and the silk of her pillowcase. She longed to feel the warm breeze that drifted through her open window on a summer's day and to lean back in her bed and watch the lights of the sunset dance on her ceiling. Her parents had done all they could to protect her, and now...

How had she repaid them? She fell into the clutches of the very enemy they had struggled to protect her from. She was barred in a cage with crippled wings, crippled thoughts, and a crippled courage.

Why!!! WHY!!!! WHAT DID I DO?!!! her thoughts screamed and she sobbed openly, hands trembling with her cries. Her body was tired, her mind was exhausted; curling her wings close, she held them like a feathered blanket and rocked back and forth, whispering small prayers to retrieve the faith that was fleeing from her. She couldn't find the comfort she longed to grasp, or the innocence she'd kept her whole life; for some reason, she couldn't get a hold on any of it. It was just... Gone.

She imagined the window panes back at the school, where she sat at the end of the day. The golden hue of the sunset would be beautiful until the night grasped it, then it would fade away; but then she would see the stars. In a pitch-dark world, the stars would scatter for miles, and she could sit and watch them all, unchanging, in the sky. She tried to remember the emotions from moments like those, but they felt out of reach. It was gone, like sunlight enveloped by night. All she could do was wait for the morning.

Lilly looked up in surprise when she heard footsteps coming down the stairs. It wasn't a melody, more like a drum beat: a war drum of wrath approaching. Shivers of fear traveled down her spine, but deep down it felt like someone had laid a hand on her shoulder and whispered to her, *It will be okay... It will be okay...* She wasn't sure she believed it, though. To the basement of the school, her prison and her cell, someone was coming.

They weren't coming to let her go. They were coming on business.

Lilly turned her back to the door, curling her wings around her as the footsteps stopped outside the bars. A key jiggled in the lock, then in came Kibbsty, dressed in slacks and a long-sleeve shirt that looked all too formal for the occasion.

"Not as feisty now, are you?" His huff carried through the cell, and he clicked the keys back onto his belt. Lilly kept her back to him as frustration bubbled inside her and made her arms tremble. She wanted nothing to do with this man, who had destroyed her home and killed her parents. She was terrified, but after everything he had put her through, she was angry more than anything. "Come, now. Don't be that way. It's your own fault we had to clip your precious feathers," he spat, and Lilly's wings curled and uncurled in frustration.

"You're an evil man," Lilly hissed darkly. The words came out with such force she almost felt ashamed. Then the images played back through her mind: her parents' expressions of fear, their wedding rings, the family photos she'd never see again. All the pain she felt was caused by him, all the moments she could never have back. She wished she could take back the day she turned around and saw him standing in the aisle next to her.

"You did this to yourself, you know." He spoke casually, wandering across the cell and spinning his hat in his hands. Lilly tried to tune him out, but he continued. "If you hadn't been so eager to get out into the city, to leave your home, I would never have found you. If you weren't there buying your hair dye, Scarlet couldn't have told me of the little Strand that had evaded our detection; clever girl with her photographic memory, once she saw you, she could easily pick you out of a crowd. You made it too easy though, wandering back into the store. Your parents seemed like smart people. Too bad you didn't share that trait."

"Shut up!" Lilly yelled, turning around with her wings trembling, trying to keep his words from taking hold. "This is all *your* fault. You chased us and you...you—"

"I what, dear? I *killed* them? They were standing in my way. I gave them a chance to turn you over and they refused. I'm a reasonable man; I'm willing to make deals and bargains, just like I'm willing now. Don't be foolish like they were. If you cooperate, maybe you can go back to your pathetic friends and enjoy that new 'home' you've been hiding in. I'm sure your parents would be so proud."

"You can forget it. I'll never work with you!" Her voice was getting louder, her anger overflowing as the tears from her eyes. She longed for something to throw at him, hands clenching and unclenching in rage. Kibbsty stopped and smiled all too sweetly.

"Fine. We'll do this the hard way."

He closed the gap between them before she could react and his fist slammed into the side of her head, sending Lilly crashing to the ground. Staggered and pained, she started to get up, but was kicked so hard in the stomach she flew backward into the wall. Kibbsty's attack was calm but calculated, preventing any counter-attack she could have managed. Meanwhile, he continued speaking. "I've tried being nice, but you're so *stubborn*. You stupid girl, you've been nothing but trouble since the night you escaped!" Lilly tried to scramble out of the way, but was driven to the ground again as his fists rained down on her wings and back. She tried to shield herself, but it got worse until she lay in a timid pile on the ground, beaten and shaken. Kibbsty was panting and the fire in his eyes was inhuman. Pulling his gloves tighter, he nodded.

"But no more. Now, you stop being my problem."

Blood was in Lilly's mouth, and she spat it out, but her body felt too bruised and damaged to move. She couldn't get her limbs to work right, and it felt like she was carrying a ton of bricks on her back. Bruises and cuts covered her body, and she wondered how she could fight back against someone like this. But her soul wouldn't let her give up, even when she was beaten almost to the core; she had to fight him. She couldn't—wouldn't—give up yet.

Slowly she sat up, hugging her stomach, her eyes filled with a slow-burning defiant fire. All of her questioning, her confusion, and her fear condensed into the rage she felt now. She didn't care why it had happened, only who was to blame, and that gave her the strength to fight. She couldn't let him win. Not this time. "What you're doing is wrong. My parents knew that, and I know that! We Strands, we're gifted with something, and you want to play God and make others have the same abilities. But you can't! You have no idea what that would do to normal people. If I helped you, I could be responsible for destroying the lives of others!"

"Do you think you can stop me?" hissed Kibbsty, tightening his fists. "Do you think you can stand in my way? All you are is a pawn; one I need for my research, and one whose blood I need fresh, whether it's freshly dead or still alive. Your cooperation is desired, but unnecessary. I'm going to complete my experiments one way or the other. You're noble, yet so foolish. You could have saved yourself time and time again, and yet you insist on being difficult. But it's all going to hit you eventually." He grabbed her by the hair with one hand, and pulled her head back. Lilly let out a gasp and slammed her wings upside his head, but he grabbed them and wrenched so hard she felt a crack. Pain shot up her spine and she whimpered, but she refused to give in. Her parents had been brave. She could be brave, too.

"Give me your arm!" he bellowed, but she pulled away, glaring back. He moved again and she slapped him, thrashing in defiance. Kibbsty snarled and dropped her, pinning her against the ground with his foot, digging the heel of his boot into her back. With his other leg he kicked, aiming for her head, but she slipped away, trying her best to reach the door. She was dealt several more blows until she crumbled again and he wrenched her to her feet, this time by the throat. The pressure on her neck was too much. Her body was screaming, her lungs were gasping, and stars fluttered in front of her eyes. She stopped squirming, focusing on prying his fingers apart, and he smiled with satisfaction.

"One more time. You give me your arm, or I'll bring my students down here. I'm sure they can persuade you better than I can."

"You're...sick..." Lilly spat, but it was a weak insult. She was losing strength. Kibbsty grabbed her wrist and flipped it upward, and Lilly weakly fought him, but the hold on her neck was too much. It seemed like he had finally succeeded...

When Lilly bit him. Hard.

"Ahgh!!!" he cried and dropped Lilly once more. She dove between his legs this time, then kicked Kibbsty, sending him into the wall. Somehow she managed to grab the keys from his belt and was able to dart out of the cell. With a victorious glare, she slammed the door behind her and locked it. The clang that echoed when it shut was the most wonderful sound she'd heard since she came here. Even with pain crippling her body, she took relief in that success. She watched as Kibbsty staggered to his feet, breathing deeply with relief. Then he took her by surprise as his voice bellowed forth with inhuman rage, "SHE'S ESCAPED!!! GET THAT STUPID BRAT YOU LAZY GOOD-FOR-NOTHINGS!!!"

The sense of victory vanished, adrenaline surged, and Lilly rushed toward the stairs as laughter roared behind her. She should have run while she had the chance, but now it felt too late. Her body screamed as she took the steps in twos but she pushed on, making a desperate break for freedom. Then she found just what she dreaded: a wall of students standing calmly by, waiting for her.

Her eyes widened, and she let the keys drop to the ground with a clatter. Tray was by the door, electricity crawling toward her, and Cory was behind him. Trish, Pete and Tara were still coming around the corner, Tara yelling something to an unfamiliar Firestone student. Strangely enough, they all stood together so naturally that she forgot her panicked flight. Her confusion stalled her as she noticed the students from Charity Academy mixed with those from Firestone: a mix of what she thought could be friends here with her enemies. It was a betrayal she couldn't understand. She had classes with some of these students, spent lunchtimes just down the row from them, and they were with the enemy? It just couldn't be...

"I don't know what you did to Kibbsty, but I can tell you already, you're not going like the results." Ice crystals started drifting across the ground, and Lilly scuttled backward, eyes frantically seeking escape. There was a whoosh and a thud as one of the students shot something at her, and behind her a strong breeze was starting to grow. It roared like the anger of the students, gaining power as they stood waiting for someone to strike first. But as Tray raised his hand, ready to move, water roared in front of him and engulfed the hallway. Lilly's heart leapt, and she felt herself fall to her knees in relief.

"Jake...You made it," she whispered.

The students scuttled back and Cory quickly froze the majority of the water with an irritated expression. Another student punched a hole in the ice with his bare hand, and ropes slivered through the opening dangerously. Nodding to the others, Tray led the way to reach the oncoming arrivals, their motions battle-familiar as they turned toward the school entrance. A tiger was the first to break the line, colliding with puppeteered ropes that were rapidly trying to bind her. Her roars of fury echoed, together with the sounds of electricity, water, and a violent wind. A mass of chaos was erupting in the hallways, but it was rapidly moving away from Lilly. Lilly found a moment of peace, but it wasn't enough.

The pain from Kibbsty's attack was starting to catch up to her, and she knew she needed to get the collar off her neck that was stopping her powers. Struggling with the metal, she couldn't even loosen it. Lightheadedness was beginning to build, and just when it was about to take hold, she heard a voice.

"Need some help?"

Lilly looked up as one of the twins hurried over, and she sighed with relief. "Please! I can't get it off!" she gasped, and he nodded, skidding to a halt at her side.

"Hold on and stay perfectly still!" The boy turned into a peregrine falcon, jumped on her shoulder, then carefully took his claw and ran it down the collar until she heard a quiet click. As soon as it fell to the ground, Lilly focused on healing as best as she could. Slowly, her powers flickered to life and relief spread through her battered body. <Learned that trick from Meg when they tried to use one of those on Dryk. We spent weeks trying to get that dumb thing off until she sorted that out.>

"Glad to know it still works," Lilly sighed quietly. She leaned her head against the wall while her body repaired itself, and the falcon perched on the stairs next to her in a protective vigil. She focused her energy on the larger wounds, like her wings and her battered ribs; the small cuts could heal later, and while bruises were uncomfortable, they weren't life threatening. Bones repaired themselves, cuts mended, and then there was the strange sensation of feathers re-growing where they had been clipped. That was the sensation that she was most grateful for. Her feathers returning meant she would fly again, something she had been fearful would never happen. The earth was no longer her captor, and that gave her the strength to continue, and an almost drunk ecstasy filled her heart. Feather by feather, one injury at a time she let the healing continue, reflexively touching her new feathers in dizzy relief. When she finally opened her eyes, the golden brown eyes were still watching her, so she gave a smile as she got to her feet.

The smile faltered as Wyvr spoke.

<Feel like lending a hand with the fight?> his voice inquired, his head tilting inquisitively. Lilly felt reluctance and fear make themselves known.

You can do this, she told herself, but her nod was forced at best. She had gotten away from Kibbsty; she could help now, couldn't she? As the bird leapt into flight and circled above her, Lilly slowly followed. She had to be brave now. *You can do this.*

The struggle had shifted into the laboratory, and it was mayhem. Closest to the door, Tray had turned off Jake's powers while Cory tried to nail the helpless victim with blasts of ice. At Jake's side Kat struggled to help him, warning him of every attack, and a swoop of feathers identified one of the twins going to even the odds. Lilly circled in the sky, still weak, trying to decide what to do. Her eyes darted to and fro, uncertain how to help. Should she intervene, fly away, or go guard Kibbsty? For now, she decided to watch, and wait for an opening.

It was strange seeing a battle like this, where the very earth and all its elements seemed to be fighting. There was a surging mass of plants in the far corner, lashing and trying to keep hold on what looked like an anthropomorphic leopard. Another boy looked like he was made entirely of flames, and he was laughing hysterically as a pack of wolves darted around him, unable to draw close and howling angrily. Seth was battling furiously with Zen, the telekinesis hardly holding off the gusts of air rapidly trying to become cyclones. The students of Charity Academy were holding their ground against Firestone merely by numbers: the one thing the students did have at this dark school was battle training. Where Charity was fighting to restrain, many of the students of Firestone were aiming to kill. Lilly barely cried out in time as a giant spider dropped from the ceiling, almost succeeding in biting the back of Michaela's neck. The classmate from her flying class barely managed to evade the attack, snapping with fury and lashing out with her talons as their battle made its way toward the ground.

"Hehehe. Lookit what's come to me skies! It's a wee bitty pigeon!" cackled a voice, and Lilly turned to find herself face to face with a harpy-like creature, scantly clothed in a black skirt and tattered top. Inky black eyes sat perched atop a crooked beak and black wings like a raven's had replaced the girl's arms on either side. Lilly felt unsettled as she looked at this girl, who was shockingly beautiful and hideously ugly at the same time. With talons glittering, she took a wicked slash at Lilly, who flew backward rapidly.

"Stop it! Stay back!"

The cackle sounded again and the black wings fluttered so close to her head, Lilly could see the details in the feathers. At the same time, sharp pain shot through her back as the talons raked her from just below her wingtips to her waist. The harpy's voice hissed in her ear, "Run, Pigeon! Run!!!"

All thoughts of trying to help vanished as Lilly reflexively obeyed the instructions.

The terror was crippling to the sheltered girl. For someone whose instinct was to fly away from people who attacked her, facing someone who also had wings left her blinded by hysteria. Her assailant was quick as lightning and her talons were sharp like knives. Within a couple of seconds, Lilly was herded across the sky in a disoriented flight. The laughter resounded with every swooping attack, and Lilly could barely fly, her wings damaged in multiple places. Like a shark that had tasted blood, the force intensified. The next blow hit Lilly's leg, so fast and strong it sliced clear to the bone. The blood started pouring before the claw had left her skin, and a leg slammed into her stomach, followed by a ravaging cut to her thigh. The force caused Lilly to buckle in pain, and her wings folded like paper as her body was thrown into shock. Claws ripped at her wings even as she fell, and by the time she hit the floor, her feathers littered the ground, blood splattered around her. Her body refused to move, so profusely damaged by the harpy's fury. Her powers flickered with effort, healing just fast enough for her to cling to life as the girl leaned close and snarled in her ear.

"Well, Pigeon. Any last words?"

Lilly couldn't speak, couldn't think. She cried helplessly and struggled to crawl away as the taloned foot pressed against her back. Fearful, she waited for the death blow, when the attack was interrupted.

There was a tremendous roar, and Harper let out a screech, claws clattering along the tiles of the room as she scrambled into the air. Lilly looked up in time to see a tiger leap over her, claws outstretched, catching the tips of the harpy's wings and yanking backward. The screeches and curses that flew from Harper's mouth slurred to the point that they were indistinguishable, and the tiger's paw came back with feathers on all claws, while Harper crash-landed, sprawling on the ground. There was a thud as the cat neatly returned to all fours, and its low growl rumbled again as Harper hissed.

"Pigeon, you're lucky you got your friend t' watch your back... You wouldn' be so tough wit'out her, would ya?"

The tiger lashed out a paw, and Harper jumped backward, just out of reach. Both faces had looks of rage, and both fur and feather were standing on end in aggression. Lilly used the distraction to heal as much as she could, but exhaustion prolonged the process. Her wings were so covered in dirt and blood she knew even if she healed them, flying might be out of the question. To make things worse, in the middle of this already terrible situation, a new assailant approached.

"Hey, giant kitty! Why are you spoiling my girl's fun?"

The tiger recoiled, tail catching Lilly and knocking her to the ground. Through her obstructed view, Lilly could see the flickers of a fire, and the crackles were loud in her ear, though fur was pressed close to her face. <Stay down, Lilly!> Meg's voice warned in her head.

"How do you like it when something's bigger than you?"

A roar stung in Lilly's ears, and the feline reared onto her hind legs in fear. From beneath her, Lilly watched the immense shape of a dragon rise up, formed from flames, wings spanning impressively to all sides. The pyrotechnic student was to the left of it, fueling his creation with more fire from a small lighter, and the flames burned greedily on whatever they came in contact with, whether it was fallen feathers or fur. Sweat clung to Lilly's brow as the heat pressed against her body, and Meg's large paws barely missed clipping Lilly's shoulder as she stood protectively over her friend. Lilly was unprepared for a situation like this, inexperienced with the challenges of battle. Her wings trembled as the flames got closer and she struggled to stay out of their path, but there was nothing she could do to defend herself against something so elemental.

The mouth of the dragon opened, ready to devour them, when a wave of water crashed down on the flames, reducing the dragon to steam. Relief filled her heart while the smell of singed fur filled her nose. Meg moved out of her way, giving Lilly room to breathe, but neither teen moved with any hurry this time. The battle was waning and students were dispersing, but as the steam faded, Lilly found herself unable to stand.

An ache started filling her body; her pain was coming back, and the more she tried to focus on healing it and finding peace, the worse it got. Letting out a whimper, she hugged her stomach, and the others looked at her with worry.

"Lilly, are you okay?" Meg whispered, putting a hand on her shoulder. Lilly tried to speak, but doubled over in agony. She felt like someone was punching her repeatedly in the stomach, each blow more intense than the last. Her eyes were filled with panic as she looked around, trying to identify the source of this agony; something was wrong. For some reason, her body wasn't healing anymore, and the day's abuses were catching up to her.

There was an evil laugh, one with an Irish sound to it, and Lilly flinched as she caught sight of Tray. Jake ran to where the boy was and pulled him to his feet. "What are you doing, you idiot! You're suppressing her powers, aren't you?!!!" he yelled, and Tray started chuckling, wiping blood from his lip.

"What do you think I'm doin'? Tha' brat asked for it, and I'm givin' it to her," he hissed back, and roared with laughter. Jake punched him, throwing him to the ground; he was glowering with anger.

"Well stop it, or I'll stop it for you!" growled Jake, but Tray kept sniggering.

"Think you c'n try to scare me, just because you like the lass? Don't threaten me, *boy*. You try to hurt me, I'm takin' her with me." The echoes of his amusement added a chilling emphasis to his threat.

Lilly fell to her knees, letting out a cry which turned into a sob, footsteps returning to her side. Jake yelled for Meg and Kat to get help, but she didn't know if they left or not. She thought she heard punching, fighting, and then the haunting laughter stopped. What was happening? What was wrong?

She let out another gasp as searing fire shot through her, and her eyes stared at the ground in dumb confusion. She felt something trickling from her mouth, but didn't take her hands from her stomach, as if they could soften the pain. Gradually, a crimson stain appeared on the ground, dripping steadily from her lips. She trembled in disbelief.

"Lilly! Lilly, hang in there!" Jake yelled, but Lilly couldn't hear it. It felt like every cell in her body was failing and tearing her apart from the inside. Beads of sweat rolled along her forehead, and the fall of every drop of blood brought new waves of pain. She felt like she was dying, dying in slow anguish.

"Jake! What's wrong? What's happening?" she gasped, looking up at him, but he seemed as horrified as she was. Her wings were splayed, her mind overrun by her questions. She wanted it to end. She couldn't take it! The world was crashing, fire and inferno, pain and torture. *Why was this happening? Why did it hurt so much?* Could *it hurt this much?*

Voices sounded distant, the world was slowly spinning in a tilting motion... Round and around it waltzed, dancing in front of her eyes, slowly reaching out to her, then pulling away. The faces, so sad... So lost... So confused....

"Lilly, don't give up! Force your powers to work, don't give up yet! You have too much talent, too much life, too much hope to die now. You have too much left to do, Lilly! Don't let go! Fight it!" Jake encouraged, taking her by the shoulders and staring hard into her face. It was enough to break through her thoughts and catch her attention, but the pain obscured his words.

Lilly looked at him pitifully. *Fight it?* How could she fight pain? How could she stop it? She couldn't find relief, and the more her brain sought it, the more the pain increased.

Help me... Please...

She screamed as a torrent of pure anguish washed through her, feeling like it would split her in two, and she couldn't take it anymore. Jake had his hands on her shoulders, trying to talk to her, but it didn't matter. It was too much! "MAKE IT STOP!!!! JUST STOP!!!" she wailed, and suddenly…

It did.

The pain was still there, but something had changed. The room was eerily quiet, muffled, and foggy. She glanced up in confusion, and Jake's expression reflected the bewilderment she felt. "Lilly… Oh, Lilly…"

Everyone was still. Meg was mid-jump with her arm suspended and her mouth open; Kat was yelling and pointing at Tray, who was unconscious on the ground. Everything was frozen, suspended in the air. Like they were hung by strings, dirt and smoke hovered in the air the same way. She must be hallucinating… There was no way to explain this.

"Lilly, I think I know what your third gift is now. You can stop time, and you took me with you..."

There was no time to wonder, no time to think. Lilly felt her body growing weak and let out a whimper, putting out her hand to hold herself up. Jake was there, kneeling next to her, and put a hand on her back to comfort her and to coach her through it. "Lilly, listen. Third Strands don't survive because they get sick, but you've been fighting that sickness. You need to keep fighting it. Tray tried stopping your healing, and maybe that set it off, but we don't have time to question it. You just need to use your healing. Come on. You're so close!"

Lilly gasped, holding her stomach so tightly it felt she would break her arms. She shook her head stubbornly and whimpered in response, "I can't! It's too hard to keep my powers going!" she gasped, and Jake gently brushed the blood away, shaking his head.

"You can, Lilly. I know you can! I've seen the will you have! You held on, even when your home was taken from you, and you made the best of things! You fought the pain in your heart then, and you can fight this pain now. You can do this; fight this plague, this illness that killed off everyone like you! You are the last Third Strand, maybe the *only* one that lived! Don't give up now, don't you *dare* give up now!"

Lilly gasped again, and slowly nodded. She forced her body to continue, and step by step she kept her powers going and forced the healing to take over. The breeze of the ocean, a sunset, a quiet night, the stars above, sitting in the rain, flying on a warm summer's day; she focused on these good thoughts, and her powers started activating. It was slow, though; she felt like she was facing an uphill battle against a giant wall of injuries.

Slowly, dull warmth filled her limbs. It rose from her wingtips, working slowly and painfully. It seemed like each bone had to be repaired, and every feather had to be replaced. Skin was restored, and the damage that had been done to her wings slowly vanished. Her back was slowly being healed, and the cuts were mended for good this time. Her legs re-healed, then her head. Blood was still dried on her back, but no more fresh blood came. Her heart was pounding now, and the healing recreated the cells that been destroyed. Her insides stopped aching, and she could take her hands away to put them back on the ground.

"Keep going. Keep going, Lilly, you're almost there."

"I can't, Jake... I *can't*! Holding time, trying to heal, I don't think I can—"

"Don't be afraid! Don't doubt! Doubting is only going to make it harder to get through this!"

As the pain started returning, Lilly felt bitter, and her voice lashed out against his reassurance. "Jake, what do you know? You have never hurt this much! You can't understand!" she gasped, instantly regretting what she said. Jake stared deep into her eyes. He looked like the blind child he was without his powers, a crippled soul that had just been slapped.

"Lilly, I do understand, because I've felt pain too, and heartache. You know that story about Fin and Dr. Allina? Well, Fin was my brother. Dr. Allina adopted me after my parents were killed in a car crash. I was afraid and I was alone. My own brother was killed in that car, and I was the only one who made it. The *only* one. Then came Dr. Allina. She adopted me, took me in. I was her son. I was happy. And you know what happened? She didn't know I had gifts. Mine arrived before Fin's, and I made Fin promise not to tell anyone, because I thought people would freak out. Fin promised.

"Then he found out he had gifts too, and we were both thrilled. Finally, someone else could know my secret. Then he was killed, *defending* me. He was shot protecting me when Dr. Kibbsty mixed us up and almost kidnapped me instead. I'd lost my parents and I lost a second brother, and it was hard to let Dr. Allina be a mom after that when it felt like I was just replacing Fin.

"So don't tell me I haven't felt pain, because I have. I lost my family too, and I pushed away my...my mom when we needed each other the most. I'm not perfect, but as angry as I was, I kept fighting. I wanted to let go, I hung on, because that's what Fin would have wanted. That's what your mother and father would have wanted. And that's what you want."

Lilly looked at him with teary eyes and nodded. "But what if it's not enough? What if I die anyway?"

"Then it'll be okay. Lilly, you know where you're going in the afterlife, don't you? If you live, it'll be great. But if you don't, it just might be better. Maybe not for me or your friends who are still here. But you'll be fine wherever you go."

Lilly nodded slowly, and let out a tiny sob, tears rolling down her face. "I know it could be better, but I'm not ready yet."

"I'm not ready yet either," Jake quietly admitted. "But what happens, happens. Please don't give up yet. Give it all you've got, Lilly. You're so close. You can make it."

That was the final push she needed. Reaching into her gut, Lilly pulled out everything she had and started fighting back. The healing traveled the rest of the way and finished its work. She kept fighting, straining for the finish, and slowly opened her eyes, looking weakly at Jake.

"You going to be okay?" he whispered, and she felt herself nod.

"Yeah, Jake, I'm going to be okay," she said, returning them to normal time, and collapsing in his arms.

CHAPTER TWENTY

HOME

Jake sighed and looked in the hospital wing window. The cleanliness was both unnerving and irritating. He never did like hospitals; they were too clean for him, stripped of life by disinfectants and bleach. Even outside the door, the polished walls were too white, the room too stark, and it was hard to think of anything other than illness when you faced something that empty. The nurse was checking on Lilly, her silhouette a halo of color on the blank walls. The injured teen had been resting for several days, and her healing was stalled, too much energy expended from keeping herself alive. Lilly was frail and weak, and to Jake her wings looked like they could crumple into powder. She was less a bird and more of a butterfly, vulnerable and easily damaged. In the hallway, it was as if he was looking into a display case at a museum; this was nothing but an empty background for something once colorful and alive.

Her brush with death had scared everyone, and the only person it seemed to hit harder than Meg and Kat was him. He didn't feel like things would be the same again. Inwardly, he felt angry and bitter. Everything had been thrown away in the conflict with Kibbsty—not just once, but multiple times. He'd taken Lilly's parents, and Jake's brother, and then tried to take Lilly's life. All the man knew was she was that part of his research, a little pawn of his, and Jake hated that she had been used like that.

Yet, Jake was in wonder as he looked through the window. The face as white as the sheets it was laying on was the face of the only surviving Third Strand. She was the last of a kind they thought was extinct, that all regarded as a myth. That was a fact that could change things for them all.

The funny thing was that Kibbsty had gone after her specifically, without knowing she had three strands. He just wanted to study her wings, study her bones. The skeleton he had been so fascinated by was attached to something even rarer. No one knew they were fighting over someone so important.

Now the secret was out. It wouldn't take long for people to hear that Lilly was a Third Strand, *the* Third Strand, and from now on life would never be even relatively normal. Lilly was in danger.

But at least she was alive.

As time went on, school resumed its normal schedule. Classes continued, people stopped talking about the fight at Firestone, and everyone slowly stopped waiting to hear about Lilly. Jake wasn't like them; waiting just wasn't enough. He stayed by her side while she recovered, helping when he could and anticipating the moment she would wake up. Jake believed what she had said, he knew she would be okay. It would just take time.

Although he wanted to look after her, it was depressing. Someone who used to be so alive, bringing a smile to every class and a laugh to every hallway, was now quiet and beaten, struggling to make it through each day.

"I'm sorry," Jake whispered one day, gently folding the sheet under her chin. "I said I would look after you, but I failed. I know I shouldn't blame myself, and I want to blame Kibbsty, but sometimes it makes it feel better. Like if I blame myself, I can forgive myself and say at least someone took the blame..." Jake sighed and looked at her, struggling to relieve his guilt-ridden conscience. "I promise: I'll do whatever I can to keep you safe this time. I can't promise it'll work, but I'm not going to give up; you didn't, and I won't either."

The room's quiet was unnerving, but Jake didn't mind it as much anymore. After spending so many days sitting here waiting, the quiet was the only company he had. It was friend and enemy.

Unexpectedly, he felt a feather brush his face and he turned as Lilly stirred. Quiet eyes flickered open and she rolled over slowly, looking into his face. "Hey," she whispered, and Jake smiled back.

"Hey, yourself. You feeling okay?" he whispered. She nodded, wincing slightly.

"Tired, but okay," she said, and leaned into her pillows. "Jake..."

"Hush." Jake held up a finger and smiled. "Don't say anything. You should be resting. You've had a long couple of weeks and you need to heal."

The young girl nodded, pulling the sheets closer as she settled back. Finally she seemed to settle on what she wanted to say. "Thanks. Thanks for being here for me."

"Any time, Lilly."

There was silence as they awkwardly tried to think of anything else to say. Lilly felt emotions said and unsaid, but for now it was better left that way. Slowly sinking back into the pillows, she sighed and smiled softly before glancing back at Jake. "You know, I don't know what will happen from here. I guess I'm still scared, but at least I have you guys. I think, I think I know one thing." She closed her eyes and felt herself drifting to sleep, but her words were clear. "Right now, I'm home."

CHAPTER TWENTY-ONE

REFORMED TACTICS

"What happened?"

The question was placed like a gun on the table, carrying an unspoken threat. The gathered teens glanced at each other, many still nursing injuries from the battle that had overwhelmed them. Their leader's dark expression demanded an answer, and finally one of the more slender teens spoke up.

"There were too many of them. We weren't prepared for an attack like that. If the others weren't in China—"

"I don't want your excuses," Kibbsty hissed, and the boy drifted back, gulping quietly. "The girl: why is she still not here in front of me? *What happened?*"

From the back of the group, the dark-eyed harpy stepped forward. Chin held high, she met their leader's face and hissed under her breath, "The pigeon's not normal. I *saw*. One second, she was swimmin' wit' the fishes, then she *healed*. An' all I did was blink."

Kibbsty's hand lashed out and caught her arm, earning a screech of pain. As her legs buckled, he snarled into her face, "She's got wings: that's one Strand. We know she heals: that's the second. There's no way she has that much control over her healing already."

"She hasn't," spoke up Tara, pushing herself to the front. "Kibbsty, she's got *another* power. She should have died, but it was like… It was like she *stopped time*."

The older man slowly released Harper's arm and straightened, processing the information. He glanced around the room, his frown deeper, but the rage subsided. It contradicted everything they knew, but that didn't seem to bother him. A look of delight filled his features, and the students risked a breath of relief. "Well, I think this changes things." He leaned back against the wall and dismissed the teens. They scattered before he changed his mind, and a slow chuckle vibrated through the room.

Footsteps paced in a circle, matching the swirling of thoughts in his head. Already, plans were forming, and he suddenly felt he had much to prepare for. "A Third Strand," he mused. "Turns out I was looking for a breakthrough, and one fell right into my lap." The battle didn't feel like such a loss now. In fact, it felt like a victory.

In the trash can, a file rested, and he strode over casually and pulled it out, purposefully placing it back on the table. Carefully written notes, questions, they were all becoming clearer now.

"Little Lilly Douglas. Maybe it's a good thing I didn't kill you, after all."

PART TWO:

STANDING TALL

CHAPTER ONE

TO THE DOGS

The sound of constant dripping rang out in the darkness. It was slow but steady, and a puddle formed on the hard stone floor. The dripping substance was heavier than water, a still liquid, and even in the black room there was a reflective tint of crimson. The walls echoed like a pity-filled voice, soiled by innocent blood, and the floor reverberated its reply. Both carried their silent burdens, disquieted by the torment they had witnessed. Wish as they might, even they were helpless to cease Lilly's suffering, and the young girl was alone in the cruel dungeon with nothing for comfort.

A sigh interrupted the unbroken pattern, and it finished in time for another 'drip' to sound. Slowly, Lilly lifted her head, her eyes searching the dungeon for something she couldn't seem to find. She kept moving her eyes about, but after a third glance, she sank against her shackles, too weak to even hold her head upright. In the dark, shadows traced her jawline and nestled under her chin, overlapping dark, ugly bruises that covered her face and neck. Long, ugly red marks marked her cheek, and her arms were cut, the wounds still open and raw. Her back was tender with a smattering of bruises and cuts, but it was her wings that were the worst to gaze upon: they were limp, broken, and the feathers were soaked with blood... The white was no longer snowy, but ashy with dirt, brown with grime, and red with gore. It was from these feather tips that the crimson stains kissed the ground.

In the mind of the once lively, hopeful girl, she tried to trace back, searching for the story that had brought her here and some memory to give her peace. The pain of the thoughts almost stopped her, but in her beaten state, fear was easily overpowered. Slowly, like the tiny hands of a child, her mind searched, looking for the lost traces of her memories. She let the gentle drip of her blood create the rhythm, the heartbeat, to *carry her back in time...*

CHAPTER TWO

TUG AND WAR

"Class, please welcome Nathan Artemas. He just joined Charity Academy with his brother Eric, our new art director," Mr. Pekinessi announced. The blond student was about seventeen years old, with his hair curled around his ears and bright blue eyes. As he stood at the front of the band room, the students paused where they were in order to give a polite greeting. "Nathan plays guitar, so Jake, it looks like you might have some competition."

From the guitar section, Jake's face flickered through an array of emotions, finally settling on a confident smile. His posture was complacent, but his eyes were defiant at the idea of someone trying to take his place as lead guitar. He watched the new kid smile brightly, then sit in the open seat.

"Hey. How are you?" Nathan beamed again, and Jake shrugged. In the background, his peers resumed tuning their instruments.

"I'm good. I've been better." Jake stretched his legs in front of him as he picked up his guitar and plugged it into its amp. "So, played long?"

The smiled never seemed to fade from Nathan's face. Jake hated it already. "Been playing since I was about five. My dad taught me, and I've been keeping with it ever since." The blond pulled his guitar from his case; it was a silver and blue with smooth, rounded edges and a royal blue bridge. The tuning pegs were gleaming silver and the strings were bright and well cared for. Next to Jake's red and black guitar, with its sharp points and dark pegs, it was like a little blue fish next to a dark shark. "I'm so glad my bro took the job at this school. I've been dying to come for ages, but mom and dad were afraid to draw attention to our gifts. They told us as long as we were safe, they wanted us to live normal lives. For a while, we did that, then Eric realized we would drive each other insane alone, after we lost them. So here we are." Nathan's voice was accompanied by the soft hum of his guitar as he tuned each string with care. Jake's sat limply in his lap, untouched.

"That's...great, Nathan—"

"Aw, you can call me Nate." The grin beamed brightly, and the strings continued to sing along.

"Nate, then..." Jake's eyes flickered for a moment, and he turned to his own guitar. Somewhere inside him, his temper had sparked, and each word Nate said increased his irritation. His eyesight flickered from one type of vision to another, as if desperate to find some way to tone down the glow of Nate's smile. Meanwhile, his thoughts were moving just as rapidly. Jake had always been lead guitar. Although he owned a bass, he preferred his Flying V. It was a custom-made electric with sleek black paint and a glossy neck with a crescent moon on the end where his tuning pegs nestled. The dials were blood red with a flaming paint job that licked its way from one pointed end to the other. About five years of savings, earned from work, birthdays, and Christmas, went into that guitar. So why would he hang it up for his bass?

Now, this Nathan guy... He also had an electric guitar. Out of the corner of his eye, Jake could see the brand name glistening on the blue paint. It was nice, but Nate could do rhythms. He didn't have a right to challenge Jake. It would be fine. Jake was sure of this.

Until the new kid turned on his amp and started playing.

Jake felt his fingers slide soundlessly down the fingerboard, and he tried to keep calm. The band room grew quiet, startled by the playing, and Nate continued to strum out a song, unnoticing. His notes were sharp and pure, and his intonation was incredible. The hum of the strings made a watery grumble, capturing tranquility and mystery in the music. The more he played, the paler

Jake could feel his face becoming. By the time he'd finished warming up, Jake's knuckles had turned as white as his face, clamped around the neck of his guitar.

"Uh, Jake..."

His head jerked up and he found himself facing Lilly, who seemed uncertain whether or not she should interrupt. His eyebrows knitted into a line, and he scowled. "What?"

His anger softened as Lilly winced visibly, and her wings almost trembled as she continued. "Mr. Pekinessi wants you and Nate to talk to him," she whispered, and scurried back to her seat before he could bite off a harsh reply. Nate turned and sat his guitar down and silently, Jake followed. The two teens moved across the room and stopped in front of the teacher's desk. For the first time, Jake found himself face to face with Nate. Jake wasn't short, but Nathan was at least two inches taller. That small difference left Jake seemingly shadowed by Nathan. It was a feeling Jake didn't enjoy.

"Well boys, it seems we have two lead guitars now. It's not a big problem, but I think it would be nice if one of you played bass with Chuy."

Out of the corner of his eye, Jake could see the lanky guitarist with the long obsidian neck of his bass resting lightly in his hand. The guitar was enormous, even in Jake's eyes. But it had to be; Chuy was 6'11", and his custom bass was just perfect to rest in the soft loops of his arms. Jake didn't know much about Chuy, so of course he couldn't imagine playing bass with him. He felt shadowed by Nate's two inches, and Chuy's height would practically engulf him.

"So, what? You want us to audition or something?" Jake worded his question carefully, dropping it on the table and letting it sit there. His hopes of a 'no' soon vanished, as Mr. Pekinessi smiled.

"Well actually, that's just what I had in mind. I thought while the rest of the class branches off to work in their groups, you two could try out."

Despair. Agony. Disbelief. "I guess so." Jake almost lost it, but with a quick shake of his head, shrugged. "Why not?"

"Great. I'll be over as soon as I get the beginner level students going." Mr. Pekinese gave a quick smile, then headed toward a small group of kids sitting in the corner. With head high and chin set, Jake strode to the back of the room and snatched up his guitar. Nate followed, cheerfully oblivious in his wake.

"This is cool, huh Jake? I've never got to audition before! Although I'm real sorry I'm challenging you. You don't mind, do you? 'Cause if you do, I would understand. I'd just tell Mr. P—"

"No," Jake cut him off quickly, with a wave of his hand. Inside, he was burning with frustration at Nate. The kid was trying so dang hard to be nice, but it only made Jake more frustrated. "What happens, happens. May the best guitarist win."

Eventually, Mr. P returned, and faced Jake. The teen took a deep breath and with a set chin, he played with everything he had. And yet, he had a feeling it wouldn't be enough.

Lilly sat with her legs crossed, gently stroking the wings of the little bird on her finger. The lovebird gave a twitter of happiness and fluffed up, but Lilly only sighed sadly. After band class with Jake, she'd looped back to the aviary, where she sat among the rafters and sought the comfort of the animals housed here. Even her fellow fliers couldn't cheer her up, though.

It was hard to believe it had only been a month ago when Jake first showed her the aviary. It was New Year's, back when they were almost inseparable. Dr. Allina let the students keep a few birds here as pets, and it was a warm shelter that was quiet and secluded. The two Strands sat and talked for what felt like hours, while Lilly held the different birds. She and Jake got to know each other on a more basic level that day: conversations about favorite colors and different classes they enjoyed transitioned to best childhood memories. They didn't touch on the sadder memories; they tried to connect like teens who weren't Strands. She had enjoyed that day, and it had strengthened her feelings for Jake. She started admitting to herself that maybe she could see them being a couple.

Today, as she sat there alone, none of that happiness remained. It felt like she and Jake were being virtually torn apart, and as lovely and beautiful as these birds were, all Lilly felt now was a reminder of everything she was losing.

She'd been at this school for five months, and time had passed swiftly. After the terrifying event at Firestone, she had trouble resuming her normal school schedule, but Jake had been great back then. He stayed with her, helped her catch up on homework, and gradually they developed a close relationship. He helped her through everything, which was more than she could have hoped for. It wasn't easy, though. Her fellow students had trouble accepting her new identity as a Third Strand, and Lilly clung to her established friendships to get through it. She felt like a freak, with that extra strand of lilac hair. She was a myth, something that shouldn't exist, and they made their thoughts known. The tension had drained Lilly's spirit and added to the feelings of betrayal. They were supposed to be on the same side, but everyone treated her differently. Jake hadn't, though. He stood by her.

At least, he had at first.

She wasn't sure when it started happening. Gradually the signs started showing, and tender moments turned into tense arguments. His expressions went from caring to annoyed, and Lilly transitioned from innocent to just naïve. She was still sad, he thought she should get over it; she thought people were picking on her, he thought she was being a baby. Jake grew up in a world that didn't understand him, and he learned to adapt to that. Lilly was still adjusting, and it was clear Jake was impatient with her progress.

It became clear about a week ago. The school had a game of tug-o-war, and Lilly was injured trying to help her side win. It had been an accident, but Jake acted like she did it on purpose because she knew she could heal. It was the first time he snapped at her, and his cutting words took her by surprise. Today in band class her presence had irritated him again. She wasn't sure what was happening, but she knew things were changing between them.

It was all moving so quickly. One minute she was struggling with the idea of possibly dating someone, the next, anticipating an inevitable break up. Could they break up? Had they ever been together?

Maybe she had been naïve about that, too.

"As you know, Valentine's Day is coming up, and Dr. Allina has decided to organize a small dance after classes on the fourteenth." A low murmur filled the room as the teacher held up a hand for silence. "I know it's exciting, but it's a large project that you can't expect the staff to do alone. So each student is asked to help out at least once in the coming days, preparing decorations or setting up on the thirteenth. You can do it with a friend or alone, as long as you're helping, and with everyone pitching in, it should be a night to remember."

In the back of the room, Meg shot a glance at Lilly, and the emotions written on her face startled Meg. Lilly didn't seem excited. In fact, she looked like she was going to cry. Meg looked back to the board and tried to understand. Then it clicked. Lilly and Jake had hardly spoken since the tug-o-war incident. And if Jake was still mad, then the dance wouldn't exactly be something Lilly would look forward to.

Poor kid, Meg thought. Lilly was going to celebrate her first Valentine's Day in the middle of this mess.

"Lilly, dear, why don't you and Meg move to sewing machine five for today?"

Meg looked up in surprise and blinked at the lean figure of Ms. MacLeah. Her hand was pointed to one of the silver-plated machines plugged into the wall at the left end of the classroom. A smudged Sharpie "5" was sloppily written on its face, and Lilly was already moving to get it. When she returned, Meg began fiddling with the gears of their sewing machine, adjusting the settings and checking that it was plugged in correctly. Finally, she

174

reached for the thread as she talked to Lilly. "You seem...preoccupied," Meg said, her voice directed to Lilly, but her eyes on the thread. Through this crook, down this crevice, behind here... She heard Lilly sigh, and a feather brushed Meg's shoulder.

"It's, well, I was looking forward to Valentine's Day so much, and then this... Jake's mad, and I don't know what to do." Meg's heart twisted and she fumbled to thread her needle. She nodded her head to hide the mistake, and squinted attentively at the pointed object's eye.

"Have you tried talking to him?" Meg asked wispily, her eyes squinting at the bobbing strand.

"Yes!" Meg jerked, and her finger pricked on the sharp needle point. Meg yelped, popping her finger in her mouth as Lilly continued, unnoticing. "But he just ignores me. I finally gave up. Maybe he has, too..." As Meg watched Lilly's face fall, she tried not to be distracted by the possibilities set before her. Lilly and Jake were having a falling-out... That meant—*No*. Meg purposefully lined up her squares of fabric, her face rigid and blank. She wouldn't go there. Stubbornly, Meg pressed the pedal, the hum of the machine filling the air. Each sharp punch of the needle through the square felt like it went through Meg's heart. *Twunk, thwack thwack. Twunk, thwack thwack.* Meg diligently guided her feelings, like the silk through that needle, and in the same way she prepared for the stabbing blow.

"Don't give up, Lilly." *Twunk, thwack thwack.* "It's just a rough spot. Give it time."

Lilly sighed as she fiddled to align and cut her own squares. "I want to..." *Snip.* Meg's eyes flickered, the blades of the scissors reflecting light into her eyes. "But, I don't know. I'm just tired. I don't know if it'll work out. We were sort of together, but it's not like he ever really asked me out. Maybe it's better to let it go." *Snip. Snip.* It was as if Lilly, too, was commiserating with the fabric they were working with, as if the red felt she held were her own feelings and dreams. *Snip. Snip.* On the other side, Meg sat, the machine *thwack-thwacking.*

Snip-thwack-thwack-snip-thwack-thwack.

What a miserable pair we are...

Unexpectedly, Meg felt the fabric jerk, and looked in horror at the tangled silk. She'd lost focus and now the string was knotted and tangled from the bobbin to the needle. Looking from the thread to her friend, it was clear to Meg what to do.

"Lilly, give it one last shot. He could be frustrated, but don't give up until you know it's over."

"You think I should?" Lilly whispered.

"I *know* it," Meg said, nodding her head sharply.

Slowly, Lilly smiled and returned the nod. "Okay. I'll give it one last shot."

Meg gave her a smile and a "Thatta girl," then took the tangled fabric and threw it away. The red thread glimmered from the waste bin, abandoned and glimmering like a piece of her battered heart.

If only Meg could throw away her feelings so easily.

"Dr. Allina?"

"Yes, Jenny?" A young girl came in the door, the youngest girl at Charity. She was thirteen and Asian, with bright almond eyes and silky black hair. Dr. Allina had to admit, she was a bit surprised. Jenny rarely came to speak with her, usually only if she was relaying a message for one of the teachers. "Is something wrong?"

"Kat and Tag are having a giant game of Risk in the Home Ec room."

The statement was so odd, Dr. Allina almost broke into a fit of chuckles. Then again, at a school like Charity, you heard all kinds of things. "A giant…Risk game?"

"Glass Risk, to be exact. Tag stole Kiln's powers and they made themselves some giant pieces to play with. Mitch locked the door so no one could stop them before the game is over. Or, that was how it started. Once Kat took over Europe Tag got bored. Now the doors won't unlock."

"Are any of the teachers on hand?"

"Oh, yes. Mr. Murphy and Ms. MacLeah are there, I was just sent here to alert you of the situation. They should be able to handle things, they just wanted me to let you know. Everyone else is still working on preparations for the dance."

"And how is that going?"

"Once people started to pitch in, it helped a lot. I was a little worried after the balloon disaster, but the gym is finally covered in decorations, and it seems this will be a nice dance after all." Jenny's cheeks flushed slightly, and it seemed she was trying to suppress a smile. The elder woman smiled at her, and her eyes twinkled with insight.

"Are you going with anyone in particular, Jenny?" she asked. Jenny giggled.

"Well...yeah. Sal asked me to go with him, and I said yes." She made a noise like a schoolgirl, shuffling her feet, and Dr. Allina grinned.

"Well, I'm glad things worked out, then. Thank you, Jenny. You can go back to class now." As the door closed, Dr. Allina sighed and rubbed her head. There were always things to deal with around this school. If it wasn't Freddy stuck in the dishwasher, it was Caleb breaking a wall or Joanna sneaking food to wolves. She was a mother to all of these children, and sometimes it was difficult to keep them all in line. Even with other teachers around, there was an enormous weight on her shoulders, and with Kibbsty and his operations constantly threatening her 'children'... Sometimes she felt very weary at the end of the day.

Dr. Allina shuffled some papers and files, arranging them more neatly on her desk. One managed to catch her attention and make her pause: Lilly's student file. Dr. Allina didn't have to open it; she knew most of what it contained. It was a simple record of what information they had for Lilly: the names of her parents, where she was born, the little she had told them about her past. She had one of the smallest files of all the students here. Some, like Meg, had birth certificates, medical records, and such, while others, like Kat, had files composed of flimsy first-hand accounts. Lilly had never given much for them to write down and go by.

With all the chaos, Dr. Allina had never bothered to sit her down and discuss it with her. So the file remained thin.

Now she leafed through what little she had. It was a very short summary, but there was one interesting thing she always had to stop at: it was a piece of paper that listed the powers Lilly had. It read simply: **Number of Strands: Three**. Those words always made her look back. Though she knew Lilly was a Third Strand, it was still hard for Dr. Allina to believe. It was a miracle to say the least, and that was enough to draw the eye. It was a sight she had to appreciate.

Turning the page, there were the medical records Dr. Allina had written up from the time Lilly had been in the hospital wing, so very close to death, and it proved the words from the pages before. She was very special, but she was also very fragile.

Her extra strand was a looming threat, even above Dr. Kibbsty's threats on her life. As much as they tried to protect her, Dr. Allina knew one day that could be out of their hands, and she may look back only to write another set of numbers next to those of Lilly's birthday: date of death. Looking toward the filing cabinets, the doctor already knew there were files in there like that, from Fin and two others who hadn't made it. The pain in her heart for them was great, like a knife she couldn't remove. Looking back at the file, she pushed it to the side as a single tear fell down her face.

She hoped she would never have to feel the same pain again.

Sleep was elusive, nightmares chasing her from one hour to the next, and Lilly found herself restlessly sitting awake in bed. Her roommates slept soundly, but for her, peace could not be found. In the end, she resolved to get some air and wrapped herself in a bathrobe before heading to the window.

The wind ruffled the curtains and drifted around her with the chill of the night. Her hair brushed against her ears and her feathers trembled as she climbed out. The cold roof shingles made her toes curl as much as her wings, and she pulled the robe in close as she crept up and away. Every step was difficult for her to manage, the tiles difficult to balance on. One wrong move and she would fall, and she didn't know if she could open her wings fast enough to catch herself, perhaps only enough to slow her decent. But the longing in her heart wouldn't quiet; the need for air wouldn't settle.

Her delicate feet made it to the chimney from the commons, and she sank down next to it, using her wings as a blanket and feathers as a pillow. She looked up at the inky black sky and sighed. In the forest they lived in, there were hardly any lights, and the school put off a dim blue glow that preserved the nature of the land. The stars scattered the sky like beads of light hung from the sky. An ethereal flashlight created the light that glittered for her tonight.

The peace didn't last. Her mind was racing too much, her heart aching too deeply. What was missing? Why was she so confused? Why was she alone?

"I just want to belong," Lilly whispered, and let her head rest on her knees. Tears crept down her face as she leaned against the pillar. For a while she stayed there, until a noise interrupted her rest.

"Looks like some bird has wandered from her *cage*." Disbelief shot through her as Lilly leapt to her feet, turning to face the intruder. It was Cory.

"What are you doing here?!" Her voice sounded weak and afraid. How was he back at the school, and how did he find her? The ice in his eyes petrified her, holding her in place. A pain filled her gut like the sting of an old wound, and she couldn't even try to be brave. He sensed her fear. With a laugh, he stepped close, hands in his pockets casually.

"After all the chaos you caused, I figured congrats were in order. Well played. You sure didn't seem like the devious sort to me, but I guess you proved us wrong." The chill in his voice became even icier, pricking against her skin. The sarcasm bit through with every icy stab of air. "I guess you really aren't the fragile little thing you make yourself out to be. I'm sure we'll be more careful next time we cross *you*, won't we." The air dropped a couple of degrees as his brows knitted together, while Lilly quickly backed away. Her wings brushed the chimney, and before she could yell or speak, Cory covered her mouth, his slim figure closing the distance in a blur. "I wouldn't scream if I were you." His nails dug into the sides of her face and she tried to pull back. "I'd hate to make this unpleasant. After all, we're just having a chat, aren't we? Just a chat between *friends*." His breath turned chilly and frost hit her face. The force behind the threat carried, but Lilly couldn't stand his touch.

"Get away! Just go away!" She ducked out of his grip with a rush of desperation, and then bolted into the air. There was a second where the air felt warmer as her wings lifted her higher, and it was followed by the faint hope that she might be free. Then, like icy fingers, Cory's irritation surged into a blast of cold wind and caught her lungs within its grip. It tightened and squeezed the scream from her lungs, until Lilly went rigid and tumbled from the sky.

Like a sheet of ice driven into her lungs, her circulatory system seemed to collapse inward. Everything in Lilly lost meaning, and her heart froze temporarily. Her wings stiffened, her healing couldn't start; even her back was stiff and unmoving. The air rushed past her in a hurricane of cold, and she slammed back into the roof, the pain blistering and swelling within her. Choking like a fish without water, she writhed in pain, willing her body to work. With a shudder, the air leaked slowly in and she gasped for it, tears trickling down her face. As life returned, all she could think of was that she had risked her safety just to escape the torment of her dreams; one demon brought another.

Cold laughter swirled around her, as Cory chuckled to himself. "Lilly, Lilly. I thought we weren't going to make this messy. You can't fight me. Why make it worse?" Lilly recoiled from the words, spitting and gagging in disgust. In a rage of pain, she threw a shingle at him, and Cory growled as it hit the side of his face. The long red stripe seemed to appear magically as he traced his finger along it, eyes slanting angrily. "Fine, then. We'll make this *messy*." With a roar of rage, he formed a stick of ice and drove it down at her. She readied for the impact, and the air rippled to a still.

Lilly scrambled out of the way before her time freeze released, but her body still hadn't recovered. In the state of shock it was in, she stumbled drunkenly, hitting the roof hard. She winced. She heard ice shatter behind her and a bitter curse of anger. Before she could move, Cory grabbed her by the back of the neck and wrenched her backward. His nails dug in deep, the pain pushing through her numb skin, and there was a hiss behind her. As he grabbed her face with his other hand and turned her around, his eyes suddenly rounded. With one last angry huff, he sent her flying back into the roof and she laid there, shivering and crying.

Someone approached and lifted her up, her trembling becoming wild and uncontrollable. Like a child pulled out of freezing water she cried, curling up in familiar arms. As the gentle whisper soothed her, she sank into the darkness, like a cold and lonely arm enveloping her. "It's okay... We're here..." The darkness filled her and she fell limp in Meg's arms, listening to the sounds of her tears against the rooftop. *Drip, drip, drip.* "We're here."

CHAPTER THREE

ARRAY OF MASKS

Drip, drip, drip... The memories shattered as a voice rustled around her, echoing down to where she was hunched against the wall of her cell. For a few moments she struggled to orient herself in time. She was back at Firestone, and those days at Charity were months ago. Lilly felt a sense of loss as she struggled to hold onto the images in her mind; as sad as she'd been at that time, anything was better than being here. Pain returned as the numbness in her mind slipped away. She was forced to face reality and the danger it entailed.

In her gut there was a moment of fear, as a chilly voice reverberated to where she was. "Don't worry, Kibbsty. I won't spoil your project. I just want to take a look." The laughter that followed made her stomach churn. Upstairs, she heard a rumble of amusement, as if Kibbsty knew there would be more than 'looking' on the behalf of the former.

"Just make sure you don't 'look' too much. You taint her blood, I'll have your hide." But the amusement showed, and footsteps started coming down the stairs as the door closed. Around the corner, Lilly recoiled as Cory came into view.

"Hiya, Lilly," Cory said, leaning against the wall, arms crossed and face empty. He looked calm at first, like a cat who had finally cornered its prey and was enjoying the final capture. Then that cold, icy grin crept across his face. He reached behind his back and pulled out a pair of keys, jingling them. "Kibbsty says I get to visit our prisoner!" He laughed and stepped forward, working one of the keys into the lock. Lilly cringed and curled away as far as she could, facing the wall and using her weak wings as a shield for her body.

"Please... Please leave me alone..." she whimpered, tears rolling down her face, mixing with the dried blood on her cheeks. The door clicked open and Cory laughed, walking forward and putting the keys back in his pocket.

"Don't worry, I will... As soon as I'm done with what I've come to do." Lilly was surprised when she heard no further movement and she looked up into Cory's face, surprised when she saw it softening. He held a finger to his lips before she said anything and knelt beside her, listening closely. Then he sighed and turned to her now ashen face. "Kibbsty wasn't kidding when he said he beat the—" there was a loud click as he unlocked the shackle around her wrists and her neck, then gently set her on the ground. "—out of you. Don't say anything, just listen." Stunned to silence, she obeyed.

"I know you think I hate you, and after all I've done to you, I would probably think the same. But I've had a change of...^{heart?} I guess you could say. When I listened to all the things Kibbsty's been saying he's going to do to you, and has done... It made me sick that he would torture someone like you, when I knew that you *didn't* really deserve it. And when I looked in the mirror, I saw that same...*monster* staring back at me, and I couldn't take it. I can't even begin to apologize for what I've done, but I hope this is a start."

He reached out and held his hand over her wrists. She couldn't suppress her sigh of relief and closed her eyes, enjoying the cold that numbed the pain. As the air cooled, it felt like ice on a painful wound, and she fell momentarily into a dreamlike rest. But Cory reached out and touched her cheek, causing her to flinch, his hand cold and unexpected. "I can't stay down here long, and the pain will probably come back as soon as I re-shackle you. So you have to listen closely while you can, got it, Firecracker? Kibbsty's getting sick of waiting and he's decided if you don't give in soon, he's just going to torture you worse, and trust me, you don't want that." He paused here, listening as footsteps moved closer, then away above them. When he spoke again, it was so quickly and quietly, Lilly had to tilt her head close to hear.

"There's a batch of students here, the ones who used to work undercover at Charity Academy. We're sick of the way Kibbsty treats us and have decided keeping you safe will be the first thing we do to spite him. Oh sure, we won't do it upfront, but we've convinced him that if you bend to his wishes, you can stay at this school like a regular student, that way you won't turn problematic on him too soon. We have to keep up our front around him, so don't come running to us for friendship or you may find yourself in trouble. There's no one in this school you can really trust. Heck, probably not even me. But your friends don't seem to be coming anytime soon, and we're the only hope you've got. Understand?" The chill was back in Cory's voice now, the one Lilly recognized from the past, but it was warning her rather than threatening her. "Don't expect life here to be easy, Firecracker. If you go along with Kibbsty, you'll probably find this is the hardest year of your life. But at least you'll be alive. And while you're alive, there's always hope of getting out of here. Angels like you don't belong in hells like this."

Then, like a dream, the ice-boy lifted her back up and re-chained her hands and her neck. The pain started to come back and Lilly let out a whimper, tears returning to her eyes. But she mustered enough strength to look at Cory, and whispered, "Thank you."

Cory froze at the door to the cell, and let out a gruff snarl. "Don't thank me yet, not until you realize what you're signing up for. You're at Firestone Academy, Lilly, and you're going to have to get a spine to survive. People here, they don't like people like you. You're going to be alone, and you're going to have to deal with it. This alone is a risk for me, and I don't know why I'm doing it." The air was icy, and Lilly shivered as he continued. "Don't expect anyone's pity or help, although it could come at times you don't expect it. One day we could be the ones helping you up, another day we'll be the ones throwing you down. But you gotta fight through it, like you always do. Firecracker—that is the only way you'll make it through here—you have to harden your heart." He turned around, and his eyes were walls of ice. "And whatever happens, don't lose faith. If you didn't have that, you'd be gone already. Keep your head down, or at the first sign of weakness, we'll take you out." The door was shut and he was leaning against the bars of the cell, frost biting Lilly's face.

"Good luck, Firecracker. Oh, and by the way—" Lilly let out a scream of shock as something whistled past her ear and shattered against the wall next to her, leaving shards of ice in her hair and clothes. "—stay sharp. We can't be trusted." And with an artic wind following him, he bounced up the stairs with his icy laugh following him out. Lilly sank against her bindings, heart hammering in her chest, threatening burst at any moment. *What on earth is going on here?* she wondered, and closed her eyes, retreating *back into her mind.*

Chapter Four

Unrequited Feelings

"Ow!"

"Sit still! It only hurts if you pull away!"

"I pulled away because it hurts! Why don't you go get Lilly ready or something?"

"Not until I finish with you. Now *sit still!*"

"I'm going to get you for this," Kat growled, then flinched as Meg tapped her on the head with the brush.

"You'll thank me later." Reluctantly, Kat exhaled and allowed Meg to continue brushing. "We've been roommates for how long, you'd think you'd trust me by now," Meg scolded, but there was something sentimental in her voice. "Guess that's part of being friends though."

"I'm not sure you can call us friends at this point. Six years, I think you're more of a sister," Kat remarked, flashing a smile over her shoulder. Meg chuckled in reply. "Even back before Charity was built and we stayed in the Brumby, you were pinning me down and trying to dress me up like a Barbie doll. Guess you didn't outgrow that." The twap on top of her head only made her snicker more.

"It wasn't like I could dress up Jake or the other guys. Although Emre's hair was pretty long back then..." Meg reminisced. "I sort of miss those days, honestly. Breakfast in the mornings with Dr. Allina, short school lessons and free afternoons. When she explained she was building a school, I never imagined it would turn out so big." Meg glanced out the window toward the lake where their old schoolhouse used to be. Kat followed her glance and nodded.

"I feel that way about a lot of things. Remember Atsuka? She's off in New York somewhere doing fashion design."

"She was always really nice. Hard to get in touch with her now that she's famous..." Meg frowned. She fluffed Kat's hair and sighed. "Those were the good ol' days..."

"Seems like ages ago, back then things were simpler. Just us against the world. I think we all believed we could be super heroes one day. It's hard to feel that way now." Conversations with Lilly came to mind, and Kat felt fears rise that she had trouble admitting. The future seemed sad. So instead, she returned to memories of the past. "When I thought of the 'good times' fading, I always thought that meant you and Jake dating and me being a third wheel. But..." she trailed off awkwardly, glancing at Meg as she touched on what she knew would be a sore subject. Meg sighed, and moved to tie a ribbon in Kat's hair.

"The school got finished, Jake got his second strand, and our threesome became a twosome. It wasn't meant to be," Meg added sadly. "Jake's just part of the crowd now."

"Not to you," Kat insisted. Meg jumped, and Kat put a finger on Meg's collarbone accusingly. "You will never see him as 'just part of the crowd.'"

"What do you mean?" Meg squeaked. "He hardly talks to us!"

Kat shook her head. "I've seen the way you look at him. And I've never heard you admit you like him. Even when he and Lilly got close, you wouldn't speak up! You just keep watching, waiting for him to get a clue. Why didn't you tell him?" She twisted in Meg's grip, undoing the bow she had carefully made. Meg just shrugged and glanced away.

"I didn't want to ruin things. We had so much fun together. All those days at the lake, and games in the forest. I kept waiting for the right time. Then he pulled away, and now... Now he has Lilly," Meg whispered, her voice giving away the pain in her heart. "I would never try to tell him, and risk hurting her. I waited too long. And that's my fault."

"Meg, I think Lilly and Jake already know it's not going to work between them. If it doesn't, don't lose him again. I care about Lilly, but I also care about you, and she wouldn't have dreamed of going out with him if she knew how you felt." Kat got up and put a hand on Meg's shoulder. She chewed her lip and sighed. "If nothing else, try to find a way to be his friend again. Talk to him. Obviously, whatever you're doing now isn't working."

Meg slowly nodded and looked out the window, and the deepening night stared back at her. "Maybe I will. But not tonight. Lilly deserves a chance to be happy. I'm not going to get in the way of that." Kat agreed, and Meg went to get dressed. But now the animal-shifter was torn between two choices: she loved Jake, but she could never intentionally hurt her friend. So would she keep sacrificing her own dreams, or would she gain the nerve to talk to him?

Lilly looked around the dance and spotted Jake. If he had seen her, he didn't show it. He was to the left of the room talking with Nate, of all people. Lilly couldn't help but wonder when the two of them became friends. So far, a fair number of students had arrived. There was Tina, who was talking to Jenny, Sal, and Carlos at the left side of the room, and Chuy was hanging out with Nate and Jake, wordless as always. Meg had scampered off with Kat to say hi to Joanna, and Mary Beth was sitting at a table with Sarah and Kent. Wyvr and Dryk were off to the side in matching outfits, though one had a blue shirt and the other green. She assumed the rest of the students would show up later.

Lilly looked down at herself and her thundering heart grew louder. She was in a summery dress with spaghetti straps and a pair of white dress shoes Meg had long outgrown. All three of the girls' dresses were new, made by a girl named Asuka who could make outfits by opening drawers, and pulling out garments in the sizes needed. (It had been a surprise for everyone, Asuka didn't usually stay at the school. She was a clothing designer out in the real world, but dropped by every once in a while to give clothes to Dr. Allina and the students.) Even though it was nice to get an outfit that wasn't secondhand, Lilly felt out of place. It felt like, even with everyone else dressed up too, she was somehow more exposed. Her wings against her back felt like they were under a searchlight, drawing attention to her, and her lack of companions made her feel like she was left hanging, caught up with nowhere to go to.

"Hey Lilly," called a voice, and Lilly turned to face Karen. Her heart lightened considerably. Karen always seemed to show up when Lilly felt the loneliest. Lilly smiled and her wings rustled at her side.

"Hi, Karen. How are you?" Lilly asked, turning to the lavender-eyed girl. Sal and Jenny moved on to talk to Kat in the corner of her eye, and Carlos was talking to Tina.

Karen returned the expression. "I'm good. I really love the dresses Asuka made for us. Everyone looks amazing!" Karen waved her arm around, and Lilly followed her gaze. There was Meg, in a gorgeous black dress with a white ribbon tied around her waist. Kat was next to her in a punk style dress with a black-pleated skirt. Lilly's eyes flickered to Karen's perfect lilac dress, with a side-cut of pleats and a halter top of loose fabric. She had to agree. The dresses were amazing, and the other students looked just as great.

"Asuka has a lot of talent. Although I still feel a little uncomfortable dressed like this. I guess part of me still feels like going out means staying bundled up in a giant jacket." Her wings gave a slight twitch and she curled them in closer, rubbing her arms nervously.

"Well, don't think about it so much then. Just have a little fun and enjoy the freedom." Lilly looked skeptical, but she didn't resist as Karen took her arm and dragged her toward the buffet table. "Come on, let's get some punch!" A short while later she found herself clutching a little pink cup with a darker red liquid. As she stared into its surface, someone walked up beside her.

"G'day, Lilly. How're you this evening?"

Lilly looked up as a twin approached on either side of her. She quickly glanced from one to the other, unable to guess who had spoken. They sounded alike, and as she watched, they smiled in unison. Then the twin in the green shirt chuckled. "Don't look so startled. You act like we're ghosts or something. Look at her face, Wyvr. You'd think we'd done something wrong."

Wyvr, in the blue shirt, grinned wider. "Nah, she's just nervous because she can' tell us apart. Ain't ya?"

Lilly blushed, but laughed in surrender. "I hate to admit it, but it's true. You just look so much alike! I never know what to say. Sometimes I think I should just yell, 'hey Dryk!' and see who looks."

Dryk laughed and moved over by his brother. "Aw, I'm touched. Don't fret about it. You just need to get an inside source." His eyes twinkled. Lilly cocked her head inquisitively as Karen moved off to talk to someone else.

"What do you mean?" she asked.

Wyvr smiled wider. "Well, I think what Dryk is goin' at, is the only people who know how to tell us apart is, well, us!"

"Well, can you tell *me* so I won't be so embarrassed around you?" Lilly asked politely. The twins crossed their arms and looked at her with mocking suspicion.

"I don't know, Wyvr. What do you think? Can she be trusted?" Dryk asked, glancing to his twin.

"I don't know, Dryk. She could just rat out our secret and spoil everythin,'" teased Wyvr in return. Lilly looked helplessly between them.

"Aw, come on! I promise I won't tell!" she said, holding up one arm as if making a pledge. "Honest!"

"Well..." they both said thoughtfully.

"Please?" Lilly begged. She edged up closer, standing on her toes. "Please?!"

Dryk grinned mischievously. "Well, I guess I might tell you, but—"

"There's one condition," finished his twin. They grinned.

"What? What is it?"

"You have to dance with us!" they declared. Lilly went from playful to mortified.

"D-dance? But I don't dance!" she squeaked.

Dryk shrugged. "Then I guess you don't get to learn how to tell us apart."

Lilly stuck out her lip unhappily and her wings dropped. Part of her wanted to give into the nervousness and just let the deal go, but another half wanted to take Karen's advice and have a little fun. After considering it for a moment she sighed. "Fine! I'll..." She looked down, but could see the twins starting to look hopeful. "Dance with you..." she finished.

Wyvr gave a whoop and Dryk grinned. The former jumped forward and grabbed Lilly's hand. "I get the first go!" he laughed.

As she was pivoted toward the dance floor, Lilly found her heels digging in. "Aw, come on guys! I don't want to dance *now*! The dance floor is empty! We'll get laughed at!"

"Not if we have fun," Wyvr smiled. Each boy took an arm, then calmly lifted and carried her to the floor. Lilly squealed and complained, but Dryk laughed and Wyvr smiled encouragingly.

"Aw, don't fuss. It'll be fine, trust us. We're your Aussie guardians. We won't let anyone laugh at you unless you're laughing with them. Right, Dryk?"

"Right. We're here to uphold your honor."

Their courage made her relax, and finally she relented. "Okay, fine... But nothing that I'll regret!" Lilly spat out at the last minute, but even as she did, she was whisked across the dance floor, unable to figure out if they were even going to agree to her conditions. A new song started playing, and Lilly found herself twirled in the first beat, and looking up at Wyvr's smile.

"You ready? Trust us, you'll have fun." He took both of her hands and smiled reassuringly. And Lilly took a deep breath, and let go.

> *It's Friday night, and everything's moving,*
> *The lights are bright, it's so confusing.*
> *I feel a little out of my element.*

She was slowly spun, and smiled.

> *Twirling 'round, everything's spinning,*
> *I'm lost, and don't know which way I'm going,*

Her eyes caught sight of Jake.

> *I wonder where these feelings came from.*

She stumbled, and Dryk righted her with a steady hand.

Because through the crowwwds,

"Careful there," he cautioned.

I can't seem to look away.

"Sorry," Lilly whispered.

I'm dancing herrre,

Her eyes flickered.

But I'm staring at your faaaace...

She tried to look away, but kept gazing at Jake, twirling across the floor.

Why can't I just let go and just melt into the scene,

Her heart thundered.

I feel like there's still hope left in you and left in me,

She tried to close her eyes...

But as the lights go flashing by...

The words bit into her heart.

And I keep spinning 'round,
I wonder if I'll ever—

She tripped.

—hit the ground.

"You okay?" Wyvr asked, taking her from Dryk. He danced a little slower, and Lilly shook her head.

"It's nothing. Just a little nervous." She smiled and tried to enjoy what she was doing. The dance had no real structure, instead filled with lighthearted spins and movements with no patterns. She laughed as Dryk slipped in and she was traded off again, the second verse starting.

The lights go down, everyone's slowing,
I can't decide what I'm doing,
I'm lost between point A and point B.

But letting go was easier said than done.

Then I see—

Jake was talking to Meg.

You standing with her,

He was asking her to dance.

It makes no sense, but how could you miss her?

She did look great in her dress....

She's everything I could never be...

The lights went strobe. The music slowed to a pulse again.

Because in your arrrms,

They were awfully close...

She looks like she could fly,

Why wasn't that Lilly?

And you're dancing theeere...

It didn't make any sense...

And I feel like I could cry.

Her eyes watered and she hastily looked away, pulling closer as Wyvr took her.

Why can't I just let go and just melt out of your life?

She never thought loosing Jake would hurt like this.

I feel like I'm chasing dreams that only bring me strife,

She said to give it another shot... Meg was....

But as the lights,

In...

Shine upon your face,
I wonder if,

She was in...

I'll ever leave this place!

She was in love with him!

I'm losing all, sense of re-al-i-ty!

It couldn't be! And... What if he felt the same way? Her knees felt weak and she felt a little queasy. As Dryk took her he looked a little concerned, shifting so he had a stronger grip on her right hand to keep her upright.

"Are you okay?"

It's Friday night, and I'm going crazy,

"I...."

I'm so sad, I'm losing everything,

Lilly took a deep breath and smiled.

And yet I just let it walk away.

"I'll be fine. I thought we were dancing?" She smiled.

There was a time, I wouldn't have given up,
But looking now, it's all I can do not to,
Cry away everything I have.

Dryk shrugged and they kept dancing, smooth loops of movement.

Because as I daaance,
She closed her eyes.
I pretend I don't care,
It was too ironic.
But I'm wonderiiing...
She could see Jake smiling out of the corner of her eye…
If you even know I'm there.
At Meg.
We were so clooose,
It was so strange...
But now we're so far.
I'm holding the parts of my heart.
"Looks like I get a turn again!" Wyvr slipped in, taking her left hand gently. Lilly forced a smile.
And I still...
She—
Daaaance.... —ed.
I still dance. I dance. I'm dancing it away.
And I still...daaaance! I still dance. I dance. I'm dancing it away.
The music went a little techno, and Lilly laughed as she closed her eyes and moved to the music. Her wings moved from side to side, her hips lightly swaying. Dryk and Wyvr laughed, and each moved to take one of her arms.
It's Friday night.
They swung her into the air.
Turn up the music.
And then Dryk had her
I'll shake it off, there's nothing to it.
I'll dance until it all melts away.
She spun...and was swapped from one hand to the other in mid-twirl. She giggled.
But tonight, I'll cry on my pillow.
Wish I didn't have to lose you.
Did she really?
But for now, I will just hold on...
I will... Daaaance. I'll keep dancing. Dancing. Dance the pain away.

She melted into the music.

I will... Daaaance. I'll keep dancing. Dancing. Dance the pain away.

The music slowed and for a moment, she was left without either twin, breathing heavily. The lights dimmed... The music slowed...

It's Friday night... I'm not all right...

Her smile wavered.

But I'll dance.

The song ended and instantly, the gymnasium erupted in an enormous applause. Lilly joined, but she felt she would never forget that song. Her heart was burying the pain just like that, as she watched Meg and Jake. The look on her face, and his... They knew, and she knew, that she wouldn't get another chance. The redhead had captivated Jake, and she had lost her hold. And she was left at the end of a dance with nothing to do but turn to her dance partners, give them a smile... And ask a question.

"Okay, I danced with you. Now will you say how to tell you two apart?" She was surprised she managed to be so lighthearted amidst everything.

Wyvr grinned. "It's easy. I'm right-handed," he laughed.

"You're... Right handed?" Lilly glanced at Dryk and her eyes lit up. Suddenly, everything made sense. Through the dance, she had been swapped from hand to hand. But Dryk had always taken her right side, and Wyvr had always been on the left. It was like whenever one twin handed her off, the other slipped in perfectly. She realized now they had been playing on each other's strengths, and therefore, it left neither with a weakness. "Oh, you two are sly, you know that, don't you?" she purred slightly with laughter, and the twins gave a bow.

"Thanks for the dance, Lilly," Wyvr smiled, and they melted back into the crowd, leaving Lilly shaking her head. Then despair settled in, and one tear fell for Jake.

I will dance....

Back at the start of the dance...

Jake couldn't help but laugh as Nate told a joke about an umbrella, a wolf, and some peanut butter. It was funny, he used to really dislike Nate because he stole his position as lead guitar, but now it was like he was actually part of a section in band. He belonged to a team, instead of focusing only on his own instrument, his own parts. He, Chuy, and Nate had really gotten along well once they learned they weren't all competing for the same prize, but working to create a masterpiece. Chuy was amazingly humorous, and despite his quiet disposition, he could make Jake laugh harder than Nate by saying little more than a few words. The two of them had really made him perk up, and it was strange. What was even stranger was that the person who had started annoying him was Lilly.

It was like one day, something had driven a knife between them, and he couldn't get close to her anymore without spewing anger. When he did, he caused Lilly pain in return. Then as angry as he was at the time, seeing her in pain made him feel like a rotten person. That's when he had started distancing himself. He decided if he was only going to hurt Lilly by being close, maybe staying away wouldn't be so bad. She could learn to hate him, and then he wouldn't hurt her so much. But he still wondered: was he really hurting her less by ignoring her?

"Okay, here's another joke. There was a fisherman out hunting with his dog in July. Since he was a fisherman, he wasn't the best person to give a gun to..." Nate was off again, and Jake tuned it out. A song was starting, and as he looked around, he was surprised to see Wyvr and Dryk dragging Lilly across the dance floor. Lilly was smiling in their arms and laughing as one of them took lead and twirled her across the gym. With the first couple lines of the song, she seemed lost in the moment, but at least she was having fun. He looked away, and his mouth twitched to the side. It took him off guard. He had expected to push her away, but hadn't expected her to do so well with it. He shrugged it off. Maybe it meant that he wouldn't have to worry too much? Lilly would be okay.

As he looked to the side, he caught sight of a brilliant red, and he opened his eyes slowly, blinking with surprise. His vision jumped back to his normal contour shapes, but Jake found himself unwillingly going back to that watercolor-style sight. The next thing he knew, he was looking at Meg. He quickly glanced toward Nate again, trying to slow his heart rate. He had always known Meg; they were childhood friends. But something dawned on him in that moment. If Lilly was letting go, that meant he could too... Couldn't he?

Something moved inside him, deep within his heart. Since he'd been at this school, Meg had always been a close friend. When he was having a rough day, she was the one to brighten it. Whether it was sneaking some of his favorite candy into his book bag, or sharing her notes with him during class, she instinctively knew what he needed. He realized now he had taken that friendship for granted.

Jake remembered hanging out with Kat and Meg on a warm summer day, eating Popsicles and sitting with their feet in the lake as they talked. Back then, so many things had been different; he had still been able to see without his second strand, the school hadn't been built yet, and Kat still went by Katie. He remembered that day in particular because Meg had jumped in, sending a wave of water across the shore. He could still hear his laugh as he flicked the water out of his face before looking up to see the redhead rising out of the water. It had been a stunning sight, one he would never forget: a wild mane of red hair rippling out of the water, cascades of water droplets raining back into the lake. The light danced off everything: her laughing smile, dimpled cheeks, and glowing face. He had never looked away so quickly, as his heart had given an unnatural jump. It had taken him so off guard it had literally scared him. Kat leapt in after her, the moment was ruined, and Jake gradually forgot...until now.

Back then, he had actually toyed with the idea of one day dating Meg, but they had been friends for so long, he hadn't really wanted to consider it. Then he lost his sight to his second strand, and he pulled away from Meg, haunted by the red hair he would never truly see again; the image of her beautiful smile and her perfect hair was forever burnt into his memory.

Something about Meg was always special, in every sight he had, she stood out. Even now.

Jake had eight main types of vision: night-vision, x-ray, thermal, ultraviolet, contour, watercolor, flare, and pulse. In night vision, her hair let off light like few things could... X-ray... well, maybe not x-ray. All he could see were bones. Thermal, now that was amazing. It was like looking at a lion's mane, and he could see the heat dance off it, her face literally glowing. Ultraviolet didn't do it justice, and contour accented all of her amazing curls, but none of the color. Now watercolor, that was probably the only vision that he could really see Meg's color with; watercolor let all the colors be visible, but none of the fine details. It was like a melted painting of swirls and lights, but it did her justice, at least. Flare only showed him how intense the color was, and pulse only showed veins and blood and stuff like that, water especially. It was pretty cool, but not for this. With all those amazing types of vision, he longed for the one he remembered: the simple one, the way things were meant to be seen.

With Lilly, he didn't have those childhood memories to hold him back, but he also hadn't had time to build a connection. While his affection for her was genuine, he didn't take the time to really step back and decide if they could be compatible in a romantic way. He tried to be there, tried to hold on to what he found in Lilly. She was caring, optimistic, and always tried to see the good in things. She was loving and open, but she was also timid, perhaps too timid to be around Jake. Every time he said the wrong joke or laughed at the wrong time he felt like he stabbed her in the back. He was trying to keep her safe, but at the same time, he was the one making all the mistakes.

While Lilly's lack of courage made him want to protect her, Meg's strong personality had distanced him. Lilly was something to shelter, Meg was confident and beautiful, and always seemed so far out of his league. How could someone that strong love a blind nobody like him?

When he was younger, he thought he would be happy as long as she ended up with a great guy, someone better than him, who would make her smile. The idea that they could be together gave way to his lack of self-confidence. Kat and Meg were his best friends, and he didn't really expect them to be more. But times changed. Now... Now what did he think?

There's no way she likes you, Jake thought sadly. *Plus, you were going to date one of her best friends. She wouldn't go for it, if it hurt Lilly...* But as he looked across the dance floor, he saw the lights rippling across her hair. Even in the flare of the colors, he couldn't look away. He knew he would always regret it if he didn't try, so he moved across the floor.

"Jake," Meg's voice squeaked, and the lights laced her face in glorious watercolor; her hair was a flowing fountain of red.

"Hey, Meg, do you want to dance?" Jake blurted out, and as he went to contour he could see her eyes widen and her face curve with excitement; excitement he thought he would never see. A smile flickered across her face, nervous, but definitely excited.

"I would," she whispered. He found his heart pounding as he held out his hand, and hers slipped into his. Slowly, he led her onto the dance floor, and was facing her as the second verse ended. And she was looking at him with something, something he was afraid to register.

"You... You look really great," Jake could barely speak. Meg looked up in surprise, and her hand felt shaky in his.

"R-really?" she stuttered, eyes glowing. Somehow, he could see it in her, even if all he really 'saw' was the curve of her eyes, barely detailing her eyelashes, her cheeks, the lower and upper eyelids, a colorless vision. But somehow, he knew her eyes had sparkled, knew her face had flushed. Knew it as surely as he couldn't see the color of her hair with his eyes, but he saw it with his heart.

"You've always looked great..." Jake whispered, images of the past painting the girl before him, her hair's brilliant red, her eyes' gentle green. "Of all the things I was tormented by when I lost my sight, nothing hurt quite as bad as never seeing you the same way again." His voice grew in volume and strength as they slowly moved across the floor, she so lost in his words and he so determined to say what he needed to. "It hurt too much to look at you and not see the sparkle in your eyes. To see your face without the wreath of fire I used to gaze at. It was hard being around you, because all I felt was loss."

He shifted her hand in his, his left palm on her waist, weaving through people he barely registered. He gulped and continued speaking. "I gave up after that. Told myself I would never have you that close again. Told myself I was a blind nobody that you could never love..."

"Oh, Jake," Meg's whisper cut him off and as he looked down at her, he could see the soft shape of tears building in her eyes. He felt the palm of her hand gently touch his face, and his pulse raced. "I've always loved you for who you are... But I never thought someone like you would love someone like me!" She laughed. Jake felt like it was a dream he didn't want to wake up from.

A smile broke across his face and he pulled her into a hug; she fell into his arms, crying happy tears. "Megan, how could I *not* love someone like you?"

As the song ended, she and Jake slipped off the dance floor and back into the crowd, his hand around hers.

At the other end of the room, a girl in a pink dress brushed one tear away and slipped into the night. There, she sat on a bench, gazing at the stars and bravely letting her best friend have the happiness she herself had dreamed of.

Jake was one of the last students to leave the dance, after Meg and Kat had slipped out for the night. After helping put away the decorations, he was finally shooed to bed by Dr. Allina, and then there was nothing left to do but find his way back to the dorms. Rubbing his eyes sleepily, brain buzzing with happy memories, he almost knocked into a figure stepping out of the girl's bathrooms. In the darkness, it took a moment to recognize the sniffling figure. When he did, he felt a flicker of guilt in his gut.

"Lilly?"

Lilly looked down and swiped a hand across her face without acknowledging him, and tried to duck away. Jake just watched, his happiness mingling with guilt and unsettling his stomach. "I'm sorry, Lilly... I was hoping you'd realize by now we were... But I didn't want to hurt you." Jake's voice sounded cold and empty when he spoke. It felt like his words were nothing but that: words.

Lilly's brown eyes gazed listlessly at him for a moment, then she looked away again. "I understand..." Her voice cracked and she flinched away, breathing deeply. "I'm sorry, I..." Her shoulders shuddered deeply and she quickly hurried down the hallway, bare feet muffling the sound of her running footsteps as she rounded the corner. Part of Jake wanted to stop her, tell her she had nothing to be sorry for. Wanted to say he should have told her sooner.

Instead, all he said was: "I'm sorry too."

The morning after the dance was cold, the roof covered in the powder of an early morning flurry. Lilly sat in the snow while the school slept, gazing sadly across the grounds. The sun was raising its sleepy head, peeking lazily at her from its perch where the water's edge melted into the light. Her pants were growing wet, but she didn't care. All she was focused on were her thoughts; the images from the night before, of Meg and Jake... It was like an emotional hangover.

"Lilly! Hey, Lilly!" The sound carried through the air, soon followed by a flutter of wings. <I didn't think anyone else would be awake at this hour!> His voice drifted into her head this time as Lilly looked up in time to see a peregrine falcon flutter down from the sky and transition into a teenage boy before her. The name 'Wyvr' on the jacket clued her in on who it was. She smiled and shrugged, burying her toes on the chilly roof.

"I've always been an early bird, I guess... Something about watching the sunrise has always made me smile." Lilly watched the lake sparkle beautifully, and the light snow twinkled in the morning sun.

The solitary twin took a seat beside her, dipping his head in agreement. "Dryk and I used to do that a lot, but then we grew up, became teenagers. Got lazy," he chortled. "Oh, the way things change. Mum always had trouble keeping us under control. If one of us wasn't getting into somethin', the other was." He let his long legs stretch out in front of him, while Lilly kept hers close, her chin on her knees.

"It sounds like you two were a handful. I'm surprised you're so well-mannered now. Or maybe that's just an act."

"Hey, I try to behave. Dryk... Well, he does his best." The teasing was evident in his voice, and Lilly shook her head in amusement.

"So I take it you're the good twin, then?"

"If that makes Dryk the evil one, then I guess the world isn't too bad off."

The statement was casual enough, but Lilly felt a question spark in her mind. She leaned back a little and glanced at the boy thoughtfully. "Hey, Wyvr? How come there always seems to be one twin who's nicer and one twin who's cockier or meaner?"

Wyvr laughed, and while the remark was unexpected he went along with it good naturedly. "Oh, the timeless question of twins! One of my favorites. You know, with any two people, twins or not, they're going to be a little different. And people's definition of different is usually interpreted as good or bad. See, people can only go one way or the other. There's good, and there's bad. As much as there are grey tones in the middle, that's what there will always be in the end. Better or worse... Good or evil. Everyone leans one way or the other.

"So, you have two people: they're different. So one is always going to be closer to one side of the spectrum, and the other, likewise. You following?" The boy paused, and Lilly nodded.

"Yeah, I'm following. Continue," Lilly welcomed. Wyvr obliged.

"Okay, you have twins. Naturally, by looking so alike, they want to find some way to make themselves different from each other, because no one wants to be a clone. They want to be unique, special. It's like they are two identical polarities that want to get as far away from each other as possible. In the spectrum of the world, one will be swung toward the 'good' end, and one toward the 'bad' end. Now, it doesn't make either evil or good, just different. Sometimes, I think the world is so focused on making things good or bad, whatever is different is placed as such." Wyvr looked thoughtful, staring out at the lake, and continued talking.

"You know, I don't think either Dryk or I are 'bad' or 'meaner.' We're both gentlemen, both playful but respectful. But we have our differences. Dryk can be a bit cocky and arrogant, but he's a nice guy. I can be a bit shy and withdrawn, but I don't think it makes me better'n him, or the other way around. Now, there is another pair of twins over at Firestone. And I feel, compared to them, we're the good end of the magnet, and they're the bad, just by nature. If you had to pick a side to label, I would say that was it. But at the same time, I have to wonder... What if we're always seeing things in a 'this or that' light? We think everything is either on the good end or the bad end. Is this 'evil,' or is it 'good?' I mean, some things are tainted bad, but looking at the bigger picture, are the people we see as 'evil' really on the good swing of the balance of the world? It kinda makes you think, doesn't it?" Wyvr smiled at Lilly, and Lilly nodded thoughtfully.

"It really does..." Lilly mused for a moment and let his words swirl through her head. "I don't know. It's interesting to think about."

Wyvr stayed silent for another moment, then laughed. "Now that we've started the morning with some philosophy," he stood up, stretched, and his eyes twinkled mischievously, "let's have some real fun." Suddenly, he leapt off the roof. In mid-fall he morphed into a peregrine, gracefully shooting back into the sky, wings cutting the wind like the sharp points of a boomerang. As he arched and dived, he was a blur of feathers with laughter following him like the waves of an ocean. <Come on, Lilly. Let's see you fly!>

With a shake of her head, Lilly hugged her jacket close for a moment before jumping off the roof into the nothingness of the air. Then her wings opened behind her, and she, too, took to the skies. As she raced, wings pushing her as fast as she could go, she let her worries stay back at the school, while her heart was in the air. Up here, she was above her problems; in this little corner of the world she was given, she could be free.

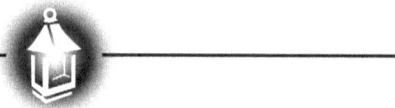

"Um, Mr. Holman, I don't think that your computer is supposed to be sparkling like that," Meg whispered, pointing to the computer at the teacher's desk. It was third period on B day, and she was in history class, where they were talking about the abolitionist movement. That was, until Mr. Holman's computer started acting odd. The other students looked up in surprise, watching lights dance across the computer screen.

Mr. Holman blinked and followed Meg's gaze. "Dear lord!" he cried, calm demeanor fading as concern took over. The middle-aged man seemed lost as to whether he should race forward or shrink back, but he finally regained control as he turned back to Meg. "Yes, dear, it's not supposed to be sparkling like that. Go to Mr. Ralf's room and ask what's happening. Get Cameron to contain it, if you can!"

Meg stumbled for a second before scurrying out of the room, while the rest of the students nervously backed away as the walls started showing trails of electricity. Seconds later, the computer let out a loud *pop!* as the screen shattered, and Mr. Holman scrambled away. Regaining a sense of authority, the teacher waved them toward the door and took the lead in the hallway. "Wyvr, Dryk, I think it would be advisable if you checked the path to the emergency exit. Class, quickly now!" Obediently, they exited.

The walls on either side crawled with electricity, like dolphins dancing in and out of water. Quindel was at the front of the group, looking awkward and nervous, his large form taking up a good bit of the hall, and Caleb moved quickly behind, for once seeming unnerved. They were all fair game in the halls, with little to protect them. This experience made them feel incredibly human.

"Mr. Holman! Maybe we should have waited in the classroom…" Mary Beth whimpered, her little notebook clutched to her chest and her pencil in her tight fingers.

"Just stay close, and keep your heads down!" the teacher answered, but his expression seemed to share her concern.

Ahead, the path widened and the students scrambled into the center of the gym, occasionally glancing upward, where the lights looked ready to explode at any minute. After what happened with the computer, it didn't seem impossible. In the middle of the room, they located Wyvr and Dryk, one sitting on the ground and the other standing over him. It was clear Mr. Holman was struggling to remain calm. "Wyvr, Dryk, is there no way out?"

The standing twin nodded, face focused on his brother. "Dryk tried to touch the door in peregrine form and got shocked something awful. I'd recommend against trying it yourself," he cautioned. Dryk flinched with pain, weakly holding to consciousness, his face pasty with sweat. He let out a moan and let himself lay back, holding his head. Wyvr looked concerned, a look of phantom pain crossing his own face.

Mr. Holman nodded, glancing fearfully at the lights. Around him, his students fed off his concern and whispered in panic. "Stay together in the center of the room. Be careful. The lights could blow any second," he instructed. His own fear tainted his instructions as the rise and fall of his breath quickened.

"Walter," came a voice, the single word bringing relief to the history teacher's expression. A frazzled-looking computers class entered—led by Mr. Ralf—then gathered with their fellow classmates. Behind them, Mr. Conrad's English class scrambled to keep up, looking just as confused and unnerved.

"Philippe, Agnus... What in the world is going on? I've never seen anything like this!" Mr. Holman exclaimed.

Mr. Ralf growled under his breath. "It's probably those Firestone kids again. The sparky one, Tray, I think. We're cut off from the rest of the school, thanks to Cameron, but it spread too far before he caught it. Now we're trapped!"

"Walter, we have to get these kids out. It won't take long before the lights blow, or a fire starts!" Mr. Conrad warned.

Mr. Holman sighed and rubbed his forehead nervously. "The twins tried the door, and Dryk is injured. I'm not going to risk any more students trying to get out."

"Use Lilly," a voice interrupted. The three teachers looked up in surprise, and Jake pointed to Lilly, who was standing fearfully with Meg. The feathered girl jerked her head up in surprise, staring at Jake.

"What?"

"Mr. Cawood, if you would, refrain from sacrificing your fellow classmates in hopes of escape," Mr. Ralf said darkly. Jake looked back at him stubbornly.

"You know she can do it! She can heal! All she has to do is open the door and we're free!" Jake looked at Lilly. "You're not scared, are you?" he added, voice unreadable.

"Jake! Stop it! We'll find another way out!" Meg stepped in, hurriedly trying to mediate the rising tension. But Lilly's expression had already changed, and she held up a hand.

"No, Meg, it's okay. I'll open the door. It's easier this way."

"Ms. Douglas, wait! I don't think that's a good idea!" Mr. Conrad yelled, but Lilly had a manner about her of someone who couldn't be reasoned with. Pride had taken over, pinching her gut. She felt belittled to be volunteered like an object; she felt insulted to be treated like a coward; but most of all, she felt hurt that Jake would turn on her so easily. The rage gave her courage as she stormed for the door, ignoring her teacher's protests. "You don't have to do this!" he cried.

Lilly turned for a moment, her fair chin stubbornly set, then she ran at the door and threw her shoulder into the bar.

Lilly had been shocked before, but it didn't ready her for the agony she experienced. A cry of pain was ripped from her mouth and she crumpled, her kinetic energy the only thing carrying her forward. She managed to throw her arm out in time to throw down the doorstop before she was jerked away, curling and convulsing with electricity. *Heal!* her mind screamed, but it was hard to obey. A few steps from the door she collapsed, too pained to move.

"Class, let's move away from the building now, quickly!" one of the professors instructed.

"Lilly! You okay?" Meg's voice asked, feet circling her cautiously. Lilly opened her eyes for a moment, trying to reassure her friend, but she felt dizzy and sick, and focused on healing instead. Around her the voices of students gathered, some grateful, some confused. They were out though, and they were going to be fine. At least, Lilly's peers were going to be. She should have been okay by now, but her insides felt scrambled and her thoughts refused to coordinate. She could hear voices as the professors tried to diffuse the situation. In the end, there was nothing she could do but give into that sensation of darkness that was becoming all too familiar.

Lilly wiped her mouth with the back of her hand and moved nauseously away from the toilet. She took the cup of water the nurse was holding out to her and gave a whisper of thanks. As she gargled, Ms. Meeks flushed away the evidence of her sickness and waited as Lilly spat into the sink.

"Ugh... I feel like everything in my stomach got fried.... It feels awful," Lilly said, washing her hands, then returning to the main room, curling up on one of the beds. The hospital wing of Charity Academy was of fair size, but Ms. Meeks kept things in order by herself. From the nurse's office out front to the inpatient area, this section of school was run by one woman. Days like today made her appreciate what that job entailed. Lilly could see Dryk laying on the bed to her right, barely conscious, and Wyvr looked up from his seat next to his twin and focused on her.

"Hey, Lilly. How you feeling?" he asked softly. Lilly let out a little moan, rolling onto her side. He chuckled slightly. "That good, huh? You sound just like Dryk, o' course, he'll prob'ly be soundin' that way longer'n you."

Lilly's eyes flicked over to them. "Is he hurt badly?" she asked.

Dryk muttered something and Wyvr chuckled. "Oh, it could have been worse. He mostly touched the plastic padding of the bar, but when he tried to fly backward, his leg hit the metal and it was just enough to give him a rude awakening." Wyvr pointed to his brother's leg. "Mild burns, stiffened muscles... And of course, feeling a little sick."

Dryk growled, "Easy for you to say, mate... You ain't the one who got barbequed."

Lilly shook her head and turned away, her laugh quickly fading. Her thoughts had grown distracted by another feeling, beyond her queasy stomach. It had trailed off to before she was shocked, to Jake's words: *Use Lilly.* It made her feel sick again, and she got up to get a drink, Wyvr and Dryk too distracted to see her leave.

At the sink, Lilly let the sound of the water filling her cup calm her, but as she turned off the faucet, the peace left. She sighed as she took a drink, and a tear broke free down her face. That tear soon gave way to more, and she found herself quietly crying, her cup spilling back into the sink.

"Lilly? Oh, Lilly... Dear, what's wrong?" It was odd how similar the nurse's voice was to her mother's.

Lilly struggled to control her tears as she wiped her hand across her eyes. "I-I'm sorry Ms. M-Meeks... I'll b-be okay," Lilly tried to say, her voice breaking and trembling.

Ms. Meeks shook her head and gently led Lilly out of the bathroom. "I think you and I both know you're not going to just 'be okay', Miss Douglas. Come on, let's sit in my office," Ms. Meeks comforted. Lilly followed quietly, and sat in the chair Ms. Meeks offered. She managed to get control of her tears, but Ms. Meeks was now set on learning what had brought those tears in the first place. "Lilly, what's bothering you?" she tenderly asked.

"It's just... These last few months have gradually grown worse. It's like everyone's started seeing me only for my powers, and they forget that I'm a person..." Lilly started, nervously fingering her feathers. It was clear she was struggling to speak out, as if it pained her to complain.

Ms. Meeks nodded to herself. "I'd like to say that no one thinks that of you, Lilly, but I do understand where you're coming from. It...pains me to see you constantly sacrificed, and although you do heal physically, I don't believe your injuries leave you entirely unharmed. Am I right?"

Lilly's lip quivered. "It's not so bad sometimes. Like when it's an accident or I'm trying to help. Those are my own choices to make. But it's almost like since then, everyone *expects* me to do that... Risk myself for others. I really wouldn't mind so much if I had more say. But my powers have suddenly taken me from heroism...to obligation."

"Lilly, I know you're trying to be nice and selfless, just helping others, but you need to speak up. You can't go on like this. While physically, it may appear you're fine, it's taking its toll mentally, and on your ability to heal. You will wear yourself out this way. As noble as it may be to help others, you're driving yourself into the ground."

Lilly felt tears prickling again. "But I can't just stop being helpful! I can't avoid using who I am for good! What if I say 'no, I'm not going to risk myself', and someone else gets hurt? It would make me feel so awful and selfish." She held her arms tightly around herself, shaking with the effort to be strong. "It... It would be more than I could handle."

"Then save your skills for the serious things. Don't let the stupid things like games and competitions become times for you to risk yourself. Say no, then in dire need, you can help. But use judgment. You're very smart, and if you talk to your friends, I'm sure they'd understand."

Lilly sighed and shook her head. "I hope so, Ms. Meeks. But for some reason, I really doubt that." She got up slowly and slipped back into the main hospital wing, where she laid back down and fell into a restless sleep. Ms. Meeks pulled out her files and finished recording her patient's diagnosis in the meantime, hoping Lilly had learned something. She'd barely finished one page when she heard someone softly walk in.

"She's not doing so well, is she, Ms. Meeks?" Wyvr asked from the doorway, his blue sweater held limp in his hand. Concern was in his face as he sighed and ran his hand through his hair. "It's how people here are treating her, isn't it?"

Ms. Meeks paused and glanced towards her sleeping patient. She seemed hesitant to speak, so Wyvr continued.

"She won't speak up for herself, you know. She just avoids confrontation. You should have seen what happened earlier... And the stories! Did she tell you about the accident in science class? Where her lab partner mixed the wrong chemicals then talked her into grabbing the beaker? Blew up in her face. Then there was this incident with the ladder and the Valentine's Day decorations... If this keeps going, she's not going to hold out for long." He looked toward the door and sighed again.

Ms. Meeks nodded. "Well, we'll just have to hope we stop this before it snowballs into chaos, Wyvr. For now let her heal, then we'll see what happens and plan accordingly."

Wyvr and Ms. Meeks talked a bit longer, then the teen left. Time passed, Lilly left the hospital wing, and almost a week leaked away. It looked like the fears Ms. Meeks and Wyvr had shared might have been for nothing.

Then one snowy morning, everything came crashing down.

The snow was an ocean of ice, spread as far as the eye could see, and Lilly found herself dragged to the rooftop with Kat. Healed from the power surge, the games were a nice distraction and had her adrenaline running in a pleasant way. The beginning of March meant the snowy day was rare, and that was enough to bring excitement from the whole school. Kat took advantage of her powers, and hit bystanders with snowballs, then ducked out of the way before they could identify the culprit. Eventually she talked Lilly into throwing one or two with her, then their truce ended and a snowball fight took its place.

It felt nice to be a kid, ducking and weaving around the grounds to avoid the frozen ammo. She didn't even mind when Meg and Jake came to join the game. They were a group again, playing in the snow and forgetting life's worries. Meg used her powers to change into a rabbit, hind legs sending waves of snow up and white fur and size making her harder to hit. Jake took advantage of his surroundings and built a fort behind one of the benches to protect himself. When the tides turned and Lilly was losing, the feathered girl changed tactics and used her wings to her advantage, but Kat wasn't to be deterred that easily.

Every detail was crystal clear as her friend took a handful of snow and with quick, error-free motions shaped a perfect snowball. When she threw it, the icy object hit Lilly in her stomach with such a surprising burst of power, her wings curled inward like a bird that had been shot, and she felt herself dropping quickly out of the sky.

THUD!

"Oh my gosh, Lilly, are you okay?" Meg's voice was the first thing she heard, and Lilly shook her head, snow flying everywhere, slingshotted from brown locks of wet hair. She turned and faced Kat, still gasping for breath.

"Gosh... Where did you learn to...throw like that!" she said with a squeak, sitting up and holding her sides as she gasped for breath.

"You're lucky there was so much snow on the ground already! You fell pretty far!" Meg said, sighing with relief. To Lilly's surprise, she whirled, growling at Jake and Kat, who were laughing on the roof not far away. "It's not funny, she could have really been hurt!" she snapped.

Jake didn't even seemed phased. "I'm sorry, Lilly, but the look on your face was priceless..." he said, unable to stop laughing.

"It's just snow, Lilly, really. You don't have to make such a big deal about it," Kat continued with a chuckle.

"But it still *hurt!*" Lilly said in offense, blinking at them in confusion. Without warning, tears were building up in her eyes. "That was the meanest thing you've ever done," she said, still gasping for air. To her amazement, they stopped laughing and Jake frowned at her instead.

"Aw, come on Lilly! Don't be that way! She wasn't trying to hurt you. There was plenty of snow," he said, voice hitting the right notes to make it sound like a whine.

Lilly's temper flared and she felt her eyebrows knitting into a glare. She looked at Kat, who was already building more snowballs. "You... You're not going to apologize? You're not sorry?" she gasped, holding her side. "I can't..." She let out a shudder, and when she opened her eyes, Kat and Jake were still in the positions they had been in before. Without thinking, she threw her wings open and flew into the sky, flying as fast as she could for the forest, heart pounding in her head. *They didn't care...* Bah-dum. *They didn't care...* Bah-dum. *How could they be that heartless?* Each beat created a painful throb in her head, and she shook, burying her face in her hands. The wind hummed around her gently, and she kept flying, before landing in the middle of the woods, falling to her knees in a blanket of snow. The cold and wet leaked through her clothing, but she just stared emptily into space. The shock of what had happened hit her like a whirlwind. She'd just had another fight with her friends; a very short one, but a fight nonetheless. Despite the whole Meg and Jake thing, they had been getting along okay. Now, as she sat alone in the snow, she couldn't believe what had just transpired.

For what seemed like ages, she just sat there, unable to grasp the situation. Then she cried. It hadn't been the snowball that hurt so much; it was who threw it, and that left a gaping hole in her gut she couldn't repair. The way Jake had laughed and Kat's unworried expression left her so confused. So empty.

"Lilly! Lilly, there you are! Are you okay?"

Slowly, Lilly looked and saw Meg, the silhouette blurry with her eyes burning from crying. "Meg..." she sobbed and threw herself into her roommate's arms, crying. "Oh, Meg! I'm so confused! I didn't mean to run off, but... It hurt! Kat hurt me with a stupid *snowball*! If she apologized, if she was sorry.... I wouldn't have, but even Jake... After you two...." She broke into a river of tears, her shoulders heaving. Taking advantage of the silence, Meg broke in.

"Oh, Lilly, it wasn't like that! She didn't realize she hit you so hard. We've been looking everywhere for you since. And Jake... Lilly, he's not the heartless monster you're making him!"

"Maybe to you he's not," Lilly muttered bitterly, then sighed sadly. "He still could have at least felt worried..." she whispered.

Meg nodded slowly. "Maybe he just forgets you're not that tough. And you having healing powers and all..."

"It doesn't mean I don't feel pain!" Lilly's severity surprised her, but Meg had stricken a geyser of fresh feelings. "Everyone thinks because I heal faster, it makes me invincible or robotic! But I'm not!" Her wings lashed with anger as rivulets of water poured down her face. "When I break a bone, it's just as horrible! When I burn my arm, it's the same as if you had! I can only heal my *body*, Meg. Don't tell me they expect me to heal emotionally as well!"

Meg took a step back, but as she spoke, Lilly felt like Meg had cut a wound deeper than any other. "Sometimes you act like you can."

"I act like it?" Her heart pounded. "How?"

"You bounce back, Lilly, so we think you're okay... No one realizes you're still upset," she whispered.

Lilly trembled. She didn't want to hear this. "Does that mean I want to be treated like a doormat? 'Step on Lilly, she'll heal.' 'Feathers, can you grab that beaker?' 'I'm sorry, but you can just heal that burn.' These last few months have been horrible! Meg, I'm just being *used*. Don't you see that? Even by you."

"Lilly! No! What—"

"You all do! Like Jake with the power surge, even that stupid game of tug-o-war! At first you all apologized and were worried and cared! Now I'm..." She cradled her stomach and wrenched away from Meg's touch. "I'm just an object."

"Oh, Hun, no! Stop that! I'm... Oh, I'm so sorry—"

"Are you?" whispered Lilly, looking up in pain. "You don't believe me, do you? I'm not over exaggerating, Meg. Whatever you think, my feelings don't heal the same way my body does. I trusted you! I trusted all of you! And you walked all over me." With a soundless cry, Lilly's feathers rippled across her wings and she threw herself at the sky, Meg screaming after, morphing and morphing as Lilly flew further away. Lilly was running...

And she didn't care who saw her do it.

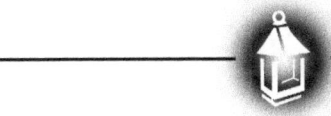

Somewhere above an unfamiliar city, Lilly lost all sense of direction. She'd stayed out of sight, and even in her hurt, she had protected her friends' secrecy. In a country field she landed, exhausted and tired. She'd flown at least for an hour on an empty stomach, and now her body screamed for food with her wings aching and tired.

Spotting a garden, she tucked in her wings, hiding them before making her way over. Whispering a small apology for stealing, she dug up a few carrots and a potato, and tried not to feel too guilty. Lilly snuck away to a more secluded willow tree, and at its base, she ate. The flavors were bland but her protesting stomach encouraged her to eat. The taste of dirt lingered in her mouth, but once it was gone she sat with empty hands, wishing there were more.

She didn't get a chance to consider her hunger much longer when a cold breeze froze her with shock, as something metal clamped tightly around her neck.

"You aren't going anywhere. You could say your flight plans are being 'delayed.'" Icy laughter gave way to a searing pain in her arms, and Lilly screamed to get free. Her mouth was covered immediately, nails digging painfully into her cheek. "Now, now, none of that. We don't want to be rough, do we boys?"

Lilly's eyes grew to the size of disks as Tray stepped forward. "I don't know. I could enjoy being a little rough to that—"

"Cory! Tray! Are you trying to get us caught? Just get her, and go!" The wind buffeted them slightly as Zen crossed his arms at them and shook his head. As Lilly turned to see her captor's face, she saw the silver-haired boy give a little shrug before his fist hit her head, and everything went dark.

As Lilly's body crumpled, Cory felt a twinge of pity. It startled him so much, he let her drop face first to the ground. With a mild curse, he grabbed her by the back of the shirt and hoisted her up, throwing the limp body over his shoulders. It was like holding a small bag of potatoes, not a human girl.

Zen gave a grunt to his left, and they slipped one by one into the shadows. To his right, Tray kept glancing at Lilly's body as if plotting how best to strike his revenge. Cory shrugged it off. Right now this girl was too valuable to do much to. Even the blow had been risky. Kibbsty would probably be worried Cory had rattled her precious brains with his fist... Truth was, Cory had been a little afraid himself when he picked her up. A girl this light, her bones must be made of toothpicks.

"Ugh..."

Cory almost dropped her a second time, but masked it with a shifting movement, as if he were repositioning Lilly. As he walked, he tried to keep a straight face, but he was in clear, cold shock. Her lips were moving softly next to his ear, the whisper inaudible to anyone but him... And even he wasn't meant to hear it.

Lilly was praying.

Pray all you want, girl, but the devil's the only one who'll hear your prayers now, Cory thought, but to his surprise, he hoped that if there was a God, He heard.

She'd need all the prayers she could get.

"She's gone!" Meg's scream shattered the silence of the morning as she burst into the gym, a flurry of snow in her wake. She slipped on the slick floor and fell, stumbling toward the storage room where a group of students stood. Dryk and Wyvr peered at her in shared confusion, setting down the sleds they had been digging out.

"Who is?"

"Lilly! She's gone! S-she ran away! I c-couldn't stop her! We g-gotta do something!" Meg cried, streams of tears racing down her face. The few people in the gym quickly moved forward, and Kent caught Meg before she fell again.

"Whoa, Meg, calm down. Jenny, get the nurse or Dr. Allina or someone! Meg, we can't understand you while you're wailing like that. Take a deep breath and calm down. You understand?" Kent calmly reasoned with her. Wyvr looked pale next to him, and

Jenny had disappeared in a flash of light. The only others with them were Dryk, Michaela, and Sal, and they all looked uncomfortable.

Meg slowly sank to the floor and struggled to explain. "She got upset b-because Kat hit her r-really hard with a s-snowball. She s-said everyone has b-been treating her badly b-because she can heal. I d-didn't think it was such a b-big deal but she got so upset s-she left! None of us can f-find her now."

"Oh, Meg... Tell me you didn't act like it was okay to hurt her because she can heal!" Wyvr spoke suddenly, and he frowned.

Meg sniffled. "I didn't realize it w-was a big deal to her..."

Wyvr growled and snapped at the air. "This is exactly what Ms. Meeks and her have been talkin' about. Meg, that poor girl has been struggling so much lately, and it's because the whole school treats her like this! She can only take so much!"

"She w-was struggling? Why?" Meg whispered.

Wyvr sighed. "Because you forget she's just a kid, Meg. Everyone expects her to be okay with being hurt, so they forget that just because she heals physically doesn't mean she forgets it, or doesn't feel pain like we do. She's been so sheltered and protected. She wants to be loved and looked after. And yet everyone throws her to the wolves and tells her to fend for herself! Meg, that hurts her more than broken bones or cuts, because it's like no one cares about her anymore," Wyvr tried to explain.

Dryk nodded, shifting on his crutches. "It's not going to be easy to earn her trust back now, even if we do find her."

"Poor Lilly... Can't we try, though?" Kent asked softly, and Meg burst into a fresh wave of tears.

Wyvr nodded sharply. "We *will* try. She deserves as much. Kent, watch Meg and tell everyone what's happening. Dryk and I will see if we can help track her."

"Watch these," Dryk instructed Sal as he held out his crutches, and with a nod to his twin, they morphed into falcons, Dryk's wings fluttering in the air before he was even fully morphed so his injured leg didn't need to help him launch into the air. Wyvr hopped up next to him and they quickly flew into the daylight, catching a few thermals to carry them higher, but mostly relying on the wind.

<Where do you think she went?> Dryk asked, wheeling low over the trees, sharp eyes scanning.

<My guess is she just went away, as far and fast as she could,> Wyvr answered, and pointed his beak forward. <I can only guess she took a straight path and hope we can find a clue that we're on the right track. When someone's upset, they can be careless... We can only hope we catch that carelessness.>

Wyvr and Dryk pin-wheeled lower, sharp eyes on the ground and wings pointed like Australian boomerangs, slicing through the air. As they kept flying, their hopes started fading, and they were just about to turn back when Dryk saw a glimmer of white.

<Eh, Wyvr! You see that? It looks like somethin's in that tree,> chattered Dryk, and Wyvr pointed his eyes, circling lower.

<It's a piece of paper... And it's folded, like a note.> Wyvr said thoughtfully as he dipped lower. Finally he landed, cautiously edging forward, uncertain of the validity of this. A familiar scent hit his nose—not quite right but not enough for concern—and he shook off his distrust to focus on what he smelled. <Lilly,> he whispered.

<Well, read it! Open it! Get it, or somethin'!> His brother let out a little noise, swooping low and tapping his brother on the head with closed talons. Egged on by his twin, Wyvr gave in and reached out with a claw, pulling the paper closer. Using one foot and his beak, he managed to gently open the paper, then he smoothed it out with a wing. Then he read it aloud to his brother.

<'If you've found this note and you know who it's from, then you can go ahead and go back. I'm going home. If I can't stay there, I'll find some other place to live. But I can't go back to the school. Just please don't try to follow me.' And it's signed: 'Lilly.' I don't believe it, Dryk. She really left...> Wyvr whispered, staring at the handwriting, which looked too much like Lilly's to doubt. Dryk glided somewhere above, and a sad noise made it to Wyvr's mind.

<Lilly's really gone? Aw, poor thing... This irks me, Wyvr. We should have done something before it got this bad! But now... Do we just let her go?> Dryk asked. Wyvr stared at the note and sighed.

<I think for a little bit, that's all we can do. We have to wait for her to calm down, then we'll go and try to find her, convince her to come back. But we have to give her room, or she'll run again,> Wyvr answered thoughtfully, and carefully re-folded the note before picking it up in his beak and launching back into the sky. With a little effort, he managed to get up to the same altitude as his brother. He struggled a little to keep aloft, but was determined to carry his burden. With a nod to his brother, they started back to the academy with heavy hearts, but accepting attitudes. Meanwhile, off in the distance, a young girl was in the hands of her enemies, and no one was there to hear her cries for help.

When Lilly came to her senses, her head was screaming in pain and her heart in terror. Each body part sent her mixed messages that jumbled together in her head.

Cold floor? It feels like tile, but harder, slick...grout-less...seamless, smooth... Humming, like machines, clothing shuffling, like a long dress or... A lab coat.

"Yeow!" Lilly yelped as someone yanked her head back, and she was facing Dr. Kibbsty. She never got used to that face, that wiry hair... That catlike smile.

"Ah, Lilly, so nice of you to join us again. But I'm dreadfully sorry, nap time is over for now. Tray?"

Lilly whimpered and scrambled to her feet as a shock of electricity nearly sent her back to the ground, and her muscles lurched as she tried to move, her wings twitching in pain. "I'm up!" she said, her voice a squawk of pain, then Kibbsty nodded and Tray stopped. She could see his disappointed frown to her left, and her heart pounded even harder.

"Very good. Now, you've been here before, and I'm sure you know we can make this hard or easy. All I want is a blood test. Is that sooo much to ask? You know how that collar works. You know you can't escape. So, what do you say?"

As he reached for her arm, Lilly jerked her hand back and surprised herself by biting him on the hand. Kibbsty snarled angrily and snatched his hand away, but his eyes only narrowed as he pointed at her neck.

"I should warn you, that collar's been updated. A friend at your school helped us with it. Luther, I believe his name was—a charming, fitting name. Last time, you escaped and healed your wounds instantly, but we've found a way to keep your injuries in place. We break something, even if the collar comes off, your powers won't be able to recognize the damage."

This information, she couldn't grasp it. "You're lying..." she said, but her voice held fear. His smile didn't do anything but intensify it.

"Oh, I'm afraid not." Without warning, his hand lashed forward and grabbed Lilly's wrist.

"Oh, my God!" Cory leapt back as Lilly let out a pain-filled scream that made his hair stand on end, and his throat tightened with nausea. No blood had been spilled, but the loud snap he had heard sounded like wood, though it had been bone. When Lilly refused to let Kibbsty take her blood, he'd snapped her wrist. With his *bare hands.*

Kibbsty turned to Cory as the girl behind him writhed in agony, a smug smile on his face. "What's the matter, boy? Too gruesome for you?"

Cory acted quickly and covered his sickness with ease. "I forgot her bones were hollow. I've never seen something break like that. And the sound..."

Kibbsty laughed, and his eyes twinkled. "Want to hear it again?" he asked malevolently. Cory shook his head calmly, but inside he felt sick.

"Nah. If you break all her bones, you'll never get to study them."

Kibbsty pondered this and shrugged. "I guess you're right. Run her through the x-ray again. I want to study that break."

It's like she's not even human, Cory thought in horror, going over to the girl. The pain on her face was unimaginable, and he knew it would only get worse when her adrenaline subsided. Even now she fought him, struggling to hit him with her wings. He calmly brushed them aside and unbuckled her from the rings in the floor, holding the ends of the chains together like one large leash. As the right chain touched her arm, she cried out and stumbled after him, her focus now on preventing as much pain as possible by not resisting.

"Get in there," Cory said, steering her toward the x-ray machine Kibbsty had designed for cases such as these. It was a spacious, large machine, long enough and wide enough for all sizes and shapes. Lilly's wings were snapped easily to the table, and she only resisted when Cory reached for her arm.

"Don't, please... I won't fight... Just don't."

The plea caught Cory off-guard as he automatically reached to snap her in anyway. But his fingers hovered above her forearm. "Keep your arm flat and don't move an inch," he hissed, and pushed the button so she disappeared into the machine before he could change his mind. But he could still see her face as she had whispered to him, and his stomach knotted.

I'm sorry... For once, I really am...

The images flickered across Kibbsty's computer screen, and even if it was only the bones he was looking at, he was fascinated.

"Look at this, Cory! It's amazing! Intriguing... Oh, if only that brat would let me get a decent tissue sample as well! If I could duplicate this... Oh..." He seemed lost in a dream for a moment, then turned to the boy.

"You chained her up well?" he asked suddenly, and the boy nodded.

"After you and Tray got done with her, I doubt she'd get anywhere," Cory said. Kibbsty studied him. This boy was so hard to read. His icy hair and eyes coupled with his cold personality made him difficult to decipher, and no emotions ever leaked through. Yet, Kibbsty almost could have sworn he caught a hint of disapproval.

"Do you think it was too much?" he ventured cautiously. Cory merely shrugged.

"You want her DNA, but you're going to ruin a perfectly good specimen by being so rough with her. X-rays and diagrams can only tell you so much. You had trouble with the samples before. You still need her," Cory said simply. As the teen left, Kibbsty had given a little bob of his shoulders and waved it off.

"Eh, double check her restraints anyway. Tomorrow you can look in on her for me," Kibbsty said, and Cory gave a smile that reassured Kibbsty of his loyalty.

"I'd love to," he grinned, and with an icy laugh, he'd disappeared, and Kibbsty couldn't help but shake his head.

"That boy is as lively as a hunk of ice," he sighed, and went back to work, lost in the read out on his computer. Then he was too distracted to waste more time thinking about it.

"Fascinating… Just *fascinating*."

Chapter Five

Bluffing to Live

I know you think I hate you, and after all I've done to you, I would probably think the same... Memories. *There's a batch of students here, the ones who used to work undercover at Charity Academy...* Time. *Good luck, Firecracker.* Questions. They just kept dropping, falling, bringing her back to the present.

Lilly was awakened from an exhausted slumber, and her tired eyes blinked to focus. As her ears perked to listen, she realized someone was at the door, talking. Dates scattered through her thoughts, her last few memories fading. March, it was March. The pain in her arm emphasized the date.

"Well, Miss Priss, Kibbsty's called for you. So straighten up and get to your feet. I ain't gonna carry you, either, so you better move quickly." Lilly yelped in pain as he uncuffed her hands and she fell, striking the floor hard. Then cold hands yanked her up, and Cory snarled. "Stand," he ordered, and as Lilly struggled for her footing, she fearfully wondered if the conversation she'd had with Cory really occurred. The chill in the air brought her senses around, and as she stumbled forward, half carried, half walking, Cory sighed. "Move it! For a firecracker, you know, you sure are slow." Shock jolted her brain the rest of the way into wakefulness, as she tried not to turn and stare at him. *Firecracker...* It hadn't been a dream. Despite the rough treatment, she knew the conversation had been real. So she gathered her courage, and forced herself to walk.

"Kibbsty, I think you're being too rough with this kid. Any more beatings and I'm going to be carrying her up the stairs, and I'm not paid enough to do that," snapped Cory, as he threw Lilly to the floor. As her knees struck concrete, she let out a little whimper, but kept her face blank. She could hear them moving, and slowly looked up to see Kibbsty glaring down at her.

"You don't get paid at all, but maybe you're right. We can't have her die before we're done with her, now can we?" He laughed and grabbed the back of her shirt, hauling her to her feet. She trembled but didn't pull away, slumping weakly against his hold. Her eyes still burned with passion and perseverance though, as he dragged her toward a chair and plopped her down in it.

"Now come into my office, Lilly. We all know you've put up a good fight, but look at you. You're not going to be able to keep this up much longer. So I've made a decision, a 'deal,' you might call it. You agree to let me do my testing, and I'll let you stay here as a student. That means no more chains, no more dungeon, and regular meals and classes, just like everyone else. Now, wouldn't that be an improvement?"

Lilly was about to spit that she would never agree to his testing, then remembered Cory's warning. She wavered, confused in a way she had never been before. Her heart was wavering inside her, and she was torn between one option and the other. Slowly, wordlessly, she extended her arm, suppressing her fears and forcing herself to surrender.

"Very good choice, Miss Douglas. Cory, bring that tray."

Lilly tightened her jaw, suppressing her sobs, and only when the needle went into her skin did she dare let herself cry. Her tears flowed like blood, raining down on the needle, her arm, and her shirt. Kibbsty gloated with satisfaction when he finally drew away, and waved his hand to Cory to remove her. Lilly was too weak and ashamed to resist, and Cory threw her over his shoulder like a rag doll. But this time, he wasn't taking her to the dungeon; he was taking her the other way. Even knowing she wasn't going back to that wall didn't stop her sniffling. She could feel blood running down her arm, reminding her of what she'd done.

A short way down the hallway Cory set her down, and she sank against the wall. "Give me your arm," he said, and she reluctantly offered it to him. He reached out, and to her surprise, his eyes started glowing, and water started to trickle from beneath his hand. It washed off her arm, and then his hand grew colder as he pressed his palm to her forearm. Lilly winced until he finally drew his hand away. Then wordlessly, he slipped one arm under her legs and one behind her back and started to carry her. Then she heard him speak again.

<Don't respond to my voice. Just close your eyes and keep your face straight.>

Lilly was grateful for the warning because it took effort not to respond. She tried to pinpoint where his voice came from, then her eyes almost snapped open. He was speaking in her head like Meg and Wyvr could, but they only did that as animals. <Cory? Are you a telepath? Can... Can you hear me?>

<Yes, just don't speak out loud, Firecracker. This isn't something I do normally. But it's too hard to speak to you...voice to voice, so I decided I would risk it. You tell anyone, girl, and you're *so* dead.>

Lilly almost nodded, and then remembered she wasn't supposed to respond. She shifted in his arms, feeling weaker and more tired than before. <I won't... You can trust me.>

<Hmph.> She could almost see his sour face and the way his mouth twitched when he grunted. His footsteps grew slower, and from the way she was shifted, Lilly guessed they were climbing stairs. <You can do what you want, but you still can't trust *us*. Every step you take here will be a risk: for me, for you, and everyone else. Now that Kibbsty has your blood, it's more dangerous than ever. You're not as valuable anymore. But there may be some way that you'll be safe, even now... Just, do that thing you do... Praying, right? I don't believe in it, but if it helps you, you should do it.>

Lilly listened closely, and then dared herself to respond. <Cory, will you talk to me more? Telepathically?>

She could sense a tense pause on Cory's end. Slowly, the response came. <I'm not sure if it will be safe. If you even give someone a hint that I can talk to you like this, they'll find out. I'm sorry. Maybe sometime I might, but for now, just rest.> His voice unexpectedly shifted. "Your bones may be hollow, but you're still annoying to carry." Lilly was jolted in his arms and winced slightly, but didn't open her eyes. She knew what he was doing, and she was getting better about playing along.

<Well, thanks for being there. I know you care, despite what you do,> Lilly dared to whisper back. To her surprise, Cory didn't bite back with the sharp response she had come to expect.

<You have no idea, Firecracker...> came back a whisper, so soft Lilly didn't know if she had imagined it. Then Cory flopped her on a bed, and she was out as soon as she hit the mattress.

Cory looked down at the bed where Lilly was sleeping, his face blank and emotionless. His heart was hammering to the beat of a war drum. Knowing everything he'd done and would have to do to her was unbearable to think about. His mouth twitched unwillingly, and after a moment of hesitation, he pulled a blanket over her and tucked it around her head. He was careful not to make a noise doing it so the surveillance speakers wouldn't pick it up, but also determined to make sure the corners were tucked next to her face. When he looked at her, he didn't see the brown-haired girl with the stripe of lilac to the left of her face. He saw blonde curls and long eyelashes: the face of a sister he thought he'd forgotten.

As his hand brushed her cheek, his heart lurched and he quickly turned and marched out of the room, closing the door roughly. The memories were still there, overwhelming him. His sister would be about the same age now. What if that had been her at this school, going through this? He could see her frowning in his mind as she watched what he was doing. It was getting harder to ignore the guilt chipping away at him.

Cory's steps sounded loud to his ears, echoing through the empty hall. It was a sharp, resounding rhythm, falling and then fading like ice breaking in a frozen cave. No one would hear him at this time of day; this was a school after all, though sometimes people were excused from class to cause mischief. Perhaps that was what surprised him so much when he heard a voice call out, and Cory had to hold himself back from throwing an icicle in that direction. Considering who it was, it wouldn't have been an unusual reaction.

"Talked Kibbsty into letting her go to school with us, did you?" Tray scoffed, and Cory could hear him lean against the wall. With his back turned, Cory could still picture Tray easily. Tray was tall and lanky, with a strawberry-blond mop of hair. His face was very freckled, with spots of acne, and his ears were a little large for his face. Cory thought he looked like a windmill, all arms and legs, but Tray was trained to use that to his advantage. Many students had learned that the Irish power surge could land a punch, and despite his gangling proportions they didn't underestimate him. Right now, his arms would be crossed and one leg would be slightly bent from his lounging position. His angled face would be curled in a disapproving sneer, with his eyebrows beginning to knit. Cory decided there was no point in turning. He could already see Tray.

"If she's dead, she won't be any good."

"To Kibbsty, maybe. But she's more trouble to us alive. You're becomin' a real pet of his, Cory. And I don't like it."

There was a crackle, and Cory moved just in time to avoid getting shocked. In a fluid movement, he caught Tray by the neck and pinned him against the wall. He could feel the icy power vanish from his body, and he glared deeply into Tray's eyes.

"You got a problem, you face it like a man. You're still Kibbsty's pet, so stop being a punk and listen. If you get a fight started between students, it will get you spat on the floor quicker than that brat you hate so much. We stay in line or loose it all. Remember that next time. I'm sure your mom would appreciate your efforts."

"Don'...bring her up," Tray said, but his face had become ashen. Cory let go and watched him slump against the wall. "I just hate that...thing, so much." His eyes were closed, and his face wrinkled with anger.

"So do I, but she's only a girl. She'll do her part, then you can have her. But Kibbsty won't be happy if you act up now." Cory's face was etched and solid. He turned and continued down the hall. "Later."

"Later," Tray quietly agreed.

This girl was creating a whole world of trouble and they barely got her out of the dungeons.

Cory opened a door and disappeared into math class.

Lilly stirred, her eyes struggling to open. Her body was weak and her head throbbing. Something jabbed her, and she curled away. Then she was yanked roughly to her feet, a cry escaping her mouth.

"If I have to tell you to wake up one more time, I swear I'll break your other arm!" Cory's voice snarled in her ear, and agonizing pain crossed her wrist with chills of cold air. His grip was tight across the bruised flesh, even if her broken arm was untouched at her side.

"Stop, please! I'm awake!" she sobbed and clawed at his tight fingers. "Let go!"

Lilly's eyes widened fearfully as Cory's face pulled closer, his eyes dangerous and chilled. "You need to learn your place, Firecracker. An attitude like that will only get you in trouble."

Somewhere in the back of her mind, that statement clicked. He was preparing her for school. It was hard to believe he was hurting her with good intentions. Lilly weakly slumped, tears rolling down her face, until Cory let go and she dropped to the floor.

"What do you want?" she whispered, staring at the ground.

Cory snarled, bristling slightly with annoyance. "Kibbsty says you're stuck with me. I have to take you to my classes and keep you out of trouble. Make sure the guys don't bust you too fast, stuff like that. I ain't happy about it. I'm not a babysitter." Lilly listened carefully to all the hidden clues in that statement. She was going to classes with Cory, and the icy boy had to keep up a front. This was dangerous for both of them, and he was doing it to protect her. To do that, he was going to have to hurt her. Lilly flinched away.

"I can barely stand. He expects me to take classes? I'm sure I'll learn a lot if I pass out."

Cory growled. "You got enough fire to spit out sasses like that, you got enough strength to move it. I'm not going to wait for you forever. Everyone already thinks I must be soft or something to be looking out for you. I don't intend to prove them right. Stay out of my way, or I'll make you wish you'd stayed in that dungeon."

Lilly staggered to her feet, falling back into the bed, knees knocking the baseboard. The pain brought her senses to life as she struggled to breathe, the collar feeling tighter this morning. She turned and glared at Cory. "If I have to be stuck with you jerks, it's starting to look nicer down there," she spat breathlessly. Cory raised his hand as if to strike her, then stopped, glowering at her.

"Get dressed, I'll be back. You better be ready." He slipped out of the room, leaving a wake of cold behind him.

Lilly slowly pushed herself onto weak ankles, her wings fluttering painfully for balance. She wouldn't have much time, if she read Cory right. She limped to a table in the corner, where she found a very simple outfit. It was a sweater with jaggedly cut slits in the back, and a pair of jeans. They looked like they would fit, but not as comfortably as the clothes Meg had altered for her. She took them back to the bed, and with a bit of a struggle, changed into them, pulling the sweater over her soiled underclothes and shirt. She felt like a mess, bloody and dirty, but it wasn't like anyone would care. She looked like what everyone thought she was: trash.

"Miss Priss, you're going to make me late! Let's go!" <Seriously, move it. You don't want to get caught being tardy here.>

"I'm coming," Lilly whispered, hobbling to the door and finding Cory slouched outside. He didn't say a word, merely started to walk, leaving her stumbling to catch up.

<You're limping.>

Lilly's heart flopped as she struggled to keep up. The comment took her off guard. <All this dropping and yanking bruised my legs pretty badly.>

"Can't you go any faster?" Cory's voice was harsh and angry as he turned to look at her. His eyes focused sharply on her leg. Lilly knew what he was doing; he was creating a reason to turn and look back at her. Lilly staggered, the muscles straining to move.

"I'm trying," she whimpered.

Cory snarled, "Try harder." When Lilly's pace didn't increase, he whirled around and scooped her up, slinging her over his shoulder. "I won't be late because of a feather brain like you," he cursed, and started striding down the hall, moving quickly and smoothly. It seemed that within seconds he was dumping her again, outside a doorway. He growled and walked in, letting her scuttle behind. Then she was in the classroom, plain enough it could have been a dungeon.

"Cory, you're trailin' a mouse. Want us to dispose of it?" a voice sneered behind her, and Lilly darted to the side as a green-haired girl entered the room.

"Leave her. Kibbsty told me to look after her, to make sure no one damages his precious experiment before he's done." His voice came from the other corner of the class, where he was lounging at a desk, feet on the table top. The girl smirked, leaning down closer to view Lilly.

"Ain't this the church mouse we caught last time? The one that kept getting away?"

"The same."

"Sly little devil. You don't look so pippy now," she laughed. Lilly couldn't stop the glare from knitting her eyebrows together. The girl smiled wickedly. "Can she dance, Frost?"

"You don't want to try. She may have her powers suppressed, but she doesn't need them to be a pain. Although maybe she learned her lesson after slapping Kibbsty."

Trish chuckled and drew back, sneering. "That takes spunk. You might survive here yet. Cherry'll kill you, you know that, don't you? She already says you're bein' too obedient to Kibbsty. Now you're his guard dog? I didn't know you could be so compliant." She swaggered over and sat on the table next to him. Cory puffed a wisp of icy air.

"Bite me."

"Trish! Where's Frost? I swear I'll wring his neck... Cory! What's this I hear about—" As Cherry burst into the room, she froze, her eyes focusing on Lilly. "You."

"Don't go pickin' fights, Cherry. Kibbsty's still usin' her," warned Trish. Lilly backed away as the dark eyes sharpened on her.

"This brat! What she *doin'* here? You know what everyone'll say! Does Tray know?"

"Can't you tell? He's been spitting sparks all morning."

"I wondered, but still. How long?"

Trish shrugged. "Who knows? Depends on her usefulness. Same as the rest of us."

Someone growled angrily, pushing in behind Cherry. "She is *not* like the rest of us."

"Xzin, you're back!" Cherry said, voice cheering considerably. Xzin turned, facing Lilly, and glared more forcefully.

<Don't look in his eyes,> came Cory's warning, and Lilly made her eyes dart away, nervously backing up further. Xzin moved and took a seat, letting it slide. "She's one of them heroic types. Noble, but stupid."

Lilly felt her heart burning, but turned and slipped deeper into the shadows.

She watched from there as Cherry gave a curt nod.

"So how was China?" Trish purred.

"Grim. I don't want to talk about it. Teacher coming." All teens slipped into their chairs at that signal except for Lilly, who was left where she was standing. At the last moment, two students slipped in and sat down before a tall, dark-haired woman entered.

"Where's the new girl?" Trish threw her thumb in Lilly's direction, and the teacher's gaze sharpened on her. "You, come over here." Lilly obediently moved from where she had been cornered, and that sharp glare raked her from top to bottom; it finally settled on her face. "You're the most recent student, are you?" Lilly nodded. "Well, it makes no difference who you are in my classroom. Cherry, give her some paper and a pencil, and we'll start class. Sit next to the ice cube."

The ice cube? Lilly thought, giggling in her head and taking a seat next to Cory. Cherry tossed a pencil at her and it nearly hit her in the face, bouncing on the table and rolling to a stop at the edge. The paper followed, deposited with equal roughness. Lilly barely collected both before the woman began speaking, mostly to her. "This is chemistry class, and in this school, we grade by result, not by effort. Each student works alone and is responsible for his or her own education. This is not a normal school, child, so I highly suggest you forget whatever lifestyle you had before you got here. Your learning is your survival. Keep that in mind.

"In this class we do not and will not just learn concepts, we will see and apply. There is always danger in the chemistry we do, so you will be expected to maintain strict discipline. Tardiness will be dealt with severely, as will failure. And one more thing." Lilly found herself looking into the eyes of a terrifyingly serious woman. "You are with the best of the best, Miss Douglas. You want to make it? You'll have to fight for it." Then, of all things, she *smiled*. "I'm Ms. Knox. Welcome to Firestone. Now turn to page 427."

Lilly's eyes darted for the book in question. Something brushed her foot, and she ducked down, grabbing the spine of the thick chemistry book. The other students already had theirs, quietly turning pages. Lilly mimicked until she saw page 427. It was about the elements Thallium and Mercury.

"Hey, Thall, Mar: looks like we got to you," Cory remarked, and one of the students Lilly saw slip in late looked up. His hair was silver with blue highlights, matching the girl seated nearby. His dull grey eyes blinked as a poisonous smile curled across his mouth.

"Finally."

Ms. Knox gave a soft chuckle. "You could show a bit more enthusiasm." She went to the board and picked up a piece of chalk. Then she wrote two sets of letters: Hg and Tl.

"We are nearing the end of our element study, but it does not mean I'll tolerate lax behavior. I expect you to pay just as close attention now as when we started. As you see, today's elements are

Thallium and Mercury, elements 80 and 81. Mercury, as you know, is a toxic element, and Thallium even more so. Both are silver in color, while one is liquid at room temperature and the other a soft metal."

As she spoke, she drew more onto the diagrams on the board. The element numbers, mass... Stuff like that. Then she drew a rough sketch of each. Lilly couldn't help following closely. Something in her gut suggested it was wise. On paper, she took notes from the board in her tight, neat script. At the same time, she was observing the other students' actions. Cory wrote in a wide, loose and sketchy way, while Trish's handwriting was disheveled with a horrible tilt. Cherry's was very sharp, with little decorative slashes on the y's and g's, and dots decorating the edges of letters. Xzin sat to the far right, his handwriting small and jumbled, occasionally speckled with a Chinese character or two. The two silver-haired students were writing nothing, staring at the board without expression. Lilly saw all of this in her peripheral vision. It was in hazy detail, but she didn't dare trying to turn her head to sneak a peek. She remembered Cory's warning. She couldn't allow herself comfort here. Her life depended on it.

"Thallium," Ms. Knox was continuing, "was once used as a rat poison and insecticide. Why, Miss Everyson?"

Cherry looked up and answered, "Because it is tasteless and scent-less."

"Good. Which also makes it very deadly. Thallium and elements like it are useful in our line of work because they are almost undetectable. Thall, will you—" There was a sharp beep, and Ms. Knox's eyes knitted angrily together. "What?"

Lilly nearly recoiled as Dr. Kibbsty's voice roared from a phone at Ms. Knox's desk. "Send me Miss Douglas. Now!" he snarled, and there was a click before the teacher could answer. Lilly felt her wings quiver as the teacher turned to her.

"Cory, take her. Now, where were we..."

While Ms. Knox continued her lesson, Cory cursed and got up, grabbing her arm and dragging her behind him. She stumbled and barely managed to keep up. Her leg shot sharply with pain, and it caused Lilly to hobble heavily. Her wings fluttered as she tried to balance herself, but it did little good. She could only bear the pain and try to keep going.

Cory's walk was brisk, and he wasn't talking to her one way or the other. She didn't dare to ask him to slow down so she tried to scramble faster, eyes watering with effort. She stumbled, her legs close to giving up. Cory never paused.

Don't think about the pain... Just keep fighting... You can do it, Lilly thought. Finally, just short of her collapsing, she stepped into Kibbsty's lab, where he was snarling with anger.

"Where is she? You!" Lilly leapt back, tripping and falling just in time to miss a blow thrown at her head. Her eyes were wide with terror. "You good for nothing little—"

"What are you rambling about now?" Cory muttered calmly. Meanwhile, Lilly shrank away.

Kibbsty towered over her, his eyes sharp as daggers. "I'm sick of this brat. I've had it!" There was a strange scraping noise, and Lilly nearly screamed when she found herself staring at a vicious knife in her face. She scuttled backward and his hand lashed out, catching her throat and lifting her off the ground.

"Kibbsty, if you don't mind me asking, what's going on?" Cory said. His voice was passive and curious.

Lilly wheezed for breath, her fingers clawing to loosen Kibbsty's grip. When Cory mentioned the danger she was in, she didn't expect it to climax so soon. *I'm going to die,* she thought, kicking her dangling legs to reach the ground.

Kibbsty glared deeper into Lilly's eyes, his mouth curled and eyes slitting angrily. "This little... *Snake!* I'm going to kill her now. I took her blood work to the lab, and guess what happened? It was unworkable! I can't explain it, but somehow her DNA corrupted, deteriorated. You know what that means?" He took the knife, and slowly cut along her cheek bone. Lilly whimpered with pain. "She's of no use to me anymore."

Cory watched as Kibbsty sliced Lilly's cheek, and knew he would have to think fast if he wanted to stop the doctor from acting hastily. "Do you really think she's useless?" he ventured. Kibbsty glanced at him, but he showed no sign of dropping her.

"What good is she now? Without examining her DNA, I can't do anything! Her bone structure was useful, but with no way to reproduce it, what good is it?"

"She's the only living Third Strand, Kibbsty. You kill her, you'll lose any advances she could create. She's invaluable to your work. Think about it." Cory chose his words with caution, using all of his abilities to convince the man. Meanwhile, Lilly could only hang at his mercy. "You kill her, you destroy the link that could make your research succeed. You end up with a handful of angry teenagers, and beyond that, you lose a bargaining tool for Charity. She's more than an annoying brat: she's valuable. You really want to kill her?"

He watched Kibbsty's face curl in anger, his fingers tightening further. Lilly wept, weakly attempting to stop him. Then the fingers loosened before finally, he threw her to the ground. There she struggled for air, a hand massaging her throat. Cory was still watching when she jerked with surprise as Kibbsty hit her unguarded face. She crumpled, a scream of pain escaping, and she curled in fear at his feet. "Feel lucky, Miss Douglas. And feel very thankful you're still of use to me. Get her out of my sight before I change my mind," Kibbsty spat. The icy teen forced himself not to flinch as the doctor gave a final brutal kick, connecting with a resounding crack against Lilly's wings, and then he left her, growling across the lab. Cory waited a couple seconds, then grabbed Lilly under the stomach and carried her out.

Cory waited until he was sure it was safe, then gently set Lilly down. She was sobbing and her face was filled with pain and fear. Blood was mixed with the tears, and a horrible bruise was building from her chin to her cheekbone. He didn't even want to look at her wing. He had already felt the broken bones against his arm when he carried her. The teenage boy knew if he left her like this her wing would never heal properly. She might never fly again. His mouth curled to the left a little, then he knew what to do. He picked Lilly back up and continued down the hallway.

It didn't take long before Cory reached the common room, currently empty of students. There was a couch that he set Lilly on, then he turned toward the hall, tuning out her sniffling. "Stay there," he ordered as he left the room. It was probably unnecessary, but he wasn't taking chances today.

As Cory moved back toward the chemistry room, he kept his face cool and collected. When he walked in, he waited patiently for Ms. Knox to address him. "Cory? Do you need something?"

"Trish, please," Cory answered vacantly, and the teacher nodded. The green-haired girl rose and followed him out, mouth tight with suppressed curiosity. When the door closed behind them and they were walking down the hallway, however, she spoke.

"Where's the mouse?" she whispered. Cory didn't look at her, just nodded up ahead.

"We're going to her. I'll explain when we get there."

He entered the room where he'd left Lilly, and Trish's eyebrows went up. She whistled, "Someone was angry." Cory closed the door.

"Don't worry. This room's safe. Edward and Tray busted the camera brawling," he said, and Trish immediately went to Lilly's side. The feathered girl's eyes jerked open and she fearfully pulled away. Trish caringly reached out and touched Lilly's cheek.

"Hey, Hun. Looks like you bit off more than you could chew. I'm going to take a look at your wing, okay?" Lilly nodded her head and Trish moved to look closer. Cory could see her survey the damage, and she sighed.

"Frost, I can't have her screaming when I set her wing. You got something I can use to keep her quiet?" Trish asked, and Cory looked around, trying to think of something. Holding up a hand he snuck out of the room, and returned with a clean t-shirt. Trish caught it, then turned to Lilly. "Bite this," she instructed. Once Lilly was ready, Trish surveyed the damage. "On the count of three... One..." She took Lilly's wing in her hand and traced the break, until she knew what she was going to do. "Two." She snapped it into place. Lilly cried out, shocked by the early action, but it was muffled by the shirt she was digging her teeth into. Trish examined her work, and traced the bones again. "Again. On the count of three. One..." She set a hand on either side. Lilly braced herself. "Two..." She waited, and Lilly relaxed when the pain didn't come. Then, "Three!" Snap. Lilly curled up in agony, making indistinguishable noises of pain. Her eyes closed and streams of tears rolled down her black, bloody cheeks. Trish looked at the wing one more time, then turned to Cory.

"I set the broken segments, but that's about all I can do for her. Otherwise I put my neck on the line. I'll help you drag her back to her room, though. It will give us a reason why you needed my help. Grab an arm." The boy slipped forward and slung Lilly's left arm over his shoulder. Lilly whimpered in pain before her eyes rolled backward and her head sank forward. Cory grunted in annoyance as he shifted the dead weight.

"She's unconscious...."

They walked quickly, knowing to be gone too long would result in punishment. Ms. Knox was not the ideal teacher to face while tardy. As they walked up the stairs, Lilly's toes thumped the steps, but neither risked carrying her more gently. At least she was light and it didn't take much effort to move her.

Somewhere inside Cory's mind, he was almost concerned, but that was easily brushed aside. He couldn't get attached to this girl, or it would cost him and the others dearly. She was an outsider, and other than keeping her alive, he was responsible for nothing. As he helped Trish heave her onto the bed and as they raced back toward Chemistry, he wondered if he had risked too much by getting Trish's help. But he grunted, and his eyes grew icy solid. *Kibbsty will thank me later. Thanks to Trish, he'll actually have something to study.* As much as he told himself he did it for Kibbsty, part of him knew better.

Every time he thought of her face, so terrified, it gutted him. Those wide eyes, that soundless scream... He could almost feel icicles covering his knuckles. He knew the feeling in his heart wasn't normal for him. He was concerned, and that was a feeling he wasn't used to.

I better not get used to it, Cory thought angrily. He nodded to Ms. Knox as he took his seat, the feelings still fading. He had to be careful...and if things got too sticky, he needed to keep the resolve to do what was necessary. If she created a problem for him or the others, he would remove that threat.

As Cory resumed taking notes, he let his eyes glaze over and his heart harden, slowly emphasizing his decision in pen. They were still studying thallium, but he was thinking of something else. **Poison.** He wrote each word carefully, even with his sloppy script. **Murder.** *You can't hesitate, Cory. You know what to do if you start becoming too attached.* Slowly, he copied the last word, throwing all guilt away.

    Death.

CHAPTER SIX

BREAKING BARRIERS AND BONES

"Get up," snarled Cory's icy voice from some distant reality, and Lilly let her eyes sluggishly flicker open. Her vision swam and she whimpered, her body tender with numbed pain. She didn't even try to move, her body feverish, her mind foggy and dazed. Her eyes flickered closed again, and a rough hand shook her.

"What are you doing? Get up!" Cory cursed and grabbed her shirt front, wrenching her toward him. Lilly could barely manage a weak cry of pain, her vision filled with blurry images. She weakly tried to push his clenched fist off her T-shirt, and everything swam in front of her. Finally, she saw some sort of realization cross his face, and then he let her fall back into the pillows, snarling. "Great... I'm going to be late." The words got murky as she fell unconscious again.

"Kibbsty, you practically killed your experiment." Cory slouched into Kibbsty's lab, grumbling with annoyance. Lilly was burning with fever, and he knew she wouldn't make it long in the shape she was in. Her body couldn't handle everything it was dealing with right now. Once she caved in, it would be over for her. "She needs to have that collar off. You're killing her by suppressing her healing."

"Good riddance," huffed Kibbsty, not even looking up from his computer. "She's too much trouble anyway."

Cory didn't move. "Kibbsty, pardon me, but you're being an *idiot*." The man looked up, startled as Cory spoke, the room going icy. "She is the *only* Third Strand, and having her alive is a key to your research. You kill her, you will lose whatever breakthroughs she could bring. Don't be a child. Just because you hate her doesn't mean her death would be to your benefit."

Kibbsty's breath was starting to show as the room got colder. But his face shifted with surrender. "Sadly, you're right. I like you better when you don't sway to one side or the other with things. It's like Switzerland taking sides when you do." The man grumbled, but he was smiling. "Admittedly, it pleases me to see you so expressive. You would be a fearful person to cross. You've come a long way."

Cory huffed and turned to leave the room, disgusted. "Don't expect it of me. You're a genius, but you never realize the opportunities you have before they're gone. I'll take care of your stupid 'lab rat.' But next time I'll let her die, and you won't be so quick to play with chance."

Cory left the room, carrying a small collar in one hand and a slim silver card in the other. By the time he got back to Lilly's room, however, he feared he might already be too late. She was deathly pale, with sweat sticky on her brow and wings limp at her side. Her breath was raspy and pained, and had slowed to a weak gasp. Quickly, Cory slid a hand along her neck, stopping at the collar's edge and holding the tight restraint in his hand. Then he took the silver card and carefully ran it down the length of the creased edge. He listened closely as the teeth of the card matched up. One click, two more, and the last seven... Crack. The collar fell off and Lilly let out a weak gasp of relief.

"Hang on, Miss Priss. You need a new collar," Cory muttered, taking the light leather collar he now held. It looked like a dog collar, but laced with a thin metal strip, and a complicated lock.

Cory snapped it into place then reached out and brushed Lilly's hair out of her face.

"Cory..." whimpered Lilly weakly, and she trembled, wings giving a feeble flutter.

<Hang in there, Firecracker. It's going to be okay.> Cory's face stayed emotionless as he slowly pulled her ruffled covers back over her. Tucking her wings in and wrapping her in the cocoon of feathers and blankets, the silver-haired teen scooped her up and started carrying her to the nurse's room. Once there, he set her on the bed, and quickly went to work.

At Firestone, there was no nurse. The students could all use this room and take care of themselves, but they were at the mercy of their fellow students beyond that. In dire cases, the braver students could seek the help of Trish, the resident medical expert. Cory just hoped he could catch her before she left for class. Leaving Lilly in the medical ward, he rushed back toward the girls' dorms, slowing and composing himself just in time for two girls to round the corner. By some stroke of luck, he had crossed paths with Cherry and Trish. At least one of them he was grateful to see.

"Frost, what are you doing coming this way?" Trish asked, and Cory pointed a thumb over his shoulder.

"The mouse is sick... Really sick," he said icily, sounding annoyed. Trish didn't even hesitate in following him; they both knew what that meant. As annoying as Lilly was, her death would be a bad thing. Kibbsty would get over himself eventually, and his anger would fall on them all.

Cherry scurried back toward class, easily slipping into her own role. She would cover their backs with Ms. Knox, and hopefully they would be allowed to make up for the missed class.

Getting into the nurse's office, Cory closed the door behind them. It was one of the few surveillance-free rooms at the moment, no sound recorders or video feed. A power surge took out the old equipment, and Kibbsty hadn't bothered replacing it. The hallway outside recorded every person entering and leaving, however, so the doctor always knew when someone went in. But once inside, they could work freely, which was what they needed.

"Poor Mouse. She's burning something awful, Frost," Trish whispered, gently brushing Lilly's burning face with her hand. She quickly got up, wet a washcloth in the sink with water, and held it out to Cory. "Chill that, please." Cory barely looked up, but little ice crystals were soon crawling on the edge of the cloth. Trish retrieved it and put it on Lilly's face, above her brow and beneath her hair. The green-haired girl then touched Lilly's forehead, face twisted with concentration.

"Make an ice cube and come here," she instructed, pushing her bright hair behind her ear. "Okay, now melt it slowly into a mist over her face... You can do that, can't you?" Trish asked, and Cory gave a reluctant nod. While he typically reserved his powers for freezing, at times like this, he surrendered to breaking the norm. Meanwhile, Trish gathered a tray full of things from the cupboards and shelves before coming back and setting it on the table.

"You changed her collar. I'm assuming her healing is back on now?"

"Yeah. But she won't be able to heal this. Kibbsty tweaked that collar, remember?"

Trish nodded distantly. "I know, I know. But I'm thinking maybe I can fix that. We have the immune booster we designed In Chemistry awhile back, remember? Before we left for Charity?"

"Yeah, I do." Cory shrugged.

"Well, it may be able to jump start her healing, undo the collar's damage. If it works, it will be almost like a pacer for a patient with heart problems. It will guide her healing to the problems, and then hopefully she will be able to heal them."

Cory listened carefully, still misting Lilly while Trish filled the syringe and cleaned Lilly's arm. "Will she be strong enough, though?" Cory asked, flicking water from his hand. "She's not holding on by much, Trish. Healing herself could be beyond her abilities... I hate to tell you, but I think it's getting worse!" Cory said. Lilly's face wrinkled with the growing pain.

Trish cursed and grabbed a different needle. "I need a blood draw. She may have that warped DNA or something Kibbsty grumbled about, but I should be able to at least get an idea of how sick she is," Trish said, and Lilly murmured weakly. "Distract her," Trish instructed to Cory, and he slipped to the other side, gently tapping Lilly's shoulder.

"Hey, Firecracker, look at me," Cory said, feeling childish and stupid. But Lilly's eyes weakly opened and a tear rolled down her cheek.

"It hurts..." she whimpered, trying to pull her arm from Trish to her stomach. Trish hissed and held firm, glaring at Cory for help. Cory quickly pulled Lilly's left hand to him, and the other one stayed with Trish.

"Hey, don't do that. Trish is trying to help. What hurts?" Cory asked. To his surprise, her fingers twined around his in a painfully tight grasp.

"E-everything!" she sobbed, but kept her hands where they were. "Cory... It...It's like l-last t-time but w-worse... It hurts s-so much..." She was white and ashen, face drained of color, making her bruises contrast gruesomely.

"When last time, Lilly? What do you mean?" Cory questioned. Trish finished the blood draw, then started the immune booster.

"I'm a T-third Strand... I...I have t-too much power for my b-body to handle by itself... Without my healing, it b-breaks... I..." She was trying so hard to explain. Cory found himself squeezing her hand and nodding.

"Hey, it's okay. Your healing is back, and Trish is trying to help it fix you. Just hold on, okay? Fight like the Firecracker we know you are," Cory whispered, and brushed her sticky hair out of her face. Lilly nodded weakly and closed her eyes, breath becoming soft and labored. Even as she fought, he could see the life fading away from her frail face. He could feel that tug in his heart again, which made his hand jerk away from hers and become icy to the touch. *Don't get attached. She's nothing more than a guinea pig,* he told himself, and glanced up as Trish finished.

"I'll run tests on her blood later, but for now I think we've done all we can. From here it's up to her," Trish said, her face slowly hardening like his. Cory nodded, and looked at Lilly.

"Should we leave her like this or..."

Trish felt Lilly's face again. "Cover her with that blanket and chill the cloth one more time. We'll come back at lunch and when school's out. She'll have to hold on until then."

Cory nodded and did as she instructed, then they drifted toward the door. "You seem to have a lot of faith in her," he remarked as they left.

Trish paused and glanced back, then shrugged the comment away. "Not faith. Just hope. That's about all you can have in a place like this." Then the door clicked shut, leaving Lilly in silence.

Cory curled with pain as it raced through the pain sensors in his mind. Mercifully, the severity was minimal as Ms. Knox stopped the torture early and waved he and Trish back to their seats. The chemistry teacher was one of the few adults with powers, and hers were to inflict pain merely by wishing it. She could make it so unbearable, even the toughest students would scream in agony, but on days like today her good mood let them maintain some dignity. The mental torture didn't target anywhere specifically, it simply tricked the brain into reading signals of pain that weren't there. But it was easy to relieve the pain of bruises or cuts, it was harder to fight the tricks in your own mind.

As Cory took his pencil in a shaky hand, he tried to focus on taking notes, but his body was still recovering from his punishment. His notes from the previous day were still at the top of the page:

Element: Thallium
Primary Uses: Poison/Murder/ect. Ultimately results in **death**.

He remembered the resolve he had when he wrote that. A resolve that he would be willing to get rid of Lilly, should she prove to be too much trouble. Yet, he had caused Trish pain and trouble to save the girl. He was treading too close to a line he wouldn't cross. He'd have to keep his distance once she was well. Prove his loyalty to his peers, and to Kibbsty.

As his limbs gradually recovered, he continued taking notes on lead, but his mind was still distracted by questions. How could he stay strong when the girl was starting to spark so many memories? How could he stay neutral when he was starting to care? He turned a page in his notebook and stared at the blank page. His thoughts echoed the silence he found there.

"Frost, I'm not sure she'll make it. Her body is just so damaged, and I've done all I can. If she doesn't start healing soon, we might lose her," Trish sighed and pulled the blanket over Lilly, wrote on her clipboard, then shook her head. "I'm going to take one more look at the blood and tissue samples I have. Tell me if anything changes."

As Trish left, Cory slouched in his chair, frowning. Trish was always honest about the condition of those that came to the infirmary. While she did what she could, she was never afraid to tell someone they wouldn't make it. Lilly wouldn't be the first who had died despite Trish's efforts, but it didn't stop her from trying.

Trish had been at Firestone since it was founded. She joined because she wanted to be a nurse, and her mother insisted Dr. Kibbsty could help give her hands-on training. Trish never liked the idea, but she agreed to give it a chance. Once she was in, that choice became permanent, however, and like everyone else, she learned leaving wasn't an option. Trish didn't resist in the end. She was doing what she came to do; she was helping people. Almost every student owed their life to Trish, and that was more fulfilling than the freedom another school could offer.

Once, Cory had been battle training with Pilar when he got his hand cut on her fangs. Pilar's poison glands were active, and the adrenaline quickly spread the venom through him even as the bell rang and class ended. Cory could still remember the pain, the light headedness, and the sick, weak feeling. While he tried to wave it off as a scratch, he soon stumbled to the infirmary and passed out on the floor, where Trish found him. Her quick actions stopped the poison from spreading, and the vaccine she gave him likely saved his life. His stubbornness could have been fatal that day if she wasn't around. True, many students knew how to administer first aid themselves. They could treat broken bones, cracked knuckles, deep gashes, concussions, and sickness. Most would go to their rooms and help themselves to a first aid kit there, avoiding the infirmary if they could. With the lack of cameras, activity in the room was always questioned, and most didn't want to go through the trouble.

Cory looked at Lilly. She definitely needed to be here. Trish had moved her to one of the back rooms and had hooked her up to an I.V. to get fluids in her, along with the immune booster. She was still teetering on the edge of real danger, delusional and feverish. They had left her alone for the day, and when Trish and Cory finally managed to get back to her she was practically dead. Trish had managed to nurse her carefully back, but whether or not it would hold was another matter. Unless Lilly's healing kicked in, Cory would be able to say he'd witnessed the death of only functioning Third Strand.

Lilly moved in her sleep. Her mouth barely moved as she shivered, small fingers curling over the blanket during her feverishly murmuring. For the past hour, she'd been weakly stirring and trembling, occasionally whimpering in pain. Cory pitied her, but he was out of options. Short of ending her misery, he could only wait at this point.

"Frost! Frost, you gotta see this!" Cory looked startled for a moment, turning to see Trish standing in the doorway of the lab. Her face was filled with a wonder he'd never seen, so he quickly got up and went to her.

"What is it?" he asked.

"It's the sample I took! Cory, Kibbsty was wrong! Her DNA, the mutations, everything is there! I've never seen anything like it... Look!" Trish was breathlessly excited, and when she showed Cory what she meant, he let out a low whistle.

"I'm going to get Kibbsty. And whatever you do, don't let her die!"

"Why did it only show up now? Why not before?" After getting over the initial excitement, Kibbsty stood back while Trish worked.

"You suppressed her healing. I looked closely at her DNA, her tissue, everything. When her DNA is isolated from her healing, it literally breaks apart. Her body shuts down, starting from the smallest proteins, and disintegrating outward. Without her healing, her body just can't function. Look at any little part. Take her wings." Trish held up one of the x-rays and pointed to the bones. "Part of them is just normal bone, part is like a bird, and then there is hybrid muscle... Every part of her is intricately woven to create a perfect balance of what she is."

"We noted her muscular structure, and the unusually strong ligaments on her wings. It makes sense her healing is part of what made it possible though. I'm going to look over what you have in the main lab, and I'm leaving you and Icicle here in charge of keeping the girl alive. Once you've done your med stuff, send the samples and x-rays with Cory. I'm going to start a file on these new results. Good job, Trish. This may be the key I was waiting for. And don't worry, I'll see Ms. Knox excuses you both for what you've missed." With a nod, he swaggered off, and Cory let out an exhale, leaning against the wall.

"Trish, I love you! As long as that man is happy, we can breathe a little lighter. But please tell me the mouse is getting better. If she dies now..."

"I know. We'd all be screwed. But I think she's past the worst of it. Her powers are finally making progress, and her immune system seems strengthened by the immune booster. But we still have to cross our fingers and hope it's enough. If her body can't keep up with the healing it needs to do, she could start relapsing again." Trish took one last look at her notes, then moved back into the main room, where she sifted through another cupboard. "Get me the bottle over there, the blue one. Yeah. Thanks." She took the bottle, and with a handful of tools moved to Lilly's side. She set her supplies up on the bedside tray and readjusted her smock. Cory watched her work quietly, staying out of the way while she checked tubes and fluid levels. Then Trish finished writing on her clipboard, and nodded toward him.

"Good news. Her fever's going down. What she really needs now is fuel... Energy. I have her on nutrients in the I.V., but I think she gets energy other ways too. I'll have to study more." Trish looked thoughtful, then glanced at Cory before turning back to Lilly.

"What about sunlight? She's been stuck indoors for days with no light. Could that do anything for her? Like, vitamin D deficiency?" Cory was surprised at his own question. Trish looked intrigued.

"It could. I'd need to experiment a little. I've got a feather and a tissue sample from her wings, too, so I can try exposing them to sunlight and see how they react. A little sun couldn't hurt her regardless right now. If we move her by the windows and open the blinds we have a little time until sunset..."

Cory shrugged, and they both gave a 'why not?' sigh before moving Lilly to one of the window-side beds, where the sun's evening light gently traced her face, illuminating her silver-white wings. Trish paused from readjusting Lilly's IV, and her face softened slowly.

"Look at her, Frost. She really doesn't belong in a place like this... Even with her all beaten up like that, she still looks so innocent." Trish sighed, folded the dirty sheets from the other bed and laid them across her arm. "It breaks my heart a little. I know, we aren't supposed to get attached to 'er. She's not 'one of us,' and all that. But every time I look at her, I find myself wishing anyone was here but her. She doesn't deserve this," Trish dared whisper. Cory moved to her side, knowing how strongly she must feel to voice her feelings. He had to admit, seeing Lilly in the sunlight with her pale face tilted toward the light and slender hands gently curled across the sheet, she looked like a young child sleeping deeply after a nightmare. Her long eyelashes left thin shadows on her face, contrasting the dark bruises that covered her. The blankets barely moved with the soft rise and fall of her chest, and her mouth was parted ever so slightly in a thin 'O.' Cory wished he could take that pained look from her, give her smile back. All of her life seemed drained, and now she was just a shell gently covered in sunshine. She was a porcelain doll who was broken, almost repaired.

"It sucks that her life is in the hands of people like us," Cory spoke softly. They sat on the bed next to Lilly's and Trish sighed, nodding her head.

"She was so happy at Charity. Even with us there, trying to draw her out. She always tried to keep her chin up and take everything in stride. I feel like there is no way the girl we have is the same one. She's barely hanging on, and *we did that*." A sort of weariness crossed Trish's face, a motherly sorrow that created shadows around her cheeks, her eyes. Cory found himself moving closer and awkwardly staring at his hands.

"We're doing what we can now, Trish. We gotta keep watchin' our own backs... Yeah, maybe it's sad an' all that, but remember why we're here. If we get too attached an' then we screw up, we'll take the blows. All of us. It's the way we have to go. Lilly's not one of us. We don't watch her back, she won't watch ours. At the first chance she gets, she's outta here, and we can't mess up our own lives making hers a little more bearable. It's gonna be rough on her, yeah, but what choice do we have?"

Trish nodded and sighed, startling Cory as she laid her head on his shoulder and closed her eyes. "I guess you're right, Cory, but I wish you weren't." Cory looked at her, a little uncomfortable, but then he relaxed, moving so his arm was around her in an awkward hug.

"I know it sucks, but don't get too attached. We need you here, and you can't let yourself do anything to jeopardize that." The normal bite to his words faded, and his voice softened. For a moment, he seemed to melt, stiff posture relaxing. Trish sighed, shifting closer against him.

"Yeah, I know. I won't. But I still feel bad. I know I'll feel even worse when she recovers an' we have to treat her like trash again. She will never be able to understand that we're really looking out for her. I hate this, Frost. I can't explain how much I do. Being the 'villain.' The antagonist. Sneering in her face, kickin' her when she's down." Trish gave a bitter snarl. "Every time I play this blasted game of survival, I wish it was Kibbsty I was kicking. Or the Gemini twins, or someone who actually deserved it! But... Gosh, Frost. How much longer can we justify helping trap others into the same fate we have?"

Cory felt his arm tightening and hissed. Trish shivered as his cold breath brushed her neck. "We won't wait much longer, Trish. Our time will come. *L.A.T.E.R.*"

"Live, appease, train, endure, remember," Trish recited.

"Focus on that last one: remember. You need to remember why we're here. We aren't evil. We aren't Kibbsty, we don't do this because we want to. We only appease him while we train, prepare, and wait for the moment when we can get out."

"Or die trying," Trish sighed. Cory nodded softly.

Lilly stirred, and Trish reluctantly rose, slipping out from under Cory's arm. She laid her hand palm up on Lilly's forehead, waited a minute, and then sighed. "Fever's almost gone. It won't be long now, and she's not our problem anymore." The tone was bitter, almost sad. Cory got up, and they walked slowly away. The sun was going down in the window behind them, and Trish paused, looking up at Cory. "You don't think I'm evil... Do you?" Trish whispered, looking sorrowfully into his face. "You know the person I am out there is not the person I want to be?"

Cory reached out and pushed her swish of hair out of her face, hand pausing on her cheek. But his face was serious, stoic. "But what if the person *I* am out there is all I'll ever be? You have character, Trish. You care and feel and get angry and smile. But what if I never get back who I was? When all this is over, where will my place be in the world? What will I become?"

Trish brought her hand up and took his, twining her fingers around his. They were warm compared to Cory's, just like the rest of her. Trish was fighting, still kicking and struggling to maintain her soul. But Cory was cold, solid, and empty. He truly wondered if this life would ever end. Trish squeezed his hand, stilling the rest of his thoughts. "You'll always be welcome in my part of the world. Even if this is who you are. You're still Cory."

"Cory the tin-man, ice cube without a heart," Cory muttered.

But Trish smiled and gave him a hug, pulling herself tight against his rigid frame. "Then you can have a piece of mine."

She left Cory standing there as she pulled away, hung up her smock, and left the room. He could hear a door open in the distance, and close, but he didn't move. He stood, hands dangling limply at his side, and when he finally moved he could still feel the warmth she had left. But the questions still lingered.

Would he ever get back what he had lost? And if not, could he ever let someone care about him when he had nothing to give back?

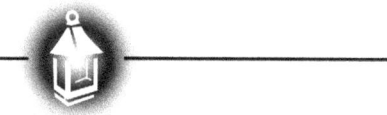

A sky of starry nightlights glimmered over Firestone, but no one admired them. The one child within their midst who would notice their beauty was sleeping, gently resting in the hospital wing bed. The dark bruises that had covered her face had faded, as well as her scratches, and only dried blood remained. Her healing had finally finished its work, so now she was simply exhausted.

The light from the stars shone dimly through the window, and Lilly stirred, eyes fluttering open. The dark, empty room was all that welcomed her. She sat up slowly and looked around in confusion, eyes growing wider. *Where was she?*

"Cory?" whispered Lilly, and she slowly pushed the sheets back to the foot of the bed. A cold chill met her feet as she swung her legs over, gently touching the cold floor. She stood shivering as she pulled her arms close, barefoot in dirty blue jeans and a T-shirt. Something tugged on her wrist and she looked down, startled to see the I.V. in her arm. She quickly removed it, and rubbing her wrist, she crept through the hospital wing. When she made it to the main nurse's office the open door welcomed her.

Stepping into the hallway, Lilly looked fearfully around, trying to make sense of where she was. She had barely taken five steps when a voice spoke behind her, "*Hola!*"

Lilly screamed and spun around, coming face-to-face with a person-shaped pillar of fire. Needless to say, she yelled again, and fell flat on her butt.

"Wahaha! *Soy Fuego*! Envy Fuego's spontaneous combustion, oh you of inferior powers!" crackled a laughing voice from with the ball of fire.

Lilly squeaked, staring up at it. "F-Fuego?"

"Yes! Fuego is the wondrous being before you! Fear Fuego!" the voice roared, and the flames jumped higher. Lilly shrank away in bewilderment. She was convinced she was still dreaming, the fever making a comeback on her recovering mind. When the flames licked closer, they felt too real and she back-pedaled into the wall. Suddenly, the fire yelped. "Ow!" The flames vanished, and a teenage boy remained, frantically patting his scorched pant leg. As the smoke thinned, he looked up sheepishly and then tried to look dignified. "Fuego forgot the non-flesh-burning part of his combustion. Second time this night," he murmured.

Lilly slowly got to her feet, still gawking at the boy before her. Her hazy mind was scrambling to keep up with his actions. He was probably only 5'6", with a spiky mullet of red hair that stuck up in the front and curled against his neck in the back. His face was covered with freckles, his eyes a hazel brown with tints of yellow-green fading from the edges. He looked young compared to some of the students here, and his face had that teenage look, still transitioning inconsistently toward adulthood. His eyes laughed with mischief, even as he inspected his charred clothing "Fuego has heard of you... Lilly, is it?" He moved closer, and studied her more carefully.

Lilly nodded and pulled her wings close. "Y-yes... That's me," she squeaked.

Fuego grinned. "*Mi amor,* she calls you *Liróna.* Dormouse, Fuego thinks is the English word? *Si...* You do look like a mouse. All skittish, like a cat is going to come out and eat you. *Fuego es no gato, pero,* Fuego does know of some cats out there who would love to eat you," the boy laughed, and grinned, then flinched slightly as he put a hand to his side. "Fuego should not laugh so much. You have distracted Fuego. Burn ointment, hospital wing:

this was Fuego's goal. Combustion near the Gemini, Fuego does not recommend."

Before he could move into the infirmary, a familiar icy voice echoed down the hallway.

"Dang it, Fuego, I'll kill you! You're like a stinkin' poltergeist, yellin' and hollerin' at every hour," Cory came snarling into view, and Lilly blushed in surprise at his half-dressed appearance. The blond teen's skin had faded scars that littered his torso, and Lilly forced herself not to stare.

Fuego growled and stuck out his tongue, a little puff of fire sputtering from his mouth. "Fuego has no fear of you!" Cory glared, and Fuego hesitated. "Well, maybe a little fear. But that will not stop Fuego!"

Cory's glare deepened, and Lilly felt a burst of icy air. Fuego yelped and jumped away like he'd been stung. His hand returned to his injured side, and he slowly circled toward the infirmary, eyes never leaving the icy teen. "Fuego will now leave in defeat. But next time, Ice Boy, Fuego may not be so surrendering!" He shook a flaming fist at Cory, then slouched off into the darkness. Lilly shivered as Cory's glare latched on her, and was horrified when his face curled with a sneer.

"Looks like Fuego's not the only one where they shouldn't be. Miss Priss is looking better."

It was a dream. It was all a dream. The fire boy and Cory's anger were just nightmares she was facing, figments of her imagination. "M-my healing f-finally came back," she stuttered. She realized she had said the wrong thing only seconds before his fist hit her face, resounding against her cheek with a sharp crack. Lilly shrieked in pain as she slammed into the floor, stunned and disoriented. Cory's foot came down hard on her back and flattened her into the floor.

She writhed for a few moments before his mouth hissed next to her ear. "That was for making me late in Chemistry," he snarled, and a cold so strong it was painful surrounded her, before a long, pointed icicle jabbed at her like a dagger. "And this is for wasting our time taking care of your sorry butt for the past two days!" Lilly could only thrash in pain as he drove it like a stake through her left wing. Then he shoved her away with his bare foot, leaving her whimpering and bleeding, the icy chill in her lungs the only thing preventing her from screaming in torment. She stared up at him, and saw no remorse on his face, not a single sign he regretted what he did. The scars she had seen moments before reminded her where she was, and what monsters this school created.

"Get used to this, Princess. Now that you're able to heal, I'm sure this is only the beginning. Later, loser." Cory laughed and started walking away, disappearing into the darkness and leaving Lilly bleeding on the floor. She struggled for breath, crawling weakly from the middle of the hall, then huddling against the wall. Her tears finally broke into sobs of anguish, as she touched her bloody wings and her bruised cheek, too sorrowful to heal. She didn't want to get better anymore. Part of her wished she had died and this torment could be over. She was about to lose all faith, when she heard a female voice whisper in the dark.

"This school isn't the place to show weakness like that."

Lilly tried to look up but her muscles wouldn't allow it. She let her head fall back down and closed her eyes, hugging her knees to her chest.

"You just going to give up, *Liróna*? Let the ice boy make you cry? *Por que*?" spoke the girl again. The voice was curious rather than comforting.

Lilly sniffled, "I'm not s-strong enough to handle this! My life has become this... This hell!" Lilly's lungs finally ripped the air they needed free, and her ribs twanged with pain. It just made her weep more. "I can't take any more of this! I want to just die here... Just let me die..." Lilly wailed, sobs shaking her entire body.

The voice softly sighed. "You aren't as strong as everyone said. They said you were a fighter. That you could take a beating and keep fire in your eyes, a burning passion in your voice. *Pero*, you sit here, wishing for *muerte*? Death? You don't seem so strong to me." The voice held a challenging bite to it, the curious tone sounding bored now.

Lilly growled, wings shaking at the insult. "You don't know who or what I am! I've fought, as long and hard as I can! But look at me! I'm gah—" Lilly's voice cut off as her jaw twanged, and each word was more painful than the last. At the moment, her anger was stronger than her pain. "I wasn't built to go through this type of torture," she defended.

"Neither were we." Lilly looked up as the girl walked into her line of sight. She moved like a viper, the Latin ring in her accent matching her appearance. "We weren't always the way we are! But you know how you learn to withstand fire? You get burnt," she snapped at Lilly, pointing a long, painted nail at the girl's nose. "No one wants pain, or darkness. No one wants a life of suffering, and all dis... *Como se dice*? Crap! But you learn to take whatever you're given and endure it, if it means that you will live. You learn to strengthen your mind, your body... Death is no satisfaction when you give up!"

"But why fight? So I can just heal and get the crap kicked out of me again and again?!"

"No, because that's how you become *fuerte*! Strong! This pain, *es* like poison in your blood. It can make you scream, and cry, and beg for mercy. But you, only *you* can decide how it affects you. You can give up, or you can drink it and use it to build up immunity. Now tell me: are you a coward? Do you really want to give up? *Hable*!"

"No!" Lilly yelled, and she jerked to her feet, throwing her right wing open at the girl. Effortlessly the girl moved to the side, and her voice hissed close to Lilly's ear.

"Good, now you are fighting. But you can do more. Again!"

Lilly threw her fist out, then the other one, helplessly trying to connect with the girl, who was quickly dodging out of the way. She laughed, eyes dancing, then caught both of Lilly's wrists and held them together.

"There's the *chica* I heard about, who gave Kibbsty so much trouble. There's the fighter. Now tell me! Do you still want to die? Because I can still make that happen." As the teen grinned, two very sharp fangs were revealed where her canine teeth belonged. Lilly glared bravely into the girl's face and growled.

"Never."

"*Que*?!"

"NEVER!"

"So heal yourself, and quit dirtying the halls with your pitiful blood. Tomorrow, you go to class like the rest of us, you keep your head high, and when life kicks your butt, don't cry and sell your sob story. How do you learn to endure the fire?" she hissed.

"You get burnt," Lilly answered. She pulled away, focusing on healing, and something amazing happened. Instead of the peace she normally felt when she healed, she was filled with fire this time; it raced through her wings, her heart, her body. It was strong and powerful, bursting with emotions and determination. It was a lake of fire, an avalanche, a rolling ocean crashing onto the beach. As it faded away, she blinked at the girl and struggled to process her thoughts.

"That's better. Get out of here, *Liróna*. You have class tomorrow, and I have a boyfriend to tend to," she laughed, and turned and started toward the infirmary, a long ripple of hair all the way down her back. Lilly jumped forward before she entered, and called out.

"Wait!"

The girl paused, and Lilly dared ask, "What's your name?"

She turned ever so slightly, and grinned wryly. "Pilar."

Then she disappeared through the doorway, and Lilly rolled the name over before going down the hallway in the direction she could only hope lead to the girls' dorms.

Lilly managed to find her room, although it was mostly by accident. She walked until she found the main laboratory, then retraced her steps until she reached the right hall. Once she was there, she knew she was right by the down feathers scattered in the ruffled sheets. A clock on the nightstand glowed red, revealing the time, 1:37 AM. Seeing that made Lilly realize her exhaustion, and she slumped into the bed, curled up tight, and fell into a sweet slumber with dreams of flying in the skies over Charity. The morning didn't grant her such a peaceful awakening.

A knock pounded on Lilly's door at an hour that felt unearthly to Lilly's tired body. She scrambled out of bed, still half asleep, only to have a handful of items thrown into her arms. As she struggled to keep hold of a pair of jeans, a hairbrush clattered to the floor. Cherry grunted and turned to leave. "I'd hurry if I were you," the girl said. "You've got about seven minutes to get to Chemistry before you're late."

Lilly quickly dumped the stuff on her bed, feeling light-headed and a little unbalanced. She quickly pulled off her clothes, then changed into the outfit she'd been given. The pants were baggy and black, with cargo pockets and other little pouches she wasn't sure were entirely necessary. They weren't her style, but they fit snugly at her waist, and she could get used to their droopy length. The T-shirt she was given was simple, with slits in the sleeves for design, and two crudely cut holes in the back for her wings. She paused before pulling it on, looking in the mirror at her undershirt, which was stained with her own blood and filth. She cringed automatically, then headed toward the small bathroom, making a note to get new undergarments and other clothes if she got the chance.

After several minutes of painful failure brushing her hair and hastily brushing her teeth, Lilly glanced at the clock and panicked at the time. Barefoot, she scrambled to class, reaching the threshold as the bell rang overhead. In a spotlight of guilt she froze as Ms. Knox turned to glare at her.

"Miss Douglas, so nice of you to join us. You are late."

"I'm sorry... I ... I..."

By the way the class had hushed, Lilly knew something bad was going to happen. Ms. Knox gave a wicked smile. "I'm sure you've heard I do not tolerate tardiness. Tell me, Miss Douglas, did you know I have powers?"

"N-no, I didn't, Ms. Knox," trembled Lilly. The rest of the class was watching with relish. Lilly took an automatic step backward in dread.

"Well, I do. It helps me teach my students to respect my authority. If it happens again, I *will* make an example out of you."

Lilly was half ready to turn and run when Ms. Knox's eyes sharpened on her, but she was waved to her seat instead.

"I expect you to be on time tomorrow."

Disappointment moved across the other student's features, but that didn't stop Lilly from feeling relieved. She tuned out their muttering of irritation until Ms. Knox held up her hand, and the room grew silent.

"Today we are having a lab to see how well you paid attention these past few days. In front of the room there are five different glasses. Each has one of the five elements you most recently learned about, mixed in a glass of water. Based on your knowledge of each element, you must identify which glass contains which element. Be warned, choosing incorrectly would be unwise." Lilly's body gave a small tremble, imagining what might make it 'unwise.' Ms. Knox continued, "Up front, there are resources to assist you. You have ten minutes. I suggest you work quickly and carefully."

Chairs scraped the floor as the students stood and made their way to the front of the class. Trish and Mar were the first to get there, looking closely at everything. Lilly was last, and wistfully wondered if she would have to do anything after all. But then Ms. Knox spoke up.

"By the way, if any of you decide to slack off, it will impact the group's grade." The class let out a groan, and Lilly felt more than one person turn to glare her way. Then they went to work.

"Frost, how about you work your magic on the water first? If we get rid of the water, we can get a better look at the elements," Cherry suggested, and Cory nodded, looking attentively at the glasses.

"One superheated glass coming up..." Cory held his hand over the liquid. Within seconds, the water started boiling and steam rose, the precipitation gathering and then freezing in Cory's hand. All that remained was dull looking metal in the bottom of the glass.

"Looks like lead," Trish said as she looked at the supplies on the table. "There's a battery. You can test its conductivity."

"I'll do it," Cherry offered. "Start on the other ones. We should be able to identify them more easily with the water gone. Frost, can you do that to the rest?"

Cory went from glass to glass removing the water, leaving four more glasses with different amounts of metals at the bottom.

"That one's mercury. It's the only liquid," Mar said, pointing. "I think this one next to it is thallium, but the sample is too small to tell."

Thall looked at it closely, then carefully reached in and touched it. "It's Thallium. I'd know my element anywhere."

"This one is lead," Cherry and Xzin confirmed. "So one of these should be gold and the other platinum."

"You can tell by the colors," Mar rolled her eyes.

"Yeah, but we need to make sure everyone participates," grumbled Cory. The main group shot another glare at Lilly.

Thall practically threw one of the beakers into Lilly's hands. "Fill that back up with water."

"Why?" Lilly squeaked unwillingly.

Thall growled, "To do something." Lilly moved to take it, when she heard Ms. Knox snap in her ear.

"Miss Douglas, tell me, how have you been contributing to this experiment?"

Lilly slowly turned, her heart thundering. "I was going to put water in this and m-make sure it didn't float to prove its gold?" she stuttered, desperately thinking of any excuse.

Ms. Knox didn't look satisfied. "I think you already proved that. You have all decided which is which. I, however, am asking what you *did,* not what you are *doing.* So what did you do?"

Lilly could barely make eye contact as she answered. "Nothing."

"How very unfortunate for you," Ms. Knox said without pity. Lilly quivered, gripping the glass she was holding more tightly. Once more, the students had hushed behind her. She vaguely wondered if she'd have to grow used to these signs of trouble. Ms. Knox was still staring at her. "Tell me, did the last punishment you received have no effect on you?"

"No, Ms. Knox. It did. I should have done more to participate." Lilly forced herself to look Ms. Knox in the eyes, even though her nerves were dancing. She was waiting for the pain to come again, but to her awe, it didn't.

"Smart move, Miss Douglas. Had you made an excuse, you would have been in trouble, but I appreciate students who own up to their mistakes. You will come in after school and clean the storage room on the second story, from top to bottom. Five thirty sharp. Don't be late." With one final glare at Lilly, she turned and sighed at Thall. "I appreciate how well you can identify your own element, Thallium, but next time, it will not be so easy for you. You and your sister need to show this much enthusiasm for the rest of my class." She turned and glared at Xzin. "And you, Xzin... If your laziness continues, you will wish you had stayed in China." She continued, giving a nod to Cory and Trish, didn't say anything to Cherry, then glanced at the clock. "We are going to start another lab now, and this time, I want to see some true effort from you."

The rest of the hour progressed at a fast pace. Ms. Knox had them scrambling all over the chemistry room gathering supplies for the first ten minutes, and Lilly had to race up the spiraling metal stairs more than one time to grab things from the storage room. She had to admit, the chemistry room was a unique and functional room. It was two stories, with the classroom on the first floor and a high, open ceiling above it. The chalkboard was enormous, and the windows spanned both stories, letting in the murky light from outside. In the back of the room were stairs that wound in a tight corkscrew up to a landing with a silver railing surrounding it, and the storage room was immediately through an open doorway, but only accessible from inside the chemistry room. It seemed ingenious to Lilly. The only way someone could get into the storage area was through the chemistry room, and Ms. Knox could easily guard her supplies. While beakers and test tubes weren't exactly appealing, Lilly could only imagine what some of the students could do with a few volatile chemicals in their hands. Although, when Lilly thought about it, someone would have to be crazy to try to steal from Ms. Knox. That would be suicide.

Lilly learned quickly that many things would be suicide with Ms. Knox, mostly through signals she got from other students. There was a fear to mess up, a timidity that traced through these normally strong students. Grades seemed to hold more impact than a scale of how they were doing, yet it was too soon to make sense of that system. All she could do was learn from was the series of mistakes and consequences Ms. Knox implemented.

During class, Lilly only encountered one more example of this system. Xzin accidentally mixed the wrong solutions together, and the result was a vial of hissing bubbles and steam that boiled onto the table where it sputtered and spat. Mar disappeared in a blur, returning milliseconds later with a cloth, students frantically helped to erase the mess. But it had been moments too long as the teacher's glare sharpened on Xzin. Then they were all looking away with pity as Xzin dropped to his knees, hands clenched into white fists, trying to hold in the pain. Lilly felt bad for him, and by the way the others respectfully looked away, she knew the feeling was mutual.

"Now, unless all of you want to be next, I suggest you finish cleaning this up, then gather your things." Lilly quickly looked for something to do, and Trish shoved an armful of bottles into her hands.

"Put these away," she said, and Lilly staggered under the weight, wings fluttering for balance. She managed to catch her footing, then made her way up the stairs to put them in the storage room.

At the landing, she shifted all the containers to her side, and used her wing to support the weight while she opened the door. Inside it was dark, with tall shelves along the walls; one supported containers full of elements arranged by their atomic numbers, and another held containers of compounds and other supplies. Thankfully, all five of the elements used by the class that day were grouped together, so those were easy to put away, but it was still a challenge to get the other jars in their places, as they contained everything from sodium to copper. Lilly sighed to herself as she shelved them, making the most of the time alone. Then she heard a creaking noise followed by a click, and the room went dark.

Lilly whirled, eyes blindly searching for the exit as fear jolted through her heart. The door had closed. *She was stuck in here.* She clutched the shelf to her right, trying to stay calm as she felt her way through the darkness. Baby steps, she could do this. Just a little set-back. Her heart leapt as she saw a sliver of light and knew she was in the right spot, but when she wiggled the handle it held firm. Her heart sank. It was locked.

Lilly jiggled the knob and pounded on the door, the fear building inside her. It was drowned out as a bell went off, and she yelled out in panic, "Hey! Let me out!" She yanked and tugged, but it held firm, and she swore she heard laughter before a distant door clicked shut. Lilly wanted to scream and pound louder but she held back, worried Ms. Knox would be angry if she made a scene. Instead, she kept knocking until she sank to the floor, pulling her legs close. As the light vanished completely, the tears started to fall.

Lilly felt pathetic sitting and crying in the storage room, letting this cruel joke get to her. But she was alone in the dark, and she didn't know any way to get out. She angrily slammed her fist into the door, the pain doing nothing for her. It certainly wasn't going to get her out, she knew that. She was still so frustrated. There was no peace in this place. All she wanted was to be out of here, to be free, to live without this constant fight for survival. That wasn't the life she had been given, though. She remembered Pilar's words in the hall the night before, distant and foggy. They traveled to the top of her mind as she sat there, and focused on that instead. *How do you withstand the fire?* the sharp voice had asked. Lilly sighed through her tears, then shuddered. *You get burnt.* She was certainly getting burnt right now. Would it really help her withstand what was to come? Why did she have to learn to withstand it? It was all so confusing... One thing was clear: she had to tough it out, whether she wanted to or not.

Getting a grip, Lilly wiped her face dry and shakily got to her feet. She closed her eyes and focused, holding the handle so she wouldn't lose her sense of direction. There had to be some way to get out, she just had to focus. Minutes passed, then hours, as Lilly wandered and felt her way around. She found tools and knives, tried to pick the lock and tried to wedge the door open. It felt helpless at first, but eventually one of the tools wedged far enough in the doorframe, and Lilly stumbled to glorious freedom.

"I was wondering how long it would take you to get out of there," came a voice from the base of the stairwell. Lilly jumped, and flinched as a light switched on. Through the stars, she could make out Ms. Knox.

"Y-you knew I was in there? And you left me there?"

Ms. Knox smirked wickedly. "You do not think I am stupid, do you dear? I have my eyes on every student in this room. This is not the first time Mar thought it would be funny to lock someone in the storage room. She thinks it is humorous to use her speed to torment others, but I must say, I am surprised you managed to get free. I was sure I would find you in there a couple hours later crying your eyes out on the floor. You do not give up, do you, Miss Douglas?"

Lilly felt a strange sort of pride rise within her, and looked boldly into the teacher's eyes. "No, Ms. Knox. I don't give up."

The strange teacher gave a rare smile that looked like a snarl on her dark face, and she nodded out the door. "Then off with you. Your next class is down the hall, room 17. It is Ms. Nakata's class, Double Agents. You are lucky. If it were my class, I would have you on your knees for being this late." There was an odd humor in her voice that Lilly was starting to recognize, and she considered it while she hurried to her next class. As evil and horrible as Lilly thought everyone was at first, as time passed she started to see patterns in their behavior. They were complex characters with different personalities, emotions, pasts. They weren't repetitive in their behaviors, and they grew and changed with time. This school, it breathed, despite how cold and solid it pretended to be. There was life to these people, one that was hard admitting.

It had been so much simpler when they all just stayed in the molds she placed them in. It was easy when Lilly could hate Tray and Cory and cower from Ms. Knox, but the more time that passed, the more she was confused about the people she encountered. With each moment here, Lilly was realizing that this was not very different from Charity, and that was perhaps the most frightening thing she could think of.

CHAPTER SEVEN

GIVE ME YOUR BEST SHOT

"*Duck*, Miss Douglas! I've never seen such a pathetic display of dodging in my life. If you don't learn from the bruises, you'll have to learn from broken bones. Is her nose bleeding, Mr. Trask?"

Cory glanced at Lilly, who was writhing on the floor holding her nose while Trish stood above her, rolling her eyes. He saw a trickle of red starting to seep between her fingers and nodded at the man standing to his left. "Yeah, looks like a good one, too. You've been practicing, haven't you, Trish?"

The green-haired girl flashed a quick grin before taking the time to adjust the wraps on her arms. The teacher shifted beside Cory, and the ice-powered teen saw a disapproving frown. Cory could have sworn the man knew Trish was goofing off, but the thick bandage covering the teacher's eyes reminded him otherwise.

Demetry Lyubov was a strange teacher; he was skilled, but also blind. Rumor was that his sight had been missing since he was a child, and that he had adapted around it. With layered silver hair, white and thin like a wig, he moved like a ghost, using his other senses. Compared to his students, his actions were liquid, flawlessly avoiding any attack. The only thing that showed Mr. Lyubov's lack of sight was the bandage that hid his eyes from view. It often took students off guard when he would turn to look at them, without actually *seeing* them.

Lilly seemed particularly skittish of the man, and rarely looked him in the face. As class progressed, it seemed she sensed the deadly nature behind his persona. Even while being beat up by Trish, her fear was reserved for their professor. Trish was striking the blows, but Mr. Lyubov was calling the shots.

"Get up, heal your nose, and suck it up. Trish, tell me, what went wrong on Miss Douglas's part?" the professor inquired, calmly tilting his head.

Trish shrugged. "She didn't block."

"Precisely. Why not, Miss Douglas?"

Lilly was shaky as she got to her feet, blood still on her hands and face. Tear stains hugged her cheeks, but she was maintaining a stiff upper lip. "I didn't react fast enough." Her wings quaked as she stood, her fear bringing a mixture of irritation and pity to Cory's heart.

The teacher waved Trish aside and stepped onto the floor next to the timid girl. He stopped in front of her and loosely gripped the long staff in his hand. Cory watched Lilly's eyes hesitantly glance at the staff, fear showing on her face. She was right to be worried. Mr. Lyubov was dangerous with the wooden rod, and if he was going to teach Lilly to dodge the way he taught all of them, she was not going to enjoy it.

The blind teacher circled slowly, face unreadable and obscured by the bandages. Meanwhile, the class stood back and watched as the fighter approached his student.

"Miss Douglas, tell me: do you always fight standing stiffly like that? Do you realize how vulnerable your stance is? No wonder Miss Carter made such quick work of you."

Lilly stared at Mr. Lyubov, unnerved by his covered eyes. Everything she did, he commented on, and if she hadn't known better, she would have guessed he was only 'blind' like Jake was. But it was more than that. It didn't matter which direction he faced, or how he was turned. He knew everything that was happening by listening. Lilly wasn't a fighter. She didn't know how to think of stances or defense. As she shifted, she felt forced to try something. Mr. Lyubov gave an annoyed sigh and frowned at her attempts.

"You're too tense. Loosen your stance and move your arms out a little. Unclench your mouth and stop bracing yourself for a blow. The point is to defend yourself against it and eventually learn to counter it. Now, when someone attacks you, you *move!*"

Lilly let out a yelp of shock as the staff cracked, and her torso folded over it, air rushing out of her lungs. She was still reeling when it recoiled backward; the teacher effortlessly slammed it into her back. Lilly crumpled to the ground, gasping for air while stars scattered across her vision.

"You wait too long and react too late. Get up."

Lilly pushed herself back to her feet, shaking and wheezing as she held her ribs. The blind teacher shifted casually, listening to her movements.

"Again."

Lilly tried to jump backward this time, but her right leg twisted, sending her crashing down as the staff connected sharply with her head. The pain was jarring, but she focused on healing quickly to prevent further blood loss today. She nimbly rolled out of the way as Mr. Lyubov hammered the staff back toward her, escaping by a wingtip.

"Better, although you use your healing as a crutch and rely too much on it. You still haven't learned to *block*. All you do is run and hide, hoping if you run you'll get away unscathed. You won't always be able to run, Miss Douglas." His tone darkened, and Lilly was glad for the bandages that blocked his disapproving expression. The staff came back to rest at his side, and his back turned. Her pulse started racing.

"I think it's time we gave Edward a chance against you. Then maybe you'll learn to move faster and run less."

The students' attitudes changed visibly and there was a certain eagerness in their expressions. Something bad was about to happen, and there was nothing Lilly could do to prevent it. From the circle, a figure stepped forward, and Lilly found herself facing her new opponent.

Edward had black hair with electric yellow tips. It was pushed together in the middle of his head in a Mohawk, ending in a braid down his neck. His eyes were blue with dark eyelashes, and he had a chiseled, clean-shaven face. Along both of his arms there were gauntlets laced up with black cord, matching yellow stripes running down the sides, and small lightning bolts at the back of the wrists. The lacing was on the underside of his arms, and small holes with silver ringlets decorated the tops. Like Mr. Lyubov, he circled her once before choosing a starting position. Lilly couldn't return his stare: the smoky eyes revealed much more than she wanted to know.

"Don't go easy on her. Make our new student learn to dodge properly."

As Edward lifted his right arm, the tension from the other students made sense. Lilly had expected a punch, or maybe some jolt of lightning, but instead, she discovered why there were holes in the back of the gauntlets. The kid was a *porcupine*. Needle-like spikes flashed to the surface of his skin, then the lethal array was thrust at her face. Lilly ducked just in time and stumbled, barely escaping the spiny forearm. Before she could regain her balance and stand, she felt a sharp pain stab through her wing.

"You got her, Edward! Remember, don't always hit with the back of your arms, use your fists as well." Lilly was struggling not to scream, her wing pinned to the floor by her flight feathers, and she thrashed her free wing backward, bashing it into his face.

"Don't lose your footing, Edward! Free up your arm and stop crouching. You're vulnerable like that."

From the corner of Lilly's panicked eyes, she could see Edward take a step back. She tried to move away, but the spikes he'd pinned her with kept her on the ground. She tugged, helplessly trying to free herself, but the spines were too numerous for her slick feathers to pull free.

"Miss Douglas, stop pulling and find a smarter way to free yourself. Get your feet under you and stage a defense if you can. Don't let Edward keep landing those blows!" The shift in assistance confused Lilly. It was hard to trust someone who was also helping your enemy. She hesitated momentarily as she considered the remarks before jumping to action. Feet tucked under her, she scooted and bent her wing in, moving so she could pull at the spines with her hands. Edward kept moving, watching for an opening.

"Use her blind spots Edward. You want to think out your actions, but don't wait too long, or she'll get herself free." Blind spots? Lilly tried to follow him, but her wings got in the way. Nervously, she pulled at the last few spines, and fell free as Edward's fist crashed down inches in front of her nose. As he stumbled past, she crab-crawled away before his angry blue eyes turned to glare at her.

"Your dumb luck is going to end soon, Miss Douglas. Think through your actions and get back on your feet. Edward, don't let her embarrass you." There was a hint of laughter in the teacher's voice, and the teen growled.

"Oh, trust me, she won't."

His right fist came flying at Lilly's cheek and she moved to avoid it, only for him to side step and slash across her face with the back of his arm. Blood gushed from the deepest cut ripped into her cheek, and she cried out in pain as she struggled to heal and move at the same time. He was in a rhythm now. One fist hit her head, the other came in a backswing, cutting into her stomach. She kept managing to slip away long enough to heal, and that seemed to anger Edward. She ducked and darted, but he kept moving faster, those sharp, thorny spikes dangerously flashing.

"Keep it up. Edward, use your spikes to your advantage. They're detachable for a reason! And Miss Douglas, you're running everywhere, but you need to do more than just flee the attack."

Panting, Lilly gave a slow nod, but didn't know how she could do anything but run. She squared her feet, facing Edward, who glared at her. Then he reached his right arm to the back of his left, and pulled three spikes free. He barely blinked, and taking one spike in his left hand, and two in his right, he slowly moved forward. The ends glittered sharply, the two inch daggers like thin, lethal blades in his hands. Lilly's heart raced faster as she tried to face her opponent. Then, he lunged.

Lilly ducked, then startled herself by dropping to her hands and swinging her leg sharply into Edwards calves. Surprised, he tripped, but as he fell he used his momentum to bury two of the free spikes into her shoulder. Her body jerked in pain, but she wasn't too worried about the annoying sting. She moved away from the boy, excited that she'd actually attempted something offensive. The happiness quickly faded as she saw the grin on Edward's face, and her pulse crawled to a stop. He got steadily back to his feet, twirling the last spine, and his mouth smirked smugly. Then the first wave of agony hit.

It was like his entire arm of spikes had driven into her shoulder, and needle-like pain burned from the two still buried in her flesh. It was like a bee sting amplified a hundred times, and it caused her muscles to spasm as she collapsed to the floor. Edward laughed and walked forward, then stopped and leaned close to her face, still sneering at her. "That's why you should always dodge," he whispered.

Lily gasped and struggled to breathe as she tried to heal away the poison, but it was like leaving a splinter in your finger while it tried to heal. Weakly, she reached up and yanked the spikes out, glaring up at Edward; in anger, she stunned the room by taking the spines and stabbing them into the boy's vulnerable leg. The reaction was a cry of pain from Edward and a gasp of shock from one of the watching students. The boy fell backward, quickly pulling the spikes before the slow-acting poison could settle in. Lilly saw blood on the spines and spots of red through the holes she'd made in his jeans, and regretted her actions as Edward snarled in fury. Her remorse strengthened as a strange noise echoed across the room. It was a crackle and popping snap like a spine changing alignment, echoed by the sound of a faint ripping from his shirt. In the corner of her eye, Lilly could see a smile slowly creep across Mr. Lyubov's face.

"Oh, this is definitely going to be messy..."

<Get in the air *now!*>

Lilly didn't think twice about the demand, just threw herself into flight. Hardly fifteen feet up, the air around her exploded with needle-pointed spines, barely missing her body, but only one punched through a feather. A roar rippled from below her as Lilly pivoted, fluttering backward and landing crouched in the beams of the gym ceiling.

"You coward! Are you going to fly away like a worthless chicken or are you going to fight like a Strand?!"

Lilly's wings quivered, but she glared bravely down. "You want to beat me up? Come and get me first!"

The teen below her was visibly angered, his back bristling with quills. He shot more of them in her direction, but Lilly easily avoided them. Many of the other students backed away to avoid flying spines, and Mr. Lyubov jumped onto one of the platforms to the left of the room, then sat there, smirking.

"You heard her, Mr. Quinn. Go get her."

With a snarl, Edward leapt onto one of the low shelves built into the wall and jumped up to reach a high rock wall above it. Lilly felt her eyebrows jerk up as the boy started scaling like a spider, quickly making it up the first third of the wall with easy handholds, barely slowing as the handholds diminished into a natural looking cliff. She couldn't help being impressed by the skill with which he climbed. She shifted on her perch, wings softly spread for balance, as he drew closer. The height had no effect on him, and his anger carried him smoothly upward, muscles flexed as he moved her way. Then he shot two thick spikes from his back, and they made a thud into the wooden beams that made Lilly's hands tingle. Lilly watched in confusion as he carefully looked at the spikes. He seemed to just be sitting there for a moment, then he launched himself into the air and caught the spikes.

"Are you insane?!" Lilly gasped. She fluttered her wings in shock, backing quickly away down the rafters.

Edward gave a pleased laugh, and using his arms for leverage he managed to climb slowly up onto the beam. "Just wait until I get my hands on you, then you'll really be asking that!"

Lilly realized a second too late that she should be flying again, but by then Edward was already standing on the rafters snarling angrily at her, his eyes flashing with a deep rage. She planted both her feet and crouched in a fighting stance, wings spread for balance. "This is my playing field. Don't underestimate me." The words sounded foreign to her, an echo of the other students who guided her at this school. She was afraid, but she was learning to act brave. It wasn't enough to scare him off, though.

Edward cackled, and straightened slightly, holding out his long arms, light dancing off the spines' glittering points. "Your fighting is based on nothing more than luck, speed, and fear. Your luck will eventually run out, your speed will fail you, and your fear will become the weakness it's meant to be. Don't make me laugh! This may be your playing field," Edward darted forward suddenly, and his fist barely missed her face, "but this is my game."

In the air, balance was Lilly's advantage, and she quickly focused on it and utilized it. Edward was enraged, but he wasn't stupid enough to use large movements that could send him falling to the ground below. Lilly, however, could be a windmill of action, because if she fell, she'd simply fly back to the rafter and start again. The trick was avoiding the spines that Edward was so keen on shooting at her. The ones on his back were particularly dangerous because he could shoot them at will, while the ones on the wrist had to either be pulled by hand or shot through the palms. Lilly could see that movement coming early enough to dodge, and felt far more comfortable here in the rafters for that reason. Her footwork was faster, her actions smoother and sharper, and Edward began to worry as Lilly kept darting backward, easily avoiding his assaults.

"Fight back!" raged Edward.

Lilly gave a shrug. "Give up." She fluttered her wings to jump out of the way of a few spines, and Edward huffed.

"You act so brave up here, but I can see the fear in your eyes. Why pretend?"

"Because as scared as I may or may not be, giving into it won't help me any," Lilly stated. She scanned her surroundings quickly, and made a jump onto another rafter, using her wings to flutter the distance, and turned as a spine grazed her cheek. She winced in pain, then turned to face him as he shifted into a pouncing position.

"I could strangle you with my bare hands!"

"You'd have to catch me first," muttered Lilly. She moved quickly across the length of the rafter and glanced back as Edward made another wild jump over, barely landing it, and catching his balance at the last possible moment. Then she had to turn and duck as a rain of quills exploded behind her again. This time, she felt prickles of pain as a few grazed her legs, and two hit her wing. That caused her to stumble, but she recovered and moved beyond the spines' shooting distance.

"You know," Edward panted, "You're actually not a terrible fighter!"

Lilly yelped as his fist grazed her chin, and stumbled backward to regain her balance. "I'd say I'm not a terrible dodger, but when it comes to fighting—" She threw a punch that didn't require much movement to dodge on Edward's part, and he returned with a slash across her wing. "—I suck!"

Edward laughed at that statement and tried to punch again, but this time Lilly brought her forearm up to block it. "Your defense is effective, but your opponent will always win until you learn to fight back." They exchanged a couple quick punches and blocks, panting with effort. "But you're too timid act viciously!"

Lilly didn't have a comeback for that remark. All she could do was throw herself flat on the rafter to avoid a high kick aimed at her face. Before she could get up, she let out a gasp of shock as a searing pain ripped through her wings, followed by a burning sensation. She didn't need to look to know he'd pinned her wing to the wood, like a stake nailing it to the timber. The shock softened the pain some, but gradually it grew to an agonizing throb. Unlike the first time, it wasn't just feathers that were stuck, and this was ten times more painful.

"How you feeling, Feathers?" Tears started to pour down her face, and her whole body shook in protest. She sank against the rafter as the numbness spread, and she found herself frozen by the poison. Edward leaned close to her face and chuckled. "That good, huh? You do realize, if we weren't in school, I would kill you now." His eyes darkened, and he shot a spine right by her head, so close it whistled in her ear. "But to clean up that mess would make me tardy for third period, and I'm not up for that sort of thing. Later, loser." He turned and walked away, leaving Lilly helplessly pinned. When he was out of sight, she closed her eyes and cried.

"So Miss Douglas, how long did you plan on laying up here?"

Lilly slowly lifted her head, barely able to do that much. Her vision swirled for a moment before it settled, and Mr. Lyubov came into view. The blind teacher was sitting casually, with one leg hanging off the beam and one leg resting on its edge. He wasn't facing her, looking didn't benefit him at all, so it wasn't surprising. She laid her head back down and gave a tiny moan. "I...can't...move," she finally spoke with effort. There was no sign of him shifting, and the only sound was his voice.

"That is a problem, isn't it? It will only get worse the longer you leave those spines in your wing, you know. I did hope you would at least try to get them out."

"I did...but..."

"Try again."

Lilly's face pulled into a grimace as she lifted her head up again. "Why do you care?" she spat out, pain turning to bitterness. "Most people...would love to just...watch me...die up here."

Mr. Lyubov shifted, but all he did was let his foot drop over the edge of the rafter. His face pointed forward, then tilted slightly in her direction. "I'm your teacher, Miss Douglas. The death of my students doesn't make an impressive résumé, even at a school like Firestone. My job is to equip my students for battle, help them grow stronger. It's not the students down there that need my teaching most. The ones that win battles are not the ones who need my words, it's those that lose. Now pull it together and get those spines out."

Slowly and painfully, Lilly lifted her hand and inched it backward over her shoulder. It was like lifting her arm with an iron glove on, but somehow she managed to move until she felt the spine. With tears running down her face, she wrapped her hand around it, and using the rest of her strength, yanked up.

"Don't stop. Finish what you've started. The hardest part is over."

Gritting her teeth, she let her hand travel blindly over her shoulder and found the second spine by touch. Once more, she removed it, body shaking with exhaustion. With a final burst of adrenaline, she caught the last one and finally pulled free of the rafter. Using the rest of her energy, her healing fought the paralysis holding her and healed the wound. Trembling, with all her energy gone, she curled her wings closed, and held limply to the rafter. "There. I'm free."

"Congratulations. Now, it's time to come back down for class. You aren't just going to lie up here all day." His tone grew sharp and commanding, and Lilly whimpered.

"Right now?"

"Now."

There was movement and a rustle, but by the time Lilly looked up, Mr. Lyubov was nowhere to be seen. Blinking away her surprise, she forced herself to get up and weakly spread her wings. Her motions were still shaky and unsteady, but at least she could move. Breathing deeply, she went to the edge of the rafters and with a quick prayer, she jumped into the air. Her body responded purely by reflex, as her wings fluttered ever so slightly, steering her in a soft loop down to the ground. She landed at the back of the group of students, and Xzin sneered at her.

"So you decided to join us? What a pity."

Lilly's feathers stood up in annoyance, and she glared. Xzin just laughed and nudged the girl next to him. "Aw, Pilar, look at the poor pigeon. She didn't like fighting Edward very much, and now she's sad."

Pilar turned and grinned, teeth glittering. "She's lucky. If I had fought 'er, she wouldn't have come back down."

By the way the Spaniard girl was looking at her, Lilly believed that statement. Even after the conversation the night before, Pilar was keeping her mask on, nice to her in private, then attacking her in public. She had no idea what the girl would do if presented the chance. Each sting of defeat seemed like a blessing in disguise.

CHAPTER EIGHT

FRAGMENTS OF THE PAST

Dryk glanced at his twin, and saw a familiar look on Wyvr's face. Beneath the crown of brown hair, his eyes were empty, distant. Even in the sunny sandlot, with the sounds of laughter carried on the breeze and their friends surrounding them, Dryk could see the faded touch of sadness linger on his brother's features. He knew why it was there, but there was little he could do to change it.

"Thinkin' about her again, aren't you Wyvr? You can't keep letting it bug you like this, mate. You know you've done what you can for now."

Wyvr sighed, and his eyes followed those playing on the baseball field, or rather, the empty lot they'd fashioned as one. The teens in front of them were dirty and sweaty, but obviously enjoying their game. He watched as Meg stepped up to the plate, wild red hair billowing from a ponytail, bat in hand as she faced Jake on the mound. Kat crouched behind her as catcher, and in the outfield Kent and Michaela were ready. Carlos was on base, as was Seth; the two boys moved tauntingly, waiting for a moment to steal a base. Jenny watched them closely from third, ready to teleport at the first sign they were going to move. As Jake pitched, Meg swung hard and connected the bat and ball, a resounding crack echoing through the lot. The baseball catapulted toward the group of bystanders.

"Duck!"

Wyvr dove as a baseball narrowly missed his face. He heard a shatter behind him, and looked up cautiously, heart slowly starting to beat again. The conversation with his twin evaporated from immediate thought.

"Geez! You tryin' to kill someone?" Dryk yelled, getting shakily to his feet. Wyvr followed suit and turned around, dusting off his jeans. Glass edges glittered in the sun from a broken window pane, and the light was swallowed by a dark, abandoned building. Wyvr found his curiosity drawn to the old structure, which was little more than walls and windows. He'd never noticed it there before, and by the way Dryk looked at it, he hadn't either.

"Aw, man! That's our last baseball!" Carlos whined from behind them, and the twins turned around to face their companions. Disappointed faces lined the lot, each staring at the window where the ball had disappeared. Dryk glanced at his brother, shifting slightly, and Wyvr gave him a nod as he morphed into a bird in a fluid motion. An equipment rescue mission couldn't be the worst way to spend his day.

With a quick thrust of his wings, he was in the air, and easily fluttered over the walls of the building. Looking down inside the skeletal remains, he easily spotted the white baseball with his sharp peregrine eyes. Dipping carefully into the structure, he flapped to a landing in front of the ball, stirring old dust as he did. He twittered slightly with agitation, and had to close his eyes as the dust cleared.

<You find it, Wyvr?> his brother's voice inquired, and Wyvr could feel the curious edge in his twin's tone.

<Yeah. Almost,> Wyvr replied. He hopped forward, squeezed under the lumber blocking the ball, and pecked until it began to shift. It was almost free when there was a creaking noise that rolled under his talons. Wyvr froze and listened closely, but it vanished as suddenly as it had come. His feathers rose along his back, and nervous energy ran through him. Cautiously he backed away, moving gently with the ball.

<Wyvr... What's wrong?> Dryk whispered, picking up on Wyvr's distress. Wyvr carefully crouched in front of the baseball, listening again.

<I thought I heard something...> Wyvr whispered back. Feeling skittish, he hopped onto the baseball and wrapped his talons around it. He was about to launch into flight when there was a rumbling quake, and the ground around him caved in.

Wyvr let out a fearful screech as he felt himself falling, a sensation he wasn't accustomed to in falcon form. He morphed back in panic, which probably saved him from a painful landing, as he slammed into a mixture of wood, dirt, and debris. More of the same came raining down on top of him until it slowed to a trickle, and Wyvr finally was left stunned, almost entirely buried in rubble.

<Wyvr! You okay? What happened?!>

Hazily, Wyvr could almost sense the deep connection with his twin, who was circling worriedly above him in bird form. Wyvr coughed, trying to breathe as the dust caught in his lungs. The cubby of rubble made it hard to move, so he shifted back into a falcon and was able to painfully wriggle to the surface, twittering softly as he splayed at the top.

<Wait up there. I'm okay, but the ground caved in. I lost the ball, too,> he wheezed, and felt relief being sent from his brother.

<Well, at least you're okay! What did you fall into?>

Wyvr slowly got to his feet, wings pointed out at angles as he tried to keep his balance. The dust was settling around him, and now he could see where he was. It looked like an old basement, a tiny room with a desk pushed tightly to the side and a small bookcase against the wall. Wyvr turned slowly around, and noted his surroundings, most of the room untouched by the cave-in. Curious, Wyvr morphed into a human and stepped off the pile of dirt with care. The ground here felt firm, and he was brave enough to walk to the desk and sift through the papers. They were very old, but still easily readable. Some were nibbled around the edges, but most were well preserved, as if this room had been tightly sealed from the world outside. As he looked closer at the papers, he let out a low whistle. The papers were dated 1943 and 1944.

<Wyvr, you find something?>

<Yeah, come down here! It's an old office from the 1940's, and there's all kinds of papers...> His thoughts carried through his brother's mental link. <Hey, I think this is a journal!>

Wyvr carefully picked up the old book he had spotted and turned it over in his hands. It was leather-bound, with worn edges, a faded cover, and a broken buckle. Delicately, he turned the page and let out a gasp.

"Whose is it?" Dryk whispered as he landed and walked to his twin's side.

"It says Avery Douglas... If it's from the 1940's like the rest of this, I wonder if it could be a relative of Lilly's!"

"What is it about?"

Wyvr carefully turned the page and paused to read. *" 'October 14th, 1943.*

" 'Research has been sluggish lately. I am beginning to think our work has no purpose. I miss my family terribly, but the Americans want to retain the secrecy of this project. No one is allowed into the city, and no one is allowed out, except maybe Shan Hyun, who transports supplies here. It is bordering on imbecilic at this point, but I suppose if it helps, what can I say? We have been here for over a year, two years come February, and I have no idea what has happened outside of this bloody little town from then until now.

" 'The rest of the scientists share my sentiments, and it has been strange to find something we coincide on. We do not often agree, especially on matters of risk regarding our research. It is madness. I do not know who thought it would be a good idea to try this, but there have been no breakthroughs to verify the validity of this experiment. This city just feels lost. We are here in the middle of nowhere, closing our eyes and wandering around with our fingers in our ears telling ourselves that nothing is wrong. My whole lifestyle has been altered by this. I miss England, and I miss the lifestyle I had. I even feel like I'm talking like an American. Dear Lord, can you imagine? It is awful enough being trapped here without realizing I am transforming into one of them.

" 'I started out so enthusiastic about this, as it was quite an honor to be chosen for this team. Now everything is falling apart. We could make one small mistake at any moment, and we would be dead before we knew what hit us. These are things that should not be tampered with, and I am starting to feel shame in taking part in this.' "

Dryk leaned close, re-reading the entry and looking at the scrawled handwriting. Wyvr turned page after page of detailed notes before reaching the last entry, halfway in. The writing was disarrayed and difficult to read, but the first line stood out clearly. "'September 4th, 1944.

"'Everyone is dead. Everyone but myself, and a young scientist Frank, who was the time keeper here at the lab. The memory will always remain vivid for me. Lucien was in a bad mood. He was drunk, grabbing chemicals, carelessly mixing them, then working with our equipment in a rage. Everyone was screaming and yelling, intent on sending him home. Then Frank came into the room and asked if I could give him a hand. He said he had walked into the containment chamber, and thought something seemed wrong with it. I followed him, of course, deciding I would be of more use working than trying to calm Lucien. Frank had just stepped in after me when we heard a bloodcurdling yell, and as I turned, a huge quake ripped through the building, and the door slammed shut. The noise... The whole room was jarred... I knew that young man saved my life. If we had not have been in that room, we would also be dead.

"'When we opened the door, the whole facility was in ruins. My coworkers, gone. I cannot begin to explain the horror of what we found. Whatever they had done, whatever had happened, had been awful.

"'Going outside, the city was in a panic. People were rushing to the factory, wives screamed for husbands, people in other buildings were hurt. It was madness. The aviary next door had every window shattered; other buildings were in ruins as well. There was a young girl running through town. She was a part-time doctor at the factory and she saved many lives by so quickly coming to our aid.

"'I felt like I was in a haze walking through the city today. Shan Hyun arrived amidst this and asked if I could tell him something to do to help. Other citizens were wandering around, some too stunned to help, some racing back and forth to assist. That young man, I have not seen him since, what with all the chaos...

"'Within the hour, the government arrived. And they are doing what they do best: they are trying to cover it up. Every citizen has individually been taken and has sworn an oath of secrecy, then they were scattered away from this city. I expect soon I shall have to as well, but I hate the thought of the government hiding something as large as this, pretending it never happened. This, my journal, I leave hidden here, and I pray that somehow it remains undiscovered. I pray that one day, someone will know what happened here...

"'We were researching something we should never have, and we paid the consequences. No one will be able to learn from it, because they will pretend it never happened.

"'And I was a part of this bloody mess.'" Wyvr let the last phrase fade into the air and stared at the words, checking the rest of the journal for more before turning back to that page. "Dryk, do you realize what this is? Charity, that's where we're at right now! The bones of that old town are right here! This old building must have been either his house, or some office of his. What if there's more hidden in this ghost town?"

"Wyvr, c'mon. Look at this place. These books were lucky to survive in the first place," remarked Dryk skeptically, but he couldn't keep the curiosity from his voice. He wasn't much of a scientist and the writing was hard to decipher, but it felt important for some reason. As much time as they spent in this city, they never dreamed they'd learn what caused its demise.

Dryk carefully sifted through the rest of the papers on the desk and finally gathered them into a pile, dirt coating his hands. He looked through the books on the shelf next, searching for anything else that might be useful. He hadn't looked through very many of them when there was a call from above.

"Dryk, Wyvr, what are you guys doing? Everyone is getting worried out there!" Kent was hovering in the air above them, slowly coming to a rest on the rubble. "Wow, you made a mess in... What is this?"

"An old office. You won't believe the stuff that's in here. We have to take some of this back to Charity, Dr. Allina needs to see this. You won't believe all the papers and notes," Dryk started. Kent interrupted, pointing at the journal in Wyvr's hand.

"What's that?" he asked.

"A journal we found. Written by an Avery Douglas. Might be a relative of Lilly's. We gotta keep this stuff. Be a good sport and help carry this."

Before long, Wyvr and Dryk had Seth, Jenny, and Kent helping them clear out the ancient office. Their baseball game forgotten, the students were soon walking back to Charity carrying dusty old papers and books, unsure of what they contained. Wyvr and Dryk staggered under some of the heavier loads; they huddled close together, trying to read the journal as they walked.

"Dryk, I don't know about you, but these numbers make my brain hurt! This man must have been brilliant," Wyvr muttered.

"Well take a break then, Wyvr. You'll get enough time to see it later. After a bath, that is. You should see yourself! People will actually be able to tell us apart for once!"

Wyvr chuckled and grinned wryly at his twin. "Fat chance. I'm wearing your shirt!"

"So you think this Avery was a relative of Lilly's?" Meg asked, jogging up between the two boys. They glanced at each other as if verifying their response, and Dryk nodded.

"It's a guess, at most. For all we know, it could be someone entirely unrelated. But it's still possible."

Meg shifted the papers she was carrying and looked distant. A dark veil seemed to cross her eyes, a familiar look. "I hope one day we'll get to show it to Lilly. She would have loved a mystery like this..."

Wyvr nodded. "She would have. It's awful how things grew so sour so quickly, but don't give up hope on her. We'll get her back. It'll just take some time and healing, on all our parts."

Meg distantly brushed dirt from her papers, trying to hide the emotions rushing across her face. Then she sighed and stopped trying to dust them, quietly letting her shoulders sink. "I just feel so terrible. I was the one who made her leave. I feel responsible."

"It wasn't just your fault, Meg. Everyone added to it in different ways, and we all hurt her. Beating ourselves up about it won't bring her back."

Meg shook her head, a deep cloud falling over her face. "I guess..." They paused as the conversation dwindled out, and continued walking in silence. Around them the city was transitioning to forest, simple shrubbery gradually changing to tangled foliage. On either side there were occasional buildings, crumbled and damaged by time. It seemed the old buildings were part of this scene as much as the trees and the grass. They were growing from the ground like weeds, littering the pathways.

A chipmunk scuttled from between the rocks and it sat, tail twitching, while watching them. Dryk's eyes glimmered with playfulness as he took note of it, when suddenly he froze. Meg nearly walked into him as Dryk handed his papers quickly to his twin and morphed soundlessly to peregrine form. Then he sat motionless in the grasses, body tense and alert.

"Guys, what are you—"

"Shh!"

The rest of the group kept walking, unnoticing, while the twins stood frozen and silent. Meg clutched the papers she was holding to her chest and looked nervously around, trying to guess why they had gone so alert. Then Dryk's voice hissed in Meg's mind.

<Someone was following us, and they left in a huge hurry....>

<Do you know who?> Meg thought back through the connection he opened. There was a long pause, and Meg could feel a strange animosity coming from not just Dryk, but Wyvr as well.

<It was one of the Gemini twins. Either could easily get away if they were spying. They must have seen us in town and followed to see what we were doing. If they heard any of that... We need to get back to Charity, and fast!> Dryk returned to human form and snatched up half of the papers, and stride for stride the twins started racing after the other students. Meg scrambled to keep up, her long legs struggling to move quickly while her arms stayed still. Every thought that raced through her head was suddenly stilled as her body jerked into survival mode, and Meg raced after the long-legged Australians.

The whole time, she could only hope they would be fast enough.

"Kibbsty. Charity found something."

This sentence was sharp and monotone, but there was still a hint of curiosity. It was rare for the normally empty voice of Mercury to hold any emotion, but Kibbsty could sense excitement almost showing through her restraint. He turned from his work on the computer and raised his eyebrows slightly. "What sort of something?"

"Papers, documents, books from the 1940s. I overheard someone mention the brat. Stuff belonged to a relative of hers. It sounded important."

"You're rarely wrong on things like this, Mercury. I'll take your word for it. Where's Thallium?"

"Ready, as always." The second cold voice made Kibbsty give a small jump, but he quickly covered it and faced the boy leaning in the doorway. Mercury had barely glanced up as her brother entered, but a look passed between their empty eyes in that moment, a silent transfer of information. Side by side, the two always caused Kibbsty to feel some apprehension. The two had a dark connection, one he never dared question. They were a force to fear, and once more he was glad they were on his side.

"Thallium, Mercury, get Cory, Trish and...Lilly." The name came in a spark of inspiration, and it surprised the twins as much as it had startled Kibbsty himself.

"Excuse me?" hissed Thallium.

Kibbsty turned in his chair, a thoughtful sneer spread across his face. The twins couldn't hide the confusion and disbelief appearing on their features, and Kibbsty wasn't sure he blamed them. But the thought had struck him suddenly and he was running with it, unable to stop. "I said, take Lilly."

"Why?"

"I think it's time to remind her that she no longer belongs there," Kibbsty continued, eyes sparkling with his plot. "Imagine how she'll take it, seeing everyone having fun and acting like she was never there."

"How can you be sure they'll act that way?" Mercury asked, grunting. "They might miss her."

Kibbsty laughed, then grinned. "You'll bring Nuo."

"Nuo? You're going to control their emotions?" The twins seemed to be growing intrigued. Kibbsty felt a bit of pride.

"Not control, just influence. Give them a boost of carefree emotions, make them relax. They'll fill in the rest. Meanwhile, you can get whatever information they found. Take the Shutterbug with you, too."

"We're not taking the papers themselves?"

"No, this is a stealth mission. All I want is the information. Cory and Trish are backup, and their job is to ensure the girl sees her friends doing fine without her. Nuo and Thallium will get rid of anyone who gets in the way and stand guard, while you get Scarlet in and extract the information. I'm counting on you and your brother to make sure everyone keeps to whatever plan you concoct. Just remember, it's an in-and-out mission."

The Gemini twins gave slow, hesitant nods. They knew better than to question him further, but this would be by far one of the strangest missions they'd been on. Normally, their missions involved things like kidnapping, blackmailing, and persuasion, but stealth missions were rare. Kibbsty normally had no problem barging into Charity and stealing things in a method that was as obvious as a punch to the face. Kibbsty seemed to favor being blunt with his actions because it kept Charity 'on its toes.' It was how he kept control. Heavy handed, like a prison guard, he kept authority by maintaining panic. As long as there was fear and uncertainty, he could rule. He enjoyed that sense of power.

As Thall and Mar went to get the students they were asked to bring, they remained silent, but their actions spoke volumes. They were confused, but they did as Kibbsty asked because, like everyone at Firestone, they knew it would be stupid not to. Every movement was a signal filled with unspoken words. Thall and Mar could read each other better than wolves in a pack. Every sigh, every hiss, all of their silence: it was symbolic of a bond closer than any other. Even when they were alone they didn't bother talking. They knew how to say enough in silence.

It wasn't long before they were standing in a classroom, with the chosen students gathered. There was confusion on a few faces, but none were as transparent as Lilly's.

"Why are we here?" Cory snapped, turning to Mar daringly.

"You're coming with us," the female twin said blankly.

"Kibbsty's orders," finished Thall.

"But... Why the mouse?" Trish's confusion showed more than the others, tracing from her forehead to the corners of her mouth. Neither Gemini twin spoke, their answer final. Trish glanced Lilly's way, and for a moment the brown-haired girl almost saw a trace of worry. It was gone so fast she figured she had imagined it, as the expression hardened to a careless shrug.

"So what's Kibbsty having us do?" Cory asked.

Thall was silent for a long moment, as if trying to splice the answer as short as possible, then growled.

"We're retrieving information. Mar will tell the two of you what to do." He tilted his head at Scarlet and Nuo. They moved soundlessly to the other end of the room with Thallium's twin, then he continued. "Kibbsty wants us to take the brat to get the rest of her belongings. He's tired of having to give her stuff. Trish, you are going with her. Cory, with me."

Lilly sat baffled as the two cold personalities moved off to the side. She now stood with Trish, terribly nervous and almost excited. What if someone saw them! Maybe they would realize she had been kidnapped. Maybe they *did* miss her, and were worried about her!

There was a bump against her stomach that jerked her back to reality, and Lilly found herself holding a backpack. Trish rolled her eyes, her brows creased with annoyance. "It's for your stuff. Let me make it very clear to you, you won't be doing anything other than getting your things and getting out. You hear?"

Lilly longed to argue, but silently nodded and took the bag. There was no warmth in Trish's eyes, no sign of anything beyond animosity. It was a sad moment, and the words Cory had spoken rang in her head. *One day we could be the ones helping you up, another day we'll be the ones throwing you down.* She accepted this quietly and put the backpack on.

"Okay. Let's go," Mar said firmly. Side by side the Gemini twins exited the room, and the rest of them followed behind.

Moving through the halls of the school was intimidating, like trying to slip through the claws of a slumbering beast. No one in the group said a word, all silent and animus. Trish stood to one side, Scarlet on the other, and Cory followed behind. Nuo, Mar and Thall all walked in front, the twins ahead of the new face. It was like they had boxed Lilly in on purpose, guaranteeing she couldn't escape. Every shadow flicker, every silent profile, all promised one thing: she was going to return with them. To this school, to this emptiness; to this terrible dungeon of an existence she longed to flee from; they were going to drag her back, and she couldn't prevent that.

It was a certainty.

They weaved to the front of the school, then toward a part of it she had yet to see: the front doors. To get there, you had to go through Kibbsty's lab, in the opposite direction of the dungeon, and through a long corridor. On the other end of the dark hallway, there was a large open corridor and two large obsidian doors. Each Gemini twin reached for an iron handle at the same time, and simultaneously pulled. A whispering noise whistled past Lilly's ear as the air from the outside world met her, and the young girl's feathers trembled with joy. Then something clicked around her wrist, and she jerked away in shock.

"Can't have you flying off, now, can we?" Cory said, giving an evil grin. Lilly opened her mouth to question his actions when a strong current of electricity ripped its way up her arm from the metal band. She screamed, falling to the ground while the group laughed with delight. Cory tossed the remote over her head. "She tries anything, give her a good reminder of where her place is."

Someone chuckled, and another person kicked her wing. "Don't worry, I'll be glad to. Now get up!"

Still trembling, Lilly forced herself to her feet and moved out the door with Cory and Trish laughing on either side of her. Crossing her arms and keeping her wings close, she could only heal and walk, trying to ignore the merciless treatment she was forced to endure. It seemed like she was in a whole different world here, completely separate from Charity. Were they really going back there? Had she ever even been there? It all seemed so far away, so distant. It felt like everything could have been a dream, and this was all that was left for her; she was in a living hell until the time she was allowed to die.

She tried to maintain hope that things could get better from here. She clung to that; it was a tiny light, a single sliver of radiance she had locked within herself. Without hope, she was a candle's flame doused by water. Day by day she would pray she would make it, pleaded she could hold on. She would be rescued from this. Certainly, someone would look for her. Help would come.

Weaving down the mountainside, the bleak setting let her fears fester, laying their frozen hands on her soul. The mood carried from the dreary school behind her and followed her like a shadow. It was no wonder the people here were as frozen as they were. How could someone maintain any sort of hope or joy in a place such as this? You would always have a cynical bitterness tainting any emotion. It would cling to the edges of your clothing, trace the curves of your sides. It was depressing to think that these students lived here. Lilly was desperately longing for freedom, but for her it *was* an option. What would she do if it wasn't? In her mind, she was kidnapped and would eventually be rescued. Charity was the home she could return to, but this *was* home for these students. What would she do if it was hers?

She looked more carefully at those she was with. Thall and Mar were the most difficult to read, exclusively isolated from their surroundings. The only thing they seemed to care about was each other. It was a strange connection, something deeper than met the eye. There was a way they read each other when they moved, and their shared emptiness, trained to keep what they truly felt to themselves. Lilly doubted even Kibbsty knew what really went on in their heads. They were unreadable and solid, consistently maintaining separation from those around them.

Nuo was new to Lilly, and she had little knowledge about him. She knew he had a sister, a dangerous girl, but Nuo himself didn't show any sort of warning signs. He was incredibly skinny, face pale and skin close to transparent. He looked like someone who rarely went outdoors, and his eyes had a milky quality to them. His hair was very downy, and it moved with the lightest breeze. The whole impression of the boy was delicate on the surface, but beneath it, he was strong. He had muscles, just enough to be in good shape, and his jaw was firmly set as he moved, driven by some unknown mission.

Scarlet was also indistinct to Lilly. Most people seemed to call her the 'Shutterbug,' although Lilly never discovered the source of that nickname. Scarlet was a breezy girl, off in her own world at times, and she had a habit of blinking rather often like something was constantly stuck in her eyes. Her hair was pin straight, with no curl or wave to it, and she wore a beanie. It was *always* a beanie, anytime Lilly saw her; that never changed. Come to think of it, little of Scarlet's clothing ever changed. It was always the same outfit, maybe in different shades, but unceasingly patterned. She had a V-neck shirt that cut off at the elbows and ended to show her midriff. The sleeves were cut in a wide bell shape and billowed with the slightest movement so much they reminded Lilly of giant sails. Both her lip and navel were pierced, each decorated with a blue and silver bead, and a large peace sign adorned her neck. Scarlet was perfectly skinny, a natural slenderness, and her pants had a way of hugging her hips until they engulfed her long legs all the way to her sandaled feet. The way she moved was smooth and predictable, but it was hard to tell if her behavior was the same.

That left Trish and Cory, who confused Lilly the most. Trish had a kind heart, but she put on a mask of hostility. The character she outwardly projected was catty and she loved to taunt and tease. But Trish's true character was different than what she displayed. She was motherly and caring, honestly concerned when others were hurt. Trish was sharpened to play this role, but glimmers of humanity shone through when Lilly least expected it.

Cory, on the other hand, was cold and empty no matter what. The ice he could create was fused with who he was as a person. Sometimes, Lilly could almost see a trace of water flow like blood beneath his hard front. He scoffed and snarled, but somewhere in him, there lurked a fragile seed of morality. It fought to be heard, but was so feeble and weak it was no match against the puppet he had become.

"Keep up," Thall instructed. He picked up the pace as they reached the bottom of the cliff, swiftly moving across the only bridge, a deadly river rushing on either side. Then the landscape took a steep dip and they made their pace a gallop to keep their footing. While the others had a more graceful step, Lilly's was clumsy. She was constantly scrambling to maintain control of her speed, fearing at any moment she would crash into Nuo and create a domino effect of people down the mountain. She wondered what the school looked like in the middle of this wilderness, and couldn't help looking back over her shoulder. For a split second she could see the obsidian fortress perched atop a wicked black mountain peak, then she was struck sharply across the head.

"Keep your eyes on the trail!"

The combination of the blow, her running, and Cory's angry snarl caused Lilly to stagger, and her wings flew open in reflex. She knew even before they made contact that she was in for pain. In slow motion, her wings crashed into Trish and Scarlet, sending the three of them cascading to the ground.

Lilly hit face first, her chin connecting with the ground as rocks sliced her flesh. There was a burning pain as Scarlet fell on her wing and the fragile bones broke. Trish landed on her side, spewing a startled exclamation. Lilly hadn't even come to a complete stop when Cory began to yell.

"What did I just say?!"

There was a mix of cursing and angry yelling, then Scarlet moved off her wing. Instead of providing relief, it created an opportunity for Cory to reach down and grab Lilly by the neck. Yanked from the ground and slammed into a tree, her body fought against the hauntingly familiar punishment.

"Tell me, you worthless twit. Does this hurt?!"

It wasn't the squeezing around her throat that caused her anguish, or even her broken wing. It wasn't the tree digging into her back, either; it was the cold. It was sudden and piercing, straight from his hand into her throat. Her breath froze inside her, her body went into shock. The rhythms inside her stalled and quieted. Heartbeat? She had none. Breathing? Gone. Her blood had

288

formed into icicles, blood splintering from the inside out. The pain was unbelievable, the cold moving through her like a mist of glass.

"Does it hurt?!"

Please stop! Please! STOP!!!!! Lilly's mind screamed with the words her mouth couldn't form. To her surprise, Cory dropped her. She didn't even feel the ground as she hit; all she felt was the cold. Her powers scrambled to save her, but it was so cold. Frigid, glacial, gelid: she felt the intensity of it, all energy drained from her. She was blanketed with the arctic.

"Frost, you may have overdone it. If you don't turn up the heat, it doesn't look like she'll make it," Trish said emptily, and Cory sighed.

"I hate when you're right."

There was a small touch on the back of her neck, and warmth melted through her. It stung unpleasantly, like jumping into warm water after rolling in the snow, but it was enough to get her breath back again, and her heart gave a feeble thump. She got to her knees, gasping for air, and hugged her sides. Before they even spoke she knew nursing the pain would not be allowed. She healed quickly, even as Cory snarled for her to stand, but her legs wouldn't move.

"You have five seconds to get your sorry butt moving again," Cory growled dangerously, as if he hadn't already caused her enough pain. Her body couldn't find the energy to heal.

Then she felt the warmth of the sun. It sent a ripple of life through her as it licked the feathers on her back in a gentle caress. It was reviving. Suddenly, she felt like a starved child who realized it was hungry, and desperately wanted more to eat. She had been barred from sunlight, chained in darkness, and now she was aware of what was taken. Reflexively, she let her wings expand, stretching to absorb the sunlight. Her healing leapt across her, mending every wound and leaving her feeling restored. The moment was short-lived. No sooner had she finished healing than Cory called out: "Time's up!" Then she was thrown to her feet and sent stumbling back into motion.

This time, Lilly kept pace, feeling invigorated and alert. Somewhere inside her, her body sparked with more life than she remembered. Being outside and feeling the sun was like a shot of caffeine to her system, energy ripping fresh through her limbs. Suddenly, she didn't care where they were going. It didn't matter how long they had to run; the longer the better. For the first time in months, she felt *alive*.

Yet... She was confused by that sensation. She realized how little she knew of her powers. With her parents, she didn't spend much time outside, so at first the need for light seemed strange. Then she remembered all the days spent by the windows, basking in the light. Firestone didn't have windows, and light was something much rarer here. What would happen if she didn't get enough sun? Why did she feel so livened? Her head was spinning with questions. As she ran, her mind chanted to the pace of her footsteps. *Why why why why why?*

Suddenly, her heart jerked in dread as she realized she shared some of Kibbsty's curiosity. He too wondered, but unlike her, he was obsessed with it. His dark heart was unshakable in his quest for the same answers that she was now starting to consider. It rattled her to realize a part of her was looking forward to hearing the answers.

"Slow now, we're at the base of the mountains. When we reach the road, we've got a vehicle to travel the rest of the way, so stay close." Scarlet shot a glance at Cory, a flash of amusement on her face before it vanished again. Lilly was continuously observing, watching their actions. They weren't just villains. Their personalities and traits shot through them in transparent wisps. They were vibrant colors that had been forced to go grayscale, but the transformation was never completed. They were muted, but the strength of who they were withstood being silenced. The world looked so different from here. Things were more than what was reflected on the surface. They hated each other, but trusted one another; they were friends and rivals at the same time. Through it all, they were brought together by need. Without the others, each faced death.

Not all quite fit the mold; Thall and Mar seemed distant. They played their own game and managed to stay detached. Nuo was still new enough to have his guard up. His eyes still had fire and a desire to escape. Yet from Cory to Trish, Scarlet, and even Tray and Cherry back at Firestone, there was definitely something. Lilly could finally see it. This was their world, and she'd intruded on it. She was an outsider, a risk factor that presented danger to their fragile society. They couldn't rely on her, because she would break away at her first chance and leave them to suffer the repercussions, so they maintained minimal attachment. They were still moral underneath it all; they pitied her pain, felt for her grief, having experienced the same things, but since she wasn't one of them, those feelings were muted. As long as she remained here, she would be seen as only an object so the others would survive.

As long as hope of rescue existed, she would be alone, abandoned to whatever wolves might care to attack her. They would watch, refusing to dampen her suffering, all because she wasn't one of them.

<Be glad we treat you badly. It means that unlike us, you still have hope of a better life than this beastly contest for survival. You still have a home with Charity. You have somewhere to run to. One day you'll thank us, because our beatings are keeping you from being dragged down with us.>

Lilly suppressed a sigh and whispered back, <I wish there was a way for you to have a way out, too.>

Cory's answer was almost inaudible. <I don't. We fight with the hope that we will be the only ones to suffer this fate, but we're done dreaming ourselves. Believe it or not, we're all rooting for you.>

<Why?>

<You carry our dreams on your wings now. We have no way to escape this lifestyle, we sealed our fates already. But we can give you what we lost. This is our mistake, and we'll find the way out, but don't you ever wish to be part of it. Be happy, because you still have everything we wish for.>

His voice stopped and didn't return. His short speech had been so sudden and quiet, it felt imagined. She wanted to ask more, longed for further conversation. But she walked in silence, only resonating emptiness all around.

"Be on guard. We're getting close."

After the short trip in the car (a cross between a dune buggy and a sports car), and another climb by foot, they were closing in on their destination. The woods were recognizable to Lilly, and her heart grew lighter with a sense of comfort. This place was still home to her. In a few moments, she would be within reach of everything she'd been torn from. Her feet wanted to rush ahead and be there again, but she controlled herself, keeping pace with her captors.

By some unseen signal, the group split. Trish and Cory moved to either side of her and shoved her off toward the right. Ahead, she occasionally saw a glitter of light, probably from the lake, which meant they had come in from the southeast. If Lilly guessed right, they were going to go in the back way toward the computer lab, travel behind the cafeteria, and try to get straight into the girls' dorms without being noticed. Stealth didn't seem to be as large of a concern as they reached the edge of the woods: the school grounds were quiet. She tried to think of which day it was and what time, while pushed forward by Trish. Despite their caution, they made it to the base of the building without problem and carefully moved forward, breathless and alert. Every sound was deafening.

"You're with me."

Trish caught her arm and led her toward the girls' dorms, while Cory disappeared around a corner. Almost robotically, Lilly scrambled up the stairs, heart beginning to thunder inside her. It felt unnatural being stealthy like this. Why was she afraid? This was where she belonged! Still, every step on the stairs was unfamiliar. It was a parallel dimension, the other side of a mirror; she had stepped into a place tainted by the viewpoint she now had. Her hands trembled as she stepped onto the landing of her floor, and she felt her fear grow as she finally reached her room.

Things looked fairly familiar at first glance. Kat's bed was extremely messy, the silver and black laptop sitting half hidden in the sheets. Meg's side of the room was spotless, as always, but things *had* changed. One of the beds was missing, and the one that had been Lilly's had an array of stuffed animals on it. A bag was sitting in the corner, open, with clothes half in and half out. It threw Lilly off, a burst of confusion buckled through her, then Trish pushed her. "Get your stuff."

Lilly scrambled into the room and hesitantly opened the closet. She quickly found a stack of boxes shoved into the far corner, and one was labeled 'Lilly's stuff.' The knife-like feeling grew sharper as she lifted it out and set it on the bed. Inside she found a stack of neatly folded clothing, a brush, a bag of knick-knacks, and some shoes. She pulled it all out and moved it to her backpack, not even bothering to look at what she took. Trish stood sentry at the door, giving her a frustrated glance to remind her to hurry. Robotically, Lilly zipped the bag shut and shot for the door, the knife twisting inside her, and then they darted back down the stairs, leaving the room behind.

They had hardly stepped into the hallway when a bell rang sharply overhead. Before Lilly had time to turn, Trish yanked her into a corner and clamped a hand over Lilly's mouth. They were between the back of the stairwell and the wall, a crevice she hadn't known existed. The sound of footsteps echoed around the corner and brought familiar faces into view. She could make out the figures of Wyvr and Dryk, and felt pain rip through her as she saw Jake and Meg, fingers affectionately entwined. But Trish had a death grip on her that held her still and prevented her from glancing further.

"So, you excited for the Spring Festival?" Kat's voice carried from around the corner. Dryk gave a large grin.

"I'm so pumped! Meivi says she'll go with me, which will be great. I'm going to show her around some more this week."

Meg grinned and punched his arm with her free hand. They paused in front of the stairs, getting into the conversation. Behind her, Trish was dead still. "Sounds like someone has a crush."

Dryk turned pink and looked away. "Like you should talk, Meg. You're the one snappin' up the bloke soon as he looks open."

Lilly never heard her reply. Another bell pealed and the group moved outside, voices dying away. As soon as Trish released her, she collapsed to her knees, tears building in her eyes.

"Aw, Mouse, I—"

Lilly cut her off, voice shaking. "I...I'm fine."

"Come on then." She waited for Lilly to gain her bearings, then hurried around the corner. Lilly started to follow when a voice caused her to jump in surprise.

"Lilly?"

Spinning around, she found herself face to face with Wyvr, whose expression was the essence of shock. She was sure hers must have matched, because she had thought he left with the others. How terrible this must look to him: her standing there, tears streaming down her face, a backpack weighing her down, and a look of fright filling her face. As his mouth began to open again, a loud clatter caused him to turn, and Lilly bolted.

She didn't know what caused her to run, but she did so as if she were fleeing for her life. Her feet pulled her away from Charity, away from every memory, every thought. She tried to run fast enough to escape the distress that was growing, but then it hit. White hot, it cut through her, until the pain mingled with the burning in her eyes.

One declaration shot home, leaving no way for her to silence it.

They weren't going to come for her.

She was alone.

Alone.

To her left, Trish strode powerfully next to her, panting to keep up. Together, they curved back toward Firestone, leaving Charity Academy behind them. Lilly turned just enough to see a solemn look in the girl's eyes, and it was followed by a sad dip of the head. Now, she was one of them.

The change clicked into place with that agonizing jolt, a simple nod inverting her life. With tears gushing down her face, a backpack pressing heavily on her back, and a shadow covering her heart, Lilly headed toward Firestone.

She had once again been torn from a place she called home.

"Wyvr, you can't stay here forever. Come on, mate! You can't keep up this wallowing."

The voice echoed up to the perch where Wyvr was sitting. His sharp falcon eyes could easily see his twin below, and he sighed inwardly, looking away. Here in the aviary he had found some time to think, but he knew it wouldn't last forever. Reluctantly, he launched off the rafters and glided to the ground. Animals were simpler to deal with, but he couldn't keep avoiding his twin.

"I gotta tell you, I'm worried about you, Wyvr. You've never been so distant before."

Wyvr sighed. "I'm sorry, Dryk. I'll be fine, I just....I can't give up on her. Something doesn't feel right about this. I thought she'd come back, and then..."

"You saw her, though. She came and she took her stuff with her. She's gone."

Wyvr shook his head as they left the aviary. "I can't accept that."

"Everyone else has. She doesn't want to be here, and it's her choice."

"I just think you're all giving up too soon."

They moved through the halls, weaving toward the boys' dorms. The light of dusk was beginning to show in the windows, leaving a glowing darkness up ahead. Wyvr had to admit, the two of them were growing further apart every day because of this. It made his heart sink. There had been a time when they were inseparable. As kids, they were like a single person, but as they grew, so did the space between them. It was unavoidable as each became his own person, but it still cut deeply.

"We'll always be close, Wyvr. Don't let it bring you down," Dryk whispered, still knowing what was on his twin's mind. "I'm sorry I brought it up."

"Don' fret, Dryk. It just sorta hit me, is all. You've always been my best mate. I just don' want that to change."

"It won't." Dryk stopped in the hall and touched his brother's shoulder, giving a soft smile. "You and I are growing apart, maybe, but no matter how far we drift, somewhere in us we'll always be together. You're my brother. And that bond will never break."

"And if you find a girl?" Wyvr couldn't help but tease softly. Dryk laughed.

"Then you'll do what I'm doing: wish the best, but always be there to bring your head out of the clouds!"

A playful tussle broke out, ending with Wyvr in a headlock and Dryk roughly rubbing Wyvr's head with his knuckles. Laughing, Wyvr wiggled free, darting away with a crooked smile.

"Jeez lil' bro, when did you get so strong?"

Dryk chortled and pranced up beside him. "While you were in art class." He winked, and side by side they continued toward the dorms, their steps much lighter. For now, life would have to go on, and Wyvr would try respect Lilly's choices. If she wasn't ready, he couldn't stop her.

He dearly hoped he wouldn't regret his choice later.

PART THREE:

HERE LIES THE BATTLE LINE

CHAPTER ONE

A REFLECTION THAT ISN'T YOU

"Tray, wait up!"

The lanky Irish boy turned and gave a nod to the girl catching up with him. Lilly smiled in return, shifting her books in her arms as she fell in stride. The passing period between classes provided an excuse for short conversations, and the casual exchanges were becoming a form of stress relief for the winged girl. It was hard to believe it had been three months since she last saw Charity Academy. Everything still felt foreign, especially the interaction between she and the other students here at Firestone. They accepted her now, acted almost friendly. It had been confusing to process. While much of her life still held danger and risk, glimpses of humanity like this kept her spirits up.

"Where're you off to, Mouse?" Tray mused, curiosity trailing into his words.

Lilly nodded her head down the hall, where the long corridor took a sharp turn. "Library. You?"

"I got World Domination in a few minutes, and thought I'd head out early. It's the same way."

"World Domination?" Lilly repeated the strange phrase, moving faster to keep pace with his long strides.

"It's not as bad as it sounds. Kibbsty was creative naming the classes back when Firestone was founded. World Domination is pretty much another term for business and stuff like that. It's really interesting." His Irish accent sounded softer today, and his words were easier to understand. "It's like Global Perspectives and Economics, all in one."

"Who teaches it?" Lilly asked. Tray shrugged.

"Killian Joltz," a smile pressed at the corners of his mouth. "Me da."

"Your dad? He teaches here?" Lilly asked, surprised. Tray nodded, looking down, and his pace lost its purposeful rhythm. Lilly slowed, pressing against the wall to avoid being shoved by anyone passing by.

"He's been here as long as I have. Mum got sick a long time ago, and he worked for Kibbsty to get the money to care for her. We've been here longer'n anyone." The hallways emptied some, and Tray seemed encouraged to keep talking. "I was a kid back then, about nine years old. The doctors told us she had cancer, so da put all the money he could into helpin' her, but he knew we wouldn't be able to do much. Then Kibbsty showed up. Said he could help her, in exchange for my da bein' a teacher at a new school o' his. My dad would do anything to help my mother, so he agreed. We came here to help Kibbsty, and in exchange Kibbsty's given mum the best medical help he could. She's still alive, but I know even he won't be able to help her for much longer. Dad don't like it too much here... Doesn't like Kibbsty's methods, and he especially doesn't like my part in things. But he can't deny the help Kibbsty's given in return. He figures, he helps the students here learn, he's just bein' a teacher. He can't change who Kibbsty is, but he can help who we become. He's walkin' a dangerous line. Me, I've been Kibbsty's right hand man, in hopes that one day we'll find someone who'll be able to help save my mom. Dad doesn't like it, but I told him to be patient...and...and..." The reality of what he was saying hit hard, and he struggled with the words.

Lilly followed his train of thought and filled in the blank. "And you found me."

Tray nodded, a snarl on his lips. "When you got away, I felt like I had just let my mom die in front of me, and the more difficult you were, the madder I got. I knew her time was ticking away, and you could be the key. You could present a solution. You could *heal.* Maybe you could make a cure. That anger started comin' out at you, because I started to forget what I was working for. I only knew I hated you, and I forgot why."

"I'm...sorry," whispered Lilly. Tray snarled.

"For what?! You never did anything to me! You were lookin' out for yourself! We, we were the ones who were doing *you* wrong! We *killed* your parents! We kidnapped you and now you're stuck in this blasted school with us! You would have done anything to help us, wouldn't you?" Tray asked, his face contorted with pain. Lilly nodded slowly. He sighed. "An' I know you would have. But we would have never lifted a finger to help you unless it meant we got something we wanted."

Lilly looked at him sadly. "But I did do something wrong, Tray. I misjudged you. I thought you were all like Kibbsty, all just evil and murdering. Maybe you are, a little bit. But most of you weren't given a different path. You're not villains. You're just kids," Lilly whispered.

Tray sighed again and started walking away. "Maybe we were, Lilly. But now we're nothing. We're in too deep to change. The only thing we can do is pray that when the time comes an' we die like we deserve, something out there will have mercy on us and at least spare our souls."

As he walked away, a tear ran down Lilly's face, and she turned and headed toward her own class. The longer she stayed here, the more her heart broke. She used to think she knew everything. She thought she was better than them, stronger, a good guy, and that they were the enemies. The more time she spent with them, the more she realized they were nothing more than lost kids, looking for a beacon of light to rescue them. In the darkness, all they could see were the walls closing in, and their hope was quickly fading. They were trapped.

For the first time, Lilly felt a real connection with them.

Lilly's pencil scratched across her paper, scrawling a sloppy equation under her own scrutinizing gaze. "Y minus lambda mu, divided by sigma." Lilly murmured, then let out a sigh, rubbing her forehead with her hands. She pulled the numbers from the problem, punched them into the equation, but still felt lost. Frustrated, she flipped to the chart with one hand, re-reading the problem at the same time. She looked at the complex table of numbers and let out a moan. "Who in their right mind expects a fourteen-year-old to get statistics? Z-scores, charts, numbers, numbers, numbers!"

Around her, the library answered with silence. Lilly sighed and let her pencil drop. Remarkably, she was holding a solid B average in all her classes, even with the crippling level of challenge. Day by day she felt more frustrated, wondering how long she could hold it. Failing meant punishment, and she had enough of that already. This week alone she'd pulled two all-nighters to get everything done. The possibility of nodding off in class was a growing chance, one she didn't want to bargain with. Miserably, she let her head sink, then a voice whispered behind her.

"Lilly, can I talk to you?"

Lilly looked up from her book, grateful for a distraction. To her surprise, Trish was standing there, a serious look on her face. Lilly nodded her head and set aside her work. "Yeah, what's up?"

Trish sat in the chair across from her, grabbed one of the books and opened it, then glanced up at her. "There's no surveillance in here, but teachers are always comin' in and out. Be ready to bluff if you see someone."

Lilly nodded and pulled her papers toward her. She had learned these survival skills through brutality, and knew not to question them. She was still picking up on the intricate signals that kept them all alive. Trish sighed and looked up at her. "I'm worried about you, Lilly. You seem to be settling in here lately. I just don't know if it's best."

Lilly tilted her head, her brows curving with confusion. "Why?"

"I just think you might be givin' up too soon," Trish said quietly.

Lilly shook her head. "Trish, I appreciate your concern, but I don't think there's any reason for it."

"Lilly, don't throw away your life." The words were forceful, and the emotions they created amplified their volume. The past few months had been a fight for survival. Training, studying, keeping under the radar; how could that be throwing away her life?

Lilly looked up at her, heart beginning to beat faster. "Trish, there's nothing to throw away." Her heart felt empty, hurt burning through her veins. Trish's green eyes continued to plead with her.

"But what if they come?"

"They aren't going to."

"But what if—"

"They won't."

"Lilly—"

"If they were going to they would have already!"

"Eventually they'll realize—"

"Then why haven't they come yet?!" She stood, shaking with effort to keep her voice down. She clutched the table with tears beginning to build, and her wings lashed. "Trish, they *aren't* coming, don't you get it?! They think I ran away! They think I hate them! They think I don't want to be there! So here I am, trapped! And I've started to get used to the idea that I'll never get out. Kibbsty will finish his experiments, then he'll get rid of me. I was the one who kept getting away, Trish. He's going to make me pay for that, I know it," Lilly whispered, shoulders shaking.

"Lilly, Hun, just give it time. Don't decide your fate so soon."

Lilly picked up her books and sighed. "I don't really have a choice."

Trish sat there as Lilly left, beaten and unmoving, and the younger girl started to regret how harsh she'd been. But walking away, her heart still burned too much to stop.

This was her life, and that was all there was to it.

CHAPTER TWO

REVELATIONS

"Look out!"

Kat dropped to the floor with a yelp, a volleyball barely missing her head. The door she had been about to step through hovered ajar, and there was a distant thud behind her. Wide eyed, she slowly rose to her feet as a small array of people ran up. She straightened her glasses and sighed, putting her hands on her hips.

"Are you okay?!" Meg yelled, running up first, jerking to a stop in front of her. Kat gave a shaky nod.

"Barely! Are you trying to kill someone?"

"Wyvr and Dryk are trying to teach us how to play netball. Apparently we fail at it," Meg said sheepishly. Behind her, Dryk was walking up, chortling with laughter.

"It's been hilarious to watch. Would probably work better with the proper equipment, though," he grinned.

Meivi gave a wide smile. "Wyvr and Dryk are great teachers, but I'm afraid we're just a bit slow." She glanced up at Dryk and flashed a smile that was as stunning as her blonde hair. Kat couldn't help but stare at her golden eyes, which she still found frighteningly beautiful. Dryk was practically drooling.

"Well, I hope next time you don't try to use my head as a target," Kat said, brushing her hands off on her pants. Then she turned around slowly. "Where'd your ball go?"

"I'll find it!" Wyvr piped up, turning into a falcon and fluttering into the hallway. The other students followed him inside and tried not to laugh as he hopped across the floor. <There it is! Rolled under the stairs!> The bird vanished for a moment, then came back, batting the ball with his beak. To everyone's surprise, a tiny feather fluttered free from it, landing in front of Wyvr's talons. A look of shock flashed across his face so unexpectedly that they all knew who it belonged to.

<Lilly.>

Without warning, Wyvr pivoted in a blur of movement and fluttered back to the stairs. Everyone stood waiting until he reappeared in human form, clutching something in his hand. Kat cocked her head in curiosity, then he opened it. There was a single green hair.

"She wasn't alone when she came back."

"Wyvr, is that a hair? How does that—"

"It's green!"

"You sure? It almost looks blonde—"

"It's *green*. I only know one person with green hair, and she's been gone for months. Why now, why with that feather?"

"Wyvr, mate, maybe you're just—"

"No!" The sharp tone as Wyvr turned on his twin surprised them all, and Kat took an automatic step back. Dryk's face flinched, but he didn't move. No one was smiling anymore. "I'm sick of you making these excuses! Why won't you listen for once?! First you throw her to the wolves, then you leave her there! You were her closest friends, and you refuse to fight for her! It's awful! I'm not going to be part of it." He shoved past his brother, teeth clenched powerfully, hand scooping up the little feather.

Still, Dryk didn't move. "Where are you goin' then?"

Wyvr paused at the door. "To find her," he whispered, then the lone peregrine launched into the sky, leaving them frozen in shock. Kat turned in time to see Dryk's face crumple with pain, and Meivi reached out a hand.

"He's hurting bad," he whimpered, and sank to the ground. "There's nothing we can do but let him go."

"Dryk..." Meg started, and he looked up with a soft smile.

"If anyone can find her, it's him. We just have to hope that if he's right, it's not too late."

Searing pain. Burning agony. It sliced through her like a hot knife, a raging inferno. Her body curled, her mouth open in a silent scream. She couldn't make a noise. There was the sound of quick footsteps and she felt a tiny prick in her arm, then the tide ebbed and a small flicker of relief spread. Slowly, she crawled off the platform, shaking with shock.

"Very good, Miss Douglas. You've improved much since your first day. Although Pilar, my dear, you are still frightfully deadly. That's it for today's lesson. Go ahead and pack up."

In a haze, Lilly got to her feet, holding her shoulder with one arm while the other hung limp at her side. The antidote would take a bit longer to pull all the venom out, which had slipped into her hand. Mr. Lyubov drifted away to speak with other students, and someone laughed beside her.

Cherry grinned. "He always pairs you with Pilar. You'd think eventually she'd get tired of taking you down."

"If it was any of us, we wouldn't recover in time for our next class," Rock murmured from behind them. Lilly sighed and struggled with her bag.

"It never feels any better. I wish I could make it through one class without getting an almost-fatal injury."

"Eh, just be glad you heal fast. We've all gotten the crap beat out of us at one time or another. We just didn't get your bounce-back." Scarlet ruffled the hair on top of Lilly's head as she passed, and everyone stopped to gather their stuff.

"*Liróna*, how be that arm?"

Lilly looked up in surprise and gave a lopsided shrug to Pilar. Inwardly, she was baffled that the Spaniard was talking to her. "It's okay. Still burning, though."

Pilar gave a nod, then swung her bag onto her back. "Ah well, is better than bein' dead, no?" She waited until Lilly stood, then gave a smile. "But you fight well. Maybe one day I will be the one needing the medic. Later, Mouse." She gave Lilly a pat on the shoulder and left in an elegant swish of black. Feeling a bit frazzled by it all, Lilly took a step forward. The result was instant dizziness.

"Ugh..." The pain shot up from her arm, burst through her torso, and hit her legs with such force they buckled under her. Her thoughts went to mush, and she felt an arm catch her as she fell toward the floor, but the splintering pain was distant as everything darkened.

"Mouse, get up! Cory, how much sedative did Pilar give her?"

"She's coming around, stop whining."

"But timing is everythin—"

"Which is why I chose the amount I did. See, here she comes."

Lilly's eyes opened on cue, everything blurred and unfocused. Gradually, Cory and Trish came into view. "Wha'..."

"Shut up, just listen," Cory snapped, throwing a water bottle at her. Without direction, she took a drink, and Cory began to speak. "We're busting you out. Kibbsty is away on a business trip, talking to a board about funding to complete his research. We have less than two hours to get you to safety before his plane lands and he checks in with the Gemini. I'm taking you as far as the train yard, and you'll have to get the rest of the way yourself. But we have to move fast. And Trish..."

"Yeah?"

"In advance, I'm sorry about this." Without warning, his fist connected with her head, and her stunned face didn't have time to register what had happened before she was thrown into unconsciousness and she crashed into the ground. Cory knelt behind her, yanked her hands into a tight crisscross, then wrapped a coil of rope around them before pulling it tight. Lilly could barely hear his whisper. "You mean too much to me to risk Kibbsty thinking you're involved. It has to look like I flew the coop and let Lilly go to spite him one last time."

When that was done, he pulled out a card and ran it down the metal lock of the collar on Lilly's neck. There was a faint click, and it fell off in his hand, the release giving Lilly a surprising sense of freedom. She rubbed her neck in appreciation. "Almost ready. Just one last touch." Resolutely, he snapped the collar on Trish's neck and pushed a few buttons until a light flickered on. Then he moved to Lilly's side and effortlessly scooped her into his arms. "That will buy us some wiggle room, but there are still plenty of cameras that could give us away. What would help is a bigger head start. If you could stop time..."

The request was a challenge, as Lilly had little practice with her ability to stop time. Usually it came on reflex, and half the time she didn't remember doing it, only the slight shiver before and after she escaped the time stream. She knew she needed to be confident if she ever wanted to get out of here, though. Anxiety was beginning to build as she gave a slow nod.

"Focus on nothing else and hold it as long as you can. Got it? On the count of three. One."

He moved to the door and shifted her so he could grip the knob.

<Two.>

Lilly held on to his arm, heart thundering.

<Three!>

With everything in her, Lilly threw her mind against time, screaming for it to stop.

Like a wave, her powers responded to the order and carried through the room. As Cory opened the door, she could feel the movement as if it were connected to her somehow. She knew that she had succeeded, and each step prickled like a distant touch. Lilly focused on holding her powers in place. In her mind, uncounted seconds ticked past, moments she had stolen from the time stream that were being used in secret. The first few were easy to capture, but as Cory moved toward the front doors, she felt time fighting for control. The movement seemed to be increasing her struggle, as each step away from their starting point tugged at her mind.

<Hold it!>

Lilly heard the echoes of Jake's encouragement when she stopped time with him, but that felt like only moments compared to this. Her face flushed, her body shook, and she gritted her teeth, mind clutching frantically to obey. Cory was running even faster somehow, desperate to reach some preordained point before she crumbled. Lilly's eyes were closed so tight, her face was pulled taut with effort. His request seemed impossible. It was like a cord strapped around her chest, pulling harder and harder against her. She didn't know when she would—

<Cory!>

She didn't warn him fast enough. She lost her grip, and they were thrown back into the time stream. Somehow he managed to cover her mouth as she let out a scream of pain at the shock, muscles curling against the invisible force. All that came out was a muffled murmur. She was jolted so viciously, her body ripped the protest from her. She latched her fingers around Cory's hand in desperate pain, but no matter how tightly she squeezed, he never flinched. Gradually it subsided, until she finally stilled and sank back. Then he carefully released her.

<Hopefully, you won't ever have to do that again,> Cory whispered quietly. He picked her up again, unusually gentle, and began to move more slowly. Meanwhile, Lilly was weakly slumped, body drained of all energy, her face ashen and pale. Her mind was hazy and recovering as Cory moved skillfully through the woods, along the abandoned forest paths. The movement of his footsteps was steady, and his heartbeat thumped softly in her ear. Without knowing it, she slipped off to sleep, the trip becoming a blur to her sleeping mind. After what felt like only moments, his voice woke her.

<We're here.>

Rather abruptly, she was deposited on her feet; she stumbled and glanced from side to side in disorientation. Her mind was thrown off by her surroundings, from the trains parked around her, to the smell that clung to the air. A dark smog seemed to hover here, of dust and steam mixing in a muddy mist. Cory pointed between some trains and spoke aloud. "Charity is that way. You can get there relatively quickly from here. You just have to follow the path."

"Are you sure no one will catch me?" Lilly felt doubtful of her success.

"Hopefully we got enough of a head start. I'm not making any promises, it's up to you at this point." Cory started to turn, but then he froze, eyes focused somewhere in the distance. Lilly heard it, too: the distant sound of running feet.

"Cory, someone's coming."

Without thinking, Lilly reached out and grabbed Cory's arm, her mind grabbing the time stream and holding it in place. In a few quick moments, Cory scooped her back up and jumped into one of the boxcars, shutting the door behind him. He did this in only a few seconds, but as he watched the girl's face, he knew it had been a few seconds too long. He barely had Lilly's mouth covered when her powers recoiled on her; even with the sound muffled, the cry of agony resonated in his head. It sent chills through Cory like he had never felt before; it was an unearthly sound, coming from such an innocent, angelic figure, it made him want to do anything to stop her suffering. Then there was silence. Her body went limp, and the air was deadly still.

"Lilly?" he whispered, then screamed. <Lilly!!!>

3 years earlier...

"Cory! Cory, wake up! Come on, you promised! You can't play that game with me. You promised!"

"Ugh...." His face pressed deeper into the pillow, and he tried to ignore the jabbing in his shoulder. It was like trying to ignore a hurricane billowing through the room.

"Come on! Get up! You said we could go today."

<Go away,> he protested, pulling the covers over his head.

His mind was instantly assailed by a wave of mental whining. <Wake up, wake up, wake up—>

"*Fine.* You win." Cory rolled over, and opened his eyes with a yawn. In front of him, a blonde-haired, blue-eyed girl eagerly bounced at the foot of the bed, brilliant curls spilling over her shoulders. As soon as she saw him looking, a grin burst across her features and she jumped back.

"Yay! You're awake!"

"Carla, it's still—"

"Nope, you're not getting out of this! Come on, get up! Up, up, up, up, up!"

His covers vanished, snatched away and carried out the door. With a bored expression he stared after them and fell back into the pillow.

<Downstairs, five minutes. I'll be waiting,> the voice laughed, and Cory sighed with exhaustion. Pulling his pillow over his head he muttered a few complaints into the fabric and the cold air made the back of his throat tingle. Then he sat up and rubbed his tired eyes.

Despite his frustration, a smile flicked across Cory's face as he tried to motivate his way out of bed. Carla was eleven, but her enthusiasm made her seem younger. She was a bundle of energy that bounced and sprang around any room. Some days he wished she would settle down and grow up a little, but other days he enjoyed her excitement. He wanted her to stay young forever.

<Three minutes!>

Cory grabbed a shirt and pulled it on, sluggishly hunting for pants. Sometimes it felt like his telepathy had developed just for Carla, and she used it like their own private walkie-talkie. At first he felt hesitant admitting his powers to his sister, but the more he used them the more comfortable they became. In a way, it brought them together. Their younger years of fighting had faded, and their secrets created a new bond. Some days she exploited that, but he knew she meant no harm. Like today, she just wanted to share time with him.

"Okay, I'm here," Cory murmured when he finally arrived in the kitchen. Carla seemed to forget the missed deadline as she leapt to her feet in delight.

"Hooray! Come on, let's go!"

His little sister snatched his hand and dragged him out the front door, a scarf swinging out behind her. Cory was forced to follow, the warm summer air greeting him. As they made their way across the open field, Carla was strangely out of place. She had a jacket draped over her shoulder, a duffle bag in one hand, and oddly enough, she was wearing thick socks with her little tennis shoes. Cory thought she looked like someone caught in their least favorite season, trying to force the other to come earlier. This idea strengthened as she led him to the pond and stopped in front of it.

"Carla... What exactly do you have planned?"

"Ice skating!" she announced happily, then opened the duffle bag to reveal two sets of ice skates. She pulled out both and held the larger ones out toward him. Cory stayed still, visibly confused.

"Carla, it's June. Are you crazy? Someone will—"

"Come on! You promised you'd show me! Mom and Dad won't be home until late. No one will see us!"

Cory winced as her lips pulled into a pout. Somehow, that expression hit him in the gut and the guilt was almost crippling. Those blue eyes made her look angelic and innocent. As dumb as the plan was, he couldn't say it to her face. So he cracked a smile, and sighed. "Okay. But just this once!"

"Yes!"

Cory laughed as she regained her cheerfulness, and they moved to the edge of the water. Kneeling down, he watched his sister crouch beside him, watching in fascination. He could have done this standing, but the expectation in Carla's face made him want to make it magical. He waited long enough for her to squirm with anticipation, then touched the water.

The result was a magical transition from liquid to ice. It glittered beautifully in the sunlight, perfectly frozen even on the warm June day. Carla let out a gasp of awe and reached out a hand, cautiously touching it. She looked up, fingers curling back, and whispered, "It's amazing..."

Cory smiled and stood, giving a shrug. "It's ice; it's frozen water. There's nothing that amazing about it."

Carla gasped as if he had said something revolting, and shook her head in earnest. "Cory, it's more than that. You made it freeze, in the summer! That's amazing! I'd give anything to have a super power like that!"

Cory laughed. "Super power? Carla, I don't have 'super' powers. I can just freeze things, remember? Well, mostly."

"Wait, can you do the opposite, too?" Carla suddenly asked.

Cory blinked and shrugged. "Yeah, I guess I can, but I have to freeze something first..."

"Why?"

Cory paused, an ice skate in each hand, and tried to explain it in a way she'd understand. "Basically, when something freezes, it loses energy. When it warms up, it gains it. So it's easier to take energy from things than it is to give it to them; it's easier to freeze things than it is to heat them up. When I freeze things, my body stores the energy, then uses it later on. But I need to have energy first... Does that make sense?"

Carla nodded with a wide smile. "That's so cool! How do you know so much?"

Cory sat next to her and unlaced his shoes. "Research. I stayed up late a few times searching the internet, and I checked books out from the library. I'm not positive that's how it happens, but it makes the most sense." He set his shoes down and started putting on the ice skates. "I mean, I can *feel* my powers working when I use them."

"What does it feel like?" Carla whispered, shoes half untied. Cory smiled.

"It's cool. It's like I'm reaching out with my mind and grabbing something that should be impossible to hold. It's like if you were to reach into a pool of water, and pick it up like a solid object. But it doesn't *feel* solid. It's like a fly trapped in your hand, thrashing around but still held in your grasp. Then it...like...melts into me. The energy disappears but I still *feel* it. I can call it back, and then give it to something, but it's so weird...I don't know how to describe it."

"Tell me! Tell me more!" Carla squealed, and Cory looked at the ice, pausing with his skates still untied.

"I just... I can sense things I couldn't before. I can look at the water and tap into the energy as easily as I can reach out and touch it. It's crazy being able to create snow on a summer day, or freeze

313

just a few drops in a cup of water. Everything has a new dimension I can move through." Cory sighed happily. "Man, Carla, if only you could do this, too."

Carla gave a smile and finished putting on her skates. "Hearing what it's like and seeing it is enough for me. I'm just glad I have such an awesome brother."

Cory stood, chuckling as he hobbled onto the ice. "I'm not that awesome. But I'm glad you don't hate me."

Carla came up behind him, a natural on her ice skates. "I could never hate you! You're the best big brother ever!"

"And you're the best sister."

They skated leisurely across the frozen surface, Carla's movements fluid and Cory's awkward. He wasn't a great skater, but he made the most of the moment. Carla never stopped smiling, beaming as they moved across the ice. By the time they finally returned to the bank, her cheeks were glowing and she was breathless with happiness. Cory returned the pond to its normal state, put the skates away, and together they began to walk back toward the house. Carla was bubbling with energy, asking question after question, but their happy day was broken by a voice.

"Good morning, kids. Out for a stroll?"

Cory turned cautiously as a man came up beside them, sporting a trench coat and a bristly mustache. The teen reflexively separated his sister from the man before answering. "Yeah, just a walk."

The man's eyes traveled to Carla's bag, and he gave a unsettling smile. "Ice skates? Is there a rink nearby?"

Cory glared, and a chill bit the air. Carla clutched his hand loosely and he took a step back. "What do you want?" he huffed.

The man turned and stopped in front of them. "I saw your powers a few weeks back. You haven't exactly been careful hiding them, after all. Quite extraordinary, if I do say so myself. I have a proposal for you, young man, and you'd be wise to take it."

"I'm not interested, sorry. Come on, Carla." Cory moved to walk around the man, but in a flash, he shifted, and Cory felt Carla yanked from his grasp. She screamed in shock, and Cory was moving to her defense when a sharp click cut the air.

"Now, I think you'll do best to listen to my offer," the man hissed, and Cory's insides twisted when he saw the cold black barrel pressed against his sister's forehead.

Cory's breath was ragged. "Let her go. She has nothing to do with this."

The man laughed and took a step back, the gun pressed to her face in a calm but firm grip. "Dear boy, she has everything to do with it. You clearly won't listen unless you have a reason to. Now you have a reason. Shall we sit and talk?"

Cory growled, but didn't move. "Talk. You can't threaten my sister's life and expect me to be very cooperative."

The man sighed, but seemed happy nonetheless. "Ah well, it will have to do, I suppose. My name is Dr. Kibbsty, and I run a school called Firestone Academy. It's for gifted people quite like yourself. It's still in the works, but I have a few students already under my guidance. I would be enthused if you would come and join us there."

"And if I say no?"

The gun pressed closer, and Kibbsty laughed. "Well then, I think you know what will happen."

"Cory, don't! You don't have to do anything!" Carla's voice startled them both, and the eleven-year-old's statement was fierce. Her eyes were suddenly free of the fear they had held before, and her face was uncharacteristically brave. "Whatever happens, it'll be okay, just don't go with that man!"

"Silence!"

"Cory, don't worry about me!"

A crack rang through the air, and Carla fell to her knees, whimpering with pain. A trickle of blood appeared on her temple, crimson crawling across her brow. Cory clenched his fists, but was forced to stand still as the gun moved to the back of her head.

"I said, silence. Now, Cory, what is your answer?"

"I'm not sure, I need time—"

"Cory, please don't!"

"Carla, you can't ask me to watch you die."

"Don't do this! He's a bad guy! You're not supposed to be a bad guy, Cory!"

"Silence, girl!"

"Cory, please, don't agree!"

"Silence!" Kibbsty kicked Carla flat on her face and put a foot in the small of her back. Carla quieted, but looked up at her brother with earnest eyes. Her cheeks were wet with blood and dirt, but she had shed no tears. Her lovely face was innocent and calm, even under the grime.

<It'll be okay. You're the best brother ever, Cory.>

The voice distracted him so much he didn't hear Kibbsty ask the question again, and he was looking at his sister's face as she whispered, both in his head and on her lips, <I love you.> Then the sound of the gun echoed, and Cory watched as his sister crumpled, hair stained red.

"Carla!"

"Time's up, Cory."

Cory didn't hear and recoiled backward, unable to look at his sister, unable to face her murderer. He turned away, body shaking with the shock of it all. Her words continued to echo in his mind.

"If you don't want the same fate for Kami and your parents, I suggest you accept my offer. Such talent shouldn't be wasted, and your refusal will only mean more death. I can prevent that from happening."

His voice was almost remorseful, like he regretted the measures he was taking. It was a lie, but Cory's soul bought it through his pain. Kami was only two: he couldn't imagine seeing her die, too. Carla adored her baby sister and would have been shattered by her death. He couldn't lose both of his sisters.

Suddenly, he hated his powers, especially the one that had allowed him to hear her last words. He shut off that part of his mind, shut out the memories and locked them away, desperate to escape the pain. Their secret conversations had caused this, and his desire to share his powers brought this disaster. Accepting this offer might be the only path to correct his mistake. If he left, he couldn't hurt anyone else.

Slowly, he whispered to Kibbsty, the ice freezing his soul this time instead of water. "Okay, Kibbsty. You win. I'll do it your way."

"Good man. Now, let's leave this bloody business and I'll show you the school."

Without a glance back, Cory followed Dr. Kibbsty, *and the life he once lived faded from view...*

Cory gently pushed Lilly's hair out of her face, pausing at her forehead. Her face was icy cold, her cheeks ashen, and her pulse barely detectable, but she was alive. After she collapsed, he had thought she was dead. When he checked her pulse, he found her clinging stubbornly to life, but she wouldn't last long in this state.

After they hid in the train, the Gemini twins made it impossible to escape, wandering around the boxcars looking for them. When the locomotive lurched forward, he had no choice but to sit there with Lilly and wait it out. At the next stop, Cory managed to smuggle Lilly into the forest, but now they were stuck at the base of a hill with no sense of direction. Cory mentally calculated how far they had come. The train ride had been about two hours, but the train had traveled relatively slowly. Overall, he guessed the same trek would take at least a day by foot, but carrying Lilly, it would take even longer. Now, if he could get a car.... No, he would have to stay on foot. If the Gemini twins caught any hint of their trail, it would be over in an instant. How would he keep her alive long enough to save her?

There's no way, Cory thought, cursing under his breath. Thall and Mar would guard the train station, and any other method of transportation would be too traceable or too slow. He glanced at Lilly, and repressed memories slipped to the surface of his mind. She reminded him so much of Carla, though they didn't look alike—Carla's face had been heart-shaped, her eyes almond, while Lilly's face had softer features and curves, angelic more than eye-catching—but the similarities were evident to Cory. Both had a childlike innocence, each had faith that refused to die, and if Carla were still alive, she'd be Lilly's age. Cory felt like he could see his sister again, yet once more he was watching her die.

Anger burned through him, a curse slipping out of his mouth. He tried to shut out the memories and force himself to see no more than a bratty girl. Try as he might, when he opened his eyes, there she was, deathly still and entirely undeserving of her fate.

There had to be something he could do!

But what?

<What did you *do* to her?!!>

Cory jerked in surprise as he looked for the speaker, and saw the peregrine falcon only moments before it became a boy, whose fist connected with his face. The blow was surprisingly strong, and sent him flat on his back. He had been only halfway to a standing position, so the impact sent him to the ground hard. In reflex, Cory's mind entered battle mode, and he crouched in rage, wiping blood from his mouth.

"I didn't do anything, punk, so back off!"

"I don't believe you, you conniving snake. You good for nothing—"

"Easy, Bird-boy, don't pull out your colorful Australian insults yet. Ask her yourself if you'll feel better! Just shut up before the Gemini hear you!" Cory hissed, still crouched defensively on the ground. The teen gave a low murmur, eyes never leaving Cory, then reluctantly he morphed back into a falcon.

<Lilly?> Wyvr whispered, gently nudging the girl's hand.

<Wyvr?> The voice came back in a feeble whisper, and Lilly's hand stirred, touching his wing. <Is that really you?>

<Yeah, Lilly. It's me. Are you okay? If you need me to kick the Popsicle's butt, I will. If he laid one hand on you—>

<No, he was helping me... But the Gemini twins are following... We have to...>

<Shh. That's enough for me. If you say he was bein' nice, I believe you. Just hang on, we'll get help.> Wyvr nudged her hand reassuringly and gave a tiny nod. Then he faced Cory. <She says you're helping an' I believe her, but don't think that puts us on good terms. I'll cooperate for her sake, but I'd sooner peck your eyes out than be your mate.>

<The feeling is mutual, Aussie. Sorry to tell you, the only way she's going to make it now is if we get her back to Firestone—>

<Over my dead body!>

<If we don't, it will be *her* dead body.>

Wyvr shifted uncomfortably and his feathers fluffed with agitation. The boys stilled as a plane rumbled overhead, and the bird gave a human-like sigh. <Why Firestone?>

<Trish has an immune booster that worked not too long ago. It can save her life again. In the state she's in now, her powers don't have enough strength to activate, and she's fading. That booster is the only way.>

<I...I guess we can take her there, then. But when she's better she'll be free to come back to Charity?>

<Keep her alive first, then we'll worry about that. As of right now, we have no way to get her there soon enough.>

<I can solve that problem easy. Keep watch,> Wyvr replied, then closed his eyes and reached out with his mind.

CHAPTER THREE

NOT FORGOTTEN

<Hang on, it's a big campus! She could be anywhere!> Dryk darted from room to room, looking for the young Strand. It was a Saturday, and with the lack of classes, the task was remarkably difficult to accomplish—especially when that Strand was Jenny. The teleporter had a habit of hiding in trees or on the roof to have some time alone, and finding her was turning into a scavenger hunt. Announcements were useless on days like today, when students were scattered across the grounds. All he could do was run and ask around, and was so focused on doing both, he didn't notice as Meivi came around the corner.

"Look out!"

Dryk didn't stop fast enough and knocked the girl flat on her back, staggering so he didn't fall on top of her. With a frantic apology, he helped her back to her feet, his ears a deep red. "I'm so sorry! Are you okay?"

Meivi dusted herself off and gave a wide smile. "I'm fine, Dryk. It's no problem. Where were you rushing to?" she asked, tilting her head to the side. Dryk forced himself not to stare at her eyes, then answered.

"I have to find Jenny. Have you seen her?"

A look of disappointment flashed across Meivi's face, and he realized he'd said the wrong thing. He quickly added, "Wyvr found Lilly and asked me to get help." In a rush, he threw in, "Jenny can teleport."

"Oh!" Meivi was visibly relieved. "Well, I think she's in the science lab doing some homework. Maybe if you hurry you can catch her!"

"Thank you! You're a life saver, maybe literally!" He gave her a hug in thanks, then resumed running down the hall, hoping he'd get there in time.

Cory crouched, listening carefully for footsteps. He could sense Thall and Mar, but he couldn't figure out where they were. Wyvr was perched on a branch overhead, watching with his sharp eyes.

<They're getting nearer. Cory, how close are you going to let them—>

<Wait, I have an idea. Wait for my signal.>

Assuming an air of confidence and authority, Cory stood, quietly listening to the approaching footsteps, arms across his chest. As Mar pulled into view, he gave an icy grin and tipped his head to the girl.

"Cory... How did you get here?" she hissed in disbelief.

Cory smirked icily. "Train. I wasn't far behind you when she made a break for it. Managed to hop on before it got too far. She got away before I could catch her. That time stopping is a nuisance."

"Well, she's our prey now. Track your own." Thall came up beside Mar and glared at Cory.

"Sorry, I can't have you two killing her."

Thall growled low and leaned closer, a fist forming tightly near Cory's face. "We don't take orders from you, Cory. Don't tempt us, or we'll remind you of your place."

The air suddenly lost its warmth, and the twins were left in instant pain. Mar clutched her brother's arm as they fell to their knees, her mouth open in shock. Cory hissed, "Go ahead. Test me. We'll see who has the faster strike."

He kept the cold assault until both fell unconscious. Then he brought the air back to its natural temperature and held up a hand to signal Wyvr.

"Let's move."

Cory ducked down and scooped Lilly up, then turned as a girl appeared in a flash of light. The new arrival didn't say a word, just stood uncertainly, glancing to the falcon for direction. "Cory, this is Jenny. Jenny, that's Cory. You ready?"

Both nodded, and Wyvr hopped onto Jenny's shoulder. The girl hesitantly set a hand on both Lilly and Cory.

<Hold on.>

Even with the warning, the teleportation took Cory by shock. It was like being yanked through the eye of a needle, his body folding over a thousand times in a rush of air. It wasn't painful, but there was a terrible discomfort, like having your foot fall asleep and being unable to wake it. The effect only lasted a millisecond, but when his feet touched the ground at Firestone, it took everything he had not to drop Lilly. He was still regaining his senses when Jenny let go and disappeared in a flash of light.

<Ugh... Teleportation,> Wyvr murmured. Cory was tempted to agree.

The ice-powered teen glanced around, waiting for his mind to register his surroundings. The room was very dark, but the faint outline of a counter was visible. Looking closer, he could see objects on the countertop and a glimmer of light near the door.

Trish's lab, he thought. Cautiously, he moved to the door and pressed his ear against it.

"It's too soon! You have no way of knowing if it'll work!"

"Trish, this is the best way! She's as good as dead anyway."

"Tray, think of the consequences. If it doesn't work—"

"Then I'll take the blame. I gotta go get it ready. Kibbsty'll be back soon." A door opened, and after it closed the room was silent. Unable to wait any longer, Cory shoved the door of the lab open and met a startled Trish.

"Cory! What did you do?!"

"Get the immune booster first. Explanation later," Cory snapped, moving quickly to the back of the hospital wing. Choosing the bed closest to the window, he set Lilly on it and opened the blinds. The dim evening sun was crawling through it feebly, but it would have to be enough. Wyvr perched on the pillow next to her, silently observing as Cory went to work. He washed his hands in the sink, grabbed Trish's tray of tools, then waited for her to follow.

"Okay, here's the booster. Explain," Trish said sharply, starting Lilly's treatment.

"We moved fast, but Thall and Mar got there quick. We hid in a train car, but the train left the station and we were trapped inside." He watched as Trish administered the booster, and he continued. "We ended up somewhere north, I think, when we finally got away, but they followed us. The only way we escaped was because Lilly stopped time, but she held it too long and the result..."

"Sent her into shock. Boy, you're good at kickin' the snot outta people." She sighed, checking Lilly's pulse. "She's coming around, keep goin'."

"Well, Bird-boy here showed up and got one of his Charity friends to bring us here to get the booster," Cory finished. Trish glanced more closely at the silent falcon.

"You're one of the twins. Wyvr?"

<Lucky guess,> he clicked sourly. Trish grinned.

"Nah, I just pay attention to details. You're a bit slimmer as a falcon than Dryk is. He's got more muscle, but you're faster." She ran a hand across each of Lilly's wings, checking for bone damage, and chuckled at his expression. "I enjoyed sortin' out the differences, sorry."

<No worries. So... She's okay?> He dipped his head at Lilly.

"Yeah, she should perk up soon when it kicks in. Best you stay in that form though. If someone walks in, you won't be as obvious."

Lilly slowly began to breathe normally, the color returning to her face, and her figure moved from its unnatural slump to a more peaceful rest. Trish finally stepped back and gave a little smile, but Cory could still see the worry that traced her face.

"What's wrong?" he asked softly. Trish sighed.

"Kibbsty got approval to take the next step with his research. He thinks he's sorted it out, thanks to the notes from Charity. Tray's goin' to volunteer his mum to be the guinea pig."

<What?!>

"Stay out of it, Aussie! Is he insane?!" Cory hissed. Trish growled low.

"She's dyin', Cory. She's losing to the cancer. He thinks it's his last chance."

"Kibbsty doesn't have a clue what he's doing yet! He'll kill her, and maybe the rest of us, too, if he tries anything like they did—"

<Are you talking about the diary?! How did you—>

"He's not thinking straight! Neither of them are. Cory, I tell you, as soon as Kibbsty gets here, he's gonna do it!"

"And then what? What if it works?"

Trish grew dead silent and whispered, "He's going to try giving powers to normal humans."

Cory went still and the room grew cold. "No."

"Cory, he wants to use your parents."

"I'll kill that good-for-nothing lunatic if he lays so much as one hand on them—"

"You know what would happen—"

"HE'S NOT TOUCHING MY FAMILY!"

Cory's yell caused Lilly to stir, and Wyvr, who'd been riveted by the argument, turned his attention to Lilly as her eyes fluttered open.

"Cory...."

The color drained from his face as he remembered the fate of his sister in Kibbsty's hands, and he whispered so softly Trish had to strain to hear it. "I won't let anyone else die because of me."

"What about the plan? *L.A.T.E.R.* If we fight, we might not *live.*"

"It's now, Trish. This is it. This is the last straw. It's time to say no, Trish. No more."

The finality of that statement silenced the room, and even Wyvr knew that something important was happening. Trish had a look of surprise on her face, forgetting her moment of fear. "Now? Are you sure?"

"Now. We'll spread the word, and when we're ready we end this."

"You're suggesting an all-out mutiny," Trish said softly. Cory nodded.

"Enough is enough. I'm sick of being a pawn. I'll get free from his hold, or I'll die trying," he snarled. Trish gave a slow nod, and her face grew set in determination.

"I'll fight too, then. But how do we get the word out without tipping off the wrong people?"

<I'll do it,> Wyvr input, and they turned in surprise as if they had forgotten he was there. <Just tell me who.>

Cory gave a steady nod and took a deep breath. "It's settled then. We fight."

"Where is everyone?" The doctor set his things on the table, uncomfortable in the eerie silence. Kibbsty glanced first down one hallway, then the next, and Tray grunted.

"Their rooms, the gym. Thall and Mar are still hunting down that brat."

"No word on her?"

"None."

Kibbsty tossed his bag on the desk chair and scowled. "Once I'm sure this works, I swear that monstrosity is dead. And good riddance. I bet Hayachi would have a ball with her."

"I wouldn't get her going if I were you. She acts complacent, but give her a leash and she'll use any opportunity to kill everyone and escape. As soon as she gets that collar off she'll change her mind. Why you'd want someone that dangerous—"

"She'll bend eventually. Just like the rest. It just takes time. Is the computer up?"

"Almost. It's a bit slow today."

"Let me know when it is. Cory! I was wondering when you'd show."

Tray turned in surprise as the icy teen slipped into the lab and leaned casually against the counter top. "Well, I'm here. How was the conference?"

"Good! Brilliant, really. They agreed to let me move onto the next phase, and my investor was very pleased with the progress I've already made! You're welcome to see our grand experiment."

"Experiment? What experiment?"

"Come see!" Kibbsty turned as the log-in screen of his computer pulled up, punched in his password, and paused to press his hand against the security pad. Cory cautiously came up behind him and watched as he pulled up a few files.

"Okay, Cory, look at this. I studied Lilly's DNA and found out that it contains a protein that's unlike anything I've ever seen. All of our students have this protein, and I already discovered that each of you has a mutated version for each of your powers. After a while, I found the three that were each of Lilly's gifts. The problem was sorting out which protein controls which power. I did experiments on a few lab rats and copied the DNA samples into them, but the results, I fear, weren't pretty. One ended up with wings, but it died before they were half grown. The next died almost immediately after the experiment. But the third...." Kibbsty pointed to a cage by his desk with a gleeful smile. "The third recovered spectacularly, and when he cut himself on the cage door, he healed in seconds. So far, there have been no side effects. It's extraordinary! None of the other powers I've grafted had this much success. You were right: she has been the breakthrough I needed. Not because of her third strand, but the power that it enables. The *healing*, Cory. It can change things."

Cory leaned close and looked at the rat, chuckling softly. "So now what are you going to do?"

"The next step: try it on a human. Now that I've discovered the correct protein, I can try to graft it into a human to create the same healing powers the brat has! And then you know what we'll do?"

"What?"

"We'll add more powers. The second strand," Kibbsty whispered merrily. "Oh, think of the glorious possibilities! We can splice these powers into human DNA! People would pay *millions* for that! And people would praise the team that made it possible. Once we have a few successful trials, the doors all open."

"Human trials?"

"Why, yes. Tray already agreed to let his mother be first, but I was hoping to get a healthier individual for the second. Maybe someone in your family—"

Cory gave a loud chuckle, but did not turn from the rat cage. Kibbsty's sentence trailed off as a chill crept across his body. "Oh, Kibbsty, you greedy slime ball." Slowly, he faced the doctor, his face barely masking his rage. "You're not going to try it on anyone, or so help me, I'll kill you with my bare hands."

"I'm glad you're vocalizing your opinion, boy, but you really won't have much of a say in the matter," Dr. Kibbsty answered coldly, and his hand reached toward his pocket for his gun.

Cory snarled, "Believe me, I do!" Cory's movements were unnaturally fast as his fist slammed into Kibbsty's head. The man crashed against his desk chair, falling hard to the floor. Within a second, Cory had him by the throat, but before he could make another move, Tray responded, and Cory crumpled as electricity raced through his body.

"Have you gone ravin' mad?!" Tray screamed, taking a stance in front of Kibbsty as Cory snarled up at him.

"Have *you*?! You're selling your mom to the devil, Tray! This is far enough!"

"It's her only hope! I got to—"

"It's a lie, Tray! He'd sooner kill her with the rest of us than let her live!"

"Shut your trap!" Cory curled as the electricity caused his muscles to spasm. Tray glowered down at him. "Just because you have your family all nice and healthy doesn't mean we all do."

"My family isn't all nice and healthy, you idiot! My sister is dead because of Kibbsty!"

"Well, she probably deserved it!"

Tray never had a chance to continue before the air froze inside him and his body slumped in shock. The room was colder than a freezer, temperature dropping each second with Cory's rage. "Whatever I've done or will do, Carla *never* deserved to die like that. She never had a chance, and Kibbsty's done it a hundred times. Wake up! He's *used* us. He's used us all! Think of Lilly's parents, think of Pilar's brother. Hayachi's locked in the basement and she *agreed* to be here. What does that tell you? We're stronger than him! But we hide our heads to keep them attached to our necks. And what are we afraid of? We're the ones with powers, not him!"

"I can't risk it!"

"Then you can die with him, for all I care!"

Cory raised his fist to hit the Irish boy, but before he could touch him, a wall of electricity sent him flying backwards. Cory cursed and staggered back to his feet, only to receive a blow across the back that knocked him flat again. It had come too fast and hard to be Tray, and that meant—

"Who has the faster strike now, boy?!"

Cory tried to freeze Mar as he had before, but a cackle of laughter confirmed to him that he couldn't. Snarling, he rolled away from another blow, only to feel a stinging touch on his neck that froze him in his tracks. His moment had run out, and now the tide had turned.

"Now, Cory, I hear you still have one baby sister. I'm sure we can think of some unique ways to help her join her sibling."

Cory couldn't even flinch as a foot slammed into his stomach, pain roaring through him. He told himself it was over, and for a moment prayed her threats wouldn't come true. He deserved hell for all he'd done, but his family meant everything. Then, as Mar readied herself to strike again, an explosion sent her stumbling backward.

Lilly rolled over and opened her eyes, feeling lost for a few moments, her mind slowly registering her surroundings. By now, she should have been used to waking up in the hospital wing, but it still took a few moments to realize where she was. Distant noises brought her quickly to consciousness, and she sat up so suddenly, Wyvr let out a chirp of surprise.

"Wyvr?!" Lilly yelped in shock, and the falcon hopped onto her knee and nodded. "What's going on? Was that an explosion? Where are Cory and Trish?"

<It's a fight, and Cory and Trish are part of it. It's all-out mutiny. I bet the explosion was just the beginning, Lilly. We should get out of here!>

"No! We have to help them!" Lilly jumped to her feet, but her legs couldn't support her, and she fell into the bed opposite her own.

Wyvr moved to human form and picked her up, easily depositing her on the edge of the bed. "Are you crazy?! You want to be part of that?!"

Another explosion rattled the walls, and Lilly moved to stand again, holding onto his arm. "They need help, Wyvr! They'll be killed!!!"

Wyvr took a sharp breath, as if holding in some response, then sighed. "Okay, you win. But—" he cut himself off, and sharply glared. "You have to stay here until you are fully functioning! I'm calling for backup, and until it gets here, *don't move!*"

"But—"

"*Stay!*" Without giving her a chance to argue, Wyvr returned to a falcon and flew out of the room. His leaving was followed by a loud rumble as the battle continued to rage.

Dryk sat nervously on the edge of the fountain, fidgeting with his pencil. He tapped it against his pant leg and tried to keep his emotions in check. It had been an hour since Jenny returned, but there had been no news from his brother yet. To his sides, Jenny tried to study and Meivi watched him closely. Their company felt intrusive right now. All he wanted was his brother.

<Dryk! Dryk!>

The voice was a welcome one, but the news was not. Quickly, his brother described the situation, then his voice was gone again. Without waiting, Dryk stood and turned to Jenny.

"I need a ride."

"Where're you going?" Meivi stood in concern, and Dryk tried to give her a reassuring glance.

"Wyvr needs help. There's a fight at Firestone, and I'm going."

"By yourself?!" she asked, startled.

He nodded. "I'm not bringing the others into this. This is a civil war I'm running into, and I can't ask anyone else to risk their lives. Wyvr and I, we fight together, never alone. I'll be back soon!"

"Dryk, wait!!!"

But they were already gone, a blip of light swallowed by the air.

Hushed Chinese whispers echoed through the dungeon between two slim silhouettes. The place was pitch dark, save for a small glimmer of light coming from the stairs.

"Nuo, what's happening?" Hayachi asked, glancing at the light.

"A fight, a big one. I'm getting us out of here."

The girl stood eagerly and tugged against her chains. Her powers pressed against the back of her mind, just out of her reach, but not for long. "Do you have the keys?"

The boy gave a tiny smile, then chuckled. "Even better. I have him."

Hayachi looked up in glee as Harris stepped forward. She could almost taste her freedom as she watched his arm start transforming into bolt cutters. Smoothly, she smiled at him and took a step back.

"Cory, are you all right?"

The icy teen let out a deep breath and swayed as he stood. "Thanks to you. But *good lord*, Trish! You blew the front of the lab clean off!"

"Complain later, when I'm done causing damage! We gotta find that weasel Kibbsty!"

In the first few minutes of the battle, the entire school had poured into the laboratory. It had been their chosen battleground ever since their fight over Lilly. The computer was in ruins, glass was strewn across the ground, and teens were locked in combat. For every student who was fighting against Kibbsty, one was fighting for him. Most, like Tray, were too afraid to change sides, while others, like Thall and Mar, enjoyed working for him. It was nearly impossible to know who was fighting for whom.

Cory ducked past Pete, who was trying to keep Harper down, while Fuego and Mic were having a heated confrontation that looked destined to burn something. Trish had just ducked out the front door when Cory was stopped in his tracks by an unexpected burst of pain. It only lasted a second, but it earned a scream of agony that caused many to falter in horror. Then there was a birdlike screech, and Cory turned just enough to see the peregrine form of Wyvr strike Ms. Knox across the face with his talons. She let out a cry of rage, but he was already out of range.

<You okay?> the falcon asked, circling somewhere above.

<Yeah, thanks,> Cory answered shakily back, and continued toward the door at a much slower pace. He sped up when he heard the sound of gunfire.

Lilly crept down the hallway, wings trembling as she moved. She kept her eyes sharp for danger, heart beginning to thunder but relieved to be where the action was. Before long she reached the laboratory, where the clamor had become a deafening roar. People had gradually drifted outside, with little of the front entrance in one piece, and flames and sparks flickered in the wake of ruin. Lilly had barely entered the room when a figure with blood red hair caught her eye. She didn't recognize the girl, but the fighting outside demanded her attention instead.

Wyvr quietly scanned the sky as he waited for help to arrive. He tried to aid when he could, but it was hard to tell who he should be assisting. The faces were all strangers here, the powers unpredictable. In his mind, they were all enemies, which made the task seem daunting. He was relieved when he saw a flash of light, and a second falcon zipped through the sky.

<Dryk! You made it!>

<I couldn't leave my best mate alone in a place like this.> The bird looped around his brother, then turned its eyes to the battle. <Has everyone gone mad?!>

<Nearly! Half of them are out to kill Kibbsty, and half of them won't have any of that!>

Dryk shook his head and dove at Thall, cuffing the boy hard across the shoulder, then darting out of reach. <Well, let's help the better half win!>

Kat looked at her homework and frowned, taking off her glasses and rubbing her eyes. She couldn't seem to do anything productive today, even in the quiet common room. A nagging feeling kept hitting her gut, refusing to leave her alone. Finally, she shut the book, and paced in front of the fireplace.

Something's wrong... She ran her friend's faces through her mind, from Meg to Jake to Karen, but didn't see any reason to worry.

Something's wrong... She hesitated before reaching Lilly, uncertain what she would find. The feeling nagged, refusing to be abated, so let her powers search. When she did, she let out a gasp of horror, and her eyes flew open.

"Oh, no!" Without hesitation she bolted out of the library and yelled into the hallway. "JENNY!"

Hayachi stepped through the door and breathed in the air, a gleeful smile creeping across her face. Behind her, Nuo followed, wearing a woolen cloak with a dark hood. Hayachi was wearing a matching cloak, looking more relaxed and calm than she had since she'd been dragged to this forsaken place. The rubble looked fitting after what they went through. Harris stood behind them and gave a soft whisper.

"You'll make sure my brother's fine, then?" he asked. Nuo nodded.

"We will, you have my word. Thank you for helping us," the younger teen answered, and Harris waved them off.

"I just want his safety. It's all I ever wanted." He turned and started back into the building, going inside without a backward glance.

As the two falcons circled the battlefield, it was hard to make sense of the chaos. Compared to their last battle here, this was amplified a hundred times. Nightmare-like creatures crawled across the mountaintop, dark eyes twinkling as they devoured or attacked anything in their path. The sound of rock music blasted through the school corridors, painfully loud even at the height the twins were flying. Students were cussing, fire was burning, the wind was howling; everywhere was pure chaos. Wyvr could sense the fear from his brother as they tried to make a move, uncertain where to start.

<Whose side are we on?> Dryk said quietly, glancing from one figure to another. Wyvr just twittered sadly as he tried to decide. When he chose to help, he never expected it would be this difficult. The students at Firestone were clearly more dangerous than he imagined.

Computer parts and pieces attacked a slender boy, then they fell to the ground mysteriously broken. An inky black dragon roared and faced off with one formed from fire. Someone snarled. Someone screamed. It took all Dryk's control not to shut his eyes and look away. Lilly wanted to help in this chaos? It was hard not to question why he was here the more bloodshed he saw.

A wayward spike went flying through the sky, and Dryk ducked out of the way. Meanwhile, Wyvr moved to action as he dove at a giant spider and drove it away from one of the only students he recognized. Scarlet shot him a grateful glance and scrambled away, but before Wyvr regained altitude, his mind was assaulted by a wave of terrifying hallucinations. Crashing into the ground, he flailed away from the monstrous insects rising up around him. Moments later the images faded as Dryk found his attacker.

The battlefield he returned to seemed just as frightening though.

Dr. Kibbsty crouched behind a rock and glanced at the teen beside him. Edward sat grumbling unhappily and huffed.

"Where is Tray? He's your body guard, not me."

"Silence! Pilar plucked him off, and if you know what's best, you'll do as I ask! We're almost there, and then you can have your fun and kill some of those traitors. But you need to wait until I'm down the mountain."

Edward cursed angrily, spines prickling along his arms. "Do you know how long I've wanted to kill Cory? He's pushed me around too long, and then the way he defended that brat... I swear as soon as I see him—"

Both froze as the ice Strand came into view, and before Kibbsty could stop him, Edward launched out of hiding and bolted toward his longtime rival.

Cory saw Edward only moments before he heard him, his body letting out a terrible crackle as his quills rippled forth. Cory answered with a blanket of ice, so slick and sudden Edward flew when he hit it, sending splinters of ice flying when his quills sliced across it. Kibbsty was momentarily forgotten, and both boys stood in silence, exchanging iced glares.

"You and me, Ice Boy. No powers. Let's see what you're made of without an ice cube backing your punch."

Cory chuckled softly. "Holding a grudge over combat training? Isn't that a bit immature?"

"Chicken?"

"Hardly." Cory's fist hit Edwards face, leaving a deep red mark. "Let' see how fast you can lose."

A fist fight erupted, and the two boys became blurs of movement. Meanwhile, Trish was struggling to escape Mic, who'd freed himself from Fuego. Flames snaked around her in serpentine form, and no matter how many explosions she sent at him, they just kept weaving closer. Trish screamed angry threats at him, but only maniac laughter responded.

Pilar knelt by Fuego, checking worriedly for a pulse.

Thall let out a yell of rage as Mar collapsed

In the midst of all the chaos, two figures tried to sneak past.

Suddenly, Cory landed a blow that sent Edward to his stomach, and he stood breathless, victorious over the boy. He turned in time to see Trish break free of Mic's flames when Harper's scream jerked his attention away. He turned and started to move that way when a sharp noise carried through the air, and a pain struck his side. Cory heard Trish yell in shock, and looked down at the sharp spine sticking out of his skin. As the poison and paralysis hit, he watched a crimson stain appear, and fell to the ground.

Lilly looped quickly around the edge of the fighting, unable to decide where she should help. This battle was so different from the first. When Charity and Firestone fought, it was the experienced against the amateurs, and numbers had the biggest impact. Now that the Firestone students were fighting each other, it was vicious, and somewhat personal. They were all battle trained, deadly, and matched hit for hit. Lilly couldn't find an opening to jump in, the pace too fast to keep up. She was just about to give up in frustration, when she noticed a figure to her left: Kibbsty.

"What is he up to?" Lilly whispered, creeping closer.

Kat staggered as her feet touched the ground, and as soon as she had, Jenny disappeared. The frightened girl only agreed to take her when she promised she didn't have to stay. As Kat glanced around, she began to wish they'd both stayed behind. Battle sounds rushed through her ears, and she pushed her glasses on her face as she looked hurriedly around the battlefield. Thankfully, she saw Lilly's outline, and had opened her mouth to yell when she felt a squeeze around her heart. It was unlike anything she had ever experienced, and that made her afraid. Someone shifted behind her, and a hand touched her shoulder. Kat didn't dare try to turn.

"I need you to teleport us out of here," a voice hissed.

Kat froze, heart beginning to pound. "I can't! I don't teleport!" she squeaked. The grip tightened, both on her flesh and on her heart.

"Lies! I saw you appear! That was teleportation!" the voice snarled. Kat gasped as the squeeze intensified, her knees starting to tremble and her head swimming.

"It wasn't me... Please, I can't help. I'm not lying!"

"Ugh! I don't have time to waste with this! Do it now!"

Trish knelt by Cory, checking his wound, and then pressed her jacket against it to stop the blood from flowing. The paralysis would wear off soon, but if she didn't stitch him up, he would bleed to death. He coughed raggedly, eyes fluttering open. "I swear I'll kill Edw—" he coughed, "—ard." He growled, and Trish shushed him.

"He's already got some lovely cuts from your falcon friends. He won't be fighting for a while," Trish chuckled, but it had a serious undertone. She glanced around again, then gently touched his hand. "You have a pretty nasty wound, as well. We need to get you to the hospital wing. You need stitches."

Cory grunted and nodded. "You know best."

"Come on," she whispered, and gently pulled him into a sitting position. "Let's get your butt back inside."

Kibbsty carefully aimed the gun, anger rippling through him. He had been so close, but in a single moment, it all was taken away. His research, his school. None of these students understood what he went through to make this happen. None of them realized all the sacrifices he'd made. They were going to be rich! They were going to be famous! Everything was going up in flames now, an explosion of incompatible individuals.

He had worked for years to get to this point. Groveled for money, stole for food, and submitted himself to an academic community that laughed at his work. He spent months putting up with bratty kids who grew into thankless teenagers. Now, it was all falling apart. It was just like the day he shot Dr. Allina's son: there was blood on his hands, and it was staining his work. He could feel the old burn on his arm brush the fabric of his coat, stoking his anger. Nothing was turning out as he'd planned.

It was hard to focus as he stood, shaking with rage. He tried to keep his arms steady, focusing on one last task. He gave a soft chuckle and fixed the green-haired girl in his sights, steadying his hand on the trigger. Maybe he had lost his research, but at least he would be able to ensure that some of them would pay for their actions.

The hand on her shoulder was unbearably tight, and Kat felt everything swimming. The stranger was screaming with rage, and Kat desperately searched the air for someone, anyone to help. Then she saw a tiny blur in the sky, and she knew it was her last shot. Kat opened her mouth as the squeeze grew tighter, and screamed, "WYVR!!! FIND LILLY!!!!" Then her legs buckled and she fell to her knees.

Lilly was within a few feet of Kibbsty when she watched him get to his feet. At first, she thought he was injured as she watched his unsteady movements and noted his wild expression. Careful not to draw attention to herself, she crept closer, then spotted a glimmer of silver as he raised his arms. *He had a gun.* The realization sent a wave of terror through her, and she turned, following the line of the barrel to Trish and Cory. With a cry, she found her feet throwing herself forward, and she slammed into the doctor as the gun fired. She heard a curse as she stumbled backward, then, to her shock, the ground disappeared and they plummeted into thin air.

Lilly threw open her wings, but it did little good. She slowed for a moment, then slammed into the rocky side of the mountain and spun into the air only to hit more rocks. Her wings were like toothpicks to the mountain, her body a toy for gravity. With a painful crash, she screamed as she clawed at the cliff, trying to slow her fall. Fear and pain became indistinguishable. There was no chance of survival, as the ground rushed up and her wings dangled uselessly. With a terrorized prayer, her heart wished for some escape from a terrible end, when she felt a pair of sharp claws catch her by the shirt and yank upward.

<Hold on!!!>

The tiny falcon pounded his wings, desperate to slow her, but the ground only grew. It would take seconds to hit the ground, minutes longer to die. To her shock, she felt him fly under her and morphed halfway, teen and bird at the same time. It was enough to slow them considerably, but then he turned into a teen, bunched her wings around her, and pulled her against him as they hit the ground.

The sound was terrible, and it felt even worse. She could feel his bones snap, and Wyvr cried in pain, unable to hold it in. Lilly quickly rolled to the side, unable to think of her own broken body when she looked at Wyvr's agonized face. Tears poured down her face as she stared at him, sobbing in horror. His arm was pressed against his side, his delicate ribs crushed in multiple places, and his leg was twisted at an unnatural angle. He shouldn't have been there, though. It didn't make sense.

"Why? Why did you do that?! Look at... Oh, Wyvr, look at you!" Lilly helplessly scanned his injuries, unable to process what she was seeing. "Why...?"

The Australian boy took a shaky breath, but managed to reach up and brush away a tear. "Because... Just because you can heal doesn't mean you should have to. You're worth protecting, Lilly. Having powers doesn't change that." He exhaled, gasping and hissing through his teeth. "Oh, that hurt more than I thought it would. Are you okay?"

Lilly nodded softly and sniffled, softly touching his hand. "You shouldn't have done it... You're hurt now. Oh, you stupid boy," she whispered. "You silly, stupid boy."

He grinned weakly. "Well, that's who I am. Maybe one day I'll learn, huh?"

Lilly sobbed and laughed at the same time, trying to keep it together. From the corner of her eye, she saw the lifeless form of her old foe. The sight sickened her instead of giving her relief. His bloodied and broken body seemed frail and fragile, and Lilly found herself staring at the body of nothing more than a beaten man, with her enemy nowhere in sight.

To her surprise, tears started to trickle down her face; she let out a shaky breath and just stared at the body. She thought she should feel some sort of joy. Some sort of accomplishment that this man would no longer terrorize them, but her heart didn't know how to hold malice in the face of so much destruction.

"Lilly, what's the matter? Why are you so upset? I mean, Kibbsty got what he deserved."

Lilly sobbed, "I don't know if anyone deserved this. I feel so confused after being here for so long. Everyone I thought I understood, I didn't. I only knew Kibbsty as my enemy." She took a deep breath and tried again. "Remember that morning when we were talking about how things are just tainted evil or good? Being here, I saw that. Met people I thought were evil, found out they had good in them. I guess I thought I would see that glimmer of good in Kibbsty, but I was too late." She broke into deeper crying, and she felt his strong arm pull her close to his undamaged side.

"Lilly, Kibbsty made his own choices, and his fate was out of your hands. No one knows what he thought when he fell, and no one knows where his heart was when he died. Everyone has a chance to choose their own fate. In the end, we only control our own."

Kibbsty was gone. So why was there no joy? No sense of freedom? He made his choice, but that still felt like a hollow consolation.

Slowly, the tears stopped and Lilly calmed, curling close in Wyvr's arms. But those would not be the last tears she would cry that night; a few moments later, they heard more dark tidings.

"Kat!"

The girl felt numb as she rushed toward her friend's side, the silhouette slumped in the mud, and glasses discarded at her side. As Lilly sank to her knees, she tearfully brushed stray locks from the girl's face, hands shaking with disbelief. "Oh, Kat, what are you doing here?" she whispered tearfully, voice cracking with fear.

"I...sensed danger. You almost died. I had to come...help...or you would have..." Kat gasped, hand clutched over her heart. As Lilly took her hand, she could feel the pulse galloping unevenly under her fingers, sometimes racing too fast, sometimes thumping too slow. She finally pulled her hand away, unable to feel it any longer.

"How did you... What happened?"

Kat struggle to breathe for a moment, and a quiet voice nearby spoke up instead. "Hayachi," whispered Nuo. His arms were wrapped around his legs, and he gazed quietly at the ground, sniffling softly. "She thought your friend could teleport, and demanded her to teleport us out. Her powers control blood. Your friend's heart, Hayachi injured it. Your friend is dying."

"Can't you make Hayachi fix it?"

Nuo looked up, tears rolling down his face. He shook his head and glanced out into the mountains. "Hayachi killed Mar, and Thall took after her. Both vanished in the battle. I fear..." He sobbed softly, losing track of his words as he bowed his head. "I'm sorry for your loss."

Kat coughed hard and shook as she touched Lilly's hand, giving a tiny smile. "Don't cry, Lilly. At least you're safe. It's not all bad."

"How isn't it?" Lilly whispered. "Look at this place! It's awful... All of this is awful... I never wanted anyone to get hurt because of me. You shouldn't have been here. This wasn't your fight."

Kat smiled and closed her eyes, beginning to breathe more evenly. The pulse under Lilly's hands was slowing, even as her own picked up speed. She traced the back of her friend's hand, trying to find something comforting to do. But Kat's serene expression remained on its own. "I had to. You're my friend, and I couldn't let that happen to you. You always had a smile, despite everything that happened. You always looked up when things went bad, and I wanted to be like you. Now I've run out of excuses. I have hope there is something better. I feel at peace with that. You helped me feel okay with that. I just wish," she grimaced, pausing to compose herself. "I wish I could be here to help you through the years coming up. There's danger, so much danger, and but there was no time to warn you of it all."

Her breathing grew softer with every word, and Lilly held her hand tighter, too tight. She couldn't let go, not now, not here. But no matter how tightly she gripped, she could still feel Kat slipping away. "Soon, all of this will be just a memory, but I have faith. I just hope you keep that too."

Quietly, Kat's breath stilled, and Lilly finally released her lifeless hand. Around her, an eerie stillness slipped across the muddy cliff side, where blood stained the rocks and the earth. There was no victory here tonight, and Lilly didn't know if there would ever be one. This world was filled with loss, and that pain never went away.

She remembered the flight that had torn her from her home. She remembered the struggle of losing her parents. The girl she was back then couldn't have handled this, couldn't have done what she did tonight. She would never have stayed at this school after the battle started, and she wouldn't have tried to stop Kibbsty from hurting her friends. That was the old Lilly. Somehow she felt she could get through this now.

The girl sitting here was stronger. She had learned to fight, learned to deal with loss, and was becoming her own person. Her friends and her enemies shaped her, and regardless of what happened tonight, that still mattered. As Kat always said, the future was unpredictable, ever-changing, out of their hands. Tonight, there was death. There were tears, there was pain, but there was also healing. A school was free from its captivity, and the students now stood lost, without a purpose and without a leader. They were standing together now. The battle lines were vanishing, and together, they would have to shape their own future, no matter how dark it seemed. She just had to keep faith that something better would come from this all.

Lilly stood and moved back toward the building she had fought so hard to escape. The sight before her was grim, but she faced it as bravely as she could.

She was done running away.

PREVIEW OF BOOK #2

CONFLUENCE

CHAPTER ONE

THE CHARITY DOCUMENTS

Two eyes scanned their surroundings, taking in the limited light and reflecting a pale yellow sheen. A soft intake of air melted into a low growl as the figured waited, before footsteps approached from somewhere in the shadows.

"It's time to move."

The waiting was over.

There was a stirring in the darkness as a shadow drifted down from the trees. Above their heads leaves rustled, and a metal latch clicked softly into place.

"Remember, we need as much time as possible."

"Just watch our backs, Scope," the voice retorted. Scope's hand flagged them forward with dismissal. On cue, the figure moved, now racing over the grassy lawn.

Moisture misted the air as black-furred paws galloped by; moving at a speed almost equal, the shadow glided after him, low enough to the ground that the thin membrane of wings nearly touched the dew. Scope, the last remaining by the fence, knelt and traced the viewfinder she was looking through, watching the other figures approach the building. She touched her earpiece and whispered into it.

"Bane, you're clear. Send Enigma in."

Scope flicked her goggles down, and the outline of a large animal filled her sight. In the green hue of night vision, she watched as Bane moved, and a girl landed lightly on his shoulders, crouching against the air current. With a few more strides, he met the building, coiled his muscles, and leapt skyward. Claws caught the slick texture of the stone, and in a hazy emerald hue Scope watched him throw himself and Enigma against gravity. Suddenly, they disappeared and reappeared again, another ten feet up. It was like weaving a needle and thread through the exterior of the edifice. One last jump and the two were at the seventh floor. Scope couldn't help but smile at the way they executed the last step of their climb. As soon as they reappeared, the animal figure of Bane melted into a tall muscular man, who caught the ledge with strong hands, swinging his body lightly to the wall. Enigma seemed to flutter for a second, and then she daintily resettled like a circus gymnast, one foot on each of Bane's shoulders.

Once they were there, Scope quickly lifted her handgun, a single bullet loaded. She focused on the window, and slightly to the left of Enigma's head, she aligned the crosshairs. Led by instinct, she fired the single shot; the whole action was complete in a blur. In her ear, she heard a crack and the girl's tiny intake of breath. Scope chuckled into the mic.

"You should trust my shooting by now, Em."

She thought she caught a rude gesture before Enigma lifted the window and vanished inside. Bane muscled his way in after her, and they became only outlines in the dim room. Time to lead the way.

"Okay, the files should be under CHARITY 1944. They are a hard copy, hidden behind the primary file cabinet."

Inside, Enigma nodded and motioned for Bane to move the metal cabinet. The boy took a step forward, and his body melted halfway to the animal form he had taken before, eyes a glowing gold again in the middle of his humanoid face. The muscles across his arms and torso flexed, and then he lifted it from the floor, brought it forward two feet, and set it back down. With her wings folded against her back, Enigma came forward and traced her hand down the wall. She knelt at the trim, and popped a small section free.

"There's a safety switch hidden against the baseboard. Make sure you hit it before opening the safe."

Bane had already taken care of it, so Enigma focused on the lock. A few quick spins and the tumblers aligned, letting the metal door swing open. Inside, hundreds of files were nested, each with a crisp label. Resisting the urge to look at all of them, Enigma carefully found the one Scope mentioned, and reached out her gloved hands to pull it free. It was thin, with a black clip holding everything in.

"That's it, now get out."

Enigma lightly fluttered backward while Bane shut the safe. She smiled as the lock reengaged, happy things had gone so smoothly. Setting down the files, she knelt and quickly put the trim back into place. All that was left was the filing cabinet now. Bane was already moving it back.

Unfortunately, it landed a bit too loudly on the ground as it was dropped into place.

"Move!"

In a blur, Bane was at the window and climbing down the wall in a half-feline form. Enigma was quick on his tail, only to freeze at the pane, remembering the folder she'd set down.

"Get out of there, they're coming!"

Enigma darted back and grabbed the papers as the door flew open. Terror-stricken, the girl crouched in the corner and a thin beam of light hit the open window.

"Someone's broken in! Quick, sound the—"

There was a thud as a tranquilizer dart buried itself in the man's neck, and Enigma leapt onto the cabinet as he tumbled to the floor. She turned, ready to leap out the window, when gunfire erupted at the glass. With a yelp, she recoiled and teleported backward instead, barely making it into the hallway, wingtips centimeters from the wall. In front of her stood a bewildered man, his mouth half open in a startled cry.

Enigma reacted as quickly as she could, rushing toward him with her wings thrown open and mouth curled into a hiss. As he backpedalled, tripping and sending his flashlight to the ground, Enigma leapt over him, picking up speed. Within a few strides, she was going fast enough to teleport to the end of the hall, and barely missed a group of guards that were exiting the elevator.

"What the hell is *that*?!"

"Quick Em, go down the stairs!"

Clutching the files, Enigma shot into the stairwell and took a daring leap headfirst from the railing. Her wings roared with air as she plummeted down the six stories, and with a burst of instinct she adjusted her bat-like membrane and sailed toward the first story exit. She ripped past the door in a hasty teleport, appearing in a large lobby area and almost crashing into some terrifying shape that dominated the room. Her reflexes sent her into an overshot arch, then shakily she landed on the back of what she decided was a stuffed grizzly bear.

"Scope, I need some help here," Enigma whispered fearfully. She glanced around for some means of escape, clinging unsteadily to her furry perch. She was about ten feet off the ground, and the door glimmered mockingly with its thin glass panes. It would have to do, since Scope wasn't giving her an alternative. Crouching, she readied for her leap to freedom, when pain sliced through her left shoulder. Hot fire spread through her nerves, and Enigma let out a scream, leaping into the air for dear life as a second shot narrowly missed her head. Her teleport went haywire, coming short of the door, but a second one brought her into the night. Her descent was too fast, her flight chaotic. Her third and fourth teleport brought her crashing with her nose in front of the fence, but she was too exhausted to reach the other side.

Suddenly, someone grabbed the back of her shirt and yanked her upward, then she found herself clutching Bane as his panther form raced through the trees, tears and blood staining his fur.

"You waited," she whispered, panting with exhaustion.

"You had the files," Scope's voice said bitterly in her ear. Enigma couldn't help but smile. The sound of a motorcycle roared to life somewhere to her left, and Enigma glanced at the headlights, wishing she could see Scope's face.

"Admit it. You like us, Scope."

The mic was silent, then a small scoff answered, *"Just don't bleed to death. Or on the papers. We'll talk when we're back at base."*

Enigma was dizzy from blood loss by the time they got back to the house, and Bane had to carry her inside. She hated feeling so helpless, but trying to move made her feel weak with nausea. Enigma had been shot before, but this was far more painful. She consoled herself with the fact at least the files were okay; Scope had taken them and put them away. Enigma could see the troublesome papers on the other side of the room.

Bane was sitting in one of the spare chairs in the kitchen next to her. The look on his face wasn't reassuring. Scope's expression matched it.

"Man, Kiddo… This is going to be messy."

"How...bad?"

"They were pretty close when they shot you. Could have taken your arm off, but luckily it looks like it only hit your shoulder with a ricochet. Shattered the bone, though. Your left wing is pretty badly damaged at the base, too. Hang tight, we need to see how deep the bullet went."

Scope motioned for Bane to hold the winged girl down, then she put on a pair of medical gloves, adjusted a new lens in front of her eyes and picked up a tool. "Don't let her thrash."

Enigma couldn't see her, but the intensified pain told her Scope was still there. "Yeah, your shoulder is messed up. I found the bullet, though. Just hang on. I need to get it out."

It felt like Enigma was being stabbed in the back. Scope was being careful, but her flesh was on fire, and Enigma was in agony. There was finally a small clatter, and the bullet was on the metal tray.

"You're lucky, it could have been worse. They could have hit your heart."

"Just fix it as well as you can," Enigma hissed.

For the next few hours, Scope pried and poked Enigma's shoulder. She straightened the bone fragments out as much as possible, stitched up the wound, then bandaged the wing and

351

shoulder. Afterward, she put both in an improvised sling, and Bane finally let Enigma up.

"The wing…how bad is it?"

"You will heal. It only got nicked. They aren't real wings anyway."

Enigma started to open her mouth, but Scope stopped her.

"Don't get offended. I only mean you're like a squirrel. You glide. If you could fly, this would be really serious. As it is, there are fewer muscles you have to worry about being damaged." Scope tossed her gloves on the tray and went to wash her hands. Enigma slowly sat on the couch, and glanced at Bane where he sat on the other end. After sitting in silence for a few moments, she touched his shoulder lightly.

"You haven't spoken all night, Bane."

His dark eyes flicked her way finally, and he shrugged. "I'm glad you're okay."

"He was worried," Scope cooed, walking back in. Bane's face gave away no embarrassment or denial, and Scope poked his shoulder. "No joke though, scared us both. We thought…" She trailed off.

Enigma shivered. "So did I. I just hope these files were worth it."

"Only one way to see."

Bane picked Enigma up and carried her to the main room. Her face flushed as he did, a mixture of embarrassment and fatigue. Gently, he set her on the couch and sat on the chair beside her. Scope brought the folder over and knelt, putting it on the side table between the three of them. With a look of both fear and excitement, Scope undid the binder clip and peeled the cover back to reveal the first sheet.

"'Classified files, Charity 1901-1944.' Wait, wait, Charity, *Idaho*? Charity was—"

Scope interrupted Enigma with a low whisper, "A town."

"These are the only files left, apparently. That's not much," Bane whispered. They rustled through a few of the papers, frowns deepening with every movement.

"It says the majority of the documents were destroyed. Convenient cover-up if you ask me. So we have the basic stuff,

some historical files, photos, and then information on 'relocation.'"
Scope flicked the first piece of paper to the side and opened the
first folder labeled 'Miscellaneous.' To the left hand side, a piece
of paper was clipped with 'UPDATE: July 21, 2002' written on it.
Scope let her eyes move to the other side of the folder where a
paper had the same 'classified' header. "Okay, let's see... Founded
April 19th, 1901 by Olivia Merritt. 166 citizens, 123 housing
units.... Final citizen count?" Scope let her finger linger, then kept
scanning. "Open town meeting government style, coordinates.
Those could be useful. Elevation..."

"Their government sounds archaic," Enigma whispered. Scope
nodded, pausing as she read the section on location.

"It's all so strange. This town was in the middle of nowhere,
and... Oh wow."

Bane gave a low whistle, pointing. "'Early February 1942,
Charity became the location for the Lantern Project,'" he read.

Enigma gave a shudder and whispered, "Scope, this sounds a
little fishy to me. I know that area. There's no record of anything
like this. How could all of this just vanish?"

Scope started flipping pages again and stopped in the back of
the historical files. She pulled out the Citizen List and started
skimming purposefully.

"Scope, what are you looking for?"

Scope held up a hand for silence and kept looking. Names
popped out, but none of them were right. Artists, scientists, then
finally—

"There. Bill Harker. Inventor, age 29.'

"What's the big deal?" Enigma asked curiously.

"He was...my great-grandfather," Scope said, a shadow
crossing her features. Setting the files down, she ran a hand
through her hair and tried to absorb the information. Her friends
looked expectant, so she tried to bring them up to speed. "Okay, so,
years back I had a cousin that tracked me down. Kid named Harris,
mechanical arm, weird shapeshifting powers. He did some research
for a guy, and in return, he got a lot of information on his family
tree. He wanted to see if his powers could be genetic or something.
When he met me, he figured he was right. We argued a bit and I
blew him off. I mean, my mom abandoned me as a baby and lied to

everyone about it, so I've never been great on family reunions, you know? Next thing I know, Harris vanished, and I just kept working with you two. That seemed to be the end of that until recently, when Harris tracked me down again and told me what happened. Super villain school, some crazy crap that made our adventures seem pretty tame."

"I remember you mentioning that," Enigma said. Scope nodded and sighed.

"What I didn't tell you was he gave me a lead he thought I should look into. He said he heard rumors about some files that could tell us more about our powers and why we have them. When he looked into our family, he found the names of our great-grandparents. He said to check for them when I found the files. And I only found one of those names on this list."

"And that would mean…?"

"We think these people are the reason we have powers. They are our ancestors. It's the first real lead we've ever had to why we turned out like this."

Bane picked up the list and glanced over it. His face was unreadable, but it was like he was looking for some clue he couldn't find. "And how'd he know about these papers again?"

"Harris told me some other Strands found a bunch of files hidden in an old room. He didn't see most of them, but Scarlet noticed one page had 'The Lantern Project' written on it, and their leader seemed pretty intrigued by that. Harris thought it was something important. Last week I tracked down a source, and she squealed that she had been asked in 2002 to move the files to a safer location. She told me how to get them."

"We were wondering where you went off to," Enigma whispered. She leaned forward to gaze at the photograph folder, but the movement was too much. She teetered, and Bane gently set her back securely on the couch. Wordlessly, he handed her the file so she could see, then moved slightly behind her to look as well, half sitting on the table with the rest of him balanced between the furniture. Carefully, they pulled the paperclip off the stack of photos, and Enigma held one up. It was a group of men, a few of them smiling, one looking away slightly. They seemed young, happy, and looked accomplished. Turning it over, the back read:

"'Scientists of the Lantern Project (left to right). Glen Wray, Frank Jones, Ned Marcum, Lucien Alden, Howard Jerome, Avery Douglas. October 1st, 1944.'" Enigma paused, unknowingly reading aloud, and studied the last name. "Why does the name 'Douglas' sound so familiar?"

"It's the last name of that girl Harris told us about. That could be a relative of hers." Scope knowingly gazed at the photo. She glanced over all the files, and let out her breath. "If my guess is right, that won't be the only name that will sound familiar. We have to show this to them."

"Who?" Bane said gruffly. Scope sighed.

"The other Strands. Like it or not, they have more information we need. Those files they found can answer a lot of this. This is the key to the mystery of who we are!"

"So what's our plan?" Enigma said weakly.

Scope looked at the photo of the scientists and exhaled deeply. "We go to Charity Academy tomorrow. We work out this mystery, and go from there."

It was said quietly, but didn't invite argument as other two silently agreed. The three teens sat for a moment, considering what they'd learned, and then Bane gently took the files from Enigma and gruffly told her to sleep. As the girl ruefully obeyed, he and Scope put the files back in order and tucked them away into their safe, a protective box disguised as a dusty old suitcase. After they were locked away, Scope and Bane went to their separate sleeping areas and settled in for the night.

Scope was the last to fall asleep, watching from her loft bed in the corner of the room. From there, she could see everything, eyes taking in even the limited light. She could make out the couches, the worn furniture, and the silhouettes of her friends. This was their home; tiny, underground, no bigger than twenty square feet including the kitchen, bathroom and storage room. Here, they had spent the past five years on and off, banded together against a world that would never understand them.

Scope was only nineteen, but in a way, she felt like a mother to the younger Strands. Bane was eighteen and Enigma was the youngest at sixteen, but Scope still felt responsible for their wellbeing. When plans went wrong and one of them got hurt, she felt guilty for the incident, like she did today. The files would have been a shallow victory if she lost either of her companions. Though she acted distant, she didn't know where she would be without them.

In the dim light from the lamp that never seemed to shut completely off, Scope watched Bane pad over in panther form to the base of the couch and lay down protectively in front of the sleeping Enigma. In her sleep, the other girl's hand slipped down and touched his head, in a silent but meaningful gesture. Scope smiled slightly at the obvious feelings between the two, but also felt sad by the distance they seemed inclined to keep. Life had never presented the right setting to see what could develop.

They had been on the road for so long, leaving this house for months at a time exploring, searching. They were law breakers, obeying no one. Working out feelings was the least of their problems. They were living by their own rules most of the time.

Scope lay back and closed her eyes, slipping into extremely light sleep, still aware of what was around her. It had been the three of them for so long. She would have a lot of trouble letting her friends go. The change would be so hard. But some day she'd have to. She knew this couldn't last forever.

It's time though. They look up to you, you're their leader. It's time to be part of the world again.

As she finally let her thoughts drift, she wondered if it would be that easy.

CHAPTER TWO

AN UNCERTAIN FUTURE

Six faces pressed themselves closer to the edge of the window, the group of teens desperate to see inside the room. Lilly grumbled as the falcon on her shoulder adjusted for a better position, and a few muffled profanities were answered by a chorus of shushing sounds. The summer sunshine was burning down on their backs, but no one wanted to move. Their attention was intent on the figures on the other side of the pane. Inside, Dr. Allina stood in front of the gathered staff members. Their voices were muffled by the windows, but the students still watched their facial expressions. Something was happening, and the students were desperate to know what.

It was the beginning of June, and school was out for the summer. A few of the teens had made their way home to visit family, so the school was quieter than normal. Taking advantage of the calm, the teachers at Charity Academy had gathered for a meeting, and their expressions looked grim. As the students watched outside the window, Dr. Allina addressed the staff members, and a stranger stood next to her that none of them recognized. This was the cause of their concern; there was a visitor at the school.

"I don't like it," Cory said, frowning suspiciously. He crossed his arms across his chest and grumbled slightly. The ice Strand was one of the few teens who wasn't looking in the window, but he didn't need to look to know something was up. A new student, he'd arrived less than a month ago, and his personality remained unchanged through the transition.

"I bet they just have to figure out what to do with the seniors this year. They can' stay here forever, so eventually they'll have to get jobs or somethin'…" Trish remarked, tucking locks of green hair behind her ear before glancing at the glass once more.

"I wish we could get in there and listen," Lilly said. She curled her wings in tighter, the feathers tight against her shoulders, running down her sides and nestling against her legs. The falcon on her shoulder twittered in agreement, and both hunkered closer to the pane with worry. Footsteps caused the group to turn, and two boys came into view. Both had brown hair, with auburn, copper, and black highlights, one styled short and spiky, while the other's fell just short of shoulder length.

"That's Michael Adams. He works with the police department in Boise. Old acquaintance of Dr. Allina," the long-haired boy said. "I've never seen him around unless something was wrong *out there*. He was the one who arrested Andy and I. He isn't one of *us*."

"What do you mean, Emre?"

Emre glanced at his companion and sighed. "He's…normal. He's not a Strand. He helps track us though, and introduces us to Dr. Allina. Meg would remember him."

The redhead nearest to the window glanced up, then away. "I do. He was the one who brought me here. Back before Alana found us, his team had a bigger role in tracking us down. I haven't seen him here recently, though." Her expression darkened the longer she thought about it. Lilly touched her arm gently.

"I'm sure there's a good reason for it. Maybe it's just because Firestone closed or something like that."

"I wish it could be that simple," Andy answered. "He doesn't come here for things like that. He's always left the management of Charity up to Dr. Allina. It's when there are people looking for us, or we've had a slip up when he flags us down. If he's here, it can't be something good. I just wish we could hear what… Is Jesle or Tami around?"

"Haven't seen them…" Meg answered and crossed her arms, stepping away from the window. "I think Tami and Tania went home for the summer. I guess we'll probably just have to wait and see what they decide to tell us when this is over. Maybe Jake will know…" The redhead glanced hopefully at the pane, then the group gradually started to disperse. For a moment, there was a flicker of sadness as she thought of the one person who would have been able to tell her if something was wrong. With that depressing thought, Meg moved in the direction of the greenhouse to sooth her chaotic thoughts.

On the other side of the window, the adults stood in worried silence, their attention focused on the problem at hand. No one thought to glance at the window where the students were trying to listen. They were all staring at a stack of files on the desk. The English classroom looked empty without students sitting in it, and the adults seemed out of place in this setting. But the problem at hand required all their input, and Dr. Allina's office was not large enough for the staff meeting.

"I just don't see how it's possible to make this work. We knew this when Asuka left: there is only so long they can go to school here before having to find another solution. What do you plan to do? Turn all of them into teachers when they graduate? Cassidy, half of your students are already in the wrong grades or lacking the education they need. You have Hailey and Jenny with the freshmen because we don't have an 8th grade, your 9th graders are in the same English classes as your 12th graders. I am helping all I can, but if you hope these kids can be part of society eventually we have to sort something out." Michael's face was wrinkled into a frown. He scanned the room at the few adults that were gathered, wondering. They needed to come up with a plan or this would all come crashing down on their heads.

"We can add a C day maybe? I can teach upper level social studies, or come up with college level course work," offered one of the youngest staff members. Dr. Allina gave a rueful smile.

"That's very sweet of you, Basil, but your schedules are already overloaded as it is. And finding some form of normalcy is as important for you as it is for the students. A 25-year-old woman like yourself should be out mingling and traveling, not stuck here in the middle of the mountains teaching. I wanted you to at least take the summer off, not standing around solving this problem."

"We chose this, just like the students. They're like our kids, Cassidy," the woman next to her said. There were agreeing nods around the room.

"We're just at a crossroad. This is not an ending, just a growing point. I don't think we need to panic quite yet."

The expressions were varied. Some looked doubtful, others hopeful, one or two almost defiant. No one wanted to instigate false hope for their future, but hope was all they'd had the past few years. As more students showed up, the staff felt the strain on their resources. This was not just a small handful of children they could hide under their skirts and raise in private. Suddenly, this was a school and they were raising a new generation that needed to find their place in the world. Even with Michael's help keeping the authorities off their trail, incidents were bound to occur, and they needed a plan. Soon.

"So what do you suggest we do? Send the students home? They have nowhere else," one of the teachers remarked while picking at the paint stains on his hands.

The officer frowned and pushed his hand through his hair. "I'm suggesting you start preparing them. Teach them to hide. Teach them to run. Playing student forever lets them get complacent. I know you want to protect them, but it's time for a little reality check. We chose to build this school—regardless of the risks, I will stand by it—but there is only so much I can do."

"The students take classes to control their powers. Some of them even have battle training. They aren't naïve, Michael," Dr. Allina insisted.

"Battle training isn't what they need. You want them to fight officers, the government? You want to put a target on them? They need to blend in! Hoping they'll be accepted and everyone will be fine with these kids wandering around isn't proving they're naïve. It's proving *you* are. Tell your students, Cassidy. Tell them the truth. Tell them the world is taking notice and they need to be ready to disperse before it's too late. There are too many. It's bound to draw attention since they're all gathered in one place. And after your incident with Firestone, I don't know what else to suggest. One of your students died, Allina. And now you're telling me some of those villains dispersed back into society? They are going to find out. You just need to decide how you'll handle it."

Dr. Allina glanced at her teachers, reading their expressions as they considered her friend's words. It was clear at least a few agreed with the officer: Angus was always worrying about the danger, and Professor Wagner had his own experiences that made him cautious. But hiding was dangerous in its own ways. It delayed the inevitable. "Whatever happens, I want them to stand together. I made this school to be a safe haven, but now it's more. We've become a family, and I'm holding onto that. I know it will be dangerous, and I will make sure they realize it as well. But all they have is each other. They need to have people they can rely on."

Dr. Allina glanced at the window, considering the choice she was making. Maybe the students could be safe if they tried blending in, but what about the students that couldn't? What good would that do in the long run? It would become a man hunt, a slow pursuit. At least this way they could turn to each other. She spun a ring around on her finger, the cold metal comforting as she faced her staff members. She had made many tough choices while forming this school, but this was by far the most difficult. She was deciding their futures.

It didn't feel fair.

"You're a good friend, Michael, and you've risked a lot helping us. I value your advice more than you know. But this may be one of the times we disagree." The officer nodded, and adjusted his coat as if to hide his disappointment. The other staff members listened quietly as the verdict was announced. "I'm not sending the students anywhere."

May 29.

That was the day that set all of this in motion. The battle at Firestone uprooted the Strands that had lived there, and a few never lived to see the aftermath. Kat had just turned sixteen. Lilly never had the chance to celebrate with her. Unlike the death of her parents, which took time to acknowledge and know for certain, there was no denying what had happened. Lilly had to let her go, and the pain was instantaneous and crippling.

May 29.

That night felt like a hazy memory. As the fighting stilled, Lilly was forced to deal with the chaos that was left behind. With Kibbsty's death, many students lost the nerve to fight, but others were still caught in echoes of rage he had planted in their hearts.

Tray was unpredictable once he woke up at the end of the battle. The wild terror on his face bordered desperation as he struggled to leave the infirmary. With poison still in his system, he staggered to the floor, deliriously crying once he realized Kibbsty was gone. "She'll die, she'll die..." he repeated emptily, until Professor Joltz found him. Lilly tried not to listen as the father consoled his son, but it hurt to watch the two of them, knowing her own parents weren't there to console her.

Wyvr was in bad shape. While Dryk went for help, Wyvr laid in the infirmary, his face drained of color. Lilly tried to go back for Kat, momentarily convinced she would feel cold being left outside. Then the reality returned, and she teetered in the doorway. She couldn't help Kat, and there were too many other people who were injured.

There were others who stood outside, lost, trying to decide what to do. Some were hurt but refused help, rebuffing the idea that they had lost the battle.

Lost. In the end, it felt like everyone lost that day.

Now, three weeks later, Lilly sat by the lake and stared at the water. The weather was warm, it was a perfect day to be outside relaxing. That's what the other students were doing. Kat's death had been hard on them all, but there was something resilient in the other Strands; a subtle understanding that they had to move forward. Lilly, meanwhile, just lingered in the past, reliving the memories without feeling any sense she was letting her friend go. She wasn't ready for the change yet.

She kept thinking of that day, listing the names of her fellow students, unable to think of them as enemies. It was easier for the handful that came back to Charity—Fuego and Pilar, Tray and Cory, Trish and Cherry—but the others she still wondered about. Thall disappeared, hunting Hayachi. No one knew where Harris went after the battle started. Xzin laughed at the idea of going to Charity Academy. Scarlet went home. Lilly didn't know why that bothered her, or why she felt disappointed, but it was just another thing she couldn't stop thinking about. They were all Strands. They should be on the same side.

Curling her wings around her, she felt the sting of tears as she buried her head in her knees.

"How're you feeling?"

The voice tore Lilly from her thoughts, and she looked up with an unsteady smile as Meg sat on the ground next to her. The grass was moist, but Meg ignored it much the way her roommate had. Lilly's thoughts snagged on the question like barbed wire, bringing everything to a halt. She frowned and looked at the water, sighing as she did.

"Not so good, honestly." A light wind created small waves, and the water lapped at her feet. Lilly watched it as she tried to form coherent thoughts, pressing her chin into her knees. "I miss her." Her voice was quiet, and she felt guilty for saying it out loud. Meg just nodded her head, sharing the sad expression.

"I miss her, too." They sat in silence for a few moments, the fabric of their shoes gradually dampening, until Meg reached out and rested a hand on Lilly's arm. "She would hate to see us sad, though. Heck, she'd want us to be getting into trouble or doing something fun. She hated to see anyone stuck in the past."

Emotions tightened Lilly's throat and she squeezed her eyes shut, trying to hold tears at bay. Her wings curled closer to her sides, crisscrossing behind her and brushing against the dirt. "It's not fair," she whispered, her breath catching and forming a sob. "It wasn't her fight. If I had… if I hadn't…"

"Lilly…"

"Kat's dead, Meg. No matter how many times I tell myself that, it just doesn't feel real. I walk into our room and I expect to see her sitting there. We go to dinner, and there's an empty seat I don't expect. I know she wouldn't want me to be sad, but it—" she paused, and the statement rushed out of her mouth despite her attempts to stop it, "It was my fault she was there." Sobs broke free as she buried her face in her hands, and her wings covered her body in a cocoon. Meg touched the feathers cautiously, as the emotions she had pent up the last few weeks broke free. She tried to be strong, tried to push through it, but with all the stress building up and the lack of distractions, it was impossible to escape the depression.

When Lilly had returned to Charity, she couldn't even say Kat's name; she could remember standing on the grassy lawn, watching the faces around her as the news spread. While Lilly was in shock, Meg was hysterical, and the memories of her screaming reverberated through Lilly now. Lilly half wished avoiding the conversation would bring Kat back, but the weight of verbalizing what had happened destroyed that glow of hope. When she looked up at Meg, she could see the shimmer of tears in her eyes, and she desperately searched for some form of comfort in her friend's expression. Meg just looked back at the water.

"Kat was there because she was your friend and she sensed you were in danger. She went to protect you. Maybe you wouldn't have needed saving if you were somewhere else, but the choice was Kat's to make." Lilly sniffled, her guilt only building. Meg sighed. "Lilly, Kat and I spent a lot of time together. Her biggest fear was that her powers were going to do more harm than good. She hated knowing the future, trying to decide when she needed to act or when to let things go. She was scared she would see something she didn't want to, and she always tried to hide it by acting out. I wasn't there when she…When she died…But I know saving a friend is not something she'd regret. She did what she thought she had to do."

The words were comforting, but the ache didn't go away. Lilly slowly uncurled her wings and collapsed into Meg's arms, feeling cold droplets sinking down to her scalp as her friend's own tears fell. As the water of the lake rippled closer, they sat and let the tide come. Maybe Kat wouldn't have wanted them to feel sad.

But she wasn't there to cheer them up. Because of Lilly.

Back in the building, the hallways were quiet, the occassional murmur of voices echoing eerily through the halls. The students who stayed behind for the summer drifted around the grounds like ghosts, and those who were indoors were extra quiet with Officer Adams around. In the past, students might have taken advantage of the staff meeting and caused chaos while the teachers were busy. Recent events had sobered them all, even the frew transfers from Firestone. Many took small road trips together or went camping instead to get rid of their extra energy.

At a school this small, everyone was touched by tragedy. Whether the students got along or not, it didn't remove the sting caused by their absence. It showed itself in little ways: Caleb hadn't skateboarded all month, Tag refused to steal powers, and Meg wouldn't go in the library. The staff were less obvious, but the signs were still there. A quivering lip, a break in in a voice, a hasty exit from a room. There hadn't been enough time to heal.

Yet, they had to move on. It was evident by the staff meeting, emphasized by the officer's warnings. Dr. Allina could hear the words as she moved through the halls, the other adults retreating to their rooms. She longed to give these children time to heal, a chance to breathe. But the danger surrounding them left little time for that. She had to tell them; that was only fair. She wasn't sending them away, but that didn't mean disaster couldn't overtake them anyway.

Going to her office, she pulled out her laptop and opened up a blank document, stared at the cursor and the expanse of white before her. She thought about what she could type, how she could explain what the meeting had revealed. She tried to think of how to tell her students what had been decided. In the end, the cursor just kept blinking, and it gradually blurred, distorted by the moisture in her eyes.

Slowly, she typed the words she wished she could find the courage to say, before letting her head fall into her hands and letting the sobs roll free.

I promised I could protect you. I lied.

CHAPTER THREE

PERCEPTION

"You're aiming too high."

The guard paused with his finger on the trigger and glanced over his shoulder at the fair-skinned woman behind him. Her hair was a vivid white in the sunlight, and her sunglasses obscured the rest of her face with their dark lenses as she lounged in the chair on the concrete. He looked back at his target and grumbled under his breath as he rolled his shoulders back.

"Stay out of it. You don't know the first thing about shooting, sweetheart." He resumed his stance and fired at the target on the other side of the range. The bullet nicked the top half of the sign, and he swore and set the gun down on the display. Next to him, his fellow guards chuckled. "Fluke. There is no way you knew that would happen." He glared over his shoulder, and the female shrugged and looked back down at her book. Begrudgingly, he picked the weapon up and took aim again.

"Try to the right more."

The gun fired, the bullet clipped the grass to the left of the target; more laughter and more swearing resounded. Ever so slowly, the woman turned the page on her book, and the guard exhaled through his nose. Before he even aimed, she pointed a slim finger to the right again. This time, he adjusted his position and the bullet clipped the center circle. There was no pleasure in the accomplishment though, merely irritation as he tossed the weapon carelessly down. "I'm sick of that brat! How come she has to be out here anyway? This isn't a pool for her to lounge around by. It's weird."

"Orders from the house, Reynolds. You'd do well to watch how she's treated," a new voice came from up the path, and the girl lifted her head ever so slightly in response. The suited male strode forward and set a hand on the back of her seat.

"Jensen," she said pleasantly, face not moving from her book.

"Evelyn. How is our new security staff doing?" He gave a hard look at the previously armed man in particular, and the girl gave a smug chuckle.

"They're doing adequately, with the exception of Reynolds there. He's got a habit of having tunnel vision and refusing to take things like wind direction into account when aiming." The man glared but it didn't look like the girl was watching. She was still looking at her book. "Maverick has potential though. He responds well to distraction, rarely misses, and is comfortable with both hands. I'd suspect he's really a lefty but was trained to shoot right handed." A flicker of surprise crossed one of the guard's faces, and he fidgeted uncomfortably. Jensen gave a slight smile at his reaction.

"I take it you are a lefty?"

"Yes, but how could she…"

"Check in with the front house. We've got some work for you. Consider it a promotion." Jensen smiled slightly, and the bewildered man put his weapon away before obediently heading toward the building. The other guards turned back to their work quietly, but Reynolds took a step forward it frustration.

"She wasn't even paying attention! You're just going to take her word on it?"

"I'd quit while you're ahead."

"No! I think it's crap you let this spoiled little girl run your security staff. She's barely into adulthood and you have her marching around like she owns the place."

Ever so slowly, Evelyn reached up and pushed her sunglasses to the top of her head. The book snapped shut as she slipped to her feet, then she turned her full attention to the angry man, grey-blue eyes intent on his face. Several of the other guards took a few steps back, and Evelyn gave the most sugary sweet smile she could manage, a subtly threatening gesture.

"I apologize if you I've offended you with my actions, Mr. Reynolds. I can see by your behavior and lack of respect for authority you regard yourself as better than others and have a need to prove yourself." The man's mouth twitched, but Evelyn continued, leaving no opening for him to argue. "You worked in the military; you risked your life but when the battle was over, no one gave you the respect you deserved. In fact, likely quite the opposite. They took one look at your injuries, sent you straight to a desk job and declared you should stay there and be comfortable making money and building a cushy little life. But you weren't content with that. Even with a busted leg you tried time and time again to get positions like a security guard and bodyguard, but you never got the job and always blamed it on your injuries. Well, I'll be the first to tell you, Mr. Reynolds, it is not your skill that is being questioned but your lack of respect for those who have seniority over you. You see your teammates as competition, your coworkers as in your way, and your employers as too blind to notice your potential. Oh, there is potential. You have a steady hand and keen eyesight, but you overcorrect yourself and don't pay attention to your surroundings.

"So, let's make things clear, shall we? When you're on the grounds, you answer to me. When you work, you answer to me. If I say go, you go, and you will do so whether you think I'm watching or not. Because no matter how 'distracted,' I may appear, I will be marking you down for every slip-up, every disrespectful grunt, and every snide glance. If I act like I own the place, it's because *I do*, and you *will* learn to respect that. Am I clear?"

The man straightened his posture slowly, eyes somewhere between fearful and impressed. His hand moved up into a crisp salute, and then with a wave of her hand, Evelyn dismissed him. His posture as he left was still brimming with defiant energy, but now it was contained and focused. The fair-haired female handed her book to her companion and slipped her sunglasses back over her eyes.

"You think we should keep him around?" Jensen said quietly. Evelyn gave a light smile, watching the figure disappearing in front of them.

"I think we should promote him. He's driven, and while Maverick is skilled, he doesn't have as much desire to prove himself. Put the two of them together, they will push each other the way we need them to. Let my parents know."

As Jensen headed back toward the main house, Evelyn quietly turned and wandered through the gardens. It was a peaceful day at least, but not quiet. In her world, there was always noise, and little relief from the clamor. Her world was filled with the echoes of information, echoes she grew up with and learned to adapt to. Few people knew the extent of her abilities, and even then, it felt like no one understood.

Know-it-all. Freak. Spoiled brat. She had heard it all, and by now, she learned not to let it offend her. She carried herself with confidence and let the insults wash over, abandoned. She didn't particularly feel invincible. There was just no other way to survive. She was cursed by her abilities, the flow of mental noise with no off button.

She paused at a rose bush, running her fingers across the petals. [*Red rose. Common, traditional. 16 petals, aphids on left leaf.*] As always, the Echoes were just eager to chatter information, useful or not. Shutting her eyes and sighing, Evelyn tried to clear her thoughts. The same abilities that made her an asset to her family made her feel like an outcast with everyone else. She thought eventually her parent's research would create an understanding of what her powers really were. She hoped with time she could learn to control them. In the meantime, there were only more questions.

There was a rustle behind her, and the noise flickered quickly through her mind. [*Slight limp, heavy footsteps but little noise from surrounding vegetation: Kyle Reynolds.*]

"I take it you had more questions, Mr. Reynolds," she remarked without turning. There was the slight movement of his physical flinch backward, and the slim girl calmly turned.

"What you do isn't normal, kid," he remarked. "You a mind reader? Telepathic? It doesn't make sense." His expression revealed confusion and a touch of suspicion, but no fear. That was a first. Evelyn folded her hands in front of her and relaxed her stance.

"You tell me, Mr. Reynolds. What am I, if not 'normal'?"

He glanced at her calm expression, moving uncomfortably. Her face was calm, unthreatened, and it affected his defensive demeanor. He came in expecting to ask the questions, but now she had turned the tables. He suppressed his emotions, however, and spoke. "You could be anything... Maybe some type of mutant? All I know is what you do shouldn't be possible. You knew Maverick was left handed, where to shoot, and now you knew it was me before you even turned. And that's on top of what you knew about my military background. That's not stuff I post on my resume." His tone took a dark tone and Evelyn chuckled.

"One only needs to watch to learn those things; your body language, your limp, the way you hold yourself. I am not a mind reader. Just..." she searched for the right word. "Observant."

"More like hyper-observant. You did it all without looking up from your book," he insisted.

Evelyn sighed, and her hands moved to her hips. "So what if I am? Then what? Will you go and tell the world? That's not your style, is it? I admire your tenacity, but you need to think things through. This world is filled with unexplainable things, and how you deal with them will determine how you survive. Challenging the wrong person will end your journey rather quickly. I'm tame compared to some of the others."

His stance changed again, posture more submissive this time. Evelyn let her own arms drop in response. "There are more...like you?" he whispered.

Evelyn chuckled, "No, not necessarily. The only trait we really share is that we are 'different.' We are the things of fantasy and science-fiction. You would use the term 'mutant,' perhaps 'super human.' In a few moments, you'll go inside and get transferred to the Alpha Facility. There, you will find the answers to your questions. You will be in charge of guarding and containing the teens we have there. And a word of advice..."

She leaned closer and smirked ever so slightly. "If I were you, I'd stop being surprised by my little parlor tricks. Compared to the individuals you'll face there, I am as human as they get." With that, she moved back toward the building, leaving a speechless Reynolds in her wake.

Acknowledgements

They say it takes a village to raise a child, but I think the same holds true for a novel. Thankfully, I've had a very talented village.

Thanks to my editors for the wonderful work they've done preparing my novel for print. Marc: the early edits you did and creative input gave me the confidence to get through later months. Diamond: your endless patience with me helped shape my story into the book I always dreamed it could be. While I blush at every error, your jokes and optimism made the process feel fun.

Thanks to my publisher, Fantastic Journeys Publishing, for taking on this project and helping get my book to print. Your encouragement, feedback and guidance was something I relied on and will continue to appreciate as this journey continues.

Thanks to my family for their endless support of my writing.

Thanks to every Beta reader whose feedback helped and will help shape this book in the future.

Thanks to my friends, whether online or in person: you guys talked me through every panic attack and helped me keep going.

Thanks to my readers. You are what keeps me writing.

Last, but not least, thanks to my Heavenly Father. You gave me hope when I lost faith.

Forever grateful,
- Mati Raine

Mati Raine has been writing for about as long as she's been drawing: both have been lifelong obsessions. While it's somewhat challenging from time to time to split herself between hobbies, the push and pull relationship creates a harmony in her life. When she's not working on her next novel she can be found busy with one craft project or another, and her weekends are often spent traveling for her art business.

Mati's favorite events are renaissance faires and fandom conventions, but pretty much anywhere she can let out her inner nerd works just fine.

Explore character files, blueprints and more at

www.archipelagobook.net

www.ingramcontent.com/pod-product-compliance
Lightning Source LLC
Chambersburg PA
CBHW070906260626
47162CB00007B/2577